CHRISTI

(1902-1983) was born at Rockdale, Sydney. Her father was a naturalist in the Government Fisheries Department and from him she inherited the naturalist's eye which she brought to her writing. Her mother died when she was two and her father remarried, Christina Stead becoming the eldest of seven children. Educated at Sydney Girls' High School, she then studied at Sydney Teachers' College. She taught in schools for one year but her voice failed and so she transferred to the Correspondence School before returning to College as a demonstrator of psychology, and working in city schools. She resigned from teaching in 1924, after further voice trouble.

Christina Stead left Australia in 1928 and took a job with a London grain merchant. The man who appointed her, William Blake, a novelist and political economist, later became her husband. She arrived in London ill and weak and began to write her first novel, *Seven Poor Men of Sydney*, as something to leave behind her if she died. From London she travelled to Paris, becoming a secretary in a bank, where she worked from 1930-1935. William Blake secretly submitted the manuscript of the novel to Sylvia Beach for her assessment and *Seven Poor Men of Sydney* was published in 1934. That year Christina Stead's collection of short stories, *The Salzburg Tales* also appeared. She and Blake then moved to Spain, where they lived until the outbreak of the Civil War. They settled in the USA in 1937.

A formidable and entirely individual writer, Christina Stead stated at the outbreak of the Second World War that she was not 'puritan or party . . . nor political, but on the side of those who have suffered oppression, injustice, coercion, prejudice, and have been harried from birth'. By this time she had also published *The Beauties and Furies* (1936) and *House of all Nations* (1938). With *The Man Who Loved Children* (1940) Christina Stead's reputation continued to rise. She went on to publish *For Love Alone* (1944), *Letty Fox: Her Luck* (1946), *A Little Tea, A Little Chat* (1948), *The People with the Dogs* (1952), *Cotters' England* (1966), a collection of four novellas *The Puzzleheaded Girl* (1967), *The Little Hotel* (1974) and *Miss Herbert (The Suburban Wife)* 1976.

In 1943 Christina Stead moved to Hollywood as Senior Writer for MGM but then went on to New York where she became an instructor at New York University, working there from 1943-1944. In 1947 she and Blake moved to Europe. They married in 1952 and in 1953 they settled in Surbiton, on the outskirts of London, where they remained until Blake's death in 1968. Christina Stead visited Australia as Fellow in Creative Arts at the Australian National University, Canberra, in 1969. Returning to England in the same year, she suffered a heart attack, from which she slowly recovered. Christina Stead returned finally to Australia in 1974 and in 1980 was awarded an Emeritus Fellowship by the University. She also became an honorary member of the American Academy and Institute of Arts and Letters in 1982.

Acclaimed in the *New York Times Book Review* as 'one of the most distinguished novelists writing in English, her work is respected by many writers, including Angela Carter, who described her as a 'profoundly serious, deeply accomplished and magically illuminating novelist'. Christina Stead died in Sydney in 1983 at the age of 80.

Virago publish eight of her twelve works of fiction and will shortly publish *The Salzburg Tales*.

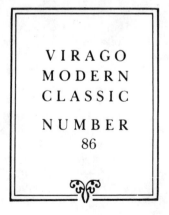

VIRAGO
MODERN
CLASSIC
NUMBER
86

THE
BEAUTIES AND
FURIES

Christina Stead

Virago

Published by VIRAGO PRESS Limited 1982
41 William IV Street, London WC2N 4DB

Reprinted 1985

First published in Great Britain by
Peter Davies Limited 1936

Virago edition offset from first British edition

Copyright © Christina Stead 1936

British Library Cataloguing in Publication Data

Stead, Christina
  The beauties and furies.—(Virago modern
  classics).
  I. Title
  823[F]   PR9169.3.S75
  ISBN 0-86068-175-0

The front cover shows a detail from
Portrait of Lucie Beynis, 1929, 79 × 64.5cm by
Grace Crowley, Australian, 1890-1979
Art Gallery of New South Wales, bought 1965.

Printed in Finland by Werner Söderström Oy,
a member of Finnprint

LIST OF CHARACTERS

ELVIRA WESTERN, a runaway wife.
PAUL WESTERN, M.D., her husband.
OLIVER FENTON, her lover, a student.
ADAM CINIPS, her brother, a dyer.
SARA STEELE, a distant cousin of Paul.

COROMANDEL, a young Frenchwoman.
M. PAINDEBLED, her father, an antiquary.
AMELIE, her insane mother.

ANNIBALE MARPURGO, a lace-buyer.
ANTOINE and
GEORGES FUSEAUX, brothers, lace-jobbers.
BLANCHE D'ANIZY, a French actress.
SEPTENNAT, political columnist, her lover.
MAURICE BLANE, journalist, her lover.
ANDREW FULTON, café loafer.

And others.

THE
BEAUTIES AND
FURIES

CHAPTER I

THE express flew towards Paris over the flooded March swamps. In a parlour-car, the melancholy dark young woman looked out persistently at the sand-dunes, cement-mills, pines, the war-cemetery with stone banners like folded umbrellas, the fields under water, the bristling ponds with deserted boats and the little naked trees which marked the horizon-searching roads. Her lips moved almost imperceptibly. The sky was clearing after weeks of rain. Opposite to her sat a man she judged to be an Italian; the initials on his tobacco-pouch were A. M. in gilt script, he wore a diamond tiepin and he was about forty. Across the aisle a rouged blonde with a cigarette-holder ordered Evian water and drawled about a hunt ball and 'Esmé, a perfect darling, terrific at charades.' The small dark woman was slipping her new shoe off her swollen right foot when she saw the Italian looking at her sociably. She drew a letter out of her bag and tried to pretend that she had just got it, hurriedly, in the morning's mail, as she left for the train. The address, in a student's script, said 'Mrs. Paul Western, Mecklenburgh Square, London,' and had a French stamp. Mrs. Western rather slowly took out the letter and read it from the beginning, although these were the very words that she had been repeating by heart during the journey. It said:

ELVIRA, MY DEAR,—Paris is bitter cold, with slate-blue skies, and yet I am already looking forward to the spring, but all you can look forward to in your blue-nose London is arthritis-March, neuralgia-April, coldsore-May, sniffle-June, macadamsick-July, cheappetrol-August, fireless-September, influenza-October, and four coffin-months to follow. I don't say, How can any woman resist my entreaties, but just, How can any young woman resist Paris in the spring? How can you resist me in the spring ? It's against nature and all the authorities ! On moonlight nights, when everyone walks with his shade, I pretend we are here together. You are the moon of beauty and I a moonstruck poet. My little glass of water on the bedroom table, when the moon sails high above the narrow street, shines with one eye, a little moon, and I go out. The skies are starling-dark—your hair ; the town and its towers discoloured—your breast ; the river, curdled, bubbling—your voice ; the glistening brown buds of the first-sprouters—your eyes. I lie awake at night, my body sinks like a crust shillyshallying to the silt of a dull canal, my brain floats. I begin to see all that tame, familiar country between Paris and the Channel, the Channel and London. I see you at home, grumping over a meal with Paul, or by yourself by the fire, contented in habitual melancholy. I feel the stuff of your diffident dresses, hear your cool voice dropping disconsolate words like water from a tap : you odd creature ! I'm afraid to do it often, because I lie awake a long time afterwards, open to sights, scents, sounds. Asleep, I know you are not with me, and I devise all sorts of ways of getting to you. I am up home in Northampton saving up to come to London, working in my father's bakery, the Polack beside me singing unintelligible songs, covered with sweat from the heat, sweeping, scraping and saving and learning under an oil-lamp. Or I am sitting for examinations in a row and cannot see you till I pass them all. Or I am in Paris for seven years, confined in the Archives, and all sorts of worries begin : Will she be dead in seven years ? Will I ? Will she have a child and forget me ? I sob in these dreams and wake up in the morning crying. The next day I can't work at all, but nod over my desk at the Archives. Only once or twice I dreamed we were going to be married : I made all preparations for the wedding : we went to the registrar ; coming out of the registry office, men working on the road took off their hats and sang the Wedding March. That was the happiest moment of the whole year when I dreamed that ! . . .

Yesterday evening, I went to the Salle Bullier to a protest meeting about the Scottsboro' boys. There was a free-for-all. (She skipped half a page.) A dick eyed me : I eyed him. Afterwards, they kept off me, because I was well dressed. I saw His Nibs standing offside fingering his pockets, while three husky cops set on some undersized workmen singing out 'Down with all tyrants! Down with the cops!' Gods, I was glad I was amateur lightweight champ. at college. I was taken up with the rest but released at the station—because of my clothes. . . .

When I think of you there, a doctor's wife, Elvira, sitting with those stodgy women who go to your church and think Mr. Baldwin is such a nice man, I can't believe it's you, the woman I love. I know it isn't. Oh, do wake up, come to life before it is too late: before the thorns interlock and crib you for ever. Will you go on doing that till you are forty, fifty, old? Paul is thirty-eight already; he has no right to make you old too. . . . Can't you be young, enjoy the youth and young love you never had. . . . I love you, you love me, we both love each other: you be good to me and I will be good to you: that is the beginning of a Polish wedding-song. . . . How can you resist me? . . . You are buried alive. Wake up, Elvira, come to me, come to me. . . . I think of you day and night: my whole life is yours, I'll breathe my whole life into you. I worship you: I only breathe to make you happy. You know me, I am not a boy: I am serious beyond my years, ambitious, my heart is a flame, I have no mental rheumatism, and I only love you. Now and for ever, Yours,

OLIVER FENTON.

Elvira once more caught the curious, friendly glance of the Italian. She looked indifferently along the car where the cloths were now being laid for lunch. A very old Anglican clergyman shook his wattled chin at two young officers going out to Bombay:

'Indubitably a don, pronounced them *Ahoy! Foo Gah Kaze.* I suppose to you young men I am almost pre-historic; indeed it is fifty years since old Brown, my tutor, murmured them with perhaps a touch of more than donnish melancholy. . . . I assure you gentlemen that this novel accent resembled to me more the inebriate hail of some strayed Celestials seeking their junk along the sombre quays than those melancholy-sweet sounds that Horace himself murmured when he first wrote down this little lament: " *Eheu, fugaces, Postume, Postume, labuntur anni*. . . ." I was at Sir Charles Mopoke's the other evening for supper : you know Sir Charles, of course, one of the few remaining in the tradition of Lord Grey —and found his son there, Lester, fresh from Oxford. I asked him whether there, or at that other place where such matters are said to be dealt with less conservatively, these *chinoiseries* are allowed in the pure Augustan. " Well," he said, " I've known much quality short on quantity, but the sign of a true liberal is conservatism in his Latin, homespun is often classic, but what you have there is modern shoddy." Very apt, I thought. But of course another tongue beguiles your frontier nights ? O, a little Sanskrit, Pushtu . . .'

Elvira heard a clear, malicious cantillation :

> ' The fleeting years glide by, alas,
> The civilising tax-collector,
> With the latest range-detector,
> Remains to watch the Khyber pass.'

Elvira looked at the Italian a moment. The husband of the rouged blonde said :

' The cuckoo should come early this year, he has a five-year cycle. I shall miss him. What a pity ! I know by instinct the night before he comes for the first time. I told Rudges when he comes to do the garden to note the date and, if possible, the hour, in chalk or charcoal on the coalshed.'

Elvira heard the malicious voice of the Italian :

' Cuckoo-lore ! Hedge-sparrow scholars ! Pipeclay artists ! Couturiers of the woad epoch ! The women no hips and the men all haws ! The women—I am not speaking of your race, Madame. You have Celtic blood, I think.'

' I have Welsh blood,' said Elvira Western, with a fashionable drawl. ' As for the cuckoo-lore, as you call it, I rather admire it. When you think that they call us a nation of shopkeepers, and on the train, amongst officers and gentlemen, you can hear about nothing but charades and Horace and . . .'

' Wordsworth loved the earth of England,' stated the old clergyman to the young officers.

' —Wordsworth,' said Elvira.

' To think that the English navy is worse off than at any time since the Armada and the fate of 450,000,000 people, their bread, their civilisation, depend on it . . .' said a bronzed and whitehaired old man.

' —and when you think that a tiny little island rules 450,000,000 people,' continued Elvira, ' I think it shows a great deal of sangfroid, don't you ? '

' It shows a race built for Empire,' agreed the Italian.

' Brown Jack is the best of his breed,' said a voice.

' A horse-race,' concluded the Italian.

' Of sea-horses,' Elvira reproved.

' Hi, hi, very good.'

' Are you and Madame having lunch ? ' asked the waiter.

' I am having lunch,' corrected Elvira.

' And so will I,' said the Italian.

He apologised for the bad manners of waiters on international trains. ' I resent this habit of assuming that every woman will let a man pay for her food,' he said brutally.

' Because they live on tips themselves,' said Elvira.

' An excellent observation : men think naturally in economic classes.'

She sighed. ' We all live by somebody's favour.'

At lunch he divided his wine with her. His name was Annibale Marpurgo. He was a lace-buyer and had just come from Calais, where he had been inspecting new designs and buying job-lots of last season's goods. She found an opportunity to say :

' My friends will be waiting at the other end.'

Marpurgo smiled. ' And with impatience ! '

She looked at him in fright, thinking, ' Do I give myself away so easily ? ' She got out her cigarettes, offered him one. He called the waiter, speaking good French, with excessive unction, flattered him in a commanding tone, almost pawed him, almost pushed him, using his hands on which his nails and two rings glittered, discussing at length the quality of the cigars in stock. Elvira, looking at his glittering tiepin through the cigarette-smoke, began to recollect how she had scurried round that very morning, early in foggy London, getting her two bags downstairs. She had lain awake nearly all night thinking of the note she would write to Paul: '. . . you say yourself we are unhappy, we might as well be divorced the way we live. I am going away for a little while to see whether we will feel differently. Perhaps it is all over: our love is dead. Perhaps we never really loved each other. I am taking my freedom; you always say I am free. . . .' After writing it and putting it in place, first in front of the clock, next on his desk, she had fallen asleep. She had had to walk to Theobald's Road to get a taxi, so early in the morning. Now, at the other end, Oliver waited. 'No one can say I don't take chances!' She smiled to herself through the smoke.

The sun was setting as they sped through the high dark woods of Chantilly, an express half-hour from Paris. The sky was clearing still, there was a blowy sunset with gold surf and dark-blotted clouds. As they drew nearer to Paris, she began to talk to Marpurgo again. He came out from a French review, *La Revue Historique*, ostentatiously held, to tell her that his brother, a painter, had died in Paris, years ago. He had been to Paris himself to study, when he was twenty: he had not known whether to study art, law or medicine, equally called: 'I had *velléités*—one should have in life one clear call.'

'Who has?' asked Elvira. 'My husband meant to be a broker: and he's a doctor.'

She blushed. Marpurgo went on after a moment.

'I design my own commercial designs, in collaboration with the house-designers. The beautiful laces lie on the shelves for years, the *meisterstück* of most designers is never sold—it's too dear. I sometimes buy a small piece for my own collection. It is my only vice. I am—a lonely man. Paris is Klingsor's garden, to me. I wander round, torn by all the curiosity-shops : there are pieces there from the prime-time of laces, when hundreds of thousands of francs went into cobwebs. My collection is of no mean value. . . .' The clumsy idiom came trippingly off his tongue. Elvira thought, ' He has taken great pains to make himself an Englishman.' She said :

' I don't wear lace. I like hemstitched and hand-embroidered things. When I was at school they did not allow us to wear lace : the headmistress thought it was unladylike. Hand-drawn lawn and hand-embroidery.' She giggled. ' There were two wards there of the richest woman in the kingdom : they had the plainest clothes of all, to prevent them from becoming giddy.'

He smiled.

' You would never wear what is not delicate and fine, by instinct. You are all that is woman. I should like to show you some of the pieces in my collection. You would change your mind about lace then. It was created for beauties, and you are one,' he added in a lower tone.

' Do you think so ? '

' A beauty who has never reigned,' he said harshly.

She was frightened, looking at the ugly poverty-stricken suburb announcing the Gare du Nord. She got out of the train in trepidation, not noticing that she had dropped her gloves. In a flash she saw a dazzling white, smiling face running towards her through the crowd. Oliver's hat was in his hand, and he did not notice the people who turned to stare and smile at him. Like a clap of thunder she was enfolded tightly, almost lifted off her feet.

People smiled. He said, ' I knew you would come. O my darling ! '

She stood still as a stone trying to keep her feet, feeling her hat tipping to one side. He kissed her cheeks, neck and hands. She was glad that Oliver was such a hand-

some youth. Then, she took the gloves that Marpurgo
apologetically held out to her and said timidly, ' Oliver,
this is Mr. Marpurgo : we met on the train. Mr. Fenton.'

Their porters, the bags shouldered, waited with bored
impatience at a little distance.

' Let's be going,' exclaimed Oliver : ' look how he
taps his foot ! ' He said something to the porter and
added : ' Gods, aren't they different from the milk-meek
English, with their yessir-ing. You can see that this
country has had a revolution . . .'

' —three,' proffered Marpurgo.

' —three. Didn't you notice a difference as soon
as you struck Calais, Elvira ? Oh, how I wanted to
make the journey with you, to see your reactions ! To
see the expressions on your face as you saw France !
Aren't they men ! Look at my porter ! Do you see how
he looks back at me exclaiming with that indifferent
mockery ! It's a pleasure to meet workmen who feel
their equality with you. How do you like being in
France, Elvira ? '

She did not have time to reply to his rejoicing, she had
only smiled in a flustered fashion, when Marpurgo said:
' I have that feeling : I'm an old French chauvinist.
Whether the men are actually as intelligent and free as
their verbal facility makes them seem, I don't know, but
truth or illusion, it's pleasant. I'm glad you're a francophile.'

' I always was, by instinct,' said Oliver.

' Why be francophile, or the opposite ? ' queried
Elvira. ' It is best to say what you see. Prejudice
irritates me.'

Oliver looked at her delightedly. ' And did you have
a good crossing ? I was so afraid of you, that you might
change your mind at the last moment. What should I
have done ? I was awake all night ! ' He looked into
her face hotly, ignoring Marpurgo. She shut her eyes
for a second.

Marpurgo, peering, said to Oliver :

'I see you have *La Vérité* under your arm : are you a Trotskyist ? '

'No ; are you ? '

'Not wholly, but the man is a genius, and you can't dismiss him with the consecrated name, counter-revolutionist. After all, he's the greatest general of the century.'

'Oliver loves politics,' explained Elvira.

Oliver was looking at her profoundly and did not seem to hear.

Marpurgo, with an air of collusion, like someone slipping in the password of a secret society, rapped out :

'I believe perpetual revolution is the only cure for thermidorian degeneration.'

'We must remember that a general has a professional interest in war and can't shine in engineering,' remarked Oliver.

'We'll have no 9th Thermidor because we have no Robespierre,' Marpurgo plodded along regretfully.

Oliver caught the ball: 'We won't see communism until we see it in France.'

Elvira began to laugh. 'Oh, Oliver, I had almost forgotten your litanies : have you been doing this ever since I last saw you ? '

Oliver threw her a loving look. Marpurgo insinuated, with acid pleasantness :

'Isn't she wonderful ? There is something divine in women : without dialectic, without knowledge of the subject, they divine our weaknesses. They have unconscious perception of form, litany-form, incantation-form. But then, they are helped by the conviction that all men of talent are merely medicine-men, leaping, painted, howling, a kitchen-conviction of the cooks' union that flesh is veal-cutlet but talent is just a game we get up amongst ourselves when we're fed. And for the most part, it's true of course. There's too much priest in all of us. Word-drunk, the woman leads us home to table.'

Oliver laughed, his face flaming towards Elvira.

' I've been waiting an hour in the café opposite, Elvira.
I couldn't keep down-town.   I had to be up here near the
station.   If telepathy existed, you should have got here
ever so much sooner : I was trying to make the engine-
driver outstrip his schedule.   I drank three Amer-Picons !
And I'm perfectly sober.'

' I made her drink a little wine,' said Marpurgo.

' Can I drop you somewhere ? ' asked Oliver.   ' Where
do you stop, right or left bank ? '

' Many thanks indeed.   No.   I'll drop off at some hotel
along the Boulevard Haussmann : that's nearer my
business.   May I call for you and take you out to dinner
one night ? '

' We're at the Royal Odéon for a few days.   Thanks
very much for taking care of Mrs. Western.   You know
my name—Fenton ? '

' Oh, we're sure to meet some time,' smiled Marpurgo.
' Brother marxists usually do—and brother fantasts.'
He twinkled at Oliver.   ' We're both cabbalist fantastics.
I sense it : we're serious artificers of form, but jocund
about content.'

Oliver from the window of the taxi exclaimed :

' Dialectics, being flexible, is a rigid discipline.'

' I must discuss that with you,' twinkled Marpurgo :
' if you'll discuss it with a business-man.   But I'm a sort
of fabulist, the Arabian Nights is my natural background,
and I don't know whether you have noticed how skelet-
ally economic the concepts of those Arabian Knights are.
Definitely hegelian concepts ! '

The last they saw of him was his slender white hand
waving out of a black taxi window; his mockery,
dandyism, strange accent, half Mile End Road and half
Piccadilly, remained with them in the air for some
moments.   Then Oliver took Elvira's hands and covered
them with kisses.   A shop which had just lighted up
blazed with the bizarre word ' Quincaillerie.'   The taxi
slid down the slippery street in contrary direction from
all the working-people hurrying heel and toe, flat arch

and muddy heel, towards the suburban trains of the Gare du Nord. Oliver looked out at the stream and sighed.

'To think that such a people, intelligent, class-conscious, revolutionary, should support a capitalist class—it's incredible. There are some things I can't understand at all,' he explained to Elvira. 'Look at them, look at them, the sanest people on earth : why do they go on with their burdens ? They only have to lay them down and they are free. Why do they go on ? '

Elvira's impatient voice came from the corner :

'Why ? Because they're hungry and tired and their wives won't let them leave their jobs.'

'There aren't so many like you, free, willing to take a chance. How I admire you, and worship you ! You'll never know how much. I live for you.'

A street-lamp lighted her banded brows and dilated eyes. He said :

'When I got your telegram on Saturday, I thought I had gone queer with waiting and was seeing things. I had to tack it up on my bedroom wall and I kept looking at it all the evening before I believed it. I didn't sleep that night, or Sunday night—until nearly morning, and then I fell into a golden, happy sleep. To-night is Monday night—to-night I will sleep. . . .' After a silence he said with emotion, 'Why did you make me wait all the week-end ? Where is Paul ? What did he say ? '

'Paul's in the country, on an estate near Luton : he was invited out by a patient of his, Sir Frederick Charles, or Sir Charles Frederick, I don't know what. A bachelor week-end. These men love to get each other off into stag huddles in the week-ends : they get crushes on each other—his patients are in the City, and the City is a sort of stag-party. I was nearly mad with trying to decide what to do after I got your letter. I thought if Paul goes away this week-end, I go : if he stays, I stay. He went. Before he went, we had a scene, of course. I couldn't help asking him why he went and left me alone. He knows I hate to be alone. When he comes back to-day, he'll get a jolt,' she ended bitterly, shrugging her shoulders.

'You won't have any more trouble—in your life! Think of that: here's someone who loves you dearer than all the world. Put your head on my shoulder. . . .'

It gave her a crick in the neck. She seized the first opportunity to sit up and look out.

'Oh, aren't the fountains pretty?'

'They don't play yet: it's too cold. That's the Régence where Napoleon played chess—Alekhine too, the champion. This is the Louvre. Look at the Tuileries, like the Garden of Eden at night: that double chain of jewels is the Champs Elysées: those two great bland clockfaces are the Gare d'Orsay. Look, look at the silky, sulky Seine. . . .' He laughed, rollicked, triumphed.

'Oliver, where are we going?'

'Don't ask. You'll see!'

'A hotel?'

'Yes, an old-fashioned hotel, with high, grand, elegant rooms, long brocade curtains. You'll like it.'

'Do we have to show our passports in the hotel?'

'No, I just fill in a sheet—Mr. and Mrs. Fenton. Don't worry, darling: even if they knew they wouldn't say anything. The French are human on human relationships. All they ask is, Do you pay your bills? If you do, you pass.'

She breathed freely. 'That's—capitalism, isn't it?' She wanted to please him.

'Yes: but when the relation is expressed in such simple terms, it is the easier to break down a system. In England it is just the opposite.'

'Yes, and then in England the people have a sense of humour: they don't take every little thing as a serious issue. They are more sophisticated.'

'Paul says . . . ' Oliver gibed gently.

'Paul believes in England: he is a patriot. Whatever his personal faults, he is faithful to his principles.'

'That is, he has no sense of humour'—Oliver peered

into her face, grinning—'when it comes to business. Don't you realise he sells his conservatism; it excuses English medicine's being in a backwater.'

After a while, she said, uncomfortably, 'In a way.'

There were few clients in the hotel. The room, on the first floor, twenty feet high, with long French windows, looked through blue brocaded curtains into the rue de l'Odéon. When the boy had left the bags and gone with Oliver's excessive tip, Oliver rushed over to her.

'Look around, Elvira: this is our first home.'

She withdrew her hands and went into the bathroom.

'It is rather nice, isn't it?'

While she was powdering her uncoloured face, Oliver came and looked over her shoulder.

'What a perfect couple we are! Aren't we made for each other? Two darkies, eh?'

When she had first seen him in London she had been shocked and repelled by his great beauty, his small, dark-red mouth, his long thick black lashes curling on a red and white cheek. She smiled at his vanity now.

'Your mother must have been a beautiful woman.'

'Oh, when she was eighteen, she was the rose of Sharon and the lily of the valley! But when I knew her she was already thick and podgy with an immense, immense bosom dressed in frills of speckled voile.'

'Freudians can't accuse you of an Oedipus complex, then. I must seem thin to you.'

'You're beautiful,' he said, 'but you don't know how to dress. A French woman built like you would build up her bosom. I'll take you to a dressmaker who will study your style and bring out your femininity. You must go, the very first thing, to the Printemps, or to Antoine, and have your hair done too. Oh, you'll spend fortunes on yourself before you've been in Paris long. You'll be quite a different woman. You can dress, you know. You'll be splendid when you're dressed like a French woman. Everyone will say, How adaptable she is.'

She gave him a long surprised look and began to laugh.

' Oliver, so I don't suit you ?   You brought me over
to make me a French woman.   You're an incredible
chauvinist.'

' I love you and I love France : I want to be happy
with the two together.'

' Let's go down. We don't want to be staying here.'

' What does it matter if they think we're honey-
mooners ?   They like it here : they're sympathetic.'

' Oh—let's go down.'

She swept out of the door.

In the lounge Marpurgo was sitting with a sheaf of
papers. Oliver nodded to him. He started up towards
them.

' Madame ! Please forgive me. I seem to be sleuthing
you. I went to the Royal-Haussmann. A person went
ahead of me through the revolving door that I must not
on any account meet—that is, if I am to have peace. I
was flustered, quite flustered, and got into the taxi again.
I am tired of my old hotel in the rue du Bac, and every
other hotel in Paris went out of my head. I said to the
driver, "Anywhere you like ! " and I found myself here.
I didn't know till I got inside that it was your hotel. He
no doubt heard your directions and assumed we were
friends ! Nadir of indiscretion.' He smiled at Elvira.
' Intention usurps coincidence in *my* system ! You see,
I believe in affinities, in fatality, and that only fate can
force its own hand. However, fate bows to neighbourliness. It's only till to-morrow, till I can regain my senses.'
He laughed. ' This person was not a lady, no, no : I
have no " buried life and Paris in the spring," but the
old anchoret has spiritual foes. . . .' He bowed himself
back to his chair and fell at once to his reading. He had
some Perrier water in front of him.

Oliver said : ' That's an idea. Let's go into the bar.
Yes ! Now, yes. We're going to do everything to-night,
have all the fun, because to-night's my wedding-night.'

' And so we go into the bar ?   What about the three
Amer-Picons ? '

'No cracks : I'm going to boss you from now on.
You're going to find out what you've been missing all
your life. You've been a nice lady : I'm going to make
you into à grand girl.'

She laughed. 'Dress doesn't suit, airs don't suit ;
thanks very much. What a terrible fellow you are ! Do
you think you'll recognise me when you've finished
making me over ? '

'Nothing could alter the you that I love.'

'I'm glad of that.'

When they sat down on the plump leather seats and he
had turned on the light in the unfrequented bar, he seized
her hands and leaned forward, looking starrily, dizzily,
with extravagant romance, into her eyes.

'Do you like being with me, Elvira ? How does it
feel ? '

'Look, here's the waiter.'

'*Garçon, deux portos !* We'll have dinner in a restaurant
in the Place de l'Odéon, the "Sucking-Pig" is its
name, but in French, and then we'll take coffee on the
boulevards, perhaps in the Boul' Mich', that's short
for the Boulevard St. Michel, the students' boulevard,
the Latin Quarter, if you like. Now, Elvira, I want you
to look at everything without prejudice. I want you to
get Paris into your blood. Forget everything you've
seen up to now, forget everything you've read, heard,
imagined, and just look. I want to see you soak up
Paris. I won't tell you much : I'm likely to influence you.
I want you to get your impression. Afterwards, we'll
go to a nine-o'clock theatre—they have them here : it
gives you time to have dinner in a civilised fashion ; or
the pictures—you'll see pictures here, despite the censor-
ship, that never get to England at all ; or a long drive to
the Bois de Boulogne. Haven't you dreamed ever since
you were a girl at school of driving in the Bois de
Boulogne ? You remember the pictures of the drags, the
gay old boys in grey bell-toppers : remember Guy de
Maupassant ? It's not like that now, of course, infinitely

more decorous. But you'll see it yourself. Perhaps you're tired.'

' I'm a little tired, Oliver. Let's rest here, have dinner and just walk a little.'

' Just whatever you like, darling. This is your night.'

' Listen to that *fool*,' exclaimed Elvira angrily.

The Italian was arguing with the bell-boy. The bell-boy said in broken English :

' We not 'ave the *Humanité*, sir, we 'ave the *Intransigeant* and *Paris-soir*.'

' No,' said Marpurgo, ' I want the *Humanité*. It has a good name—Humanity it means, doesn't it ? '

' Yes, sir.'

' I like its name ; I want that paper. Order it for me to-morrow.'

' Yes, sir.'

The bell-boy lunged off, with his tip. Presently the dignified porter appeared, saluting :

' Excuse, sir, the boy tell you want the *Humanité* : you will not like that paper, sir. Will I order the *Matin* ? '

' No, I want the *Humanité*. I like the name. Humanity is a lovely word, and here you believe in liberty, equality, fraternity, don't you ? You even have it up over your prisons, don't you ? The French are admirable people, a great revolutionary people : I come here because I admire their free spirit. I want to get your paper about humanity.'

The porter looked cautiously, heavily at him. ' *Je vous demande pardon, Monsieur*, but it is not about humanity : it is about *politique*. It is for working-people.'

' Well, I work, you work : get it : get it in the morning.'

The porter cried in desperation : ' Monsieur, you don't understand ; it is the journal of the reds.'

Elvira said impatiently, ' Oh, can't the porter see that man is making a fool of him ! What fun is there in it ? Imitation Mark Twain ! Marpurgo seems to like acting to mystify waiters and so on. He was doing it in the train. It's cheap snobbery.'

Oliver laughed. 'That Italian is a card : do you hear his accent ? He speaks perfect French, the rascal. I'm going to send the bell-boy upstairs for my *Humanité*. That will shock 'em.'

'Oliver, please don't.'

'Oh, Elvira : where's your sense of humour ? He's real fun, that man. I'm surprised you had the brains to pick him up.' He twinkled engagingly and went off. The Italian bowed to her again, and they stood laughing. Presently the bell-boy, amused because of the tip, appeared with Oliver's paper. The two men came over to Elvira.

'I was only pretending ignorance, of course, to teach them a lesson. I did it in my last lush hotel, but they were more cunning; they agreed at once and forgot it every morning.'

Elvira looked unsmiling into her drink.

'I'm sure you think that's childish, Madame ! '

'Yes, rather.'

'We are : we do our best to remain young to match the eternal youth of women.' Elvira flashed an insolent look at him, thinking, ' He knows already that I am older than Oliver : what is the use of trying to conceal anything from this gumshoe ? ' Marpurgo was bending over in a debile pose, looking at his small, pointed, polished shoes.

'You have never been in Paris before ? ' he said politely to Elvira. 'And you ? ' he asked Oliver, ignoring Elvira. Oliver told him he had been there two years before when he was an undergraduate, during the summer vacation, staying in the apartment of a friend, a student at the Beaux-Arts. Elvira said, ' Alec Bute, you mean ? '

'Yes, that dear fellow ; a painter,' explained Oliver to Marpurgo with a puzzled smile, conscious of some antagonism between the other two ; ' but it was only for ten days. We only saw a bit of Paris and then ran out to

Chartres, where he was doing some painting in an old
street. Then my cash ran out. My uncle put me through
the University,' he added: 'I have a scholarship the
last two years.'

Marpurgo nodded. 'I was a student here when
twenty. I spent half a year and then the war broke out.
I went through the war and came back to Paris at twenty-
five, but my academic career was finished. I couldn't go
back and study at that age—or thought I couldn't. Now
I regret it. But my father's health was failing. I went
into the business. Then—my, er, politics are not popular
in Italy. I naturalised in England, without changing my
name always. But the year I spent here at twenty '—he
bent towards them, gathering them both into his lap, as
it were, like a fowl with drooping wing running after her
family—' here,' he repeated slowly, thoughtfully, looking
at the red port he had consented to take, as an exceptional
thing, ' in the land of enchantment where the glasses are
full of dissolved pearl, jasper, sard, ruby, topaz, curling
cornelian, where there are more false diamonds and false
eyelashes than anywhere else, where the gowns are more
elegant, the complexions more enamelled, laces finer,
shoes smaller, heels higher, the gait more billowy, the
fans better painted and the breasts set more to advantage
than in all the world ; where that violent liquor love
concealed in the heart's smoky hard jewel, is finer strained
and thicker distilled, more adulterated and oftener
aspersed, the blood flows wilder in passion and revolt,
the beds are oftener stained with blood and love and the
river oftener thickened with blood and tears : the garden
of lovers, joy of youth, nest of revolution, city of the
thrice-fired blood ! '

Oliver sat back in his chair watching with dark, jealous,
appreciative eyes. Elvira smiled faintly. She occasionally
cast a glance over Marpurgo from head to foot, sizing
him up, his thin body, cold, bright eyes and dark fluty
mouth. Marpurgo acknowledged one of these glances
and smiled: he said in a lower key, hurriedly, to Elvira:

'I hurry away and hurry back—the cornices, the river, the soft sky—it makes me restless.' He turned his insistent sapphire disks upon them both, leaning forward on his stick, his shoulders rounded.

'It is impossible to rest here. You must get up and go, walk, talk, write, spend, speculate, invent: I don't know whether it was so before the revolution, but it is so now. And yet we spend a whole life here uncreative and go away, regretting the glorious years spent in Paris, and die sniffing the dry scent of those weeds we sowed here and carefully cut and pressed. I read in my history book when I was at school that, in the beginning of the ninth century, the " king and his nobles vegetated in Paris." I suppose the climate was the same. When you are here you have your place in the sun.'

'Then Paris has simply got you,' said Elvira with her habitual quiet disdain : ' but it would not get me : you are like that, that is all. You like this kind of life, busily frittered away.'

Still bending on his stick, with his eyes on the floor, serious, he said :

'I don't know why, really, I didn't become French instead of English. First, because I didn't want to be conscripted, second because I am afraid of frittering away my time here : I am fated to it, knit by numerous threads to it, but I have never done well by it and yet I feel I will be fulfilled here, one day. You have the same feeling about a marvellously beautiful woman when you sit beside her —you have not done well by her, knit her nimbly into all your minutes of life. Every slow word she lets fall, every recalcitrant charm that somehow escapes though she sulks, every small curve is perfectly sensual and stirring : you have not seized all those particles, you have let them drop, float away in the air—others have caught them, strange eyes of louts and gentlemen, wine in glasses, mirrors, plate-glass windows : she is busy making herself up already, preparing, restless, getting on her gloves, settling her furs to go to another rendezvous . . .

even when she is shooting off some sibilant insolence at you, she is thinking of being somewhere else. Only her mirror possesses her in plenitude. . . .'

His eyes were appealing to Elvira. Oliver, watching Marpurgo, said to himself, ' He is an ascetic, he despises women and yet he is lonely, he tries to net them with eloquence, and then he lets them fly free again ; when he has amused her now he will tire of her and give her to me. . . .'

Marpurgo drained his glass and lifted his right hand, dark, softly muscular, supplicating them to hear him out :

' When I stand in the Place de la Concorde, I think of when I will be dead and in the Elysian fields. I say, Rise not before me, Paris, when I am dead, to disturb my shadow walking. I hope your rushing wheels and glittering spokes, orchestras, first violins and barkers, ten-o'clock theatres and singers on the Tertre, screams, klaxons in E flat major, your " Arise, damned of the earth," tramping feet and dramas of the rue de la Goutte d'Or, the sprouting of leaves, lapping of waves, jingling of your praetorian guard, clinking of glasses, scraping of palettes and tapping of typewriters, will not penetrate the earth too deep. I should like to live shabbily a little while, undisturbed by the dreams both gay and miserable which I dreamed in your coverlet. And the joy and hope here would discontent me with death, I should want to live again. In the myriad discontents here is the gestation of the new world, that dawn is the only peace for the wild, wicked, selfish, unsmiling, lonely human heart. . . . The streets here are patined with the days of man's life.'

Marpurgo closed his eyes for a minute, and opened them wide, serious.

' A song of the lovers of Paris to the lovers in Paris ; but why Paris ? She should have been called Hellene. . . . For her good patriots desert their fatherlands. . . . Another vermouth ? No ? Can I take you to dinner ? The Capucines is on the Grands Boulevards, very good— you can see the Baron de Rothschild there sometimes—

if you like a *filet mignon*—but you'll see : wonderful cigars. The last is very important, spiritually, for spiritual adventures ! Do you smoke, Mr. Fenton ? '

Oliver said with a touch of bad humour :

' I am not yet in the stage of spiritual adventures.'

' Some never reach them, lying becalmed off Cytherea.' Marpurgo laughed to himself. ' But that's not for you. Well, let's walk a bit—to the Seine, and then a taxi if you like : otherwise, we can keep walking.' He wrapped his loose French coat round him and sent Elvira forward with a bright gnomish courtesy, his face wrinkled in a smile : he followed after them both with his head planted forward in his shoulders, his shoulders bowed, his feet put forward firmly, splayed ; he seemed to limp slightly. He folded the *Humanité* into his pocket and paddled out, nodding to the bell-boy and porter as if they were in his own mansion, speaking to all and sundry in fluent French. He saw them through the revolving door holding hands covertly. When he got out he said : ' We will have dinner and then I'll let you off, while I avoid spiritual adventures in my chess-club. You honour me by spending your first evening in Paris with me, and I don't want to take advantage of your goodness. I will go and play chess at the " Régence "—you know it ? There is a good orchestra there, a café orchestra, but good : the first violinist is a Hungarian, I sometimes get him to play the real thing for me. If you want to go there later for coffee, you will like it. But if you intend to go to the theatre or the pictures,' he waved his hand at the billposts announcing the beginning of a Beethoven cycle and turned to Oliver deferentially. ' Did you get in to hear the Leners last year ? I was at the Queen's Hall, heard Maple Wood conducting the Brahms second in D Major, he blurred the delicious second subject in the usual way—there are after all only two conductors who can do that, Stokowski and Mengelberg——'

He stopped, maliciously. ' Are you a musician, Mrs. Western ? '

' Oh, no,' she said in her soft metallic voice, ' no, I just learned music, with geography, fancy-work and painting, in the ordinary way, for five or six years, but I have no real talent for it : we learned painting from an R.A. and music from a composer, I forget his name : when I'm lonely I play Chopin's Nocturnes, the Moonlight Sonata——'

' —in C sharp minor, Op. 27, no. 2,' murmured Marpurgo.

' I don't know,' said Elvira. ' I don't know that the name matters.'

Oliver, who had been dreaming, only said :

' I love to hear a woman playing in a house : it's always been a dream of mine, a woman's hand wandering over the ivories—when I have a house—a woman, a soft, reluctant voice, music, flowers.' He turned and smiled into Elvira's eyes.

She took her hand from his arm with irritation, looking for her powder-puff in her purse. ' A woman is a human being, not an aesthetic gratification.' There was silence : Marpurgo smiled.

The advertisements in red, blue and green neon tubes bloomed softly in and out, crowds passed along the grisette boulevards, the boulevards with open lap, decked out and beckoning. The broad, blue-crayoned streets were full of hoots, horns and wind instruments of motor-cars, hurried animals hailing as they passed. The rue Laffitte thundered, the cafés were full, their terraces, glassed-in against the cold, were planted with clients, like conservatories with pot-plants, the stoves burned bright. The gutters were frozen black, heaps of snow still lay under the trees. Friends let out of work met each other and hurried by, men with evening papers, girls with neat belted waists, streamed along. Marpurgo expanded, sniffing up a thousand details with the animal delight of a dog reconnoitring fenceposts. He made them sit down in a small bar in the rue du 4 Septembre opposite a great bank, saying if they were not going to the theatre, they had plenty of time, it was best not to eat till eight o'clock. He ordered two drinks for them, but himself took Perrier water, and described the profession, character and intentions of various persons who passed, old sleuth and boulevardier.

Oliver lent himself joyfully to the game, but Marpurgo sniffed at his conclusions. ' It takes years, Fenton, to get the right mixture of malice, melodrama, sentimentality, ethnology, psychology ; when you get it right, you shake together, toss it off and immediately the people under your eyes become translucent : drunkenness of the human cocktail.'

Elvira looked the women over and sipped her drink.

' There's no one to check you up.'

Marpurgo cackled, and in a moment, ' Look there,' he said.

A thin middle-aged man on the second floor of the bank building, between the undrawn curtains, was imitating a ballet-dancer to amuse some person whose thin saffron hand grasped one of the sand-coloured velvet curtains. The dancer looked fawnishly out of the lozenge-paned windows at the thinning boulevard to see if he was observed, and then resumed his ballet with a coquettish expression, his face sharpened like a lead-pencil, pallid, with receding hair and small head ; now high, now low, he went, advancing and retreating, patting the air with outstretched hand, marking different heights as he rose from a stooping pirouette. Suddenly, he stopped, clapped his hands softly, bowed a number of times, then, with a twirl, smiled, blew a kiss and retired behind the other curtain. The small hand which he entertained disappeared. The dancer reappeared, talking rapidly, gesticulating, shrugging his shoulders, shaping with his hands a pair of legs of enormous size, tapering down to a pair of svelte ankles. He retired beyond the chandelier.

' Well ? ' said Marpurgo.

Elvira admitted :

' Luck is with you.'

' It always is,' said Marpurgo, ' always. I am a Parisian.'

Oliver stopped grinning to say :

' Lots of funny things happen to you. When I was here last, I got blotto one evening. The next day I was sleepy ; as I came along to the bus-stop Sèvres-Babylone, I found myself zigzagging on the pavement with my head doddling on my breast. I went into the nearest doorway and sank down on the two steps in the entry. When I woke up I was in the concierge's loge, on her sofa with a warm black hair rug over me. A woman was singing in the kitchen with a noise of pots. I heard the gas flaring and the canary chirping—heavy filet lace curtains with crocheted bunches of grapes hung on the glass door, on the wall the traditional engraving "The Last Roll-call of the Girondins in the Conciergerie." The concierge came in : she was a pretty young woman with dark hair and a new pink jumper. She came close to look at me and asked me if I was sick. I lay looking up at her for a while, not wanting to speak at all : then I said no, and she came a little closer to peer at me, and put her hand on my forehead. It was twilight : an extraordinary psychic event took place, I took her hand, kissed it violently and drew her into my arms.' He laughed. ' She slapped my face, called me a filthy young thing, opened the door and turned me out. On my honour, I don't know to this day what possessed me.'

' You got slapped for a psychic event,' said Elvira coolly.

Marpurgo remarked : ' There are hours when we expect the human race to act naturally, ideally—we usually get slapped for our pains : akin to the hour when you are afraid you will be impelled to get up and dance in church. Come, children, we must eat : then I am off to the field of battle. I go to the Régence for preference because I have refused money to every sponger there for years, and now they let me alone.'

He gave them a fine dinner, himself eating little and

taking long over it, nibbling luxuriously. When the
filtered coffee came he called round the cigars with
importance and bought four Corona-coronas. Through
the blue smoke he entertained them with a story of dis-
pute between master and men in a progressive lacehouse ;
the designs executed on the Jacquard lace-machines are
controlled through pierced cardboards hinged together
which pass over a roller, in the manner of a player-piano.
The cards are pierced either by hand or by an automatic
card-piercing machine, operated with a keyboard, like a
linotype machine. The débris from the piercing usually
belongs to the operator ; he sells it, and the few centimes
it produces are his. The owner of the progressive factory
considered that the débris was his and commandeered it
for the sake of the few centimes. Marpurgo described
the man, Monsieur Boutdelaize, a gay, inventive man, a
great whoremaster and buyer-out of bankrupt inventors ;
he rarely made a fine lace, specialised in commonplace
commercial designs and threads, was full of sharp prac-
tice, skimped on thread, showed old lace for new, was
out to break the trade-unions and ruin all leaders of the
men. He thought the world would get poorer and
poorer and its wealth be concentrated in the hands of
men like himself, crafty, inventive, unscrupulous men.
He was a high-class engineer and chemist himself.

Oliver said :

' Taking the short view, he is right ; money is only
made at present by men who combine the technician and
financier, the old-fashioned man of the métier is ruined.'

' What is the subject of your essay ? ' asked Marpurgo.

' The French Workers' Movement from the Commune
to the Amsterdam Congress of 1904,' said Oliver.

' Why 1904 ? '

' I can't get at the Archives much later than that,'
explained Oliver. ' They're not open, you know, till a
generation has passed. That makes all investigation safe
for the existing order.'

' You don't have to depend on the Archives ; you can

use newspaper files, you can go to the provincial newspapers,' suggested Marpurgo.

'I don't want to press it too hard : I want to look like
a socialist who knows the amenities,' gibed Oliver. 'I
want to get a job, in other words Elvira doesn't want
to be the mother of revolutions !' He laughed at her
sitting there with her critical, indolent, mute eyes. 'I
don't want to cut up,' said Oliver. 'My family are bakers
and poor working-class people. I know what it is to be
suburban, believe what's in the newspapers and admire
the family life of the King and Queen. I'll be a labour
educator. I'll edit books of essays on social problems—
I've done my bit in doing that. I know the working-
class, you must gradually foment their revolt. They
revolt, not us : we're the bourgeoisie. We can't do
anything : their revolt will come in its time. The hour
is no longer with *blanquistes*.'

He drank his liqueur : his gestures were becoming
frequent, his eyes more fiery, his sidelong smiles to Elvira
more silky : he was getting drunk. Marpurgo permitted
some of his spite to creep through, seeing it would not
be noticed ; he said abruptly :

'Why not do the English workers' movement ? '

Oliver giggled.

'The old question ! Opportunism, pure and simple,
dear boy : I must get a position before I can spout fire :
the " fool-red fury of the Seine " has been accepted as a
weakness of the French character, not as a stage in the
dialectics of history : it can get past the examining body
as a piece of exotic learning, like the quaint customs of
the Aruntas. I doubt if I could be sufficiently patron-
ising about the English workers to have the same effect
on my superiors. After, after !'

Marpurgo sneered. 'After, when you are well-
established, you will go foot-loose among the intellectuals,
dazzling them and the masses but well removed by a
pretty line of footlights. You have talent, but you're an
arriviste ! '

Oliver waved his hand. ' As Lenin calls it, I am being seduced by the " refined corruption of the petty-bourgeois state ! " Not at all : look at G. B. S. ! Has he been a fount of criticism or not ? Is it better to be a bad little black Shetland pony curried and favour-curried, fed and silk-fed, finally disrupting the family through the Freud-ian dreams of the wife and daughter, or a hardheaded mule, kicking against the brick wall of the stable and getting nothing but turnip-peel and the stick ? I shall disrupt them through their dreams ! Like G. B. S. Like all the slink-eyed, bristle-backed darlings the petty-bourgeois take into their lap : to deceive and be deceived.'

' To be honest is a poor man's folly,' sneered Marpurgo.

' Fortunately I have the folly in me through my father and mother : in the meantime I have to do better than them, or I will have to sweat like them and never get a moment to think. I have to be my own Alma Mater.' His brow puckered and darkened, he brought his hand down flat on the table.

Marpurgo looked at him with curiosity and said finally : ' I know a few of the professors at the School of Economics through Lensky. But I also know Edwards and Jamieson, leading brokers in Throgmorton Street and Austin Friars, respectively : if you ever think of going into business, let me know. You would make a very successful business-man.'

Oliver flushed. ' I'd like to go into business ! I'd like to deal with something real. My father always said to me, " I'm dealing with real things, bread : people can live on bread alone." He isn't at all impressed with my scholarship and success : he just says, " I do real work, I make and sell bread. People can live for bread alone." For the majority, it is all they hope to get. He is right.' He looked at Marpurgo merrily, appealingly. ' Get me a job, in lace, in anything : I'll take it at once.'

Elvira looked interested. ' It's not a bad idea : you can't be king of a chat-parlour all your life ! Unless you have the divine flame, you know, that makes a man a bookworm, it's better to do something else. And a man like you, Oliver, so lively and so taking, and so—' she laughed and blew her cigarette-smoke into the air and did not speak for a minute, slewing her gelatinous eyes roguishly on him, '—such a natural two-timer,' she finished, ' you'd be a wonderful business-man.'

' When I was thirteen, I won my first scholarship,' lamented Oliver : ' I saw it as a way out of the baking business : I took it. Since then it has been nothing but essays. The boys I went to school with were clerks, counter-jumpers, insurance-salesmen, weavers, coal-miners, long ago : married, have children, are getting the dole and belong to labour-unions, and I've never faced one of the issues of life. I'm still a schoolboy.' He hiccoughed. He put his shapely small hand on Marpurgo's coat. ' You get me a job, Marpurgo, and I'll take it at once. I'm keen to do some work.'

Marpurgo laughed paternally, satisfied with his work.

' I'll introduce you to my firm here, Georges and Antoine Fuseaux : I know a house in Calais also, cotton importers, who need a bright young man, and I'll ask in Nottingham when I'm there in a few months. But you had better finish your essay and get your doctor's degree first : a doctor's degree goes well, even in business : then consider, there are so many graduates who are waiters and chauffeurs now. You can't allow yourself to be less educated than the "hideous proletariat," an expression of Paul Bourget, you that have come so far and will undoubtedly go farther.'

' I'll take anything that offers, even so,' said Oliver impetuously, looking languorously, the next moment, at Elvira.

Elvira, getting sleepier and more numb with the good food, warmth, cigar smoke and voices of men, spread her charms around, gave them the benefit of her eyes, thought of her body, knowing by experience that that made her an enchantress. She smiled deeply to herself with the full realisation of her female powers. Marpurgo watched her putting out her flowers : they went on talking of politics and Oliver's essay, but lazily linking one expected remark to another. The misanthrope in Marpurgo came out, rubbed his hands and stretched. He left them very readily after dinner, treadling away through the thinned crowds down the Avenue de l'Opéra.

'A misanthropic dervish, a thwarted play-actor,' crowed Oliver, following Marpurgo's back, with enchanted eyes.

'I hope he doesn't adopt us,' murmured Elvira. 'He will want to show us all Paris. He bores me with his speeches. It's a city like others, isn't it ? People work in it ! '

'It's not workaday Paris for us to-night : he knows it —and then, didn't he say he likes to sit next to a beautiful woman ? '

Oliver looked at her thoughtful face and unreadable eyes and lifted her hand to his lips as they walked. Elvira went walking straight ahead, leaning on him, swaying a little, a buddhist expression, which he took for content, on her broad, still features. Their room looked on to the steps of the Odéon. The people were just streaming out, the women with long robes like night-dresses under their cloaks.

Elvira turned into the room, took in the yellow-plated bedstead, the wallpaper covered with red palm-leaves, the red carpet, the red and grey chairs, and murmured, dashed : 'It's so trite, isn't it ? It depresses me so : couldn't we have found something not so much like a hotel bedroom?' She laughed. 'Think of all the couples who have slept here before us ! They make it stale, don't they ? ' She lifted china eyes to Oliver. 'Life's a pattern, and we're just shuttles rushing in and out thinking we are making jerks up and down freely.' She sat down on the edge of the bed. 'When Paul divorces me, this room and this night will be mentioned in the evidence.'

Oliver rushed over, took both her hands and looked into her eyes. 'Oh, what is it? Remorse? No, no. You're tired. We should not have gone with that pestiferous Italian : we should have spent this evening, our evening, alone quietly. I blame myself. . . .'

'I wonder at myself ; I wouldn't have come away unless I had done it in a rush : all the way to Paris I was concentrating on you, to forget about Paul, and now I am exhausted, morally exhausted.'

Oliver, stroking her smooth sable hair, smiled to himself.

'You need someone to look after you, and you've got him now. I thought this was a beautiful room ! Remember my digs in Brunswick Square ? You went there —once—you remember?—that evening I knew——' He kissed her forehead. 'Well, we'll move if you don't like this room to-morrow. Now, shall I unpack for you ? '

'If you like.' He dragged her cases about, full of love, dived his hands into her clothes, let the water run for her bath. Soon she was cheerful again, finding it a huge joke that she had packed one stocking in one case and one in another. When Elvira came from her bath she had on the mandarin robe Paul had bought her in Greek Street, three years ago. She had never worn it. It was of transparent net, but heavily encrusted with gold thread. She heard Oliver draw in his breath sharply and walked softly about the room for a while pretending to unpack : all the lights were on and Oliver had taken out a new red, grey and black silk dressing-gown : they looked like a couple of butterflies. She reclined on her pillow while Oliver was bathing, her hair scented, smelling the fresh linen, and thought she had never felt so easy since she was a girl at boarding-school. She had been happy with all her life arranged for her. Oliver heard her laugh.

'Oliver ! I'm laughing because I'm glad I ran away.' He hurried to rejoin her : she was stretching her arms. 'I should like to wear this robe all night, I feel so grand in it.' He stood, like a robed priest, looking at her intently.

'Elvira, you're lovelier now than I've ever seen you! You have a secret beauty, a bloom that only comes out when you're in the house : and now it is brightest of all.'

She laughed softly. 'Oh, I shall sleep so well to-night : I am rosy with sleep. Yes, I will sleep all night in this mandarin robe, to celebrate my adventure. You must lie still as a stone all night, or you will crush it.' She laughed to herself gutturally.

'No, Elvira : it's harsh, it'll hurt your skin.'

'Yes, I say.'

'Perversity!'

She opened her eyes wide and looked up at the ceiling.

'I am bitter and perverse : no one wants me when they know me ; and I am egotistic, too. I like to spend money, I like to eat chocolates, I like to waste time. Now you know me : there's no more to me!' She laughed provocatively. She would have liked, though, to sleep all night alone wrapped in her gold-embroidered coat, with Oliver in another bed, but near : it was appropriate to the dark and glorious turrets of the Louvre, the coronet of the Champs Elysées, the great translucent clocks of the Gare d'Orsay, the neon tubes. She was so tired that she wished Oliver had not been there and she had been able to sleep all night alone wrapped in glory, an immured citadel busy with the traffic of dreams. A sleepy glutton, doped with foretaste, she would have put off the moment of joy. She wanted so to keep him enslaved, not to gratify him.

When they woke in the morning she wished still to lie and stretch, but Oliver got up, rang the bell, poured out her coffee, arranged her pillow, brought her her dressing-gown, eventually pulled her out of bed and made her dress.

The bells of Paris rang nine o'clock as they set out. It was cold in the frosty March air, the snow lay in the corners, groins and niches, on the turrets and cornices,

and hung on the breasts and noses of the statues in the
Tuileries. In the garden of the Beaux-Arts a shivering
dove with feathers blown the wrong way sat on the neck
of a dirty, mossy torso with snow on its back. Elvira's
eyes hurt, her colourless cheeks reddened, she was cross
at being waked so early and having coffee poured into
her and being dragged out by the scruff of the neck,
and being rushed along at this pace to see a romantic
commonplace like the Latin Quarter. It was there
before : it had been there since Abelard : it would be
there this afternoon. There were no bounds to Oliver's
enthusiasm. She thought, I hope he won't be like this
all the time and completely spoil the town for me.

He showed her the engravings and bookbindings on
the Quai Voltaire, and half-sang as he went. ' When I
was here, when we were here, the chaps and I, two years
ago, in June, Alec Bute was leaving the Beaux-Arts; they
always give them a send-off and they go singing round
the streets at midnight and breaking a few glasses in the
cafés : it's the regular thing, it's permitted . . . we had a
grand time. Gee, I wish you'd been there. We drank a
lovely soft Chambertin here—there they make an *entre-
côte Bercy*—oo, la, la !—we ate like kings : there always
used to stand a middle-aged prostitute with one leg. We
used to chivvy her and stand her drinks. There a
motherly old soul, with a black apron and crocheted
shawl, left off drinking a mug of bread-soup to sell me
a copy of Brantôme's *Gay Ladies* at thirty francs, the
crook. A lot she cared what was in it : she saw a young
forny fool ! '

His gay laughter rang on the air. He saw that she was
cold and took her to a bar where they stood up at the zinc
counter and had coffee. He got into a halting conversation with a workman speaking atrocious slang on the
subject of German rearmament and the funeral of a young
workman killed in an encounter with the police ; he was
in agreement with him, with everyone : he was out-
rageously, indecently merry. ' And all on account of me,'

thought Elvira, 'because he slept with me last night: aren't men childish? I slept with him, am I giving war-whoops?' She widened her united brows, made her semi-mongol face candid and austere, cast a wistful glance from her china eyes up at the moulding of the ceiling. Oliver was recalled by her silence and the infolding of her beauties from his boyish gallopading: he became silent, his hand crept down and found hers. He ordered another glass of coffee and drank it, with a wary eye on her, and without a word. Then they went on—book-shops, schools, famous old streets, gardens, the École de Droit, the Luxembourg, Montparnasse. To please him she submitted to it, hanging on to his arm until eleven-thirty, and then peevishly quit and sat down on a café terrace. He was all solicitude. 'What a stupid child I am! I have no consideration, to drag you like that: I'm used to hoofing it about with great hulking students. It shows I haven't squired too many ladies, at least. . . .' He chattered and looked brightly into her face for approval.

She smiled and said, when they had ordered another coffee to set them up: 'What about the concierge the time you fell asleep in the street?'

'Oh, what a memory! I'll have to watch my step.'

'I remember everything you've ever said,' she volunteered. 'Do you remember the day you asked me if I'd ever had a lover and said that to take one was as hard a step for a chaste married woman as for a virgin, and required as much persuasion?'

He blushed.

'You were so anxious to find out.'

'I always knew you hadn't,' he said seriously. 'You can always tell, you know.'

She cast him a silky look. 'Is that so? And then I remember the day we went out tramping. I had on my oldest hat and coat and was terribly ashamed you met me like that. And just when we were going past the glass in the door of the baker's shop you said you had dreamed about me the night before and dreamed I was the madonna.'

Oliver had a guilty look. ' I say,' he protested. ' I'll never tell you anything after this ; you've got a prize memory.'

' For conversations,' she emended.

By chattering she endeavoured to keep him there, but presently his dragoman passion got the better of him and he was careering off again, showing her a hundred things. She thought, in despair, ' I'll never be able to keep this up. After all, he's five years younger than me, and strong as a horse, coming from that working-class family.' Towards five o'clock she was ready to cry, when, un-expectedly, he took her towards home. She was ready to cry from relief when she saw the Opéra in the distance. The taxi deposited them in a few minutes at the hotel. They went upstairs, and then Oliver, surprisingly, said he would go out to the barber's. She thought, ' I'll take a bath : otherwise I'll never get through the evening.' She loved taking baths of all sorts, hot-water baths, Turkish baths, sunbaths. She lived through her skin and would have liked to have slaves to massage her and roll her in oils and powders. Oliver came back presently and asked eagerly, ' Did anyone call ? '

' No. Did you expect someone ? '

' No, no : I just—I thought I heard someone asking for Madame Fenton when I was going out.'

She looked at him doubtfully. ' Who would be here asking for me as Madame Fenton ? '

' How do I know ? ' He laughed. ' Perhaps I had the name in my head.' He gave her a strange look. ' I was no sooner out than I longed to be back : I saw at least ten women like you on the boulevard : you are a European type.' She stood in the shadow of the bro-caded curtain, against the wall, looking at him. He came nearer. ' Elvira, you missed me too. I can tell by the look in your eyes, a man can always tell.'

She put her hands on his breast. ' Oliver, let's go

away from Paris : I'm tired of Marpurgo. Let's be alone,
in a forest, or something. You spoke of Fontainebleau
in London. Let's go there, away from Paris and all its
scenes and love-episodes. It makes me feel cheap, and
I'm not cheap. I don't want Annibale hanging round
noting how we get on.'

' Yes, yes, I want to. I thought you liked Paris.
Let's go.'

She smiled. ' Let's go.'

He gave her another strange look. She murmured :
' It's too restless here. Let's get away where we can get
to know each other.'

He swayed towards her. ' I'm going to love you every
minute of the day, all your life—not just affection but
active, creative love. I used to be a selfish bastard—
with you I've got someone to live for and care for myself,
for I don't care if you impose on me. I'll like it. I want
someone's foot on my neck.'

She said, ' Paul—Oliver, kiss me ! '

She had a prosaic, experienced, brutal behaviour that
Oliver had never met before and that fired him : he had
thought her a cool, gentle creature.

CHAPTER II

A PUFF of heat and the smell of roasting chestnuts wel-
comed Marpurgo as he turned down the rue du Faubourg
Montmartre, one of the busiest streets in Paris. His
gaudy, busy, populace-loving soul rejoiced as he thrust
through the small-shouldered crowd, past the glass
doors and nickel bars of cafés serving late breakfasts of
coffee, beef extract, white wine and little breads, past the
loafers standing in the doors of bag-shops, shoe-shops
and theatres, of passport-photographers, erotic underwear
manufacturers, past pimps, pickpockets, unemployed
workmen and theatrical artists, girls with shiny bags and
high heels, restaurants and every brand of little commerce. The cold straked sky meandered down the
street between the irregular chimney-pots. Poor men
went past with their hands in their pockets and the
collars of their faded purplish suits turned up : pouter-
pigeon girls from the cheap hotels of iron bedsteads and
honeycomb quilts down that way, strutted by, marking
time with their heels, with high colour but stomachs
empty, pulling short coatees of imitation karakul about
their waists. A peddler selling pencils pulled out some
obscene photographs under the flap of his torn coat and
showed them to Marpurgo. A woman with a baby in
a shawl begged : ' I haven't eaten since yesterday, sir ;
give me six sous for milk.' Marpurgo passed on wilfully
with his eyes on the ground. Farther along a man lay in
a doorway with his hat over his red whiskers. Marpurgo
waked him up to put two francs into his hand. As he
did so, a voice said :
   ' Good morning, philanthropist ! '

Marpurgo turned suspiciously and said hastily :

' This is my propitiatory for the day. There were two others offering, one sold cheap heart's-ease, the other cheap heartache : I'm an ascetic ; I like to go down two turnings and up an alley for sensual enjoyment, and official gratitude is heartburn to me : so I waked up a chap who wasn't looking for it, and wondered what the devil I wanted with him.'

' Well, as long as he got it,' said the speaker, a business and café friend, ' and you're happy. How are you ? My wife wants you to come to dinner—say this day next week ? She sent a special message when she heard you were expected back, that she will keep the evening just for you. She got that history of music you suggested and has been studying ever since : I haven't seen her so serious since she left school. We've positively had nothing for dinner but *truites à la Bach* and *soufflé à la Offenbach* since you left.'

The cold wind still blew, but Marpurgo went on his way cheered. ' The offering worked,' he said to himself. ' I'll have a lucky day.' He turned into an old mansion used now as a commercial house. He treadled up the wide, worn axial staircase and pushed open the great black door on the first floor. On it was a board : ' Fuseaux & Cie : Tulles et Dentelles.' A clerk worked at a sloping desk by the courtyard window with a card-board shade over his eyes. A typist clicked in an adjoining office overlooking the street. She called out with affection, ' Good morning, Monsieur Marpurgo. They are both there. They expect you.' He crept in towards her to have a private word, when a clear, lazily exasperated voice came from another office, saying :

' Listen, what's the use of you trying to kid me ? You didn't send them the cheque. I know you, Georgie ; you always delay cheques two days and cash payments three days to a week. You hoped there'd be a war or a moratorium last night or this morning, so that you wouldn't have to pay. You've been doing it the fifteen years you've been in business : I suppose one of these days you'll be right. In the meantime, it's irritating.'

Marpurgo said very low, to the typist :

' It injures the credit of the firm.'

From the other office a voice graver, but very like the other, replied sharply :

' You save a day's interest—that's the way you make money. If one of us throws it away, one of us has got to save it. We owe him the money, don't we ? Why should we be in a hurry ? Let him be in a hurry. I told Mlle Rose to send it off yesterday. She forgot.'

The girl whispered :

' He told me to keep it till to-day.'

' Of course, of course,' nodded Marpurgo. ' Have you got any letters for me ? '

' I kept them,' deplored the girl, ' but Monsieur Georges went through my desk one Saturday afternoon after I had gone and found them all. He told me I should give them all mail. Afterwards I could only keep one. Here it is.'

Marpurgo looked at the Swiss postmark.

' From my wife.'

' Yes, that's why I kept it.'

He tapped Mlle Rose on the hand with an air of complicity by way of thanks and said, as he slipped it into his pocket :

' Kings crash, banks close, wars are declared, presidents fail to be re-elected, soldiers die in battle and workmen on the picket line, prize-fighters perish, but fragile Clara Marpurgo, tottering along life's slippery course, who was supposed to take the final leap before the age of sixteen, prophecy of an outspoken mitral murmur, still persists and is a lady and has a psyche withal. They tell me she blooms there like a flower, surrounded by pitying friends, whom she entertains with sour-sweet Christian tales of her husband who fears so much for her health and lives in Paris. She never could love me because of her heart : that was a relief

for me : she married me to provide sick comforts. Her
father had just died of heart disease and her mother
taught the piano to keep them both. Clara was to
die at sixteen, and she stopped growing at twelve.
When I first saw her I was fascinated by her sickness,
her airs, her parasitism. 'There is the wife for me,' I
thought, 'a purely selfish, childish, undeveloped Dresden
china soul, who will never have a thought for me, will
never make me a home, never bind me to domesticity,
who will make life a dream, keep the house shaded and
tranquil, and irritate me into action.'

'You really thought that at the time ? ' asked Mlle
Rose.

'Yes : I was a very young man and I wanted to be a
philosopher, but not an academic philosopher. I left
school at fourteen to learn men before I formulated any
theories.'

'Why are you in the lace business ? ' asked Mlle Rose.

'Men of genius usually ruin themselves for some
fantasy, or for their families, that's why there are so few
that succeed. There are really hundreds of thousands
of men of genius in the world. Well, my wife was my
ruinous fantasy and my bloodsucking family in one.
And, like most men, my need for spiritual intercourse
increased as old age approached. Now I bitterly regret
and hate my flowerlike parasite.'

'You are not old,' deprecated Mlle Rose.

'Thank you, but I am nearly forty : I have already
reached my autumn. I was a man at fourteen, I am in
decay at forty : I am in dissolution. I doubt, hate,
despise, ridicule, embroil, slander. The disease helps,'
he struck his breast. 'If I had actually married a healthy
woman who would have had her way and had children,
I should be better off now : I'd take sun and blood from
my sons. I should have had such sons. . . .' He laughed.
'No doubt they would have been loose-knit slubber-
degullions, something monstrous and gawky with
inflexible ideas—sons are usually a failure too.' He

patted her wrist. 'You're young : don't take any notice of me. It's a comfort to talk to you : I think you like me a little.'

'Yes, sir, I do, and I wish you were happy.'

He knocked softly at the door and put his head through as he slowly opened it, laughing with a peaked smile and cracked voice.

'Ah, the man himself,' cried Antoine Fuseaux, getting up and shaking Marpurgo's hand. 'Hullo, Marpurgo, how have you been ? Some of those job-lots were grand stuff : I don't know whether we'll get them all off, but they're certainly high quality.'

'Some of them have been on the shelves for five years : did you notice those fine Vals ? Raguse hated to see them go as job-lots, but I guess the million francs were welcome. He's practically closed down.'

'A million francs of back-numbers,' said Georges. 'Raguse must have got the impression that we'd gone in for philanthropy on a large scale. We bought out his old stock in Calais and we'll certainly have to give it away this end, it's so out of date.'

'Where are your eyes, Georges ? It's exquisite lace.'

'At thirty francs a metre, they'll probably be putting it on their beach pyjamas next summer,' drawled Georges.

'How are you feeling, though, Georges ? Is your rheumatism better ? Did you get away to Deauville ? '

'I don't get away, you know that, Marpurgo : there's too much work—someone's got to stay here. Otherwise the clients'll think the firm's changed hands and they'll expect to see on the door, " Mlle Rose and Albert Porteplume, Tulles et Dentelles." '

'Monsieur Raguse sent his kindest compliments to you both,' said Marpurgo politely. 'What a sweet man ! He particularly said he hoped Monsieur Antoine would soon be going to Calais.'

'Certainly, he doesn't like me. I sometimes remember I'm in business,' interjected Georges. 'Certainly, tell him Antoine'll go up there to have dinner with him any time. That's all he's got to do. We're not in business : we're running a greeters' club.'

Marpurgo continued nonchalantly to Antoine :

' Poor fellow. He has one winder, one spinner, two men only, the oldest with him, on the Jacquard machines, one designer instead of a dozen, and a man who comes in occasionally to punch the Jacquard cards. It is miserable. He'd shut up shop and save money if it were not for his name, Raguse, which is linked with the history of Calais. I remember when the whole building used to tremble with the machines ; now the courtyard is grown with weeds and the two machines work fitfully on little stock Valenciennes.'

Antoine, leaning back in his swivel-chair, with his hands in his pockets, and his eyes on the map of France, babbled :

' I like old Raguse; he's a lovely man, but he's history. He's history, he's a monument. That's just the trouble with him, that he's tied up with the history of Calais. . . .'

' You can't make lace out of knotted thread,' scolded Georges. Antoine talked on : '. . . Raguse is a gentle-man manufacturer. We're not in the candlestick age : we don't wear knee-breeches and ruffles. He ought to wake up and realise lace is proletarian now. What you want is pretentious, embossed, cheap, washable flowing stuff to put on cheap voile nighties. You don't want a design, because it gets hacked up anyway. And then you're competing with rayon. It's no go. You can't be a what-d'ye-callum minnesinger to-day. To-day you've got to be a cheap-jack, a thug, a bastard. You've got to forget art and steal your competitor's best selling designs. Like Boutdelaize. It's the age of vandals. You got to be like the chaps that followed what-d'ye-callum —Marpurgo, you're the learned mug round here, you know the name of the chap——'

' Attila ? '

' Yes, that's it, like the barbarians that followed Attila. This is an age of decay—you can plunder, you

can't lay up treasures or build. If you do someone else
will take them. Like Boutdelaize. He's just a plain
bandit. He was born for to-day. You've got to be a
man of your time.'

'Venus de Milo wouldn't become Miss Europe to-
day,' put in Georges. 'It'd be like the chaps who
invented the first fire-balloon putting fire into an aero-
plane and sending it up covered with fancywork. Raguse
makes lace for Looie Dizweet, and we've got to sell to
the Galeries Lafayette, who sells to typists on 800 francs
a month who make their own camiknickers in the
Tuileries. No one has a glory-box any more. Everything's changed : everyone's poor. And the only fine
designs the Rothschilds are interested in are the arabesques on banknotes. Banknotes, gold and diamonds
are the only things that have value any more. Nobody
believes in fine laces, jewels, movables, antiques any
more. Only the dumb middle-classes, who still hang
on to Aunt Annie's Queen Anne mirror, which they
think is worth £200, but which only brings £5 in a sale.
The chaps with money have bent steel, frosted glass
and fancy geometry on curtains. The only commercial
money is in something the unemployed can buy, or
something their sisters, who work as typists and keep
the family out of their pay-check, can buy, cheap,
effective, and that can be sold off the shelves in a week.
When the girls buy cheap stuff they want to change it
often. What we're doing in the lace business at a time
like this I don't know. Sell something people want.
How did Woolworth's make their money ? They saw
the world was getting down to a pauper economy. . . .'

'That's Boutdelaize's idea,' said Marpurgo.

'Come into my office, Marpurgo,' said Antoine, 'and
we'll look through the samples. Georgie's seen them
already.'

When he got Marpurgo inside his own door, he said :
'Don't listen to that moke ; you know him, he's on to
everything : he's so wise that he hangs up his pants

where he can't find them in the morning, so that he won't
pick his own pockets in the night. You don't make
money that way. We've got to have some new ideas ;
of course the business dies when you sit around and
groan like Georges. Isn't that what they're all doing—
sitting around and moaning you can't do anything ?
Now Boutdelaize is making money and so is Faubonhomme, your dyer friend. They've both got their heads
screwed on firmly though crooked. Boutdelaize uses
rotten thread and skimps on the selvedge. I'm not
against that, it's business. You've got to reckon that
you're up against rascals in business. Faubonhomme
invented the angel-skin finish for rayon, and now uses
this new glossy finish for écru lace. He undersells
Lyon for his dyeing and finishing because he uses non-
union labour and sacks every man that sabotages.
Boutdelaize knows that ninety per cent. of his competitors are out of the market, Faubonhomme knows
that eighty per cent. of Calais workers are out of a job.
They understand the world they live in : they may be
crooks, but they're hellishly smart. And you've got to
make money quick or go under to-day : this is the last act.
We boys who understand that this is the twilight of the
gods are the only ones that are going to keep our heads
up till the last minute. We won't see the end. We'll
have time to get off to Patagonia, or Iles d'Or, or Australia before trouble comes, war, or revolution or
fascism. You wrote me Boutdelaize is making money
on some colour-film process, didn't you ? I didn't
quite understand your letter. . . .'

Antoine fished in his drawer and brought out a letter
from which he read :

' " . . . *our virtuoso in financial jazz has become a chef
d'orchestre : a new Mephisto, his volant shadow moves from
Barcelona to Berlin, chaffering cockeyed souls of proletarian
Fausts who exchange little matchgirl dreams of preferred stock
and lifelong participations for the materiality of a crust, one
day to startle the yokel Everyman with a few cheap tricks in*

*white magic and retire with the contents of their pockets before
over-capitalisation has stolen their pants. . . ."* I knew
" virtuoso in financial jazz " was Boutdelaize, because
you always call him that, but what does the rest of that
spiel mean ? You'll have to write just plain French to
me, Marpurgo. You know I had no education. My
family sent me to one of the finest schools in England
and we learned the trick of washing in a trough and
eating soup and sardines off a wooden trencher. But
I ran away ; I wasn't smart enough for that even : I
can only eat soup out of a soup-plate. My folks de-
spaired of me after that and sent me to art-school. So
I learned nothing literary at all. I learned English, but
not French. Next time you write to me, do me a favour—
write it in words of three letters. Keep your white
magic for Boutdelaize. He likes it. Did he tell you
anything about the colour-film business ? '

Marpurgo smiled darkly. ' You know, I tried the
old enchanter on him ; I played the flute and the cobra
danced. He loves me like a brother—watch out for the
knife in your back, in other words. I did my mental
hula-hula, and the old fornicator fell for it : my asceti-
cism gave me a more than feminine charm. He flattered
the flatterer to flatter himself he was of my company.
A gross old whoremaster like Boutdelaize, with ten
legitimate children and three childless mistresses of the
most flamboyant sort, who seduces half his working-
girls, a vulgar devil, can't resist the seduction of metaphysics, especially pseudo-metaphysics. Doesn't Christian Science have its greatest following among business
men and bank clerks ? Boutdelaize, stinking money-
grubber, still likes to think he can attract the open-pored
person, monkey philosophers as well as working-girls
who have brothers and sisters to support. There are
plenty of men who think they seduce whores. Old
Boutdelaize is a savage, a primitive ; he lives by rule
of thumb, acts on his childish impressions, follows out
his coarse impulses with the superstition of a successful

egotist. In me he senses mysticism, post-graduate of superstition. You're all satraps, you successful business men, you want to buy everything ! You think money can buy everything, even brains, even mysticism, even poetry ! And then he thinks I'm rich. He drew plenty of bank reports on me. The reports all said I was liable to inherit a couple of million lire when my brother dies ! Like all over-smart men, he's quite a fool. He only believes in his own game.'

Antoine watched him patiently, the tips of his fingers together, his chair tilted back, a pleasant smile on his charming, thin, blond face. At the end he said, ' What did he tell you about the colour-films, Marpurgo ? Has he really got the patent ? Does the thing work ? Is it a commercial proposition, or does it cost too much ? '

Marpurgo shrugged his shoulders delicately.

' He hasn't put any money into it but is letting the inventor use the last of his own capital ; his brother's and his wife's savings have all gone into it, and now the fellow's broke. Boutdelaize has promised to buy the invention if it succeeds, and so the fellow keeps on at it. He is living in an attic in the ghetto, his wife and a child with him. Boutdelaize advanced a few guilders just to buy bread, and got in return a promise in writing that the invention would not be offered to any other promoter. When the inventor dies of hunger Boutdelaize will get the invention from the wife, or the other way about. In the meantime, Boutdelaize keeps him working at it to perfect it. I wouldn't pay too much attention to it yet. . . .'

' Think there's any chance of buying out the inventor before Boutdelaize gets it ? ' enquired Antoine lazily, as if in duty bound.

Marpurgo put away the question with his hand as he went on :

' You noticed his samples ? That incrustation with a second, different design is done by a special machine. He pays the girls twenty centimes a metre : a metre may take an hour to do. The rates vary, but he cuts his cost to a minimum. I believe this new incrustation will be taken up by all the cheap lingerie makers. I bought the whole stock. It's on a bet, but I don't think I made a mistake. The man's a pure thief, of course. You have to keep your third eye open, the primitive one in the forehead. Faubonhomme told me they have the dickens of a time stretching his laces after dyeing. He skimps on thread and requires the drying machine to pull the lace out to the proper width. The edge is always tearing, and the whole piece of lace is weakened and shoddy with the excessive strain. You've got to watch out for such lace with him.'

Antoine thoughtfully remarked : ' Well, that's your job, Marpurgo : if you know what he does, you can look out for it. He's a smart man ; I wouldn't mind putting through a deal with him. I'd get you and Toto to knock it into shape : you go up and see this inventor for me, after you've been to Lyon.'

Marpurgo had frowned. ' I wish you'd get someone else besides Pierre Brunet for your private lawyer : he's the laughing-stock of Paris. Nobody but you would employ him : you're his only client. Maître Lebrun told me the other day he has the reputation of not know-ing anything about anything : when he takes a case before a judge, he automatically loses it.'

Antoine waved his hand, airily, irritably.

' You're prejudiced, Marpurgo ; you never did like him. I know he's a bit of an ass, but my wife likes Toto, and I've known him since I was a kid. He knows my business and he wouldn't let me down. Besides, my wife says he brings us luck. If you can't go a bit crazy sometimes and have the wrong fellows along with you, what's the use of being in business ? It'd be better to do what Georges wants to do, be safe and retire. I like life. Toto's smarter than any of you think : you don't know him.'

' And he flatters you,' said Marpurgo bitterly.

Antoine laughed. 'What the deuce! He likes me.
You and Georges are always against poor Toto. Perhaps you're right: perhaps he's a mistake—but I don't
think so,' he suddenly shouted crossly. He instantly
regained his good-humour, but with a ring of command:
'About Boutdelaize, write to him and see when he's
coming to Paris next: I want you to get me in touch
with him. That man's money: I want to go in with
him on some deal.'

Marpurgo sneered gently. 'Take my advice, Antoine,
the best deal any man can get out of that man is the
worst of it. But you won't listen to me, Antoine,
what's the use? I'll write to him.'

Antoine shouted in exasperation:

'I'll listen to anyone that has something practical to
say, without hooey, without a lot of theatrical *mise en
scène*.' He resumed his normal tone: 'Scheherazades
should remember to keep their bedtime stories for light-
ing-up time. I'll listen to you every time, Marpurgo, but
you're a fantasist: you let your suspicions run away
with you. You see when he's coming to Paris, and we'll
get together. I like that crook. He won't pull the wool
over my eyes. We're both post-war men: we're both
depression-men.'

Marpurgo smiled at Antoine, veiling his eyes.

'Yes, but you have a weakness he hasn't, Toine.'

'What's that?' asked Antoine, anxious.

'A good heart,' murmured Marpurgo. 'You're kind,
sweet and generous, Antoine; essentially you're a
good man, you were born a moneymaker, but love is
in your heart. You deserve a beautiful fate, but your
crooked ingenuity pushes you into all these schemes
and into the company of these gross, brutal egotists
who think that money is all there is in life.'

'What else is there in life?' asked Antoine with
childish simplicity. Then warming to an old theme, he
expatiated: 'With money you can buy everything,
ev-ery-thing! You know that's the truth, Marpurgo.

You're a brilliant fellow, and your rigmaroles and spiels and conversation and your talking about books and philosophy is just a way of getting the better of business-men. It's a very smart way of doing it. I like you for it. You like books, you like plays, you like fine liqueurs, lectures : you like to belong to chess-clubs and sub-scribe to hotsy-totsy magazines : you like to take people out to famous restaurants. There's no harm in it ; I like you for it. You know how to live and how to graft along in a world where there isn't much to go round. But it's all money. Without money you couldn't get any of them. And I don't know whether you've noticed that you don't like anything that doesn't cost a lot ? You haven't any simple tastes, Marpurgo. It's all luxury with you. Am I right or not ? You say yourself one of your grandmothers must have slept with a doge. Am I right or not ? '

'You love your wife,' said Marpurgo. 'Is that money ? '

'She was a rich girl,' replied Fuseaux. 'All the girls I was ever sweet on were rich girls. I couldn't love a poor girl ; there's something missing—they're rough, gawky, crude, they have bad clothes, their teeth aren't fixed right, they wear cheap rouge. They're not lovable. Of course you can say they'd look just as good as Huguette, my wife, if they were dressed by Worth—but they're not, and they never will be. But rich girls are beautiful and lovable, sweet, easy to get on with : they're good fun, and they can pay for their own kiddies. They're nice human beings : the rest of the human race ought to be like them. And all because their papas had pots of money.' He laughed gaily. 'You must admit you're beaten, Marpurgo ! '

Marpurgo laughed. 'Well, I can't convince you, Antoine. I'm going to get a hair-cut.'

He got up. Fuseaux laughed and shuttled his slim long legs.

'Yes, go and pay for your hair-cut and overtip the

barber so that he'll like you.' He began spinning a
five-franc piece on the table. 'Hey, Marpurgo, I'll
spin you for five francs, heads or tails ? '

'I don't want to, Antoine,' said Marpurgo.

'Come on, heads or tails ? '

'Heads.'

Antoine spun, looked at the coin, laughed. 'I won.
Go on, you owe me five francs : pay me next week.'

'I never gamble,' said Marpurgo, 'because I never
win.'

'And I always win, in the long-run,' said Antoine.
'Why ? Because I've got the money to stand the gaff.
I quit when I win. I never play more than ten thousand
francs an evening. At the end of a year, I'm at least even.
What do you bet you fall for a rich girl, Marpurgo ?
You're getting near forty, you've been chaste, you like
refinement, elegance, you're soft, Marpurgo. I bet you
five thousand francs you fall for a rich girl before midnight, December 31, this year. Do you take me on ? '

'No, keep your money. You forget I married a poor
girl.'

'Yes, you started in life by being a bit crazy. But
you've got more sense now. You've got a sane streak
somewhere : if it weren't for that little safety brake in
your head you'd be running round with café-poets now,
or sitting in a garret writing philosophy. But something
saved you. Perhaps it was your unlucky marriage.
The only reason you can live apart from your wife and
not have her squeaking and fainting about the house,
is money.'

Marpurgo sighed. 'True enough. You have good
instincts, Fuseaux. If you only knew men better and
could get this money-monomania out of your head.
But I don't really wish it : it's the way you make money,
and you're only happy scheming for it. In that you're
an artist, fulfilling your creative destiny. I've sold
myself on the ideal stuff. I believe my own canvass.
That's why I'm spendthrift and why I'll never have

any money: money is something ideal, abstract to me, as it is to an extravagant woman. You keep me for amusement on your earnings, Antoine: I'm your whore.'

Antoine shouted with laughter. 'You old leather-skin: you do believe in that seraglio grandmother, don't you? Go on, go and get your hair-cut.'

As Marpurgo was going out of the door, Antoine called:

'Oh, Marpurgo, I want to see you in here when you come back. Have you ever heard of Lanafil? It's a wool substitute; I want you to have a look at it. I know the man who wants to put it on the market. He swears it'll put Australia and the Argentine out of business. He has some Japs and Heinies after it. I want to get your slant on him; see if you think it's hooey or horse-sense. And don't listen to that groofer Georgie; he's against it as usual. If we followed his advice we'd go to sleep in a forest and wake up with beavers after two thousand years in a peat-bog—and then sell the peat.'

Marpurgo bobbed, put his forefinger to his eyebrow in assent, and padded out.

On the way through the now empty general office, Georges Fuseaux waylaid him, with gloomy mien.

'What was Toine gassing about? He was in there all the afternoon yesterday with a funny-looking flat. Did he mention that dopey Lanafil scheme to you? Look, Marpurgo, I want you to do me a favour: persuade him not to go into it. You and I slave for the money and he defecates it away. He wants to make wool out of paper or something. It's like a scheme for growing fish in the air or inventing artificial oil. Why can't he stick to the lace business? Why does he have to be a financial wizard? I'd rather he went and played with his children and let us run the business.'

Marpurgo patted the lapel of the younger Fuseaux. 'Surely. I'll try to dissuade him, but you know, Georges, I must listen to his scheme. It's not good my vetoing

it straight away. Sabotage only makes a poet fly into
more furious fits, you know. He'll only accuse you
of being of the earth, earthy, a mole or a slow-worm.'

'A poet,' cried Georges. 'We're in business. When
I first went into this business I had a few illusions. I
thought I was doing something for the women when I
got out a nice new pattern or bought up a good line
and let them have it cheap. I thought the things went
on getting better from year to year and the human race
was benefited—progress, you know. Then I saw the
private lace museum of Paindebled in the rue Jacob
and I thought we were making it easy mechanically for
working-girls to get what fine ladies used to wear. Now
I see there just ain't any progress. Progress is just a
train that stops at every station to take up the eight-
o'clock workers and drop them in town, and then stops
at every station coming back in the evening to put them
down again. I know better now. Business is business,
and the accountant is there at the end of every six
months to tell you whether you're up or down. You
don't have to wonder, Am I doing mankind any good?
Will my work be appreciated in twenty years? I'll
beat my competitors in the long-run because I have
vision and they're money-grubbers. I'm full of bright
ideas. You can't fool yourself the way artists can.
And you can't retire when you go broke and say, He's
beaten me, but I'm the better man. In business you know
goddamnwell who is the better man. That's an advantage after all : you don't kid yourself.'

He laughed greyly, straightened his broad shoulders,
sleekly at ease in his pale grey cassimere : the filtered
light lent mauve and olive gleams to his smooth, greased
blond hair. 'Toine thinks the same too : he's not so
crazy as he sounds. If he had a screw looser he'd be
running round like these flossy lounge lizards, playing
polo or smashing himself up at bobsleigh at Saint-
Moritz. He spent a year at the Beaux-Arts, and when
they kicked him out came here full of hot-air, talking

cinquecento, Renaissance, Great Pandora and Little Pandora, the Genius of France, wanted the return of the monarchy. He got that monarchy stuff from the cheesy crowd in the Deux-Magots, those journalists he used to hang round with. He said the monarchs of France cherished the lace industry—any excuse for reading the *Action Française*, the deadest sheet on earth.'

Marpurgo smiled affectedly.

Georges continued :

' Oh, that was just measles. Now he's a republican because under a republic wages are higher and girls are working in factories, and so able to buy their own slummockies. There's a lot to that, you know ? ' He looked suspiciously at Marpurgo.

' I believe in Toine.' Marpurgo snapped his fingers softly before Georges's face. His keen, salt-blue eyes flickered. ' He's one of those transparent, endlessly becoming characters, infinitely, beautifully, involuntarily complex, like crystals ramifying on glass.'

' Fantasy should be kept out of business : business is making money,' said Georges.

Marpurgo smiled, waved his hand, and went out to lunch. He heard Georges's voice when half-way down the stairs.

' Are you taking any of those expensive business friends of yours to lunch to-day ? Why don't you let them give you a break, and treat you sometimes ? You're too open-hearted, Marpurgo ; that's your fault,' and a faint chuckle.

Marpurgo raised his profile, which bit at the air with its long droop-tipped nose.

' I am a small man, but I cannot live in my own pocket : if I were not, life would not be worth living.'

' So you live out of pocket,' said Georges's voice.

Marpurgo thought for a moment and then climbed back upstairs, with a hurt and spiteful expression. Georges had gone. Marpurgo hesitated outside the door, biting the inside of his bottom lip, getting more furious as he stood there. Suddenly the door opened and Antoine Fuseaux appeared. He looked at Marpurgo standing there with his pocket-book in his hand and a green complexion.

'Hullo,' he said. 'Are you short, Marpurgo ? Here, take five hundred. Is it enough ? '

Marpurgo shook his head. 'I have enough, thank you. Georges seems to think I have too much. He told me I was living out of pocket. Of course, I had no idea that you did not wish me to have an expense account.'

'What's the idea ? ' cried Antoine. 'Don't be so touchy, Marpurgo ! I'm surprised at you ! You know Georges : you can't take offence at him. He doesn't mean it ; he's just naturally a grouch : he always was. Go on, Marpurgo. What are you grinding your teeth about ? Temperament, temperament, temperament makes donkeys of us all. Where are you going ? To the Capucines ? Come along, I'll drop you there.'

Marpurgo's dark face softened craftily. He murmured : 'Thanks, Antoine ; I did not think you could feel that way. Georges is always crabbing about my expense accounts : I find it difficult to keep my mind on business when I know there's someone eating my back when I'm away.'

Antoine laughed. 'Nonsense, Annibale ! Gosh, you should have been a woman. Your mother must have been neurotic, Annibale. Fancy getting worried about something Georges says ! Everyone knows Georges. He doesn't mean it. He's probably hungry. You know he'll never go out to lunch, because he pretends customers may come in and find us all away. Georges is very fond of you. He's very fond of everyone, but he thinks he has to hide it, because it isn't business.'

Marpurgo smiled frankly. 'Well, I don't think you know your brother as well as outsiders do. At the same time, I hope what you say is true, and I'm willing to believe it for your sake. I'd do anything for you, Antoine : you're irresistible.'

Antoine laughed gaily, irresponsible, careless, always the sunny spoilt child, and presently shook hands with Marpurgo before he left the taxi. 'Now, run along and have a good dinner: have a *fine*: have a Corona, and you'll feel better.'

Marpurgo stood and looked after the taxi with bare head and a faint smile, and then turned into his favourite restaurant.

During lunch he read the current copy of *Mind*: he prided himself on keeping in stride with the most recent advances in modern philosophical thought, especially the English logicians and philosophers, because he appreciated their strains of whimsy and wit. He was late getting back to the firm's offices, as always, and found Antoine already there, in a good humour, his room full of smoke, and an impressive-looking fellow with an eagle-head, grey hair, hand-made boots and white linen, expounding mysteriously and wittily some scheme. Georges, crabbed but subdued, dictated some letters to Mlle Rose. Marpurgo was being wafted past Antoine's room, by his own pointed toes, when Antoine saw him and called him in.

'Marpurgo, I want you to meet Mr. Severin. This is our chief buyer, Mr. Marpurgo.'

Severin had a well-fleshed, ruddy face, large grey eyes set well apart under thick eyebrows, a large sanguine nose. He flashed his well-made dental plate at Marpurgo. 'Italian? *Ho gran piacere d'incontrarla . . .*'

Marpurgo answered in French, the language they were all using. 'You are not Italian, I think, Mr. Severin.'

Severin lowered his glance, but in a moment recovered his poise. 'My mother was Italian and my father Russian. I was born in America. I married a French-woman during the war, and my boy is going to school in Switzerland.'

Antoine laughed. 'You sound like a slippery customer: no one knows where to have you, or where to get out of your way.'

'It is bad, is it not?' said Severin charmingly to Fuseaux. 'I often get confused myself.'

'So you were in the war?' continued Marpurgo. He knew that Fuseaux valued his opinion of a man and that he had been invited in to size Severin up. Marpurgo never bated his style unless he wanted money: and despite the spotless linen, the polished hand-made shoes, his instinct told him Severin had none. Fuseaux was watching his attack. Severin's manner had changed: he was warier, and suaver, but his voice had a frank ring.

'Yes, I enlisted—a mere private: somehow or other I found myself a major. The war broke into my academic career; it broke out just three months before I took my Doctor of Science. I have never ceased regretting it: my little old mamma can never forgive the war for breaking out just before she could refer to her only son as *Dr.* Severin. She herself has lost faith in my talents. A man not in destiny's lap—evidently there's something wrong! She is not really consoled by the major, for she hates war: a real pacifist. And then my father was a professional soldier: he fought under Denikin: left her, in fact, to do it: went to Prague and spends his time scheming against Russia and sleeping with chorus girls. Mamma is a pacifist—evidently. I was invalided to Tours: there I met a lovely Tourangelle—angel was quite the word, I thought: such an accent. Actually, she came from Loches, Alfred de Vigny's town. She was born under the castle wall. I married her and thought of becoming a Frenchman. Eventually, though, we went back to America. But we see Europe nearly every year.' He smiled at Marpurgo. 'I represent—various large interests. I have been sketching out to Mr. Fuseaux some ideas I hope will prove profitable. Mere sketches: I like to get the slants of various experienced business-men on them: saves me from tangents, you know. Likewise, it sometimes leads to a little mutually profitable investment. . . .'

'Tell him about the scheme, Severin,' said Fuseaux.

Severin unfolded a white silk handkerchief with an embroidered initial and flicked his nose.

' You can tell Marpurgo anything : he's my investments manager,' added Fuseaux.

' Do you smoke ? I think you do,' said Severin to Fuseaux.

' No, no thanks, not now.'

' And you, surely ? '

Marpurgo could not resist the proffered cigar, which he sized up with quick eyes. Severin smiled.

' I get them from one supplier only in London, corner of Jermyn and Bury Streets. He imports them : the only man I know in London.'

' There's another, near Dover Street. I'll give you the address if I see you again, I've just forgotten the number. I found him out, " extensive researches," you know. When I found him I knew there was balm in Gilead.' He held his gold lighter to Severin's cigar.

' A beautiful lighter,' murmured Severin.

Marpurgo looked at it with a street urchin's cold appraisal, and said in a quick cracked voice :

' Do you like it ? It's beautiful, isn't it ? A gift—I didn't deserve.'

He sent a twinkle to Antoine, who had given it to him, and sucked at his cigar with pursed lips : he raised the cigar in his fingers and spoke in a fat, melting way, indicative of sensual content :

' Well, Lamentations and Ecclesiastes are the present texts of the world : what have you to suggest that will bring us forward to Ezra and Nehemiah ? '

' The venality of the French press is a legend : and not a golden legend, but a nickel one—you can buy silence and vociferation for a nickel.'

' They teach the same in their own public schools,' agreed Marpurgo.

' The French, like all Latins, are mad speculators—one-tenth lottery tickets when they're poor, Bayonne bonds when they're rich,' went on Severin.

Marpurgo puffed. Antoine put in impatiently :

'The point is, everyone nowadays wants to get something for nothing, that's why there'll never be communism anyhow : but the French are the only people who study how to lose their money on the Stock Exchange.'

'Exactly,' agreed Severin. 'Every newspaper here runs its financial page, and there are dozens and dozens of little daily and weekly sheets giving Bourse tips and notations. The English are mad over horse-racing . . .'

'Even the workhouses have their weekly sweepstakes,' added Antoine.

'You see chalked up in a few places *Shining-Light to win the* 2.30,' continued Severin, 'but what do you have for information sheets ? The tipsters' envelopes, very dear, and a couple of bi-weekly or weekly sheets. In France the local financial news comes out daily.'

'You forget,' said Marpurgo. 'You do the Teutonic countries an injustice : you forget they can't read or write : if they could, undoubtedly they'd read the newspapers. I tell you they're smart. When you hear a bus-conductor figuring how he will win fifty pounds through five races with an initial outlay of a tanner, you realise that was the race of Newton. I always hold the people are the unexplored mines of intelligence of the country.'

'Rats,' said Antoine. 'The average man knows he has a job, a wife and a pint of beer, or no job, no wife and no pint of beer : that's all he knows and all he'll ever know. If he were smart he'd do something about it. Would I sweat for a boss ? Not likely. If they were smart you couldn't get money out of them. I'm tired of arm-chair socialism : you know yourself, Marpurgo, you're a million times smarter than most of the work-people you meet. Of course you are, of course you are. Don't be silly, Marpurgo : if you weren't, you'd be working for eight hundred francs a month and dying at forty of old age : instead of which you're wearing a satin-lined overcoat and smoking a Corona-

corona. And are you ashamed? Of course not? Am
I ashamed when I go out in my Rolls-Royce with
Francis in livery in front, with my boots that cost eight
pounds, and my coat that cost 3000 francs? Of course
not: I'm proud of them. I like them. If they tried
to take 'em away I'd fight them for them. I don't care
whether it's right or wrong: I want 'em, and I'd fight
them for them: that's not economics, that's human
nature. And it always will be. Who could stop me,
or you, or Severin, from wanting to be better off than
the next feller? We're made that way.' His boyish
laugh kept on carolling out: he had had a good lunch.
'If they weren't dumb-bells, could any business-man
make a living, eh? Go on, Severin, tell him your scheme
for syndicating the Bourse papers.'

'As I was saying,' said Severin promptly but patiently,
'the French Bourse gamblers will read any tip, bad,
good or indifferent, and any sheet, however suspect and
whatever rumours are current about it, because of a
third fact, the incredible venality of the parliamentarians
and the judiciary: they always assume that these little
sheets can get information from high sources through
sheer blackmail. Even if they are pool-papers, the
little speculator thinks he may as well be in on the pool.
He reasons, The minister giving this information may
or may not be telling the truth: in any case the rumour
will lead to a rise (or fall) in the prices—I may as well
get in at the beginning and get out before the end of
the ripple; the same with a ramp. You've got to know
them. It may be a *canard*, they think, but someone
owns it and someone will pluck it: now I'm as smart
as the next feller. It's a republican sentiment, you see.'

'I get the point,' said Marpurgo.

'Now, the fourth point of my plan is based on the
fact that French newspapers hate to pay for cables,' went
on Severin. 'They'll print bad news, news a week old,
they'll crib, steal, invent—but they won't pay for cable
service.'

' And Havas ? ' put in Marpurgo, looking cunning and showing his rat-like teeth.

' I'd pay Havas part of the boodle, that goes without saying : the point is, I have New York backing from Wall Street pool-workers.'

Marpurgo considered. ' You could buy some cheesy little bankrupt sheet, spread the rumour through the white-slave and Bourse cafés that the backer was Wall Street, and make a rip-roaring success overnight : why wouldn't one be enough ? You've only got to start the fashion : insinuate that what you've got comes straight from the laps of the gods.'

' No. To really sell the shares *en masse*, we've got to have all the financial press behind us. Let the rumour about our machinery be confused, that which naturally springs into gamblers' minds, but nothing precise. It should be good enough especially to catch all the suckers, to draw the good coins out of the famous country wool-stockings, out of old maids' cotton bosoms, out of the funds held in trust by family lawyers. I don't want only the smart-alecs who take a flyer, the beachcombers who wait for the turn of the tide, the wise guys who cut a loss and cut a profit ; I want investment money.'

Marpurgo said : ' How about working it through existing institutions ? '

Severin snickered cleverly. ' Accounting and ladies should be beyond reproach, and that's only possible if they both stay at home. My wife is beautiful—I keep her at home.'

' And your accounting too is beautiful,' said Marpurgo.

' Severin's already got the direction of the *Herald of Dawn* to agree, provided their bosses agree. The idea, of course, is that we pose as a private cable service. Actually we get service through one of the big companies. It would be worth the while of any of them to get the Stock Exchange cables alone.'

' Another idea,' explained Severin, ' is to call ourselves a Committee or Society of Economic Survey.

We would have a board of directors, of whom, for example, leading manufacturers and middlemen like Mr. Fuseaux would be one, an advisory board, of which, say, a gentleman like yourself would be a distinguished member.'

' And you ? '

' I'm simply acting as agent for my New York friends. The directors and economists receive salaries, the directors participations, and the economists bonuses according to the amount of research done.'

' And the money ? '

' The money should be French capital,' said Severin. ' It would not do for the rumour of foreign money corrupting the Bourse to have any foundation.'

' It has possibilities, I think, Antoine, don't you ? ' murmured Marpurgo. ' We should have a detailed suggestion and think it over.'

' Knowing Mr. Fuseaux's experience, I was going to ask him to suggest details himself, as well as yourself : you both know the French and the French Stock Exchange better than myself. I, on the other hand, know the American end.'

' Who else have you spoken to about this ? ' asked Marpurgo.

' No one—except Monsieur Dacapo.' He mentioned a well-known financial Jove.

Fuseaux started. ' Dacapo ? What did he say ? '

' He's interested. I'm to see him at ten to-morrow. I told him I was going to see you next, and he wants to know what you think of it.'

Antoine Fuseaux was visibly flattered. Marpurgo crushed the end of the cigar in the ash-tray.

They promised to meet again on the following day. Antoine asked Marpurgo eagerly, when they were alone, what he thought of it. Marpurgo said :

' I don't know : I've got to think it over. That boy's no angel : I want to work out his game exactly before I give an opinion.'

' That's right : you do that. Now let's look through these patterns and get it over with.'

They spent the rest of the afternoon over the business for which Fuseaux was known. When Marpurgo was leaving, Georges came into the wash-room.

' What you doing to-night, Marpurgo? Are you eating ? '

' I'm going to the Capucines. Come along ! '

' No, I'm eating at the Pyramides ! '

' Are you still there ? '

' Yes : the grub's good. And what do I have? A chop. And I know the waiters. Come along.'

' I like the Capucines : the cuisine's excellent—they make a *filet mignon* exquisite. And the best coffee in Paris. Be my guest, Georges.'

' No ; why can't you come to the Pyramides for once? Come along, come along, come along : it's the only place you can eat quietly.'

' No, it's so dead, Georges ! I'm expecting to see a couple of new young friends of mine at the Capucines, besides.'

' Oh, well, I'll meet you after. Where'll you be? '

' Come and join us, Georges. Snap out of it ! Have some fun ! You're too gloomy for a young man.'

' I want to be quiet : I'll meet you after. Where'll you be ? Or at any rate come and have an apéritif with me at the Univers.'

Marpurgo wiped his hands. ' You win, Georges : I'll come to the Univers. It's one of the few lively places, and I want to talk to you.'

' The waiters know me : they give me service.'

They went off. Georges was pink with content at getting someone to drink with him. He for the moment forgave Marpurgo for the legendary figures in his expense account. At table he talked steadily, humourlessly, with the bumbling persistence of a bee in a basin, about business affairs. He rarely mentioned outside matters or persons, but this evening, after he had had his inevitable quinine pick-me-up, which he drank down, smacking his lips, Georges, leaning over the tablecloth, said grudgingly:

'You ought to meet the feller I was telling you about, you know who I mean!'—with exasperation—'the chap I told you about to-day, Paindebled's the name, rue Jacob: go over there some day. He has an antique-shop. Don't know how much money he makes, but he lives in the back of the shop. You know how these antique dealers live. They own the shop and live in the back on spinach and veal. He used to be a designer in Raguse's in Calais. His wife too. His wife's crazy now, but she inherited some tin from a sister who went crazy too, after getting married. They bought this antique-shop in the rue Jacob, and Paindebled's put quite a bit of cash into laces. He says it has antiquarian and aesthetic value some day translatable into real round berries. You ought to go along and give him the benefit of your canvass, Marpurgo. You'd get along like a house on fire. He invited me to dinner, but I don't want to go. I hate social events. I'm no good at them. You go along and excuse me and get to know him: then he won't bother me.'

'You come along and introduce me.'

'And get nabbed for another date? No. I'll give you a note for the lady. You take it. That's the best thing. They've got a daughter, a long high-brow blonde.'

'And you're a bachelor!'

'You've got the idea.'

'You can't fade out of parental pipe-dreams as easily as that.'

'Can't I, though? I'll use parental pipe-dreams for a smoke-screen. And you're a married man. You have nothing to fear.'

'I never mention my wife in society,' said Marpurgo.

'Well, tell 'em you're an ascetic,' grinned Georges. 'Is it a deal? You hold off the high-brow blonde, and I'll pass your expense accounts—this time.'

Marpurgo darkened, but said delicately :

' It's like you, Georges, to do *me* a favour, introduce me to your connoisseur friend and with the same motion wipe the debt off my slate by pretending I'm obliging you.'

Georges said : ' Oh, have it my way.'

' I have to telephone,' said Marpurgo : ' some young friends who wanted to have dinner with me—young lovers, hi, hi, quite a little romance, charming little adultery. . . .'

' No, go on, an adultery ? And you call that romantic ? That's like calling the postman romantic. You're romantic yourself, Marpurgo. Adultery ! ' He put the drink greedily to his lips. ' You often see a beautiful young woman, you know, all curves, married to some dry stick of a civil servant. Everyone looks at her on the street and says, What did she marry him for ? Then if she does meet another man, her own age, and in business, that she likes better, and she goes out with him, it's adultery. Of course, what did she marry him for ? She could have waited. But I suppose they're all worried they'll be old maids. They won't wait : they want a fellow to tie himself down. And then the husband is always between them and has a right to her.'

His round face looked childishly at Marpurgo, ' I——' he noticed Marpurgo's smile, ' it's nothing ; I often think, it's like putting your brand on a heifer and turning her loose on the pampas and then laying bets on what colour the calves will be.' This seemed a great joke to Georges. He went on argumentatively, ' What does she care what colour they are ? A mother's a mother to any colour calf ! '

' That's so,' Marpurgo murmured, with lowered eyes.

' You can't blame them : they want to make sure of an income before they lose their looks. We oughtn't really to blame them.'

Marpurgo coughed. ' Law is on the husband's side ; ruminating doesn't alter that.'

The face of Georges, completely softened, leaned towards Marpurgo : 'I suppose we all have girls in our lives. . . .'

Marpurgo got up testily. 'I must telephone.'

He went away. When he came back he found Georges his normal self, ready with a crusty remark. Marpurgo was discomforted.

'They must have forgotten : they went out.'

'Well, now you can come to the Pyramides with me : you've got nothing else to do.'

Marpurgo was forced to go and while away the dull, lost evening. After supper they walked to the left bank and passed along the rue Jacob where Georges pointed out the house of Paindebled, the antiquary. It was now shuttered and completely dark. A ham-and-beef shop and some other small-goods shops glowed along the next street. At the corner two street musicians sang a senti-mental song in Parisian slang.

'Delightful,' said Marpurgo, 'there's something here that will bring me back again and again. This is mellow, old, full of charm and peace.'

'*Parlez-moi d'amour*,' sang the musicians.

'These old buildings are probably full of bed-bugs, that's all,' said Georges.

They passed a boring evening which rested Georges, whose evenings were all empty. Marpurgo went home furious and restless, very hurt that Oliver and Elvira had deserted him. He went back to look at the Paindebled house when he had seen Georges home (Georges insisted on it). There was now a light burning in the top-storey. Anaemic stars were lost in the black sky above. Mar-purgo walked up and down the rue Jacob twice, talking to himself :

'Dark, dark, dark, without a ray of light ; no com-panion heart, despised and suspicioned, a lonely old wreck, alone, alone, aimless, going out with blockhead fools, adultery, heifers, ha ! I used to dream about angels of light, diamond crowns of glory. I am a genius : much

good it does me ! Where is my equal ? Much good it
does me ! Where are all the books I thought of writing ?
That imbecile Griffin published his theorem in last
month's *Mathematica*—I always made him a laughing-
stock in company. He doesn't know what's the sum of
two and two. I could have written a symphony. Nothing ! If I had been one of those who could have fooled
themselves into having a " career " ! Lumps that decor-
ate themselves with wreaths of roses. But it works.
Look at me ! I see their satire. Not even loved. No
love. There must be someone—Young Girl, can't you
see what a beautiful soul I have ? Can't you see what it
would be to have a lover who would worship with his
spirit ? *Parlez-moi d'amour.* Ha, ha, don't worry ! I
have everything. Now I'm old. There must be a way
of fighting old age. I'll wrestle with it : it can suffocate
me but I'll never be old. I won't be old, I'll love again
and better. I'll succeed. There's time. There's time.'

He found himself standing in front of the Paindebled
shutters.

He went home and to bed. He tossed as he remembered that Georges had given him all his mail opened.
'You know how I go through the mail,' Georges explained
in a take-it-or-leave-it fashion ; ' I go through the mail
backwards and just slit the letters. I didn't mean to open
your letters. I thought they were for Antoine or me.'

He had allowed himself to say spitefully :

' Why don't you hire Harris, the detective, to write
reports on the cafés I visit ? '

Georges had only said lazily :

' Don't get hot in the collar, Marpurgo. Anybody'd
think I did it purposely. As soon as I see, Dear Marpurgo, I slap 'em back again.'

Marpurgo switched on the light and took his wife's
letter, unopened, from his pocket. He read :

My dear Friend,—The weather continues charming : my
friends come and go : I continue my régime. Our old friend
Dr. Eggeli visits me regularly, and I continue the same.

Naturally I do not improve, but I do not get worse. I am grateful to God for so many peaceful, happy years of life, I whom everyone expected to die at sixteen. Only one thing lacks, my dear Annibale, and that is my husband. You are busy : you cannot realise that it is fourteen months since you visited me. Your own ill-health occupies you. How I wish we were a little better off, so that you too could spend your days by my side in some beautiful alpine resort like Pontresina. I hear that Pontresina is excellent for bronchial troubles.

I am sure you no longer believe that you have consumption. No one continues to have consumption for so many years, Dr. Eggeli tells me. But you are fatigued. I have not been much of a wife to you ; my physical indisposition has prevented that. Ours has been a spiritual relationship and has avoided the crudities of another kind. I hope that you will soon be reconciled to me, my dear friend, and that we will be able to pass the remaining years of life together. You are, after all, my husband. You are all I have in this world. I want you to come to see me. It is not very pleasant for me to sit here alone all the year round. I know your affection for me, but I am exposed to the sympathy of my friends. They think it strange that you cannot tear yourself away from Paris and London. You know the childish pictures these names call up in innocent and foolish minds. A friend actually hinted that she thought we were separated. I want you to come here to me, my dear, and give yourself a little rest while doing me a little service. I ask very little of you : you give no account of your time, your life is yours. I have lived under water in the calm pool of your life. Telegraph me when you are coming and I will engage a room for you. This little anxiety is irritating my heart and, as you know, if I am to see middle-age, I must take greater and greater care.—All my love to you as ever, affectionately,

CLARA.

P.S.—Dr. Eggeli has just told me that you can take me to Paris for the spring if you can get an easily-run apartment facing a garden. In summer we should leave again. Think this over and let me know what you are arranging when you come. This is only in case you can't get away yourself for an alpine spring.

Marpurgo, in a rich fancy-striped poplin pyjama-suit,
went and looked at himself in the long mirror. After
staring into his own eyes for a long time, he murmured :
'Why not ? What have I to live for ? At least I can
give her some pleasure. I hardly know her now. She's
so alien that she will rest me.'

He went back to bed, tossed and coughed. He woke
up once to find his heart throbbing wildly and tears in
his eyes.

CHAPTER III

It was Wednesday. All the morning Elvira was way-
ward, languid, idle, untouchable : she looked youthful
when she was so. She teased Oliver and refused to say
good-bye to him when he went out to be shaved. Then
she looked out of the window at him in the street and
laughed but would not wave. She took a handful of
chocolates and a handkerchief to the bed, and lay down
wondering what Oliver was thinking about her, and
whether her husband Paul would write to her or come
for her. She closed her eyes and ran her fingers many
times through her hair slowly until it began to crackle,
thinking disconnectedly. Then she put her hands behind
her head and began to think of the past night, addled
memories of the theatre, ' Faust ' at the Opéra which
she had not liked although they had a box to themselves,
because she had been hungry. Afterwards Oliver, eager,
leaned towards her asking, ' Well ? well ? Now what
did you think of it ? '

' I didn't like it : it was so artificial with the old-
fashioned scenery, she was so clumsy with the jewels.'

He had been so hurt and angry. She laughed to think
of it : that young man angry with her. She thought of
the street-lights, dresses, the splendid ceilings when they
promenaded in the intervals, the taxi whirling home,
Oliver's white shirt, her pale-blue silk dress, which
although dowdy had not looked worse than most there :
it was not a dress-night, and the suburban women were
in. She saw Oliver's agate eyes in their clear whites
smiling at her.

Then she thought of the days before, the winds blow-

ing, the fire roaring in the chimney, the snow, Oliver
when he began to appear so often unannounced, the
circle of her husband's men friends around her, idle
scraps of her bitter conversations with Paul, about
nothing in particular, Paul away and Oliver holding her
hand, the postman bringing her Oliver's letters, the last
hurried foggy morning with the luggage all bundled up
in the taxi, the train, the snow.

Then everything was dark, she was very tired and was
soon wrapped in a warm half-slumber, wherein she
dreamed of nothing, but seemed to be suspended, a full-
blooded great body in a dark scene where an obscure
tower or veiled monument took the centre of a vast
colourless plain. She opened her eyes placidly for a few
moments, imagining she had heard the door click;
then she closed them, and obscure images hopped into
her mind's eye. She saw a rod with two headless snakes
emerging from a dusky ivory egg, jagged lightning
issuing from the great letter O, flame coming from a peri-
winkle's shell, a lake at the end of a row of dark clipped
trees, a sea-lion creeping slowly towards her with melancholy head, a mushroom turning into a silver pheasant,
a long stretch of yellow and black strand with the fringed
sea invading it on one side and the black coarse grass on
the other. She saw two cranes drinking from a soaring
fountain, an hour-glass in the form of two swans em-
bracing two eggs, a snake swallowing a blindworm twice
wrapped round a bundle of wheat, a headless tree growing
out of a thousand-fibred root like a peacock's-tail, a
white hand balancing an empty retort, and many dull
images impossible to recognise.

She got up, walked languidly to the dressing-table,
undressed and made poses before the long mirror.
Then she walked slowly, with a childish swagger, to the
bathroom, turned on the water, and lay naked on the bed
till the bath filled. She spent a long time in the bath,
massaging herself, washing herself over and over with
love for her soft skin, watched herself floating in the

green water, like a strange sensuous water-animal, and got out to get her hand-glass so that she could see how she looked to strange eyes. She examined her head, neck and breast, grimaced to see how she looked when she was crying. She got out of the bath with reluctance, letting the water run slowly off her limbs, held up her arms in the warm air to see how slowly they dried, put her hands beneath her breasts and so carried them, glad to feel their weight, into the bedroom. She folded her hands round her waist, passed them round her thighs and looked at the profile of her belly. She glanced sideways at her olive shoulder and kissed it. She kissed her arms, tried to reach her breasts with her mouth, but could not. Then she threw herself across her bed, and with her arms raised above her head, imagined an old ivory female idol, old ivory sucking human children, she imagined children clustering over her like grapes, curtaining her. She suddenly felt naked, and getting up, put on her mandarin gown. She wandered about the room, giving her body hundreds of small attentions, using ear and nose syringes, sponges, files, scissors, chamois leather, swan's-down puffs, sticks of orange-wood, creams, powders, and the rouge that Oliver had brought her home. She rarely used rouges, but now that she had several of different kinds and a pot of dark powder for the eyes, she tried them on different parts of her naked body, and almost thoughtlessly began to move, lifting her arms, advancing and retreating. After one or two steps, she made an impatient face and began to dress. When she had put on her thin silk stockings, she stood before the mirror, admiring her legs and wondering if she would buy the new short stockings. Then she finally put on her dress, a close-fitting one of French blue, low cut, which she had almost never worn, because in London it seemed too low to suit her. She drew the belt tighter, polished her nails and divided her hair in the middle of her head so that it fell in equal curls on each side. She thought, ' I never noticed how well this dress suits me : silly what prejudices you get ! At the same time, a woman with a pretty figure who wears high-throated dresses—and occasionally a low neck, they see how white her skin is !—to be desired ! H'm, of course it is every woman's duty : instinct, that's why you do it without thinking. A pretty woman probably has more instincts : made for it, made to succeed as a woman.' She looked towards the door and started violently. Oliver was sitting on the valise in the entry looking at her.

' How long have you been there ? '

' Since before you had your bath.'

She blushed faintly and asked him to wait while she put on some powder. She kept him waiting for some time and then came forward into the dark room, with her self-absorbed smile. Oliver thought he had never noticed how thick the languorous graces clustered round her, robing her shoulders and thighs, nor how eloquent of dark enclosed beauty her body.

She loved him : she had learned to love him. His ardent eyes were fixed on her face ; she looked away slowly. He turned her face to him and looked on the tide at its full, dark, lustrous, and full of internal music. He felt, if he ventured forth on it, it would bear him without storm or whirlpool, and he would finally reach the white thread of the distant shore.

He drew her unwillingly to the window to look at Paris, just lighting up. She did not want to look out-ward. She went from the window and brought out some cigarettes.

When she had smoked two or three cigarettes, she rested her head back, so that her round uncovered throat spoke to Oliver.

She thought, ' If I wished to, I could love him without being at all attached myself : I despise sentimental women.' Paul had always been in her power : now Oliver was too. She looked at Oliver's sanguine cast. He was very unlike Paul. She trembled a little and thought of the women he must have known already. Would she be able to manage him ? But he was very young and she was a married woman. She took courage at this last idea. She would have been very lonely and aimless in life if she had not been married. Her wifely status was all she had to give her confidence. She was a timid beauty. But being so well-married, to a patient man, she had thought she would always be warm, eat, have someone to get angry when she was injured, and would hear advanced ideas without ruining her skin or eyes peering over books long enough to swallow them.

She said to herself, ' Lectures are the most natural way to learn : listening and questioning. The philosophers in Greece knew that. . . . How silent he is ! ' she now thought. His head was resting on his arm : she suddenly caught the gleam of his eyes watching her between his fingers. She got up.

' When did that man say he'd come ? Five o'clock ? It's more than that.'

' Marpurgo will be here at seven.'

She laughed.

' I was thinking just now, I spent my real honeymoon in Bath. Oh, it was so boring ! Paul would walk about and look at all the plaques on the houses telling what famous people had lived there. The place is just plastered with plaques. Paul used to worship the great when he was a younger man. It's so jejune, isn't it ? ' She looked timidly at him, to see if the word was right. ' Like children worshipping a movie-actor, or a prize-fighter. I got him to stop. They can't help it : it's no wonder to be talented. No thanks to the person himself ! Some make the best of their opportunities and some don't care to. I hate ambitious people. Then I noticed him creeping off one day when I was lying on the bed with my eyes shut. I had awful backaches on my honeymoon. I got up quietly and followed him. What do you think he was doing ? '

' Visiting the plaques,' said Oliver.

' Yes ! I believe you'd do it yourself.'

' I like looking at their busts, just as girls to marry like looking at wedding-photographs.'

They laughed.

They heard a timid knock at the door. Oliver began to grin secretly. In came a young woman with a cheap Paris overcoat and blonde hair, who looked at them both and went mildly to Elvira :

' Good evening : how arr you ? '

' Francesca ! What a surprise ! '

' I received your *télégramme*,' murmured Francesca.

' A surprise,' explained Oliver. ' I thought you would feel less lonely, Elvira. I telegraphed your friend Francesca you had arrived in her bailiwick. Now, I'll leave you two girls alone for a few minutes.' He went into the bathroom. Elvira sat down on the bed. Francesca, without taking off her coat and gloves, looked at her.

' You are happy ? Yes : that is why you are not ashamed. Who would have guessed ? And your husband ? '

' He knows. Only I came away secretly to get it over with.'

' H'm. And imagine, I used to get irritated with you because I thought you did not know love.'

' How are you now ? '

' Still working in the bank. It is very *intéressant*. Every morning we go together into the general office, and if anyone comes late he must walk in in front of the big crowd. Then the director says, Here comes Monsieur Valetvaux : he is interested in the cross-country, he cannot give his undivided attention to his work. It is amusing. Every Wednesday he gives us a speech, and says, The Bank must be your life : you must take it home with you, talk about it at the family table, think about it after dinner, read the papers to see how it will be affected, dream about it, dress for it in the morning. Most *intéressant* : I have never been in such a house at all. These Americans do everything with so much energy. But that is the secret of their success.'

'And your brother, Francesca?'

She stamped her foot: 'Oh, don't speak of him: he is *embêtant*: five years younger than me and thinks he can boss me. I cannot be out after seven at night. He takes my sister to the station when she goes out. He is opposed to my younger brother Étienne joining the sports-club. And to think he has had a married woman for mistress these five years. *C'est dégoûtant!* You English women are free.'

'You must free yourself, Francesca.'

'Oh, no, no more. You don't know what I had to go through that time I took three weeks' holiday in England when I met you. Never again: unless I run away for love.'

'You ought to do that.'

'I would do it, but I must find a man, after all, and then I will. One should do anything for love.'

Oliver reappeared smiling from the bathroom. Francesca looked towards him dubiously. 'I had better go now: I will be late home.'

'Have lunch with us next week, Francesca,' he called.

'No, no: we must eat in the refectory of the bank.'

'Well, at night, after work. We will come for you, rue Lafayette.'

'No, no: you must excuse me.'

'Well, then, meet us for an apéritif, near the Gare Montparnasse!'

'Well, yes, I will do that: just for a few minutes. I cannot do more. Mrs. Western, I have told my mother about you: perhaps you will come and see me, if Mr. Fenton is busy, one Saturday afternoon? I will take you there. On Saturday afternoon my brother Raoul is out with his *maîtresse: elle est dégoûtante, c'est une métisse, mais à un homme tout est permis*. You must come then. You will let me know, hein?'

Elvira saw her to the lift. When she came back, Oliver was nursing his foot gloomily in the arm-chair.

'It doesn't pay to see old friends in another setting:

they lose all their charm. In England she was delightful,
an elegant bas-relief of her countrywomen : here she's
just a dumb little office-girl.'

'Did you hear that about her brother ? Isn't it amaz-
ing ? The family's such an institution in France that
even illegitimate sexual relations have a place.'

Oliver frowned.

'And I bet Francesca recommended you to go back to
your husband : *une femme mariée doit être auprès de son
mari.*'

She laughed : 'Jealous ! There you're all wrong :
she kept dinning into my ears that I ought to go flat out
to it, and love one or other of you desperately : she said
I was missing something. She nearly got down on her
knees and begged me to sacrifice all for you !' Elvira
went into a peal of laughter : 'Oh, oh, can you imagine
it !' She put her handkerchief into her mouth. 'Oh,
dear, now that I think of it !'—she became more serious
—'I was really surprised : it shows you don't know a
person as well as you think you do. And in London she
had a miscarriage : she's not a virgin at all : she had a
lover. All women are deep. They don't tell you the
truth even if you're close friends with them. Not that I
care twopence : I prefer they shouldn't be virgins. It
clears a lot of nonsense out of their heads.'

She sat down, crossed her knees and wagged her silken
little foot idly, and crossed and uncrossed her soft olive
hands. She smiled at Oliver.

'How would you like me to love you madly, to get
frantic about you ?'

He went rather pale : 'I want it !'

'Oh, I couldn't : I couldn't give up my identity so
much, and you wouldn't like it !'

'So she wants you to love me, like that ?'

'I don't know about you in particular : it's just a
principle. I'm not sure she's fond of you. A French girl
likes a man with a solid status and position. And she
doesn't like the way you criticise bourgeois society while

still living on its fat.' She laughed softly. ' You know
—" do anything for the workers, but get off their backs."
I told her you were thinking of going into business,
anyhow, and she thinks you are a business-type.'

Oliver looked at her, quietly. At last he got up and
said : ' Well, if we are going to look at our lives with the
eyes of other people, what should have been a sensual
delight will be a spotted rotten orchard pear fallen to the
ground before picking.'

Elvira lit a cigarette, still enlivened with Oliver's
jealousy.

' On the rare occasions that I've dreamed dreams, I've
been fooled. I can't bear seeing myself a fool. I always
look at myself with the eyes of others. And I would
rather cut my throat than cut a figure. My pride is
against it.'

' You are deeply, passionately proud : you appear
mild. Suddenly a blue flash cuts the suffocated night :
the less stars are blotted out.'

She laughed.

' I cannot dream : I am myself a dream. I seem to
myself to be a dark, cosy dream.'

He said eagerly, ' And that dream will always be my
idea of you. You will never know how I worship you,
Elvira. You are part of me, just as a proper dye is part
of an absorbent stuff. You are my Tyrian.'

She mused. ' How do you see me ? I don't know.
I'd like to know. You know, when you are away, I
think of you as a certain rather fuzzy shape, thickness in
the air : I think of you in a typical attitude and mood, a
rather plump, dark, rosy-cheeked, prepotent shape, with
a lock of hair falling over your forehead, which has the
same white as apples, your hands moving. And I think
of you as always eager, easily irritated, spoiled, self-
conscious, ambitious in a materialist way.' She laughed
again.

' A little flabby, vain exhibitionist,' pouted Oliver, ' in
other words.'

She looked at him calmly. 'I didn't say that : no, not quite that. I see clearly : I like you, but I see you object-ively. You mustn't accept compliments from me. I never flatter anyone. I can't. I'm too honest to myself.' She let her eyes, universes of self-absorption, roll over him. 'It is not you : it is a sort of symbol of your sort of man I have when I think about you. I want to know just what sort of symbol like that you have of me.'

He seemed cast down. 'I don't think I have any symbol like that : I think of you in so many ways, in all your moods : everything you do is so dear to me——'

She went on foolishly : 'I often think it's just an attitude I have towards you, towards Paul too, of course. I can't lose my head : I never fainted, you know. People don't catch me off my guard very easily. I don't listen to conversation so much as understand the psychological weaving that is going on underneath. I see everything dissected.' She was under an impulsion to talk, and went and sat on his knee. He gripped her very tightly, his face still a little pale. With her head on his breast, playing with a button of his waistcoat, she went on, dreaming : 'When I look back, I realise that I never loved anyone. With Paul, I was a young girl, and he wanted me so much that it gave me a sort of little terror, every time I saw him looking at me and looming over me. He has that great frame, and yet he was so timid with me and so miserable without me : I just wanted to see what he imagined he could get out of me. I wanted to see if it was just living with me or sleeping with me. I wouldn't sleep with him for quite a long while : he got very depressed, and one day he let me see he thought I was not a virgin and that I was afraid to let him know. I waited a little while longer to punish him for that, and then—I couldn't give myself up to anyone.

'At last, he said he would have to go away to the country for a while if I couldn't make up my mind to live with him. Well—I did, I did, of course. The very next morning mother came to see us, quite early : I forget

now why. We were having breakfast. Paul got up and
ran to the door and took mother in his arms and kissed
her, laughing and nearly crying, if you can believe it,
saying, " Mother, mother, she was a young girl all the
time, and she loves me." Mother bridled good-humouredly and said, " Well, what did you think, man ? Don't
I know my girl ? " I looked at the two of them con-
gratulating themselves over me. I always felt a sort of
cool amusement. With you, too : I like to tell the truth.
I like to keep on analysing what I feel and just telling the
truth, it is such a satisfaction. You don't mind, do you ? '

A strangled voice said : ' No, darling : just keep on
talking.'

Warm, dreamy, she kept her cheek against his breast,
her hair falling over the other cheek and keeping out
the light. She went on :

' When Paul first brought you home, I liked you
awfully : you weren't the first. A married woman likes
lots of men, because she can like them from a safe distance : they can't get right after her, and their women,
if they have any, can't say anything because she's married.
But you hadn't any women, at first, and then you used
to dodge after me, in the house. Oh, dear, I actually had
to shut you out of the bathroom, you were so anxious to
talk to me and explain to me about the girl you picked up,
that student, so-called student, Margery something. I
used to want to take you in my arms and put your head
on my breast, you were such a child, such a boy. I knew
it wasn't the girl at all, but me ; you were talking to me
through her.'

He let surprised eyes fall on to her sleek head.

' Did you know that ? You were right ; but I didn't
know it till now.' He passed his hand gently over her
crouched shoulder. ' My dear girl.'

' I didn't mind that at all ; I could watch your feelings
as if in a play : I was safe, I didn't have to make up my
mind. Then you changed, you sort of stole in, you
started to murk about the house——'

He laughed : ' Murk ? '

' Yes, perk about in a moony way, and I knew you were looking at me. I got cooler to you because I wanted to have a long time to make up my mind. . . .'

' That you loved me.'

She laughed casually. ' Oh, no : just whether I would take you or not. You see, I had been thinking for a long time, from the time I first slept with Paul, what other man I would sleep with, just as an experiment : but I had never been able to make up my mind. Of course, don't think I don't love you : I do. Because why did I choose you otherwise ? '

' Yes.'

' When you came it used to be as if the air darkened a little, and when I thought of what you had come for, I had moments of excitement, terrified voluptuousness. I could have lived like that for years. I liked that. I always wish it was possible for women to have a sort of house-husband, one who would want them but not live with them.'

' Charming,' he murmured. ' A lapdog.'

She laughed naughtily. ' Really, you don't think we spend all our time worshipping you ! Perhaps old maids do ; not a married woman. We make men, we don't worship them.' She thought for a moment, and went on in the former tone : ' You went away, and I thought, Oh, well, this is finishing like the others : Fenton is not the fateful one. Your letters started to come. At first I was repelled, because you weren't experienced like the others, you just gave yourself away. Then your letters really moved me. I felt a little bit humble—the first time in my life, about a man—and because you were away I could imagine you better. Then I was safe, I didn't have to make up my mind. When your last letter came begging me to come to you, I thought, What's the odds ? It's got to be some time, it may as well be now. Because I knew you would never do me any harm. I thought about you all the week-end and about Paul.

Paul still broods over me and looms over me as he did in
the beginning : but you're more a companion, a brother,
more like a playmate. I thought of your breast all the
time. I wanted to see if the same sleep and darkness
comes over me on every man's breast, just the same. I
wasn't so curious about the rest, all men are the same,
practically. And I just wanted to see, if in continuing in
my own line, you know, just peering, being curious,
analysing, being objective, even in love, and I am, I
could get any new experiences.'

She lifted her head and looked at him, satisfied. She
was surprised by his estranged expression.

' Oliver, what is the matter ? '

' Nothing, my dear.'

She looked close at his face, shut his eyelids with two
fingers and opened them again. She patted the light
folds which had become marked in his cheeks, laughed
close to his mouth, kissed him.

' Oliver ! Silly boy ! Oliver, cheer up. Come on,
laugh. You aren't angry at what I told you ? '

' I'm not angry,' said a restrained voice. ' I'm not
angry, Elvira. Don't worry about me.'

She put her head on his breast again. ' Look, I'm
talking into your breast that I told you I loved : I'm
listening to your heart. What is it saying ? Something
is wrong, Oliver. I can feel a dreadful coldness in you.
What is it ? ' She sat up and got off his knee, really
startled.

' Oliver, was it my silly gabbling ? I didn't mean a
word of it. You know how you start on one track of
thinking and you go ahead and it doesn't really express
what you mean at all. It is just a way of thinking. There
are lots of ways of thinking. I'm a foolish woman.
Look, look at me ! ' She tried to turn his eyes to her.
He looked at her :

' Elvira, don't bother about me : it's nothing. You
didn't say anything wrong : you have a right to say
anything you like to me. I am your lover.'

A few fretful tears came into her eyes. She cried:
'Oh, how can you be so foolish as to take what I said
seriously? I told you it means nothing. I was reading
something in a French magazine while you were out, and
it was like that. I just copied the way the man thought.
Oh, you annoy me when you're so sensitive! I didn't
mean it.'

'You mean it, my dear,' said Oliver, seriously and
gently. 'Don't worry about me. Let's go downstairs;
perhaps Marpurgo is waiting downstairs for us.'

He got up and pulled his tie straight. She went petulantly into the bathroom to powder herself: a proud
expression came over her face. She thought, 'Let him
come round: it's just foolishness. I can't be explaining
all night.' She came out, smiling, sailing, in all the
panoply of her languor and robust female beauty. When
he looked at her, still with that alien expression—one she
had often seen, in fact, on Paul's face—she knew that he
still had a fierce, unalterable passion for her, but that its
gaiety had evaporated. She went out insolently before
him, swaying her hips, pouting her bosom, wantonly
wilful and pretty.

They walked down, and on the stairs, which were ill-
lighted, she was inspired to make a few jokes with double
meaning. 'Now you are going down a gloomy staircase
when you would rather go up,' and 'I read somewhere
that the Greeks said that a man is only tender over a
woman on two nights, the first night in the marriage-bed,
and the first night in the cemetery, the two nights of the
worm. I know why; I was thinking about it to-day
when I had my bath. It is because marriage is the
beginning of pregnancy and death feeds the seeds in the
earth. Men want to dissolve us, crush us, get rid of the
vessels of their pleasure. They want to pretend they
create alone.' She turned a disdainful, malicious face
over her shoulder, saw that he looked interested, and
was warming to her. She smiled.

'There is Marpurgo peering at us: he prides himself

on being a psychological detective. He can never guess what I was saying. To him I'm just zero.'

Marpurgo was rather distrait, though, and greeted them with more normal obtuseness than usual. However, he roused himself to enquire, satirically :

'How is the work going ? '

'I didn't work all day,' said Oliver.

'He needs the whip : you'll have to get him a job.'

'If you get me a job, I'll take it,' supplemented Oliver. 'Study is beginning to look unreal. They keep us at our books too long. The youth of man is stretching farther and farther out towards middle-age.'

He flung his rather plump body into the easy-chair.

Marpurgo smiled. 'Haeckel divided the life of man into two sharp divisions : the idealist, before marriage, the realist, after marriage.'

They sat silent, and Marpurgo kept his eyes running from one to the other.

'Are you going to the concert to-night ? ' he asked. He did not say which concert. There was an assumption between them that, as intellectuals, they always knew the musical programmes and which was the most important aesthetically of the various concerts offered.

'Do you want to go, Elvira ? ' asked Oliver with the proper amount of eagerness.

She looked helplessly at them both.

'No ? ' he laughed and pressed her hand. 'Our little lowbrow does not want to go to the concert.'

Marpurgo picked up an olive, with crooked little finger.

'She is honest : few women will admit they have little ear. To tell the truth, you're missing nothing. Only Mengelberg can conduct this symphony. It's a waste of time to hear anyone else.'

None of them wanted to go to the concert.

'Well, do you think the franc's going off : what's your odds ? '

Marpurgo drawled : 'I've got a ten-to-one bargain with

the chief that it won't go off before December 31, 1934, midnight.'

'You'll win,' said Oliver. 'They think they can get away with anything at present. Lagny and Stavisky nearly brought the state down: the coup of the 6th February was nicely managed to make people forget all about both. They are as wise in their way as the British in their own particular brand of politics: only here it's a firebrand, touch-and-go, derring-do kind. An attempted coup d'état always routs other questions in the French mind. The Irish have orange *v.* green, the Indians Hindu *v.* Mohammedan, the English labour *v.* conservative, the French Paris *v.* the provinces, when things get so bad that the ministers have to talk about " spiritual uncleanliness in high places." But the situation got a little out of hand this time. I wrote you about it.' He turned to Elvira. 'Oh, I was praying you'd come a couple of weeks earlier. I wanted you to see the true Paris, cloth-capped Paris, flowing down from Ménilmontant. The bourgeois ran home and stayed behind shut doors.'

'We heard the city was armed: we thought a revolution was coming,' said Elvira. 'I don't know what Paul will be thinking now. I am sure he imagines me sitting in streets bristling with machine-guns.'

'If I hadn't been a foreigner, and been so anxious to finish my essay,' said Oliver, 'I would have been down in the streets again with them. After one night the workers had the streets to themselves: the *fils de papa* who come out with billies for a lark after supper only ventured into areas well protected with police after that night, and after a little scuffle got themselves safely locked up until two o'clock in the morning, rowdying in the police-station and singing " We must have a king ! " The police were lenient although they got sick of the game after a few nights. They began to come out with weary faces and black-ringed sleepless eyes. They then forgot to see the fun of it all. They found they were proletarians after all. That's the virtue of even a French cop : he asks " For what ? " when he's kicked out of his material comfort. After all, he's just a natural loafer and snooper, overpaid for hitting his brother on the head. When trouble comes and he has to work and go into the firing-line, he's a worker like the rest of them, and his practical mind works it out in terms of francs and centimes. " I'm likely to get my head knocked in—for what ? For four pounds a week ? So that Chiappe can get the kudos and sit in the Municipal Council." When he gets to that point, they have to call out the Republican Guard and the negro regiments.' He said indignantly to Elvira, ' They actually had two coloured regiments here in Paris during the riots. The old Roman way : suppress the Romans with provincials, the barbarians with Romans.' He saw her eyes sparkling, and smiled. ' You like this crazy world, don't you ? You were built for life, not death. This is slightly different from Mecklenburgh Square ! '

' Paul doped me : I've been under a drug for eight years,' exclaimed Elvira : ' this is really life.' She con-fided to Marpurgo : ' When I was at school I always tried to get the socialist side in debates : or rather, the liberal side. It was conservative as only a persevering lower middle-class school for young ladies can be. I wanted to be a lawyer or run for Parliament every time I won a debate.' She laughed ruefully. ' Now look at me : a pumpkin-wife.'

' Yes, but you've left your kitchen-garden,' said Oliver hurriedly. ' I'll say to Marpurgo what Lenin said to Wells—Come back in ten years ! You won't recognise her.'

Elvira giggled : ' Oh, I knew it was coming.' She bent archly to Marpurgo. ' He is dying to make me an honest woman—politically—and sartorially—and every other way. In ten years I'll be the perfect woman. You know, Oliver, you're losing me a job. I'd never get my job back with Paul with all these embellishments. I'd frighten him. Consider what you're doing.'

Oliver stared at her passionately, without speaking. Marpurgo impatiently crushed out the end of his cigar and took them to dinner. Oliver was obsessed with the woman all through dinner.

'Have we ever known women? I love to think of a state in which women will be perfectly free. The women we know are inchoate . . . the seed of our passion is only a thread of foam threading in and out of their dark atlantic of storms and mists : Aphrodite is not yet born.'

Marpurgo bent over the table :

'To get to know another person takes as long as a degree in medicine : lots get pipped.' He bobbed up and down like a cork between the carafes of wine and water.

'I think you see best with your first eye,' drawled Elvira. 'Afterwards you just read into the person every-thing you want to : like a woman who thinks a man means " I love you madly " when he says " We are friends." I always take an outsider's view of anybody I know too well.'

'A cynic, I see,' trifled Marpurgo.

He and Elvira spent some minutes in persiflage. Oliver watched them, flushed, in increasing gloom. Marpurgo turned to him, questioning. Oliver said, 'If you want to, Elvira, I think we'll make that trip to Fontainebleau to-morrow : the air should be sweeter out there. Paris is so close, without winds ; we live in a perpetual bath of our own sweats here.'

Marpurgo slid in. 'It should be against the law to sweat in another's presence : as Herodotus says of the Persians, that they denied the right to spit or make water in another's presence.'

'Fine advice for a road-mender, for example,' laughed Elvira. 'In the Russian pictures what I love most is the way the rich-muscled oudarniks sweat and shine. A non-sweating man is not a man.'

'I sweat at night,' said Marpurgo softly. 'All my deeds seem then like sins against myself : I am convinced

that ill-health is the only sin and alone, the path to knowledge.'

Elvira laughed : ' Either you're born right or wrong :
if you're born clumsy nothing will ever go right. It's
just a matter of disposition. People love you that
you do nothing for, and hate you that you do everything for. Look at my brother Bennie, spoiled, drunk,
a waster. All the family has to keep him, mother just
worships him : and he damns the whole family.' She
pushed out the end of her cigarette and began putting
on her gloves. 'I always think—take what you want :
either you get it or you don't get it. It depends on
your nature, not on what you deserve.' Her soft drawl
stopped ; she looked brightly and cunningly at the two
men : ' Let's go : I'm bored stiff. Where to, for you,
Marpurgo ? '

' My chess-club, I think : I'm playing with a woman
this evening : a Soviet press reporter. She's cleaning up
the club, and I'll spend half an hour walking there,
plunging into a triple-bottom of melancholy, the only
way to match her new-world optimism : with every
displacement in space you can see she is aware of the
multiple play of threads in future time, which is her
present : how can I match her except by opposing to her
the bag of bad tripe we all are ? If we once abolish
property, and free women, men will be reduced to cards
and cadging : natural materialists in a materialist world.
A second paradise-lost—the last great Cabbalist falling
slimewards before the matriarchate.' He looked up
sideways at them with self-delighted smile. ' Women
cook in pots and men work out by mathematics the
one-sixtieth impurity of pure pot.'

Elvira, whose secret glamour was spread out under
the desirous looks of men passing, moved a step away
from Oliver and made him break up the conversation.
Marpurgo turned round upon himself and footed it
down the avenue without turning round. The last
glance he gave her was satiric. Elvira looked at Oliver.

'If we're going to fiddle every evening away with that man, I'm going to get another feller.'

Oliver was delighted. 'I should have thought of it before I brought you here : every woman comes into her natural rights in Paris, her sexual rights.'

She had a contralto laugh this evening. He flaunted her along the boulevard, till she marched into a café terrace ; he sat down excited at her side, but when he had had two café-cognacs, he flushed and began to talk again, because he saw two Russian women, handsome and expensive Aphrodites, near them on the terrace. They could see on the building near them the title of the royalist Russian paper, *Vozrozhdyony* (renaissance).

He waved his hand : '*They* say, What is the complete vozrajenie (repartee) to Stalinist bureaucracy ? The advent of Fascism in Germany. Socialist mankind betrayed by the phrase-mongering and opportunist diplomacy of a clique-elected Barras—they complain of social-democracy! Let them sweep their own house clean first.' The two women started to look Oliver over, coolly and guilefully, smiling, ignoring Elvira. Elvira murmured :

'A lot they care for your Russian—it's probably wrong. You're a trick, aren't you ? I've noticed before the actor in you : you have to have an audience.'

'I wasn't acting,' said Oliver earnestly. 'I didn't notice those women till you pointed them out.'

'They seem to think differently.'

'Everyone in Paris cares about politics—it's the currency of the country. A girl will pretend to be anything you like, but won't change the shade of her politics to please you : in that they'll quarrel with their best clients. In England you go to Whig hotels, in France to S.F.I.O. whores.'

Elvira pulled his sleeve ; the women seemed indifferent, although more polished than before. They were talking quietly to each other and eyeing some rich men entering the café with the cool air of great ladies. Oliver, rosily

drunk, took out his pocket-book and pretended to light
upon a paper there.

'Hello, I'd forgotten this!' He laughed. 'Listen to
this, Elvira, some of my lucubrations: tell me if you
can't stand it, it's pretty raw in some spots.' He unfolded
it and read:

'On the Magdalenian stone
In their glyptic, cryptic tongue,
Palæolithic bard, engraver,
Yearning gave her
Name and pigment, flesh and bone,
The steatopygous one:
They to graving-bone are gone,
None stay, save her,
Fresher than yesterday's scrawl
On latrine wall.
We wail at wall, bawl—
Hail, outlived stale,
Stupendous frail!
Shadowfall, waterfall, deathfall,
Have not served us at all, at all:
You persist with your lids of anemone
In the dead men's agapemone;
You remain with your bullocks and red men
Down among the dead men;
Alone alive, flesh-sucking, succulent, lusting saprophyte,
Sallow angel of the night.
You are she with diamond-pointed eyes
In her grottoed catalepsis
From her infundibular prison
Carved her mystic harmonies
On my eyes: I sit and yawn
While through my blood and marrow creeps the sepsis
And a fever-heat has risen.
I sit and gape and yawn and I say, some night, some
        dawn
Have seen her eyebuds slowly flower,
The dark-sheeted, pale almond-buds with germinating
        centres:
Centaur, satyr, ape; Kalang, Cro-Magnón!
In the power of an hour,

The shelter of a summer-shower :
I shall be the same as the past experimenters—
Food for dust—that is all ! '

His clarion voice, for which the vowels of the verse had
been carefully chosen, had risen during the reading, and
now not only the Russian women, but the other clients,
the waiters on the terrace, and the cashier at the desk
inside, were staring. The manager said, ' Shh ! Shh ! '
Elvira's face had a rare flush : she said in a strained
whisper : ' I thought Paris was fond of the arts,' and
cast a timid, would-be indignant glance at the head-
waiter. She pulled Oliver's sleeve as he looked at another
sheet of writing.

' Let's go home, Oliver : you can read it to me there.'
He was delighted.

' You like it ? It wasn't too strong for you ? You
know to whom I am referring ? ' She nodded and
flushed again. He said :

' I know, I know. When I first met you I thought, I
want that woman always to talk to, to inspire me, to hear
me out. You used to sit there all those evenings listening
to those dull discussions of business and stupid personal
philosophy, listening so well, winding the men out of
their own hearts ; and when you let some remark drop,
it was always rounded, perfect, put with wisdom.'

She pulled on her furred gloves.

' Dear, I had no idea I was so dull. I've been a slow-
poke all my life. You can make me over that way, too.'

*   *   *   *   *   *

Elvira, who knew only high-school French, thought
she heard the maid say to the valet, ' It is a honeymoon,
but they are not married,' and when Oliver came back
from buying a newspaper, eager to tell her the political
news, he found her standing in a brown study between
the curtains. She swayed towards him and he took a step
towards her ; they looked at each other in a blind way
for a moment, and then Oliver held out the paper to her.

She took it and sat down in the arm-chair, elaborately turning the pages. Oliver sat looking at her. It was only the fourth day of their passion.

She suddenly laughed. 'Why, I might be in my arm-chair at home by the fire, as I was five days ago !'

Oliver laughed and waved his hand at the panelling, the curtains, the cornices of opposite houses, and then, leaning forward with darkening eyes, at himself. In the evening they dined in a Norwegian restaurant, and Elvira, after studying for some time the painted wall above them, with a picture of Vikings and the legend 'Rolf Landgang i Frankrike,' laid down her fork and murmured, 'Oliver, I ought to write to Paul : he doesn't even know where I am : he will worry.'

Oliver laid his hand on hers. 'He won't worry yet : he knows you're with me.'

'I ought to let him know.'

Oliver sighed and shook his dark young head, but he said kindly, 'Then why don't you telephone him ?'

Elvira brightened : 'I'll telephone him at home when we get back to the hotel.'

In the hotel, after dinner, Oliver lay on the bed while she got her London call, and heard her explaining herself to her abandoned husband in a sad, intimate way. She did not even mention him. She said, 'No, no, I'm not lonely, Paul ; I am trying to find a way out.' His heart was beating to suffocation. He had dreamed for months of being her lover, and yet he could not be her lover in that strange room, in that strange city with the false telephone on the wall.

In the morning he persuaded her to go to the Forest of Fontainebleau, and there they went before lunch and took a room in the Hotel of the Black Eagle (that is, Napoleon) which is near the Palace. In the freezing sunshine they went through the bare grounds where the blue and sepia forest, tall, thick and old, melted into the luminous alleys, and at hand a white swan swam half-congealed by the high clipped birches, and the falling fountain, suddenly frozen, glittered with its stalactites over the great frozen central basin. Not a blade of grass moved and not a bird flew down the perspective of the great water, but under thickety trees, officers and children skated with coloured cloaks and gloves over a pond. Beyond, dazzling and enchanted, lay the leafless forest. In it the pines alone were green. They drove through the forest, and from an eminence, for the first time, looked far north-east to the sullen, rolling boundaries of Burgundy. They skirted a stony, shallow valley, treeless, red and yellow, and arrived quietly in the ancient town of Moret, lying around its ruined abbey and beside the still pooly reaches of a fat river over which hang willows and the balconies and turrets of improbably romantic houses. Beyond a weir and the abbey it runs through the channels of the laundries and down under a great viaduct where lie the barges. Overhead in the blue sky passed the Blue Train, bound for the Mediterranean coast. They looked up at it, with linked arms, and smiled into each other's eyes. Ever farther, farther south, seemed the promise and hope of romance. At midday nothing moved, and time alone went ambling ragged and in sabots, an idiot spectacle in that ancient village street, and passed unhailed by the wineshop and out of sight beyond the tumbling gate.

They were so in love that afternoon that they returned from Moret by taxi and pulled down the blinds to stop even the winter sun from coming into their room. A year ago, in London, Oliver leaning over her ear in a room full of people, had murmured, 'Last night I dreamed I heard you cry with love for me.' She had often thought since that she would please him by an artifice, invent a little scene for him. This afternoon, when she awakened from a profound dream, she found Oliver looking at her in ecstasy, kissing her forehead and silky tangled hair and saying :

'Now you have opened your eyes at last ! I have never been so happy in my life as this last hour.'

'I must have fallen asleep!'

He shook his head and continued to contemplate her. They were as united as twins that suck at the same breast. He said often, 'Now I know what had to be,' or 'If I had not met you it would have had to be another like you.'

They could only stay in Fontainebleau a week. They heard that Trotsky was living incognito in Barbizon. This displeased Oliver, and the brown twiggy forest road, along which amazons sometimes rode, heard his partisan acerbities.

One day she put her hand to his lips. 'I hate politics, Oliver.'

He pointed with a grim smile to the Palace, in whose grounds they walked. 'You are different from me : that nonpareil recalls to me the ruined people that built it. I look at nothing without asking, whence, why, whither ?'

'Under socialism, you'd never have a thing as beautiful as that,' said the woman. 'Life would be robbed of beauty. You would have everywhere clinics for consumption and workmen's accidents. I prefer it this way. Look how lovely it all is ! See how happy we are ! Could we be so happy in a planned city with hospitals, factories, laboratories and playgrounds, and people everywhere ? How beautiful is this silence, even this melancholy isolation ! I love the decay of this palace, this tomb closed on so many rowdy centuries. The sunrise and sunset are the only fires these panes that glitter now see. . . . I love decay,' she cried restlessly, with tears in her eyes. 'I hate that athletic, gymnasium world of oudarniks you want to build.'

'And I couldn't be bothered working at all if I didn't believe in the edification of socialism. I am a man, I want to join the front ranks of the first men of our time : I want to work marvels and see the future.'

'Over the top of a barricade,' sneered Elvira. 'Oh, you are a boy still, Oliver. Over the top of a barricade you only look into the ends of the rifles of the republican guard. Pop goes the weasand! A lot of good you've done for yourself and the rest of—humanity! You say socialism must come, don't you?'

'It must come.'

'If it must come, why should you bother about it? And if it won't come now, what's the use of your messing your life up? No one will thank you for it, and you'll only get your family into trouble. Your family sent you to the university: you ought to think of them too.'

'I paid for my own way with scholarships and tutoring,' said Oliver with pride.

'Yes, but you didn't help to keep them.'

He bit his lip. 'If you must know, Elvira, I used to do what I could, too. It's only this last year that I've blossomed out a bit. I earned more—and,' he fawned on her, suddenly brimming with love, 'I wanted to get you.'

'So you're not so inflexible and heroic,' she laughed.

'Not when you're concerned.'

'Heavens, I'm glad. I'm not at all heroic, you know: I like marshmallows and ice-cream sodas. I wouldn't give up my afternoon porto for the proletariat. And neither would you.'

He kissed the tips of her fingers. 'You're such an idiot, I have to love you. I'm going to have to give you a strenuous study course.'

'Oh, for God's sake!' she cried. 'Again! I only ask one thing: promise it.'

'When I hear it.'

'Promise you'll give up being my Messiah.'

He laughed frankly. 'All right, I promise to let you go on being your own little dud self—for a while.'

They returned to Paris. The sun shone everywhere with promise of an early spring. The year before had been hopeful and fine, but this year had begun with a tempest of political troubles and accidents: the clouds had broken about Christmas, and still there were showers, thunder and lightning. The funeral of Vuillemin, the communist youth killed in a fight with the police, took place with many thousands of mourners in fighting mood. Oliver was on tenterhooks. He was late getting home, and Elvira was always frightened that he had got into a fight or been taken to a police-station by the police to have his papers examined. If they made enquiries about his home-address they would find out about her. She had no courage at all. As it was they looked at her curiously. She had telegraphed Paul her address and kept receiving anxious telegrams from him. 'Are you safe?' 'Is there fighting in your quarter?' 'Don't you think you should get out of Paris?' 'How can you stay there alone? Come home.'

Paul had not understood that she was with Oliver Fenton. She was alternately pleased and piqued to learn this. Meanwhile Oliver was calculating that Paul would divorce her and that they would be married, say, within a year, at any rate, before he would have to take a position. Paul might like to spare her, establish domicile in Paris and divorce her there in secret.

'Even if Paul gets bitter and makes a public affair out of it,' said Oliver to Elvira, 'we will stand together. I will get a job myself. I will take a clerk's job—anything. We'll get along. I've never feared the future, and with you behind me all will be well. Love has a first option on our lives. As a matter of fact, I was thinking of going to see the Fuseaux brothers, Marpurgo's bosses. I'd like to get in there, but I suspect a little psychological difficulty . . .' He smiled.

'Jealousy?'

'A little: I'm as good at Marpurgo's game as he is. He doesn't want me to get too close to the brothers.'

Elvira looked happy and urged him to take Marpurgo out to dinner by himself. They walked along the streets, looking into the antique-shops, at the old lace. Oliver bought a book on mechanical tulles and laces. He said, 'It's of immense help to me in my essay, too. I'll bring in the struggles and early disorganisation of the Lyonnais and Calais workers.' He pressed her arm. 'I should never have thought of this without you, and, do you know, I believe I'm on the right path. What plums do the academic woods promise to young men to-day? You've got to be conformist to earn your salary, and conformity is stultifying. In business no one asks questions : you can believe what you like as long as you bring in a profit.'

That seemed an ideal solution of the question to Elvira. She told him for the first time that she was happy she had come to Paris.

* * * * * *

They often rose at twelve or two in the afternoon. On the next Sunday they walked down from the little hotel on the Boulevard St. Germain, to the Île de la Cité, through the bird market where was a crowd looking at the birds, fish and kittens, and some poor householders, unemployed boys and old women with grey hair and black aprons trying to sell their pet cats or canaries in cages. Single goldfish hung artificially in bowls as big as tennis-balls. They remarked that the French resembled the Chinese in a variety of ways: economy of space, time, money, the first three and the fourth and fifth dimensions, respectively, in their neighbourliness, love of clipped gardens, formal music, polished prose, manners, and making of silk and embroideries. It was a fine cloudy cool afternoon, with the twigs swelling now at their tips, but no one yet out and the river grey, windblown, swollen but now free of ice. Notre-Dame stood vigorous and burgherly in the clean square, its sculpture purple, yellow and bronze in the fresh river airs.

Round the empty central markets the many small shuttered streets, with barred cellars and store-rooms smelling of cheeses, fish and vegetables, and littered pavements, sent the air careering to the rain-washed sky. The sun came out more brilliantly, and the prostitutes who had the good fortune to have their regular beat on the sunny side of the streets loosened their furs with gratitude and became more nonchalant. In the shadow a corpulent one-legged girl with a cotton stocking propped herself on her crutches against a greengrocer's door, a few steps from her hotel in a cold, blasty passage. When they looked back, the girl was tapping down the street with a man, while her whole and satined sisters tapped their high heels impatiently in the sun. It was damp underfoot and cold. Elvira was drowsy. They passed a young white-skinned prostitute, and Oliver said, ' Did you notice that girl ? She must have begun at fourteen : how young she is ! '

' They all begin at fourteen, or twelve, or younger,' drawled Elvira. ' Why not ? To be thirteen and to know men must be a pleasure, whatever comes after.'

He smiled down at her—he was only an inch taller. ' You would have liked that ? Yes, you are sorry you weren't married at fourteen.' He held her arm, hand in his, and she felt his muscles tightening. Her laugh dropped out like ruby liquid from a glass.

' Perhaps.'

' Oh, how you must have regretted having to wait for Paul till you were twenty-one,' insinuated Oliver.

She said with feeling : ' Oh, I did.'

' You must be sorry for all those years when every night might have been a loving-night,' he insisted.

She said nothing.

' How many nights ? From fourteen to twenty-one— 7×365, you were born in 1905, 20 was a leap year, 1924 also, 2,557 nights, that is plus two leap-year nights. Oh, and to think of all the girls lonely in their beds all those same years and all the other years, so many thousand years of lost nights ! What a calculation for a bachelor, for a half-fledged boy groaning over his homework, for a country boy snuffing in the rich odours of the paddocks ! For a boy slouching along the pavements and wondering if he can bear to go without supper so that he can buy that young street-girl on Friday night ! '

Elvira laughed now again : 'Don't talk about it : I don't want to think about it.'

Oliver went on : 'To count all the days of our lives in which we are robbed of one desire or another? A lifetime of fulfilment can't make up for a lifetime of such repression. Every time I have a desire, I know I have been cheated all my life : every time I am satisfied, I am afraid of the next moment which will bring me back to desirous discontent.'

She pulled his sleeve petulantly. 'I don't want to walk any more, Oliver : I'm not as young as you, don't forget : don't forget you're five years my junior ! '

He touched his head, taking off his hat. 'And those grey hairs ? '

They sat down in a café in the Boulevard de Sébastopol and drank a vermouth. In the gutter a man cooked chestnuts in a stove. At hand, within the glass shelters, the café stoves with their perforated ostrich necks sent veins of heat through the cold air of the passages. An old Jew in a greenish cap with metal visor, clad in a torn overcoat bought in some rag fair, which he wore with the same fold and stoop as his cassock in Poland lately discarded, stood for some minutes, humbly, merrily obtrusive beside the stove and joked with the smart-tongued young waiter.

'Spring is coming,' said Oliver. 'Can you believe that spring will not be coming for ever? Can you believe that spring will come, summer too, autumn and winter ? We will have to go away from here eventually ! And never return.'

'Why think about it, now ? ' asked Elvira. 'I'll have another vermouth. Garçon ! La même chose.'

Oliver looked at her with admiration : in a few days she had learned all the tricks of the café, how to ring with her spoon, how to call out an order across the terrace without being loud, the right phrases, even the right intonation—at least for drinks.

'You're a smart girl, Elvira,' he said.

She spoke over the lip of the amber-filled glass :
' Does that surprise you ?   Am I different now from what
I was ? '

His long dark lips and little new dark moustache curled
round his white teeth.   ' No : only—more than I ever
knew you were.   Oh, I got the great prize in the lottery.'

' You said that before ! '

' Yes : it is in a German tale called *Immensee*, I read
at school.'

She teased : ' All you know is from school.'

He drooped his head : ' I am only a scholar : there is
plenty of wastepaper in my existence.'

She began to triumph, and raised her round chin.

' I hate the sight of ink, it is so stale with all the
platitudes it has written, and yet I only feel really
myself when I have a pen and ink in hand and am
scribbling, scribbling over reams : that was—till I met
you.   Then I changed.'

Her full lower lip drooped insolently.   ' We don't
change.'

He caught her tone, hurriedly.   ' With you, I will
change.   I will look back to this great spring all my life :
when we first joined hands and began to walk along the
crazy pavement with flowers and moss coming through
all the cracks.'

' How suburban ! ' cried Elvira.   ' I was in Hampstead
the other day : in front of one of the richest houses was
a crazy pavement : they paid about £35 for it, doubtless.
The man who would have done it best was in an asylum :
he would have done it for nothing, happy to do it.
They employed a sane man to do it, and the more there
is of it, the more dull and plain it looks, just an expanse
of conventional craziness, looking as stupid as a neander-
thal skull.   That's the suburbs all over.   That's what we
are, you see : suburban, however wild we run.   You
know quite well, in yourself, don't you, two people like
us can't go wild ?   Still it's nice to pretend to, for a while.'

' For a while,' he echoed, and going a little pale.

'Why, you strange woman : as if you were playing in a play !'

'So we all are, people like us,' she repeated with dull contentment. 'We are not fire and dew.' She laughed. 'I'm getting a little squiffy, I believe : fire and dew. From me.'

He began speaking rapidly. 'Elvira, you are a little squiffy, and I hope you remain that way. Oh, you've been sewed up in household dusters, and frozen up in cold and sooted up in that dark London house of yours. You're a mummy. I'll have to dig and dig till I find the crooked secret passage to your soul, and then I'll dig it out and carry you all off, jewels too. This is your spring, this spring, this is your feast of life beginning, your new adolescence, you will not miss any nights now : every one will be gemmy with bright lights and loving eyes and stars and kisses : you'll know what you ought to have been. You are such a beautiful woman, but you act as if your beauty were only a mask over some embalmed body, like the painted faces over the sleeping princesses in their mummy-cases.'

She saw he was not looking at her but talking himself into a mood. Her large eyes searched every lineament in his face, as if she would extract all the truth and conviction she could from him now he had roused her. He looked and found tears in her eyes.

'Dear girl.'

'I am alone in the world.'

'What do you say ? What makes you say that ?'

'I don't deceive myself.'

'If you left me, I'd die. I couldn't bear it. It's I who am alone.'

'Men don't commit suicide from love.' She laughed cruelly.

A handsome dude, strolling in with an independent air, looked her over coolly and murmured, 'Oh, the beauty !' as he passed, too low for Oliver to hear.

She flushed with beauty.

'Oliver, I think I'll have another vermouth. It's so pleasant here. I like the café-life, don't you? Why don't we have them in London? Garçon! Encore un vermouth!'

He was happy.

'You like Paris, then? You're not sorry you came? Don't you remember how I had to persuade you to come, and how frightened you were that people would look at us, or that we would meet someone we knew! Now, what do you think?'

His dark face, his young brown eyes, now bent upon her, made her smile; drinking her third vermouth, she said with a sudden warm slippery speech, as if she had found her tongue for the first time in her life:

'Oliver, I like you because you're so naïve: you really don't know what life is like, and you never will.'

'How do you know I'm not showing you what life is like? A little child shall lead them. The pleasure of innocence! Oh, what would Paul say if he knew we were so innocent?'

She nodded her head like a mandarin. 'Paul is the real innocent: he would say nothing. He is so good that I am sure he expects to win everything by kindness. Do you think there are people who believe that? Paul does. He expects to get me back by kindness: he expects to shame you by kindness. Oh dear, dear, and you're so cruel!'

Oliver suddenly put his hand in his pocket and hailed the waiter. They walked out on to the pavement, and after a few paces got into a perambulating taxi. In the taxi Oliver squeezed her hand, put her head on his shoulder, and said, 'You are quite drunk, my dear.'

She gave a bubbling laugh: 'I never felt so gay in all my life: light-headed as if a vent'l—ventilating shaft went up through my head: a flock of doves could carry me off through the air on a net. Oh dear, I am drunk. What would Paul say?' She kept laughing all the way home and saying, 'Oliver, can you imagine what Paul would say? Oh dear, can you imagine me coming home drunk in Mecklenburgh Square?'

When she was lying on the divan in their room, Oliver went downstairs to get the evening papers. He rubbed shoulders for a while with the quick-walking crowds on the boulevards, going home from work, and for a moment thought, 'What a lazy beggar I am! But what the hell—I'll only be in Paris once.' He walked up the rue de Rennes towards Montparnasse station and back again. He stopped at a bar and drank another vermouth, only his second. He walked more slowly, looking up at the rose-aproned sky. A great joy seemed to be nesting in his heart: it rose up and shook out its feathers as evening advanced; he even heard the cheeping of the newly-hatched egglings. 'What a happy man, that ever this should have come to me!' He realised his lips were moving: a woman passing looked at him. He smiled at her, full of love for all women. She had a black shopping-bag with a piece of pumpkin and an onion in it. He thought: 'When Elvira is running my house, we will be happy.' A young girl went past with make-up on; he thought: 'I must get Elvira to use a little rouge when she is pale.' He suddenly realised that he must go to the Bank in the morning. It was time they settled down. If Paul was coming to Paris, too, he should have a dovecote for Elvira's soft-bosomed heart. He sat down in a café and wrote to a friend in London to ask if he could get reviews, or a Paris letter, and offered him the usual commission, 10 per cent. on articles he placed for him. He took home the rouge and watched Elvira making herself up.

The next day Elvira, who was out of sorts with the excitement and change, lay down after lunch, and Oliver, instead of going back to the Archives, went to the address in the rue du Faubourg Montmartre where Marpurgo worked. He met Antoine and Georges Fuseaux, found Antoine disarming and Georges sulky, but he got into a bitter discussion with Antoine about whether the Russians abroad took commissions, and won the respect of Georges by saying that every young man nowadays should go into business to learn what the world is like.

'Most of our economists, even our best theoretical Marxians,' said Oliver, 'even those who write most intelligently about politics and human nature, write irritating polemic platitudes when it comes to business, because they have never been in it. Business-men are not mannequins of the class-war, and individual businesses are not patterns of the decline of capitalism.'

Georges retired into the washroom and did not come out till the voluble and charming Oliver had gone out again. Then he came forth and said darkly to Antoine:

'That kid Marpurgo brought in has good business-instincts: he'd make money if he went into commerce. I wish we had one or two like him instead of some of the fancy ladida huggermugger medicine-men we've got eating holes in the pay-roll.'

'He's an intellectual: he thinks they're angels in Russia; he's an arm-chair revolutionary: he doesn't know what's in the back of the heads of fellows,' Antoine shot off, with a wave of the hand. 'Don't bother me with sucklings: they're likely to get diarrhœa in their diapers any time they're in a jam.' He looked with irritation at Georges, and then burst into a merry laugh. 'Go on, Georgie: you've got your angels and I've got mine, and while I'm running this place only my angels will get a chance. Hard luck on you and yours. You run the accounts and see I don't overstep the mark: that's all you've got to do. You're no judge of men, Georgie. Leave that to me.'

Georges half smiled.

'According to you anyone with a clean collar, pearl studs and a cissy accent is a genius!'

'You're an ass, Georges.' Antoine with good-humoured petulance piloted his young brother to the door. 'Tell Mlle Rose to come here: I want to write a letter.'

'If it's to that Lanafil chap I wish you'd let me see it before it goes out,' was Georges's parting provocation.

' You never mind me : mind your end of the business.'

Oliver rang Georges and asked him to dinner. Georges said :

' You come out with me ; you come to dinner with me, that's the best. Listen, do you know the Hôtel Pyramides in the rue des Pyramides ? It's a wonderful restaurant. Do you want to meet me there at seven o'clock to-night ? I've got nothing else to do. We can go for a little spin and have a coffee and liqueur somewhere afterwards.'

' Good, at the Restaurant Pyramides.'

Oliver walked straight from the telephone booth to the rue des Pyramides and looked at the hotel. The restaurant card was outside the great arched stone doorway. Oliver's heart sank when he saw the prices, but his hopes rose. However, Georges paid for them both, took Oliver in his car along a route which circled about the Place des Vosges and the Archives, since Oliver had to direct him, and they ended the evening in a long session at the café called ' La Duchesse.' Georges paid for the four brandies that Oliver had, in order to have his company, and both went home well pleased. Georges concealed this outing from Antoine and Marpurgo. Oliver had confided his plans to him, told him, when half-drunk, how he went round the curiosity-shops of Paris looking at laces, and Georges told him about the nutty fellow who collected laces, Paindebled, and his highbrow blonde who went to the Sorbonne and who ought to marry a professor.

He said : ' She's a knockout on looks and she has a dowry. You're not thinking of marrying a French girl, are you ? '

' That's not likely.'

' Some other little complication ? ' asked Georges knowingly.

' Haven't we all ? '

Oliver went home drunk and laughing, and retailed the whole thing to Elvira, a very Silenus of laughter.

He said privately to Marpurgo much later: 'The captain's lady and Judy O'Grady are Ninon de l'Enclos under the skin: my dear chap, I see my dear moult, and under the glassy skin is a new creature preparing to put on another instar. You see the tender creative blood pulsing, the soft flesh: sweet creatures that create so many miracles out of mere brown dust.'

'A woman is famous for her moults,' said Marpurgo.

'My lady of metamorphosis.'

'The Spanish fly,' murmured Marpurgo. 'Cantharis mated to Kantharos, cup of Dionysus; no sound is more maddening than the buzz of a beetle in a brass cup.'

Oliver flushed, not ill-pleased. 'Cantankerous old chip! I won't confide in you any more. At any rate, we're going to Fontainebleau again for a week at least.'

'I'm going south to Lyon for a time,' said Marpurgo. 'You'll love Fontainebleau. Very wise of you to go; be happy while you can. If you're going into business you'll have few such jaunts.'

'And you?'

'I'm not married: I'm Mr. Walker, the man that wears highways threadbare, the firm of Ready, Set, Go in person, the sinister character without fire or hire; when you hear my steps in the night, does not each one lift his head and say, Whither goeth the thief? (From Nietzsche, my master, that.) I am Footman Moth, but you are the Spanish Fly and you have a weary hour to beat out yet, waiting on doormats and dancing attendance on Judy O'Grady before you find you're not so fly.'

Oliver tried to embarrass him with innocent frankness.

'Marpurgo, why are you out to get me? Why don't you like me?'

'I'm as fond of you as I should be of my own son.'

'Knowing you for a Freudian, I get the delicate innuendo.'

They shook hands and parted, arranging to meet each other when both returned to Paris.

CHAPTER IV

IT was late May : cool weather persisted but the first trees were out. They had their breakfast every morning in the Café d'Harcourt at an hour when the first apéritif-drinkers were already there. When Oliver had taken his black French hat and gone off to the Archives, Elvira took out a thin letter and slit the envelope. Her head drooped more as she read it. A woman sitting near, drinking a porto, saw tears in her eyes and her mouth loose with discouragement. She read and re-read the letter and presently sat with it folded in her hand, looking out through the heavy-meshed curtain, her lips moving slightly.

' . . . your brother told me yesterday that business is slow : there is business in gold shares which means that other shares should go down. He asked for your address and said he might rejoin you. I told him you were travelling. Archie Penn came to me for a consultation yesterday. He has gallstones, as I thought. He asked after you. I still have not the courage to tell anyone that you have left me. I haven't the energy to answer their questions. The usual Wednesday night crowd was here yesterday, with Giles Gaunt playing the fool as usual. I had a good laugh, which I needed. Since you went I have been able to realise that time has passed since we married : before, it all seemed to me just one day. My cousin Sara is coming to London, tired of her Birmingham, to see if she can open a Snack Bar in the Fleet Street or Mansion House area. I am afraid the rents are too high. . . .'

A husbandly letter. She saw Paul's great athletic body, fattened, hunched in the arm-chair opposite hers at home, his hands, veined like a river-delta, lifting and falling sketchily, sweeping as he made a point, the large nails

polished like alabaster. She heard his embarrassed bari-
tone humming tunes from weary old operas, saw him
beat time to a line of music on the dark upholstered arm
where his ash-tray hung. Sara had sent that ash-tray for
his birthday years ago. Elvira wished she had thrown
the rubbed old thing out before she left home. She saw
his dark ivory lid close over his agate eye when he was
tired at the end of the day, while he smoothed back his
smooth black greased hair, plucked out his handkerchief
and wiped his face : he fumbled and perspired out of
nervousness when he thought she was cross with him.
Her heart closed round the dark image as a glove on a
hand. She was so used to him. In the first years of their
marriage she could never get used to him, and her heart
used to throb passionately every time she saw him coming
towards her or standing in a doorway, every time she saw
his tall head bending towards her. To look into his eyes
had given her a pleasant swimming nausea. She pushed
the glass of coffee away and thought how bad it was for
the high price they charged : the milk had skins on it
which revolted her. She felt weak. The Paris air did
not suit her. In the second page Paul had written :

' Naturally these three months have been difficult for me.
I do not know whether we were happy or unhappy before.
I am definitely unhappy now—and lost. The system of
marriage is wrong when it parts out of weariness and boredom two who loved each other as much as we did.'

It was a sober letter. He was good, patient : too good,
too patient—that was how their life had become so
stiflingly dull : and she herself was naturally lethargic.
She should have married a live-wire. A large tear rolled
down her face. She pitied herself. In the last paragraph
he went on repeating himself :

' I always loved you dearly, and I used to think that if
anything happened to you I could not live, but I have lived
without you these three months, and I shall go on living.
Everyone who comes into my consulting-room has troubles

worse than mine. If you want a divorce you can have it,
when the law allows. In the meantime I am your husband,
and you can always come to me if you are in trouble or need
anything. You sound so uncertain, but that is rather like
you. You stay away three months, and still give no reason,
nor describe how you are living. What persuaded you to
take such a step? It isn't in your character. I sometimes
even imagine that there must be someone else with a
stronger will than yours who enticed you. Or was it the
result of years of pent-up irresolutions? Perhaps circumstances will decide for you and me, again? Keep in touch
with me. I enclose the money you ask for.'

Circumstances had decided already. She half-smiled
as she imagined Paul's thunderstruck expression if she
wrote: ' I am living with another man and am going to
have a child by him.' She could not make up her mind
whether to tell Oliver and watch his reactions, or to go
where she could make sure that the child would not
come yet to make hay of their amorous painlessness.
When she first knew of the child she said to herself:
' Before this I have been a larva, an ephebe: my life has
been one long yawn of boredom: now I shall never be
bored again.' A week after, the idea was not so new.
The divorce would take a long time. She would be
saddled with a child and a roving young man. Her hair
would turn grey early, she knew: her mother had gone
grey at 'thirty-two. Another tear rolled down her face.
She would be sick for nine months and nursing for nine
months—until eighteen months the child would be
crying in the night. She saw, rapidly, Oliver's rosy
cheeks, drab with fatigue and irritation. Could Oliver
love her through all that? Of course not. This second
marriage would be even worse than the first, because she
had to cope with a brilliant young man's impatience and
disappointment. She said to herself babyishly:
' I want a baby and a comfortable home: I don't want
to belong to the intelligentsia.'
The tears rolled quickly down her face. She shielded

her face with her hand while she wiped her eyes. When that was done she clinked her glass and called the waiter.

'Waiter, take this away and bring me a vermouth. Your coffee is *moche* this morning.'

'Yes, Mademoiselle.'

The insolent fellow. She would usually lip her apéritif like a gourmet, before lunch. This morning she could not be bothered finishing that either. She kept the glass before her, taking small drops to keep her occupied, while she turned Paul's letter over in her head. A dull, comforting, melancholy rumination settled on her. 'I'm a woman with two husbands and don't get much joy out of either. How many women this very minute would give their very souls for even one man?' She looked round. Opposite her, the observant port-drinker went on piling up saucers and watching her. Elvira had often seen her. She had a regular oval face, large hazel eyes, black hair bound on each side of the head, like a ballet-dancer, nails painted gold. She was made up brilliantly in a very finished style, and seemed to have used three colours of powder, yellow, purple, ochre. Elvira swept her over with two casual glances and, in doing so, met the eyes of the woman, friendly eyes introducing themselves. 'An actress, of course,' she went on thinking, 'two husbands : I suppose it's easy to get a man if you actually think about that sort of thing all the time. As a young girl I was *farouche*—I always thought I'd marry a man about ten years older than myself, and I did.' A pleasant thought plumped her soft high oval cheeks. 'At seventeen I thought I should never marry—no one had come after me, I thought. I was so shy. Now I think that friend of father's, the architect,' she laughed to herself, 'Teasdale Fortescue, who wrote poetry in the local paper about fishing trips—he was so prompt, mild, tender and avuncular—but married, of course. That was why he told me that time that he always slept alone on the back verandah. Funny. I knew nothing.' She became aware that her lip was moving slightly, and her enquiring eye

swept the café again, and again met the eye of the young
actress, who smiled and said in a perfectly-pitched
whisper :

‘ You have dropped your gloves, Madame ! ’

Elvira thanked her, and as she stooped to pick them
up, blushed. The actress nodded and murmured politely
‘ *Il n’y a pas de quoi* ’ a little louder. Still studying
Elvira’s face, she said : ‘ May I bring my apéritif to the
next table, Madame ? ’

‘ Why not, Madame ? ’ said Elvira.

The actress sat on the leather bench beside her. Elvira
noticed that in profile she had a long nose like a blade and
high round cheekbones, long-lying eyes alive with lashes,
a slightly defective chin. She suggested something
Elvira was too sluggish to place, a fox, a silver pheasant,
perhaps. The actress began to speak to her in a fluent
English with a pretty French accent. Her voice was full
of unexpected broken notes of music, her words dry,
intelligent, flattering, but she began with ominous
fluency. Elvira drank vermouth, and before she knew it
began to talk about herself under the influence of these
charmed, coquettish, manhunting eyes.

‘ I am an artiste,’ said the actress. ‘ When I was
younger I sang and danced at the Folies Bergère ; now I
am too thin to dance naked, and I sing and dance in little
cabarets in evening-dress. My name is Blanche d’Anizy,
and it is not even a stage-name ! I come from near
Château d’Anizy. When I have earned enough I will
buy some land there and go and cultivate it with my
brother. He has land there. My brother is in the
Ministère de la Guerre.’

Elvira said : ‘ I went the other night to the Folies
Bergère : we saw a beautiful young girl there, naked, in
a green aquarium light, like the dream a woman has
when she dreams she is beautiful. There also a
stageful of beautiful naked young girls, dark, with
nipples like raspberries, and blonde and pale—it satisfied
you, like a good French dinner.’

'They look beautiful like that, in the green and flesh lights, but young girls, no, they are not!'

'I don't see why not,' cried Elvira, unreasonably contentious. 'Why does everyone assume that a dancer is immoral?'

Blanche tapped her foot with irritation. '*Est-ce possible? Non, mais vraiment*, you are naïve, Madame, really *innocente*. Do you think it is possible? They are all *catins*, all. They could not live otherwise: they must be.'

'I don't think so.' Elvira made a little severe mouth.

Blanche laughed richly. 'You are amusing! One always hears that the English are *naïfs*, and it is true. You are charming,' she finished with a fresh note of irritation. 'But listen, I have been through the mill and I know, and you know nothing, you were a well brought-up young girl and then you got married, hein?'

Elvira nodded. Blanche called the garçon and repeated her order, saying aside:

'And you too, Madame?'

'No, not now.'

'Ah, you are waiting for someone, of course. Before I was sixteen, I knew the whole of life. I was making my living off men. Why not? *Les hommes, quels mufles!*' she said rapidly; '*ce sont tous des voyous.*' Her English accent deteriorated into a stage-caricature. 'Zey arr oll keds, I av no taime forr zem....'

'Well, the sort of man who hangs round a stage-door is not the best kind of man....' Elvira lighted a cigarette.

Blanche d'Anizy flashed back in an exasperated tone: 'I was married, Madame, when I was sixteen. I ran away from home because I had no freedom, and went into the Folies Bergère. At fourteen already I did not know how to sleep at night. The Latin races have hot blood. Not like your cool northern girls.'

'Indeed,' began Elvira.

'I got tired of zem and I married to *un étranger*, an Englishman. *J'ai eu tout de suite un petit garçon, mort-né, eh, pourquoi en parlerais-je ? Enfin,* a dead little boy, I say, e gave me and then e flew away, e abandonne me wizout ze sou. *Non, mais il m'a encore donné quelque chose,* e gave me also syphilis. I went into ospital. I was cured. My family would never see me again. Only my brother who was in the Ministère de la Guerre took me in, and he and his mistress looked after me. Now, Madame, I take them, they pay my rent, but,' again the stage-accent, ' I het zem.'

Blanche drank her port and said interestedly in quite a different tone :

' I have seen you, Madame, with your husband. I have seen you this morning crying over a letter. I hope no bad news ? '

Elvira smiled slightly, and looking down at Blanche's gold nails, answered :

' That letter I was crying over was from my husband. I left him. I left him for another man. He wants me to go back to him. I don't know what to do.'

' I ave seen you with another young man, very beautiful, which I thought was your husband.'

' That is Oliver, the young man I ran away with,' explained Elvira.

Blanche approved. ' He is marvellously handsome : and your husband, not so good-looking, I suppose ? '

' But you must not tell anyone. I don't know why I told you. I am upset. We pretend to be husband and wife.'

' *Naturellement,*' approved Blanche.

After Blanche had drawn out all there was to know of Elvira's story, and saw Elvira beginning to regret it acutely, she changed the subject.

When Oliver came back for lunch, mad with enthusiasm about the United Front meeting at the Mur des Fédérés, to take place a few days later, on the 27th, Blanche took another apéritif at his invitation and, while attributing to Tardieu political and financial genius and proclaiming herself a good Catholic and a good Royalist, parbleu, if the king ever returned (which she thought improbable), caricatured richly Chiappe, 'this little Napoleon of the garbage-tins of the city council'; on the other hand, she excused the pranks of the rioting Royalist students on the ground that 'these are only children, one does not lock up children,' and detested the young working men of Ménilmontant and Sébastopol, 'these rascals, blackguards, jealous impotents. Are we not in a republic,' she cried, 'where every man has his chance? More's the pity. One sees dirty types in the Government. One sees reds, Jews and freemasons.'

Oliver argued with her good-humouredly, and she was presently reduced to saying :

'Well, old thing, it will be a long time before the reds produce a Velasquez : propaganda has nothing to do with art.'

Oliver laughed, and when she said she could stand a bite, they all went off to the restaurant des Marronniers, near the Ministère, where Blanche's brother met her for lunch every day. The brother was a lively little fellow with bright brown eyes and a moustache, full of cheap puns and a merry giggle. He treated Blanche with the greatest courtesy, and they rolled their eyes at each other amorously at every joke he made. His name was Frédéric. She called him 'Fred' in English, to be chic. He was excessively formal with Elvira and said 'Madame' at every second sentence. He seemed to think Oliver a good joke. He had the mind, manners, vivacity and spitfire good-humour of a public-gardens sparrow. Although he was a poor clerk, he had saved up enough money to buy two properties in the rue de la Goutte-d'Or, a slum street under the Sacré-Cœur. He was a freemason, and laughed at priests and at the miracles at Lourdes in which Blanche professed to believe. They wrangled good-humouredly about it during lunch. Blanche ended by saying :

'Happily my little Blanche is not here : thou wouldst be ashamed to say such filth in her presence.'

'Fred' giggled:

'Ah, the little Blanche is a belle: one would not talk
religion with her: one might think of giving her her
"first communion."'

'Ah, thou hast no shame!'

After lunch Blanche accompanied Elvira back to her
hotel, with the familiarity of an old friend. Oliver went
off to his books again. Blanche went upstairs with
Elvira, took a bath in her bathroom and made her tell her
all about her husband Paul, what he looked like, how
much he earned and what their home was like in London.
When she heard that he was a doctor and that Elvira
had £200 a year income, she became more intimate than
ever, held Elvira's hand and said:

'Really, you are romantic! And Oliver did not
hesitate to break up your home? But it suits him very
well to have a—friend—with an income! But I see now.
Will you marry him, your Oliver?'

'I suppose I have to, anyhow.'

Elvira had presently told her about her infant, too.
Blanche held up her hands in horror.

'But, my little one, that cannot be! Not yet. You are
not sure. Never make the mistake of letting a thing like
that decide you. Never, never! Life is too serious and
too short. If you soon find you want to go home to
your husband, you cannot ask him to accept this Oliver's
child. A respectable woman cannot do that.'

'But Paul is different.'

'No man is different. You would lose him entirely.
He would hate you and it and take a mistress. I know—
a friend of mine— ...'

'What am I to do?'

Blanche made some suggestions. They arranged to
meet again the next day before lunch. Elvira said
impulsively:

'I'm glad I met you: French women are so human.
I was in such a tangle. I really didn't know what to do
next.'

Blanche laughed and kissed her, calling her 'my darling.'

When Oliver met her in the café that afternoon, Elvira was full of enthusiasm about her new friend. To please her, Oliver said :

'Demimondaines are not ashamed of themselves here, are they ? I walked with Frédéric to the Ministère. He was telling me about a tenant of his on the sixth floor, the attic of one of his buildings. She's a whore. He tells me the concierge is a friend of hers and was telling him last time he was there : "This poor dove is nearly starving : she is doing no business at all owing to unemployment : I took her some soup the other evening." By God, at any rate it shows a deep humanity that no winter of cruel respectability freezes. She's a human being, isn't she ? Good, then she needs soup if she's cold and hungry. And to think that my own aunt, a good, kind woman, a working-woman, turned a servant of hers out into the winter when she found she was pregnant. And she's a Christian woman, famous throughout the neighbourhood for the help she gives to people.' Oliver almost spat. 'Where there's an aristocracy, we all become aristocrats and let our neighbour be damned if he doesn't suit.'

'At the same time,' said Elvira, 'the married woman has here a status she has nowhere else on earth. You wear black, you talk gruffly and rudely, you know how to order red and white wine for a dinner, and you're queen of the earth. I call that status with a vengeance. Why ? Because they bring their husbands little bits of property. Well—this is the place for me. I'll let it be known I have £200 a year, and they'll respect me. The servants in the hotel are quite rude : on account of the riots, I suppose. Did I do them any harm ? I'm a bourgeois, but can I help it ? They can't blame me for the money my father made by his hard work. Isn't it their ideal to have a little *rente* ? Even Blanche d'Anizy only dreams of that. That chambermaid this morning was quite impertinent. I hate it. You'd think they knew we weren't married.'

Oliver laughed. 'You wear a wedding-ring, but you don't run an apartment and you have no furniture. That's the European ideal. Blanche d'Anizy can be ten times the whore—they will respect her more if she has an apartment and furniture, than you, were you ten times married. Oh, you funny little bourgeois bunch of forget-me-nots. You cling ferociously to respectability, you won't climb down a millimetre, and yet you're wickedly delinquent.' He laughed at her consumedly while Elvira got red.

'I hate their money-philosophy,' grumbled Elvira.

Oliver laughed still. 'I like it : it's frank. You know where you stand. The class struggle is expressed in one simple common denominator : no chance of fooling them. Every revolution has come after a levy. Make the poor figure their resources, and then they revolt.'

Elvira scolded. 'No one would think you were born in Nottingham. You ought to have been born in Ménilmontant. You're a blessed expatriate.'

'You think I'm naïve, don't you ?'

'Very.'

Oliver grasped her hand and kissed it. They sat looking into each other's eyes and the waiter took care not to come near them. Presently Oliver called a taxi as if they could not wait to get home. In the taxi Elvira said : 'You're right. Let's take a furnished apartment. I suffer under this disrespect.'

Light-spindles from the lacquered automobiles rolling past outside ran round in a half-circle : a golden reflection, an inch broad, fell between the drawn curtains and moved drowsily over the furniture, dusting it with gold. In the cool of the evening they came down again and sat on the terrace of the Café d'Harcourt, looking at the first olive tatters of the trees. They soon walked on again, shawled in the delicious tissues of the air.

Blanche d'Anizy was sitting on the terrace when they

passed, with a pretty young American girl with auburn hair and five men, whose professions, in Elvira's haunting of the café, she had learned, but whose names were unknown to them—three journalists, a young American *rentier*, a gynaecologist of sixty who looked like, and was, a fearful rake. Blanche waved to them casually and immediately bent forward to talk to her group in French : as they turned the corner, they saw the heads turn their way.

' I didn't see her lover there,' said Oliver with interest.

Elvira smiled satirically : ' Oh, one just pays her rent : the others just try to get her places, write up Press notices for her, buy her apéritifs and see that she gets regular meals . . . the dress-man, hat-man and lingerie-man are not there—or else they've lost their jobs and she's looking for others.'

Oliver stared at her. ' Gee, Elvira : you're a woman after all. That's the first time I've heard you say a catty thing : I always told myself I had never heard you say or seen you do a mean or unrefined thing.'

' And now you have ! '

' Of course not. She obliged with her life-history. It doesn't seem to be a secret. I suppose it's quite true.'

' Oh, it's true.'

He was silent for a while ; ' Elvira, I oughtn't to get you into company like that : you ought to have friends of your own sort. . . .'

' She's a woman and she's got sense. I admire the way she battles through. You sound a bit narrow.'

He admitted humbly : ' I did sound rather narrow ; it's just old prejudice.' He added after a moment : ' All the same, she's out for herself. I wouldn't like her to bother you, Elvira.'

' I'd like to see her,' said Elvira.

He stared at her again. ' Bravo ! If that isn't applied democracy ! You mean to say you don't feel any difference between her and you ? '

' Why should I ? Because she lives off men ? Don't I ? Paul, my father first, then you if we get married. . . .'

His eyes darkened. 'If? When. It's wicked of us, it destroys the freedom of your sex, but it is such a pleasure to work for a woman you love : no wonder women live on men. I never knew why : I was a hard-headed, cutting, cruel rationalist when I was a boy. I was a boy till I met you. . . .'

She tightened her hold on his arm to make him stop speaking : she continued. . . .'You like a person irre-spective of where or how you find them : you can perhaps make a friend of your washerwoman and hate your own cousin.' Her brow darkened while she made this oracular statement : Oliver peered at her, said nothing, but took her small oval hand in its grey kid glove. They arrived at a little café newly-installed, the Cosmos, and sat down to sample the springing of its red leatherette benches and glass inlaid tables.

'Two Campari with grenadine.'

They both got warmly, gaily, and definitely fuddled on this strong drink, and presently went to the cheap little restaurant in the rue des Canettes. Half-way through, Oliver, loving, pressing, smirking, got out of his coat pocket a sheaf of papers—copies of proclamations which he had copied down at the Archives that day.

'What do you think of this ? '

She read it : the first formation of a tulle-makers' union in Calais. With glee he pointed out the mayor's pro-clamation preparing for riots, the formation of a volun-tary militia by the local worthies. She read the papers with the patience of a good girl-scholar and then gently put them down.

'It's very interesting. I'll read them, Oliver, when I finish this. I'm afraid it'll get cold.'

After dessert, during coffee, he forced them on her again. She read the first page obediently, found it prolix, skimmed the next few pages, picked out a passage to praise and please him. She suddenly thought that in his half-drunk irresponsibility he had let his secret out—he wanted to impress her with his scholarship, show her

that his scholastic future would make him the equal of
Paul, if not his superior. His radical speeches, more
frequent than necessary, were to offset Paul's old-
fashioned conservative Liberalism. He vaunted his
youth because Paul was fifteen years his senior. He
said, ' We young ones, we of the new world, we of the
post-war world, we who were at school when the war
was on, we who never knew what it was to worship a
Fabian . . . of course, I was five when the war broke
out. . . .' The last time, yet unconscious of his reason
for saying this, she had impatiently replied, ' Don't
forget I was ten then, and a big girl : it makes a
gulf between us.' Since then he had dropped that set
of references. Then her deduction was correct. She
thought scornfully : ' I can't go living all my life with
Paul—by negatives. . . .' Her eye roamed over his impassioned face and beaming eyes, and she relented. ' He
doesn't know my doubts : he's mine : poor boy, dear
boy. . . .' She let him take her hand under the table. He
said ardently, although the eye of the cashier was on
them : ' Do you love me, darling ? '
' Yes, Oliver.'
' Oh, my dear.'
' Shh, behave : she's looking at us.'
' Let her look : she'll know we're lovers.'
Elvira flushed and withdrew her hand. ' No, no
don't.'
When they got home she showed him Paul's letter.
He read it a long time, in silence, and said sadly :
' He loves you, Elvira.'
' If you call that love : I suppose it is, though.'
' What does he mean by circumstances ? Er—you
haven't told him about me yet ? '
' No : why start trouble ? It'll come soon enough.
When he gets used to my being away I'll tell him.'
Oliver moodily unfolded his evening paper, the
Journal des Débats ; presently, with his usual brightness,
he showed her a literary criticism.

' Gods, you've got to admit their literary style is the first in Europe.'

She looked at him for a few seconds and seemed to fall into a contemplation : she was drowsy and could hardly sit upright. A voice came from her mouth by itself.

' I shall have to tell him soon.'

A startled voice exclaimed :

' Why will you have to ? '

Her dreamy voice went on :

' Oliver, it would be fearfully inconvenient if we had a baby, wouldn't it ? '

He flushed slowly and came forward, examining her. He sat down beside her and took her hands.

' My dear ! '

He kissed her hair, forehead, ears, eyes, hands, knelt beside her and buried his head on her knee. ' I have never known what it is to love you till this minute.'

He kept looking at her as if he were seeing her in a becoming new dress that flattered her shape, as they moved about the room getting ready for bed. He said : ' I can hardly believe it, it is like a dream. I sit in the library, fiddling with matters four generations old, and you are here making the new generation.'

He began to ponder. When she saw that, her face fell and she nodded to herself. When the light was out, she murmured :

' It would be foolish to have a baby now.'

He drew her close to him. ' Although we can't have it now, it makes no difference ; it only means that henceforward you are more to me than a beloved woman—you are a mother : you can bear me children.' She was so quiet that he thought she had already fallen asleep.

Two days later, when they were reckoning up their accounts, she said :

' This morning I asked Blanche d'Anizy's advice : she is going to find me a first-class *sage-femme*. So you don't have to worry. She is going to tell her that I am a student here and haven't much money. It will cost about 500 francs. Paul sent me a thousand in his letter.'

' Why did you ask Blanche d'Anizy ? '

' What other friend have I here ? She knows all about these things : in such things I could not find a better friend.'

' All right : but be sure she finds a good woman : I can't let anything happen to you,' he said helplessly.

She sat with bowed shoulders, looking darkly at the window curtains.

' We must arrange for meals to be brought to me : I am going to-morrow, with Blanche. I've already given her the 500 francs to give to the woman. It is illegal : they all risk gaol sentences : you have to be secret. They won't do it if a witness is there, a man, for instance.'

She looked at him with a faintly-curling lip. She told him all that would have to be done. He looked a little crushed. She said with a childish, pathetic pride: ' When you come home from the Archives to-morrow, come upstairs : I shall be in bed.'

' Poor love : how long will it be, three days ? '

' A month.'

He started. ' No ! Does it have to be like that ? '

' It's their method : an easy one, they say.'

He looked quite nervous. She looked round the room, tormented, and cried out :

' Oh, Oliver, how can I stay in this miserable gloomy room a month ? I feel now as if the four walls were pressing down on me : I can't bear it, I can't bear it.' She ended in a moan. He comforted her : in the dark of his shoulder she sobbed again : ' I'm all alone in the world : Paul doesn't want me now, you don't want my child.'

He drew her away from his shoulder, looked at her. ' It's yours : you can have it if you want to : whatever is yours, I'll cherish.'

She began to pace up and down the room ; she finally sat down in a chair where she could look at him from a

distance. A smile crept round the corners of her mouth,
she began to smile, to laugh, her shoulders began to
shake, and she said in a low, rippling voice :

'Oh dear, oh dear, it's so funny.' She went on giggling.
He stared at her. 'What's funny, Elvira ?'

'Oh dear, I just remembered that dream you had, when
you dreamed I was the Madonna : oh dear, and you
found it came true. Oh dear ! . . .' She held her chest,
catching for breath, writhing in her chair, her muscles
snapping like a sparking wire, leaning over in her lap
and dropping tears of hilarity, her mouth disfigured, her
eyes beginning to widen, her soft dun brow flushing, her
hair entangled. Oliver stared at her leaning forward,
on his hands ready to spring up.

'Elvira, don't : you're hysterical.'

'Oh, oh, oh ! . . .' she managed to say. 'Oh, it's too
funny : I can just see your face. . . . Oh, oh, oh ! . . .
your dream . . . come . . . true. . . .' She began to be
shaken by spasms of laughter, more like electric shocks
than laughs : her face was drawn now, now merry, her
mouth dribbled, her wide open eyes were full of tears :
she gaped and grinned.

Frightened out of his wits, Oliver started forward and
put his arms clumsily round her. Immediately, she
bent herself in the shape of a bow and fought him off
with her hands and knees.

'Go away, get away, don't touch me, don't dare touch
me !'

She flung him off and sprang up : he fell back with
dangling hands. She went into the bathroom. Presently
her sobs rose loud enough for him to hear. He went in,
sat down beside her and began speaking to her without
touching her.

'My dear, dear . . . I had no idea you felt like that
about it : how clumsy I am, how stupid I am ! Oh, why
couldn't I see ? I'm a man, but you're a woman. You're
a woman,' he said thoughtfully ; 'the most obvious
things are the things we ignore.' He kissed her. 'You

were meant to have children. You shall have it, I'll find
a way.' He said it with a tender regret. She let him
console her and take her out to supper. They were very
quiet all the evening, looking at each other with wood-
violet eyes, occasionally touching hands. They walked
along the street: it was a fine soft spring night, with the
buds and stars out. They went home late.

When he got home the next afternoon he found a note
telling him to meet Elvira and Blanche in the usual café.
Blanche said to him, frankly:

'Elvira didn't want to go to the *sage-femme* to-day:
she told me she got upset last night—so perhaps it's
better to wait a day or two. She's still got time to
decide.' Blanche was excessively friendly and introduced
them to one of the journalists, one of the small *rentiers*,
and a tenor. When Oliver and Elvira had gone off to
supper, Blanche said to the men in her practised tone of
camaraderie:

'She's in a condition—you know—he doesn't want
any such thing: of course not. A student—with not
even a sure situation in view: foolish of them—but with
new lovers these things usually happen. I offered to take
her to a *sage-femme*: she can't make up her mind: it's
natural, with the other she was barren. He just worships
her. Of course, she's quite right to take the step; these
little accidents kill a man's love. You're such selfish
brutes, a real pack of brutes—go along! And they're
not married. I told her, My little one, don't be foolish:
wait till he's regularised the situation: that is, if you're
really going to stay with him. Remember, my dear, I told
her, you are not yet divorced: your husband is kind to
you. Think, I told her. I don't like to see a woman
like that get into a mess: they're so helpless. . . .'

'She's a pretty woman,' said the little *rentier*. 'Pretty
eyes, and those brows that meet—they curdle your blood
when they turn on you. . . .'

'A sort of domesticated charm,' said one of the
journalists. 'But no fire—like a moonstone. . . .'

'It's a scrub-chinned love-affair,' said the second journalist.

Blanche shook her head. 'She'll never keep him: she doesn't really want to keep a man: considering she's a beauty, that's quite a quality, you know.'

'She'll keep him,' said the little *rentier*, 'because she's so moony, moody, down-sitting, broad-bottomed: her world wags round her basin. She's always got the look of a pregnant woman. She's one of those female women, a sluice-gate, you know. They always get men; we need that sort.' He smiled a lecherous, impotent smile.

The setting sun, falling through the rich lace curtains, sent its fire through the curling green milk of his Pernod. His eyes were little and red-rimmed at the moment, his red mouth was wet with drunkenness and sluggish desire: three other saucers stood beside him. He had the satisfaction of being the only one in their circle who could drink four Pernods without falling like a log, or being carried home raving drunk in a cab. Now he was frightfully drunk, as he knew; but they only thought he was slightly tipsy. They always said of him: 'I saw Andrew with his Pernod at the d'Harcourt,' or 'It was so early in the morning that there was no one on the terrace but Andrew and his Pernod.' He sometimes wrote letters to friends in Germany, France or England: never to America, where he came from. He knew the look of a letter containing a cheque, and gave it to Blanche or one of the others to open. They gave him the cheque, read the letter themselves and then tore it up. He had at home scores of letters from America, all unopened. Sometimes, in a fretful sober moment, he shoved a handful of them into the hand of some friend, said, 'Read them and then tear them up: don't tell me anything about them.' The gentle wastrel had a large circle of café friends: he did not care for any others. If he had a friend too close, he would not have been able to backbite him. He was very happy, with his unopened letters, his smooth-shaved chin, his well-cut old suit, his Pernod and his backbiting:

he told friends, in moments of tender drunkenness, that
he had the art of living. No one but him and the old
Greeks, and some few beachcombers, he said, had the
art of living so well. His name was Andrew Fulton.
He liked Elvira and Elvira liked him. He then walked
with her and had lunch with her, cracking a few jokes
about Oliver, at which they both laughed. When she
joined them this evening he said, ' Get rid of the kid ;
have some fun while you're young.'

She showed him the letter from Paul, and Andrew
said : ' I don't see why you three can't live together.'

' I could do it ; I'm really a liberal,' she said, putting
her hand on his arm and smiling faintly into his face.

' You're a girl for two boys,' said Fulton lewdly.
She laughed. When Oliver walked in, Fulton cried :
' I am sorry to see this pretty woman suffering the
penalty of your lust.' They all laughed but Oliver, and
a peculiar smile of satisfaction grew out of Elvira's face.

At supper Oliver asked her if she had written to Paul.

' Not yet ; when I tell him he'll come over.'

He was nervous again. ' It's you who has to decide,
you're the mother.'

She answered :

' I can't see Paul if I'm in bed : he would be upset if
he saw me in bed.'

She looked at him defiantly. He fondled her hand :

' And wouldn't I be upset ? '

She laughed drily : ' Oh, you ! You're the cause of
all : *ab ovo*. Ha ! '

' My wife ! I could never leave you now.'

' Ah ! Now ? '

' Don't quibble, don't pick at every word I say : you
know very well how I feel about you.'

She softened. ' I know ; excuse me ! I have been so
nervous with trying to make up my mind. You ought
to decide ; it's your responsibility.'

He grew graver. She went on : ' All day I was thinking
of the girls who are abandoned and who commit suicide.'

He said, trying to catch her thoughts :

'Isn't it strange, when they say the maternal instinct towards life is so strong ?'

She looked straight at him. 'It's not that ; it's the money. Where would I be now if I didn't have Paul or you to look after me ?' She had a slightly contemptuous satisfaction at seeing the thoughts in his face.

'Well, I'll desert you, then,' he said, shaking his shoulders, with a joke. 'I'll just leave you flat and see how you can swim.'

'Good of you. Do what you like : I don't give tuppence.'

They both laughed, and breathed a little irregularly. He urged her to eat.

'Have some Petit Suisse ? Some Gruyère ? A fruit-tart, surely ?'

He ate gluttonously himself, like a man just come from work. He thought she should write to Paul, but she went to bed without doing so.

For a week their indecisions went on. Oliver got to the café a few minutes before Elvira one day, and found Blanche d'Anizy installed. Blanche had drunk two ports and was just warming up. She made room for Oliver beside her ' until Elvira comes,' and he began to twit her : she had a way with her, she knew men inside out, no question. He teased her about her outrageous enamelled face, asked her if the barber gave her the best in his line and if in payment she gave him of her best. She tapped his hand : he took it and gave her a parody love-kiss. This she resented with a charming dignity. 'What are you thinking of ? Elvira will be here in a moment. I am her friend.'

Oliver was impressed and called to mind the stories he had read, the old, trite stories, of the friendship of whores. It was true, then : they had wonderful hearts : wonderful the sisterhood of women. Sturdy—something beyond mere social status. As with men, for instance : he felt a real kinship with the workmen taking their black coffees and white wines at the zinc. Communism would come, because it was such a natural principle. He began to explain all this to her, and she listened and replied seriously. It was a gag she had heard when she was quite young, and had almost forgotten : a reminder to resuscitate it. She commented with her old adage, ' A woman can learn something new from every man.'

She let a silence fall and then sighed. ' We understand each other's troubles,' she murmured ; ' we can't tell them to men ; men regard us as instruments, that's all.'

He was up in arms. ' I certainly don't. I respect women as I respect men. I'm one of the few men who doesn't instinctively feel any difference between men and women.'

Her pose and expression were beautiful and interesting.

' What is it ? ' he persisted : ' a love-affair ? '

' Don't press me,' she said. ' Why should I tell you depressing things ? You have your life to live. To you love is joy, to me, since I was sixteen, it is all sorrow. I never think I will love again, and then I do. I love men ; I cannot help it, they attract me and then I suffer for it. They mean well and then they cool off. . . . If only they did not leave me debts in their train and bills to pay.'

He suffered a slight deception to know it was about bills, but he pressed her still. She said at length, as if taking a resolution :

' Well, the clothes you see me in are all I have to my name. The hotel-keeper, the dirty dog, is keeping my bags because I could not pay. And why ? Because *he* has another mistress. Oh, he will come back to me. I know his other girl, a shopgirl—younger than me, that's all. In the meantime I have to pay the hotel-bill for the room he engaged. He comes back to see me occasion-ally, when he is tired of her schoolgirl stuff, I suppose.' She smiled beautifully at him. ' There was a time, when I was a young girl, in the country, when I would have stayed awake all night in horror if I had even read in a

tale of the existence of such a woman as I have come to
be. And yet, it has all happened so easily : I feel the
same, I feel innocent.'

He looked at her regretful, naïve expression, and was
sincerely touched. He said : 'You are innocent.
Innocence ! What is it ? You have never murdered
anyone.' He looked doubtful for a moment, and added :
'Even if you had, you would still be innocent. You are
one of those born like that : unconscious of evil, pure
from the heart.' He mused, and laughed a silvery, low,
boyish laugh. 'A year ago I would have regularly
snarled if anyone had said such a thing. Pah ! Pouf !
What a slob I was a year ago. I knew absolutely nothing
about women and nothing about men, can you beat that ?
At twenty-three.' He smiled confidingly at her.

It ended in him lending her a hundred francs and
promising never to tell Elvira, because she did not
'want to spoil their friendship.'

Elvira came in. She had been sleeping since lunch-
time, when she had drunk a heavy red wine, and had a
pink complexion like a newborn baby. Blanche soon
left them, asking as she left if Elvira wished to go with
her to the *sage-femme* soon. Elvira said airily : 'I still
have time : there's no hurry : I'll see.'

Blanche smiled, and went off to sit in the corner by
herself. Soon a plump sardonic blond fellow in a blond
raincoat stalked in, threw down his yellow journalist's
satchel beside her with a grand air, and smiled a simple
smile which was intended to be mocking. He sat opposite
her, and Blanche immediately forgot all that had gone
before, and the crowded café, to plunge into that passionate attention and those deft expressions and loving smiles
that Latin women have for their lovers. Elvira said :

'That's Septennat, Blanche's permanent. They've
been with each other off and on since she divorced her
husband. She knew him when he was a haughty, disagreeable fledgling in an embassy here. He was transferred to Poland and she lost him. When he came back

for holidays they lived together. He went to Berlin and
she lost him. They made it up again. He lost his job
through some leakage of commercial doings to a journalist. He came back here, and she kept him till he got a
job himself as journalist : it wasn't long, of course, two
or three months. They were really on their uppers then,
living on the fourth floor in the rue du Roi de Sicile, but
she says they were never so happy.'

' Looking back,' mused Oliver, ' how the dickens did
she manage to fit so many lives into one ? She's only
twenty-eight now.'

' In between she had plenty of others, but she told me
she really loved them all. She would do nothing for
money : that is, unless she loves a man. She says she
always has a tissue of growing affections and declining
loves. . . .'

' And only from them she takes money ? ' asked Oliver.

' So she says.'

' Perhaps she loves money wherever it grows,' suggested Oliver.

' Oh no, Oliver. An Indian prince offered to marry
her, and she refused until she had lived with him to see
if she really had an affection for him. She would accept
nothing from him, and he came to see her in her little
flat in Passy. She asked nothing and she got nothing,
and after the second time he did not say he would marry
her. She is quite quixotic, too.'

' He gave her nothing ? '

' No : he told her he was glad there were women in
the world who did not sell themselves but knew the
charm of a pure friendship.'

' And so—good-bye. In the meantime, who paid for
the flat ? '

' Oh, at that time she was starring at the Folies. She
had plenty of attention. She is beautiful now, when she
makes up, Oliver. I saw her the other night when she
was going to the new cabaret in the Champs Elysées,
where Maugrebon the entrepreneur, her friend, got her a

place. You wouldn't have known her : she looked like
the firebird. I should like to go and see her. She is
strange made-up—a dream,' said Elvira. ' She had to
sell her evening-dresses to live in the drought since her
last engagement : I lent her my new evening-dress, the
black tulle over gold lamé : it has a dancing skirt. Do
you like me in it ? '

' It suits you wonderfully,' said Oliver.

' Yes, I look nice in it. Well, Blanche looked—a firebird. I suddenly realised I was a dowdy little domesticated bird, like a silver wyandotte, say.' She laughed.
' I am appealing,' she concluded, ' almost always, but
some days she's downright ugly and the other days she's
so seductive that men follow her everywhere. Think
that the Minister of the Interior last year tried to rape
her in a taxi,' she said. ' I don't blame them or her.
Plenty of actresses are like that.'

He began to tell her about his day's work in the
Archives.

' Aren't you nearly finished, Oliver ? Perhaps we
should return to England now and try to settle down.
I'd like you to get a position. You see, I've almost
decided to keep the infant.'

He tapped on the table with his pencil, his eyes
lowered. She said :

' I've never felt so well in my life as now : I know now
what was wrong with me. I was always so wretched and
futile : now I feel wholesome, like new bread. That
was what was wrong with me. I must keep my
child, Oliver. It's Fate. It's ours. It's the fruit of
our adventure. It was meant to be so.'

He raised his eyes from his tapping, his eyes quiet.

' Very well, dear. Then I'll get ready and we'll go
back and I'll look for a job. Just give me a month more,
will you ? I can get something impressive ready by then,
I think. I must make a good impression if I have to ask
the professors to recommend me straight away. I'll
think it out. If you want me to do that, I'll do it. I'll

put myself in your hands. You know my principle, I'll try anything once, and no growling, eh?'

She looked at him dubiously. He nodded at her.

'Of course, if we could put it off, just for a few months, it would give me a better chance to get something : we know we love each other, we know we can have children : we're both young. That's all we need to know. I want to see you in our home first, Elvira.'

She looked at him steadily, the father and enemy of the child.

She said : 'Of course, if you feel like that, and you think it would make a bad impression on your friends, I'll go home and stay with Paul till it's all over. He'll shelter me.'

Oliver's eyes were lowered as he traced earnestly on the table.

'I have been a student : I'm relatively fond of the little nippers, but not like you are, Elvira. It doesn't mean the same to me. I can wait a bit, and I think we would be happier if we did.'

She suddenly began to cry softly, so that the tears just stood in her eyes.

'You don't want my child ; you don't want it.'

He shook his head to himself, and called the waiter for the bill. He helped her on with her coat and they went out, unnoticed by Blanche, deep in her emotions with her lover. Outside on the pavement, in the fine evening, holding to his arm, she looked at his well-set profile, his fatigued, deep eyes, and thought of the evenings at home, when Paul was at his meetings, that she had seen him thus, looking melancholy into the fire. She said low : 'It's degrading to be a woman, to have to bother about what people think, not to be able to provide for your child, to be dependent on men. If I'd kept on being secretary in that hospital, I should have been free, I should have had my job : now, he's taken me out of it, I've become a plaything ; I'm no good. I can't even have my own child when I want it : it has to wait on circumstances. Do you think I like to pretend to be your wife when I'm not ? '

Oliver walked along pressing her arm and shaking his head.

She said, ' Oh, I feel so bitter when I think that, even though I give up my old life of wifehood, there is no freedom for me, a middle-class woman without a profession. They should give me a street-walker's card. I regret it, I regret it,' she said violently. ' I made a mistake to listen to you. I'm five years older : I can't start out afresh with a young man. I've done that already with Paul. I want something else now. It was only the need of a child driving me on, and now—I can't have it. Oh, I hate society, I hate the burdens it places on women.'

' Yes, it isn't fair : women are not really free,' said Oliver.

' The real thought of the middle-class woman,' complained Elvira, ' is the problem of economic freedom and sexual freedom : they can't be attained at the same time. We are not free. The slave of the kitchen and bedroom. Even if you have a maid you're supposed to be thinking about the cooking and linen. It ought to be done by people who make a job of it and leave the women with a good education free.'

' There are plenty of women in laboratories, and in business, now.'

' I've always been idle and useless,' mourned Elvira. ' It's true, I could have gone on to do something. I came first in things often at school. I got my B.A. What good did it do ? I was born that way. Other women would have gone on and made a career. When Paul came along, I wanted him to love me but I didn't want to marry : I wanted to be myself, not a wife, with children. I wanted to do something creative : something—perhaps writing. I didn't want just to turn into a bad incubator. I didn't want to marry him, I just wanted to live platonically with him. But he wouldn't. It gave me a shock :

I thought it was so gross of him. Afterwards, of course,
I felt differently. I was a bad wife to him. Yes, I was.
Everything I have ever done was bad and inefficient. I
never had anything out of life that I should have had.
I'm pretty, and I didn't have a good time. I'm intelligent,
and I never did anything. I married, and I didn't even
have a proper home with children. I ran away with a
lover, and I'm miserable. And it's all my doing.' She
was crying : Oliver felt the tears on his hand now. ' I
am good for nothing,' she said in a lamentable tone. ' I
might as well commit suicide. You wouldn't miss me
after a month. Paul doesn't miss me now. Sara is going
to keep house for him.'

' Elvira, I can't bear to hear you talk like that. You
don't mean it. You know that Paul loved you and I love
you. And you have plenty of time to make a career and
have children if you want them.' He laughed, rousing
her. ' Cheer up ; what's all this ? You're depressed :
it's the—child perhaps.'

' I suppose so, and I've been thinking what to do : I
don't know what to do. It's that that upsets me so much.
I'd rather decide to do anything than be like this, between
wind and water. Somehow, though, I always seem to
get into a sort of jam where I have to decide something
momentous, and it tortures me. I was happy when I
knew about the baby, because it seemed to have decided
something by itself. But then, I began to think about
you and the money and it all started again. Like a
toothache. You're lucky. You're creating something.
It sounds easy to you. But I never found self-expression.
Perhaps I could have been a musician. But I haven't
got it. It's something.'

' I love you. Doesn't that mean something to you ? '
' Yes,' doubtfully.
' It will work out all right in a little while, then. All
those troubles you mentioned, even the disappointment
in life you have, will disappear when our love grows and
we settle down. We'll have a fine life together.'

'I suppose so.'

She scanned the faces and get-up of every mother with a child, thinking, 'I will be something like that.' She saw this evening that they were dusty, drawn, violently fatigued and acid faces : the children looked like blobs of flesh, their clothing rubbishy. 'Oh, not for me,' she thought, and a slight nausea began in her. She thought of her eight long quiet home-years since she married Paul, her polished floors, washed carpets, recovered chairs, her new bed-linen which felt like silk, her underclothing of silk and lawn all put away in piles, her curtains, silver dressing-table ware, vases, doyleys, the olive, yellow and smoke-blue bedroom, the red and walnut dining-room, her work-basket with an olive silk bag. She thought of her soaps and cleansing materials always in stock, and her dusters neatly arranged, the coats hanging in their entry, the shawled trees waving against the sky in summer, the Adam window on the stairs through which she looked, whenever the stairs were untrafficked, dreaming like a child, watching the birds fly up beyond the curve. If she had a baby, she would have to have a home at least as large, a nurse who would sleep with it in a separate room, and look after the washing, the bottles. She could not have it in a hotel, with Oliver without a position. Her face suddenly grew firmer. She determined to go back to Paul, if he would have her, with the baby. It would be different at home then, and Oliver—Oliver would become a patient loving friend, coming to see them, taking her for walks. Sometimes she would go to his rooms, in memory of old times. He might marry, on the rebound—but he would come back : their friendship could not be broken that way. But if he married she could not see him as before. 'Women have enough troubles,' she said to herself. 'I wouldn't bother another married woman. Even Blanche, I wouldn't take a man away from her. They know it instinctively, besides : that's why they like me.'

Oliver turned to her, smiling, patting her hand.

'Wool-gathering, Elvira? Dreams for the future?'

'I was just thinking,' she drawled, 'thinking about us, about everything.'

They went to the pictures that night. There was a moving picture of the well-worn prodigal wife pattern. Oliver wanted to leave half-way through it, when the erring wife showed signs of returning to her husband, but Elvira was absorbed. She came out elevated, convinced by the coincidence. Oliver began his usual raillery: 'Gee, why don't they think up a new story? I believe they have three since the wild west died, the sentimental hurdle-race, the repentant gold-digger, and historical heroics.'

They went to a café for coffee, as they couldn't get it at the hotel at that time of night. Since they were at Montparnasse and it was late, there were numbers of male and female prostitutes about. They sat opposite one and began a fuddled conversation about these unfortunate people, whether they began through hatred of work, or excessive sexuality, or early incest.

'Exploited labour, that's how I look at them,' said Oliver. 'I never could go to them, any more than I could sweat a workman.'

'It's all a formula,' proposed Elvira. 'You could exploit a woman in a house, making her wait on you and cook for you, turning her into an idiot with ideas about mouseholes and curtain-rods, while you wrote essays on labour-unions. It's just the same, I see no difference.'

'You're right. Lord, how we adhere to our patterns! We gibber like marionettes in trite situations. All middle-class novels are about the trials of three, all upper-class novels about mass fornication, all revolutionary novels about a bad man turned good by a tractor. There's nothing new on earth—and how well you know it, life-sick child! What's the matter with you, Elvira? Isn't there anything that gives you hope?'

'Human nature's the same all over the world, if you

aren't taken in by poinsettias in the tropics and rainbows in the north to think it's different.'

After a silence, Oliver said : ' In a way, you were happy at home, Elvira, weren't you ? You slept and had grey-footed dreams. And yet why did you come to me ? Did you love me ? '

' I am a dead soul ; life is too heavy for me to lift. I thought perhaps I just had to shrug it off as a snake shrugs off his old skin. Since I bore life in me I feel a will growing in me. But the will is the infant. When he is born, he will just leave me like an old skin. I shall be the same as before, limp, aimless. Why was I ever born ? My mother fell down a trap-door in a cellar before I was born, and nearly miscarried. I wish she had. Then Paul would have found a simpler, more extrovert wife, and your student's life wouldn't have been spoiled. You could have had women who didn't ask for too much : you could have lived cheerfully your selfish men's lives. You hate responsibilities, and I am nothing but a responsibility. I ask for too much. None of you is as generous as he'd have to be with me.'

Oliver looked down at her. ' Dearest, you only lack something, that is all : you are pretty, a true woman, often witty and gay. You lack an aim. We'll give you one. You'll have your baby.'

' Oh, I have no will,' she murmured.

He did not ask her about her own affairs, and for a week she said nothing. But she was turning her disappointments over in her mind. Every night they walked out till late, and he discoursed about his essay, his discoveries in the Archives, and his plans when the essay was handed in. One evening she said nothing the whole evening, but he kept seeing her bitter, white, contained face under the lamps : another evening, she suddenly put her hand on his lips when they were a quarter of a mile from home, and said :

' Now, don't say a word until I tell you,' and then had laughed, in childish hysteria.

The last evening she suddenly cried : ' You talk all the time and never think of me. I'll go mad with your journeymen and rates of pay. What the devil does it mean to women ? Then and now it's just the same, the world isn't made for them. Why don't we all kill ourselves ? Amuse yourselves with ephebes. Men used to like ephebes : they still do. Look at the way you admire those schoolgirls with breasts just starting and cropped hair. A passion for women before they become women, that is, for boys. You were talking aloud all through dinner to attract the attention of that little schoolgirl who can't comb her hair properly. I don't know what to do with myself. Let me go home ; don't follow me : let me go home.'

Oliver took her arm, but she shook herself free, passionately.

' Don't dare follow me or I'll scream : you're not my husband, are you ? ' She planted Oliver on the descending pavement of the Boulevard Raspail. He sat on a seat and watched her little hunched back go striding furiously until it was lost to sight half a mile down.

Men and women going past looked at the beautiful youth with dejected face : he got up and walked towards a café at the corner, one where they were not known. Inside, the walls were covered with mirrors and oil-paintings, left for sale by struggling artists. He thought, ' There are so many other and better troubles in the world than hers and mine : how the deuce do we get into this situation ? It's not a situation. It's just nervousness. I have no experience.'

A young woman beside him looked at him steadily. When he had drunk two half-litres of beer he felt more cheerful and began to scrutinise the café. A fair young girl was sitting alone, looking timid and lonely, reading intently to keep off the attentions of men sitting round. Oliver thought resentfully :

' Elvira kicks me out : I'd get a better reception from

that young thing : Elvira doesn't know when she's
well off.'

He laughed to himself. The young woman beside him
struck up a conversation. They had a friendly hour
sitting there, and when he got up to walk home, he
laughed to himself all the way home at the way in which
he would conquer Elvira's melancholy and solve all their
troubles. She was lying with wide eyes in the dark :
she turned them on him without a word. He went to
her and buried his head in the counterpane at her side.

CHAPTER V

OLIVER returned from the great United Front meeting at
the Mur des Fédérés on May 27 on foot, with a group
of French workmen. He had been called ' camarade '
so often during the day, had seen so many red flags and
so many sinewy arms lifted into the air, had heard the
' Internationale ' and ' The Young Guard ' so often, that
he was no longer himself, a piecemeal student grubbing
on collegiate benches, but a glorious foot-soldier in an
army millions strong, sure of battery, but sure of victory.
    He left the workmen near the Pont des Arts, and stood
there in the cool breeze for a while, his cheeks burning
and his chestnut hair on end. The sun setting gilded
the windows of the Louvre ; the dark chlorophyll had
now filtered through all the trees of the Tuileries : the
polished   automobiles   budged   quickly   towards   the
Champs Elysées like hard-shelled plant-bugs. Some of
the trees along the Seine were thickly tapestried, and the
air was full of floating pollen and small blown fluffs :
the boulevard trees were all lace. The Île de la Cité, an
enchanted city, with bastions and bridges, barges and
shallops, called soundlessly downstream. On the brick
quays men were still fishing for the Seine's small fry,
rust-trousered unemployed were bivouacking with small
fires, an artist was painting the river-scene, and a dark-
haired woman in her thirties was suckling a child.
Oliver leaned over the bridge in a dream. His eyes
wandered from the dome of the Académie Française to
the enchanted isle, to the flittering fires, the oleaginous
hues of the tide, and rested on the sand-coloured breast
of the woman. ' A woman is the least individual of

creatures,' he thought to himself. 'To think, in the winter I shall have a child!' He smiled to himself at the idea that if he took a boat then and there, and skipped to any South American port, to Canada or the South Seas, to Majorca or Egypt, he was free to go. 'The solutions are so easy and we can't take them. Fear, pride or indecision?' He thought: 'She takes it just as if it were natural, but for me it's a new universe: so, I am sending my seed from generation unto generation, a man full of humility.'

He was in his oldest clothes, striding with the tough easy stride of thousands of miles of walking, walking all through his life, to save money, for the pleasure of it, to school and back, to the University and back, to the houses of students he tutored and back, hiking in the week-ends. He thought: 'I'd like to take a rucksack now and bum for two years. I'd come back a changed man. You can't learn in libraries, you can only learn through men. To-day I'm a changed man. Can I go back to this fusty setting after this afternoon? What can I do with a house and a position? I'll take a cattle-boat to Canada and go across the provinces in the summer: I'll get across to the U.S.A. at Niagara and ride goods-waggons across to California, then down, Mexico and south. I'll get mixed up in some good old South American fight and have a good time—perhaps get shot, but have a good time. Elvira will sit at home and nurse my child.' He thought that the child would have dark eyes like his own and hers. 'With those eyes,' he thought, 'she can get away with anything—she'll never want for a home. Look how everyone befriends her, is sorry for her, runs around doing messages for her. It's a gift. Paul will be her faithful slave till death—the big, tender, kind mug.'

He leaned over the stone parapet of the quay again, under the rustling new leaves. In the distance the Seine curled by the Great Palace and the Trocadero towers towards the open green country beyond Saint-Cloud. 'I care for nobody, no, not I, and nobody cares for me:

the reason I fled with a woman already married, bonded, was, I believe, an unconscious reasoning for liberty. *A nous la liberté !* ' He went on, whistling. The familiar café-terrace was planted with all the familiar heads, like red-flushed cabbages. He sat down to wait for Elvira, who had told him she had a late rendezvous with the hairdresser. Folded up in one corner, talking with an air of complicity to someone unknown, was a familiar form : he looked twice and recognised Marpurgo. When he tinkled on the sugar-basin to get service, the chisel-point eyes were fixed on him. Marpurgo came over.

' Hullo, Fenton : I have a message from Mrs. Western. I went up to your room because the maid told me your key was not on the board. I met Mrs. Western coming down with two men. She introduced me to Mr. Paul Western '—his eyes questioned—' and Mr. Adam Cinips. Cinips was Mrs. Western's maiden name, I gather— her brother, it seems. She asked me to tell you that they had all gone to Mr. Western's hotel, the Madison, to discuss personal matters.'

He scanned Oliver's face carnivorously. Oliver was so exalted that he could say joyously, although his heart had begun to pump hard :

' Thanks very much. Will they come here after ? Oh —won't you sit down ? '

' Yes. Mrs. Western will meet you at the rue des Canettes restaurant alone, at 7.30 p.m.'

' I see. What will you drink ? Perrier ? '

' A brandy—I feel rather weak to-day. I was terribly excited over the United Front meeting. I walked miles and miles.' He looked down, waiting to draw Oliver. ' I'm afraid we Trotskyists proved to be good prophets : how is the United Front for temporising ? Where is the pure revolutionary party now, the enemies of the social democrats ? You'll have another Germany yet in France, everyone a socialist, everyone confused, everyone, even the police chiefs and the post officials, communists, as in Bremen in 1844, and in a few years, hey presto! a Nazi paradise. I'm afraid we're turning out to be the only true Left party.'

Oliver, angry with the bearer of evil news, exploded with indignation.

'Isn't it better to have socialists and communists a majority in the parliament and the city council than to have a majority of foul Chiappe and his gangsters? We're gerrymandered out of power. Paris is eighty per cent. red, but the boodle-barons swing the gavel. You pretend to be a socialist, even more Left than the Lefts, and that doesn't appeal to you! I wish you had been where I've been to-day! That burning flood of enthusiasm, those red flags and red wreaths, like dripping blood at the trench where lie buried the thirty thousand dead of the Paris commune, would have sweetened the most acid misanthrope, and converted the most enraged traitor to the cause of the working class.'

When he said the word 'traitor' he looked straight into Marpurgo's eyes. Then he said more softly: 'It makes you pass over all your own preoccupations, you forget your own silly little troubles, and ambitions, your own life with its single strand. I wish I had taken Elvira—but she felt sick.'

Marpurgo changed the position of his chair slightly, sipped his brandy, and leaned forward on his snakewood gold-monogrammed stick, coughing. After he had refolded his silk handkerchief, also monogrammed, he said:

'Curious what women will do! H'm. No shilly-shallying, although we men accuse them of having no minds of their own. They go straight to the point. Jettison useless baggage, situations, men—they know their own business, the receipts and security business.'

'Instinct of self-preservation and race-preservation,' said Oliver.

'Does the second come in here?'

'Why not?'

Marpurgo kept nodding his head like a mage.

'I must wait and see,' said Oliver nervously.

'She needs you,' said Marpurgo. 'Physically she can get along with Paul—a great, morbid, introverted lump of flesh; spiritually speaking, she needs you: you alone can save her.'

'From what?'

'Bourgeois sloth, the slough of despond, æsthetic inanition, intellectual sterility.'

'Should I lose the whole world to save one woman?' asked Oliver.

'That's more like it,' exclaimed Marpurgo, with an enthusiasm as apparently false as a Guy Fawkes mask. 'If you meet a woman with her own rationally selfish sangfroid, you'll escape scot-free. You young people are admirable! You suffer less and you have the same pleasure. It's a perfectly modern love-affair. . . . Only it assorts strangely with ogival learning, perpendicular degrees, medicated ogees—but I forgot, you're a student of economics, you're a Stalinist, altogether a man of your epoch.' He became confidential. 'You ought to go into business really, Oliver—I understand, by the way, you have made some steps in that direction: Georges told me he took you to dinner—you'd succeed: you're hard as granite inside.' He clasped his small restless hands. 'I wish I had been.' He leaned forward to Oliver intimately. 'I met my wife in a café with other nihilist students; she was a beauty then—and seventeen, brilliant eyes, thick bushy hair, red cheeks, a red silk blouse with Russian embroidery. I said to myself, Why drag through Dostoievskian torture for the sake of the thing? I went up to her, introduced myself, and the next day we were married. I didn't wait in the putting on any more than you wait in the putting off. In that we are alike.'

'You are making a mistake,' replied Oliver.

'You'll win, you'll win,' cried Marpurgo, like a witch now. 'Only show that you can be firm: she needs someone to direct her. Shadowy beauty steeped in quiescence needing lifelong slumber, whose name on the tomb will be the most blatant fact in her history.' He shook his head to himself.

' I need a guide too,' said Oliver.

' What would you do if she went back to Paul ? '

' I don't know. I wish I'd known women earlier. In a sense this is a tangle. Marpurgo, where are they staying—the Madison ? Why do I have to sit here and wait ? Surely it concerns me. She came to live with me ! Am I a leper, a pariah, that they can't talk to me ? I've heard about that brother of hers : he horns into everything, and out of the pulp of other people's sufferings makes up his book of expenses. And my child ! I am surprised at Elvira. She is always so delicate, good-mannered and thoughtful. She has prehensile senses for my feelings. It's really unexpected.'

' She's a child,' murmured Marpurgo. ' She has never had to face life before. It's taken her unawares.'

Oliver heard the melodramatic phrases with impatience. He said good-bye to Marpurgo and left the café, to walk about the streets until supper-time.

Marpurgo left immediately after. He walked down the rue de Tournon and across the sketchy antique Square de Furstemberg. The laces, bronzes and old silver had been rearranged in the shop of the antiquary Paindebled according to his own suggestion.

There was a flounce of machine-made cotton Chantilly and a point-de-Flandre doyley, both exquisitely fine and made in Calais in 1886. When he had first seen them in the window he had known he was going to like Paindebled. But Paindebled had many friends, all amateurs, æsthetes, old-timers. Marpurgo walked along the street to look at the yellowed, dirty old laces he knew were displayed in other small black-painted shops, a charming Feodora and some fine old imitation Bruges, a filthy valance trimmed with a good example of a lace he nevertheless disliked, Valenciennes-platt. He turned then, looking up at the old houses, the former family mansions, the portals and walls. The sky had clouded over. The long rue de l'Université stretched for half a mile behind him, leading to the Invalides. He tapped back, with philosophic stoop, past the shops to the first one with its Chantilly. After staring disconnectedly at some crude old revolutionary prints and Daumiers, he entered the dark shop which stretched back over the space of two rooms. A person who had been sitting behind a Chinese robe stretched over a lantern rose out of the gloom and came forward; a tall, handsome man of sixty, slender, his moustache, vandyke beard and thick hair still chiefly black, with candid brilliant dark eyes and delicate cherry mouth. He said:

'Good evening, Mr. Marpurgo. You came at last. I thought you had forgotten your promise. And Monsieur Georges Fuseaux—never been near me! You are busy, I suppose. Mine is a spider's business—waiting: a secular business. I shouldn't be open. I was just going to close the shop. But since you're so interested and I promised it to you the other day, I must keep my promise. Here's an old print, by the way, of an early machine. Since you're a buyer, perhaps you know the date or place of manufacture? I've searched for years and haven't been able to place it. It simply has the name, Thos. Leavers, and the date. Look, some old bonnets. If you'd come earlier, you could have seen my whole range: I have some fine ones. That's a Norman bonnet; the women wear them on Sundays and for marriages. Notice the handwork. Now, if you'll come upstairs into my salon I can show you something remarkable which I've just received and haven't had time to display properly: a black lace umbrella-cover, hand-made on machine-made tulle. It's priceless: its value is incalculable: it's been in the family of Mme de B. for two hundred years. I used to value and take care of her laces for her, and she left me this with the proviso that I must give it to a museum when I die. Would I sell such a thing? Who could buy it? No one. It must be given away. So dear that it must be given away, eh ? '

The lace umbrella-cover was a yard in diameter, with a deep Chantilly design executed by hand. It was in a case, stretched on white paper. The umbrella which had last carried it, an umbrella with an ivory handle and ivory silk cover, lay underneath. The owner let Marpurgo examine passionately its texture and workmanship and the dreamlike beauty of its design, while he discoursed on a dozen other questions of lace. His head was packed with them. It shuttled back and forward, regularly, winding out its tissue like a reel unwinding cotton.

Marpurgo, quite pale, looked at the owner. ' I can hardly believe it exists. I could contemplate it all the days of my life. It is so perfect that you are cheerful because man can contrive such things.'

' I am glad you have seen the lace towns—Lyon, Calais, Nottingham, Plauen, Saint-Gall,' said the tall man. ' I have seen them all. I was born in Saint-Pierre, the second half of the town of Calais, in 1870, that black year for the French. In that year there was much talk of the union of the two towns Calais and Saint-Pierre, which were, of course, the same town. Some seriously advised Calais to turn her attention to fishing and give up all projects of lace-making. But I was in Saint-Pierre. My father went to the war with the Saint-Pierre contingent, and alas, never returned. My mother, left with a new-born child, went into a factory there and became a winder : she wound the cotton on to a drum. In 1882, at the age of twelve, I entered the same factory and got five francs a week. At the same time a school of decorative art was definitely organised, and I went to it at the time I entered the designing studio of the firm. In due course I became chief designer of the foremost firm, from the point of view of fine and original laces, of Calais. The lace business had declined since the war, as you must know. Can I take you to have an apéritif ?

In the meantime, the métier Leavers : if you remember having seen one like it, do tell me. I cannot place it. An early one.'

They came downstairs again, and the shopkeeper, saying all the time, ' I really can't stay to show you now, I have a rendezvous, but I must just show you this,' opened some shutters and showed Marpurgo a blonde de Bayeux, a point-de-Flandre and a point-d'Angleterre insertion which he looked at with desire : he was on fire with passion when they came back into the front of the shop. Marpurgo shook hands with the designer and promised to return to see his laces the next day at ten.

Someone came running down the stairs, saying, ' Papa, papa, you are late already.' At the bottom of the dark stairway, blond as a hank of twisted silk, long, undulating, stood a young woman. Marpurgo lifted his head. She looked round the shop as if to see that the pieces of furniture and bric-à-brac were in place, and, without noticing Marpurgo, ran upstairs again.

' My daughter,' said the shopkeeper, ' Coromandel : a fine designer, but there is no place in the lace industry for her nowadays. She designs for bookbinders : her room is a forest of designs : she gets up in the night to do them. The last several nights, for example, she has been working every night : she can live without sleeping when the mood is on. I'll show you some too, to-morrow. She likes showing her work. Well, good-night, sir. I am obliged to you for calling in. I am busy now ; I have a rendezvous, or I would show you what I have now. It is fortunate you caught me then. If you have any col-leagues who have your interests, tell them to come. They will not receive the cold shoulder : tell them they will receive a hot plate of welcome : tell them I don't roll pebbles in my mouth, my tongue is hot with in-formation. Tell them I have treasures. Good, now I must go. Good-night.' He came out with Marpurgo and started putting up the shutters.

Marpurgo took off his hat with an Italian flourish. He stood on the opposite side of the street to see the man putting up his shutters. On the third storey, under the attic, Coromandel was standing. She had on a dress of embroidered yellow Swiss muslin. Her hair was down, rolled in two strands, one round the other, like a hank of silk, round her neck and down her back again. She stood looking down on him without making a gesture, shining on high like a yellow moon in the scented sweaty evening.

Marpurgo went along the street slowly. The father went in and shut his door. Marpurgo looked back and saw Coromandel still standing there. She went from the window, and he stood there, meditating. A small piece of paper blew off the window-sill. He picked it up. It was a pencil design for a courtyard lantern. In the corner was a sketch of it hanging over a grille in an archway. The legends were written in different scripts. ' I am a lamp and gate '; ' I light dusty feet home '; ' My flame's the same to rich and poor.' They were all crossed out. She had signed her name underneath, Coromandel.

He looked up to see if she was there again, but the window yawned. He folded the drawing into his pocket-book and walked off, his bright inquisitive eyes far away, up the shining dust-blue rue de l'Université, his small heart beating steadily. He returned, without thinking, by the Square de Furstemberg, and saw the standard lamp standing among the four trees. He stood at the entrance to the square, leaning on his stick. ' A lamp,' he said. He went on, feeling that a lamp had been lighted in his breast-pocket where the drawing was, folded.

He saw Oliver, Elvira, Western and Cinips on the terrace of the Deux Magots. They sat talking quietly, like old friends. Adam looked rapidly once or twice, sideways, at Paul.

' Larder-rat,' whispered Marpurgo to himself.

They saw Marpurgo come stepping across the wide end of the rue de Rennes, across the façade of the abbey church. Oliver said something to Elvira. Elvira beckoned him. Paul turned his bowed head and nodded to him. Marpurgo made to go on and then retraced his steps.

He saw that the group which appeared so quiet was half-frozen with constraint. Elvira was enjoying herself. Her words came dripping rarely, white and sweet, like sugar-cane shreds, from her sensually swollen lips. She kept smoking cigarettes and swinging her silk-clad legs. When she had finished all her own, Oliver and Paul offered theirs. She took Paul's. Marpurgo explained his national status to them all again. Adam judged the time opportune to relate that he had married an Italian wife when he was eighteen, and that they had left each other to go and live with other loves ten months after. Elvira said :

'But all Adam's loves were economic. His next girl kept him for two years.'

'She was a syndicalist and sculptress, a tigress,' affirmed Adam. 'Her husband believed in Robert Owen and taught Hebrew. It was the nine days' wonder of Birmingham. She still writes to me.'

'Adam is shade-matcher in a dyeing firm in Luton at present,' put in Paul, with mortification.

Adam began to explain rapidly :

'I spent three years at Leeds University, having a taste for chemistry and colours and finding I was a rotten painter. I got a position as chief dyer in a dye-works belonging to a felt hat-making firm. We dyed straws, felt hoods and grosgrain ribbons. I found the first day I wasn't capable of handling it. Turning out big ranges of goods when you're costed down is a different proposition. I felt like committing suicide. I was messed up with Theresa—that's the sculptress— at the time. I went and looked at headstones and thought of the obituaries in the papers. I've always had a lot

of pride. Instead, I asked the manager to take back my
contract or put it off for some years. He put it off for
three years. I went to work in the factory as a learner.
That's two years I'm there.'

Elvira laughed.

' You've been sacked four times already.'

Adam grinned.

' Oh, I tell the foreman off from time to time. He
can't stand me : they all know I'm going to be chief
presently. I experiment, and he has to show me all
their secrets. Petty secrets, but how they cherish them.
When you see how they hug some poor little process
to their breasts, and at the same time can't adopt modern
improvements, on account of cost, obstinacy, patent law
or something, you pray for socialism.' He threw back
his leonine black hair.

' That's true,' exclaimed Oliver, and plunged into a
discussion with Adam. They both bragged.

Adam's eye twinkled : he kept throwing provoking
young-buck glances at Paul. Elvira pretended to sleep,
but her eyes lighted up and she was slightly flushed,
stirred more than usual by the combat taking place
over her. She appreciated every realignment of enemies
and allies. In this mood she was desirable, fresh, younger
than ever. She was not the languid young woman
Marpurgo had seen on the train. Marpurgo turned an
enquiring eye on Oliver.

Elvira murmured :

' Oliver came and picked us up at the hotel. Thanks
for giving the message.'

At last they spoke of having dinner. Making a shot
in the dark, Marpurgo asked Paul and Adam if they
knew Paris. If not, he would take them to dinner and
to a show, or to drive.

' You are an associate,' he smiled to Adam. ' Un-
questionably, since you're in the dyeing business. I'll
put you down on the expense account as " Business
dinner, Cinips-consultation " and so forth.'

' I am so forth,' said Paul.

Marpurgo had arranged the invitation, with a sweep of the hand, to include or exclude the lovers. Oliver was now helping Elvira on with her coat : Paul had her gloves, bag and cigarettes. She took them from him with a grimace. She had a bunch of violets which Marpurgo could see had been given by Adam. He fingered them and smelled them. Paul, who had changed his collar and handkerchief and been shaved since his train-trip, looked at them all diagnostically with his yellow-shot agate eyes, grandly at a disadvantage, like a heavy-weight among flies.

Elvira and Oliver went off to supper : half-way across the boulevard Oliver took her arm. Adam grumbled, stretching his plump white body, and letting his dark eyes smoke.

' His head comes up to your tiepin, Paul. I bet you anything you like that if you two fought for her she'd be back home in Mecklenburgh, happy and content, like a shot. She's tired of it all now, but she can't climb down. Do you think I don't know my sister ? Women are primitive. What stands in place of their minds is swayed by a neat uppercut. And, mind you, I love Elvira : she's got brains, of a sort.'

Paul laughed a little in his dark voice.

' It's quite possible that you're right, Adam, but what can I do ? I'm not a cave-man, and Elvira's not a cave-woman. I know her too ; you forget that.'

Marpurgo wagged his head.

' Well, well, though I agree with Adam, about the logic of pugilism in general, I don't think the present situation can be resolved by force. Mrs. Western's is an incredibly complex, subtle nature—chiefly latent, though, so that her will only appears in common rational-mystic form known to dream doctors and psychiatrists. There is mental potency, inflexible will at the bottom of erstwhile apparent drifting.'

Paul gave Marpurgo's fur-felted head a glance of

gratitude. He put himself into Marpurgo's hands like a child, and, while Adam vainly cavorted, snorted and whinnied outside the charmed fluid stream of their intercourse, Paul came to tell Marpurgo about his work, his friends, about that close, dear brother, Giles Gaunt, with whom he had gone to college, and even (when Adam had gone to the men's room once) how he had met, loved, courted and married Elvira, how faithful and loving she had been to him, thinking only of him, anticipating what would give him pain. Marpurgo smoked one expensive cigar after another, putting his lips to the end as if it were a bubble-pipe.

'You are an angel,' said Marpurgo definitely. 'Nothing less. You are a really good man, and, of course, you suffer. Everyone in the world has a better attorney than you : you take everyone's part against yourself.'

'No, no,' protested Paul. 'I am not a good man. I have many faults. I have done harm to people. That's why I go gingerly. I know my own shortcomings.' He smiled at Marpurgo. 'I love my wife, that is all. I know her ; she is self-willed, she must be led. She is a —child. Despite her self-possession and polished manners, her cool air and way of uttering opinions— like Portia.' He laughed. 'Really, she is just Viola, loving, a little self-deprecating, self-subduing, a little masochistic. I could not believe that she had gone off by herself. This—boy—told her he needed her. We had been unhappy. No children, a declining income. I spoiled her. I should have given her a profession : made her a doctor, or a laboratory assistant. I stole her life and gave her nothing in return. I kept her like a specimen in a test-tube. She said this afternoon, " Like a foetus in alcohol. I was pickled, an exhibit." '

'Witty concretisation,' commented Marpurgo.

'Elvira got her M.A. with honours,' confirmed Paul.

'And you came to some arrangement ?'

'She is coming to stay in the hotel to-night, in order to make up her mind,' said Paul doubtfully. 'She has

to make arrangements with—this boy. It's only fair,
I suppose. She didn't tell me about him. I suppose
she was afraid to hurt me too much.'

' It must have been rather a shock to you ? '

' Several times my letters to her were returned, which
surprised me. I should have guessed. Yet—why?
She never looked at another man. She was so chaste :
infolded. She told me she would rather think of me as
her brother than her husband.'

' That's wrong,' submitted Marpurgo.

' I am afraid it must be.'

Adam came lounging back.

' Let's go somewhere else. After all, we're not in
Paris every day of our lives. Marpurgo, you know this
metropolis of sin. You look like the father of lies
himself. Let's explore.'

Marpurgo ignored him.

' Did they—she—tell you anything about—their life
here ? '

' Very little. It seems he works in the Archives and
reads her the political news, and she does nothing at all.
She sits in cafés. I am still getting over the shock.
What else is there ? '

' Well,' demurred Marpurgo. ' Well, you must not
take it that we are close friends. I met Mrs. Western
on the train coming here, by hazard of contiguity. I
always assume that fate has a joker in every pack she
deals. I worship derivation of drama, the genetics of
intimacy, at heart a boy, though through flaws in God's
fabric a misanthrope—the pterodactyl Death over-
shadowing me seems to poke his transparent digit at
the core of every man. This notwithstanding—no,
because of this, I chafe those abrasions of the spiritual
cutex we call chance acquaintance. Thus I met your
wife. But early recognised the lady was no hand-fed
one-girl harem, one of those psychological stalagmites
formed by slow calcareous drippings in the windless
caverns the bourgeois call homes. I saw an unusual

woman, in an unusual situation. I saw a genteel woman
startled by her own coup-de-tête.'

'I wish I could see people as you can,' complained
Paul. 'I do not know human beings. When I try to
imagine what they are thinking, I see nothing but the
brain-structure. Their impulsions, decisions, all their
psychological make-up just seem to me thick smoke
blown by black magic through the nerves. The brain
to me is not part of the organism : it is a cancer.'

Adam whistled. 'Paul, Paris suits you. You'll be
struck off the B.M.A. yet through getting a new idea.'

Paul laughed uncomfortably. 'With Peter Bell the
third, it was dullness for fifteen miles round; with Mr.
Marpurgo it is cerebration for fifteen miles round—even
my rheumatic brain-box.' He lowered his head and
shoulders boyishly over the table to laugh convulsively.

'Western.' Marpurgo's voice was decided, metallic.
'You're too fine a man—and it is true you do not understand people. You should not be deceived.'

'I surround myself with simple people,' said Paul
humbly.

'They did not tell you that Elvira is enceinte,' Marpurgo's voice struck across the table.

'No !'

'This is serious,' began Adam with importance.
'Paul, you can't handle this. You had better leave it
to me. You can understand,' he hurried on, before
Marpurgo could speak, 'that Mrs. Western hesitated
to tell her husband such a thing. I am glad you told us :
it puts a weapon in our hands. . . .'

'I don't want a weapon,' protested Paul.

'We will demand the truth to-night, and perhaps it
is not too late. . . .'

'What are you suggesting ? ' cried Paul.

'If she returns, would you bring up another man's
child ? ' cried Adam. 'Of course not.'

'I certainly should,' said Paul. 'If it is Elvira's, it is
mine. I must beg you, Adam, to restrain yourself and

leave this to the two of us. You are a very young man.
Especially now we must be careful what we say.'

'What? This is really decisive!' cried Adam. 'She
must be got away somewhere to think her position over
before it is too late. Paul, I am her brother. Let me
take care of her, then she is influenced by neither of
you.' Paul flinched. 'And she can make a decision
that will not be fatally foolish.'

'It's early yet,' remarked Paul. 'Marpurgo, would you
take us somewhere else? The air is rather thick here.'

When they came out they heard the familiar cry:
'*Intran:* Fourth Edition — Proposals of Monsieur
Barthou.'

They ended at the Mosque, where Marpurgo set the
Arab singers off by chanting one or two of their songs
which he had heard in Tangier. The singers went on
chanting their improvised drooling arabesques, ana-
creontics illustrated by their mean, downtrodden,
lustful eyes. Paul was more manly than he had been all
the afternoon: he relished the thick coffee. Adam,
who took a liqueur whenever it was offered to him,
began to recite his own poetic drivel in *vers libre*,
imitations of T. S. Eliot and D. H. Lawrence with a
dash of Walt Whitman, a squeamish cocktail. He
favoured them with a sonnet he had written to a girl
at Leeds University 'doing chemistry and bacteriology
—I can only go to bed with an intelligence: I like to
woo in the images of Donne and Carew.'

'Your parents spent a lot of money so that you could
get hot in words of more than one syllable,' remarked
Marpurgo roughly.

Adam retired for the night.

Marpurgo was up till nearly morning, all his mis-
deeds forgotten, singing desert songs to himself under
his breath, composing pages of a never-written novel
which would epitomise the age. He looked at his drawing of a lamp. He believed in signs and tokens. He fell
asleep saying 'A lamp, thou art a lamp unto my feet,

the lamp of life,' and so on, weaving the lovely father and visionary daughter into an impassioned legend. When he fell asleep, he woke again several times with a fevered head, thumping heart, and a host of extravagant dreams retreating from his pillow.

Elvira had sent a note to the Madison saying she could not join them that night.

Adam dramatically said :

' An idea ! You go to bed, Paul : I'm going to walk a bit.'

' Do you want some money ? '

' No, nothing : ten francs if you've got it. I came away so hurriedly that I forgot to draw from the bank.'

Paul gave him a hundred-franc note. ' Don't be too wild—the family's not as rich as it was ! ' He laughed pleasantly, patting the young man on the shoulder.

' Oh, you're mistaken. My expedition is philanthropic—I might take a coffee, that's all. It's for your good : the family good.'

Paul laughed. ' That's a name for it : do be careful.'

Adam came down to breakfast in the Deux Magots with a telegram : he showed it to Paul.

' Leaving eleven this morning. Meet me.—SARA.'

' What on earth is that ? ' expostulated Paul.

Adam grinned. ' I telegraphed Sara from the all-night bureau in the rue de Grenelle last night. This is a situation for a woman to handle. Elvira always wrote to Sara, you know : her only correspondent. I admit it's rather like a corroboree of the whole caravanserai celebrating a rite of passage, isn't it ? Still, I want you both to be happy, and I want to see that centripetal bastard flouted.'

' I have a headache this morning,' said Paul. ' I didn't sleep much last night. This thing has got to be settled. Perhaps you did the right thing. It looks cruel to go off and leave Elvira to her tergiversations, but I've got my patients to think of. It's strange : I always experience the same thing : I trust Vice-Brown, and yet I worry about my patients every minute I'm away. I had an appointment at ten this morning with Penn, quite important, and one at three this afternoon with poor Fanning. You don't know him, Adam. A tumour on the brain and a Xantippe wife. It's ten now, isn't it ? I got up this morning at seven as usual and went for a walk. You must excuse me : inactivity makes me irritable. Do you notice the woman there with one dilated pupil, the left ? A scar of childhood chicken-pox, doubtless. There's another mark just above the mole on the left eyebrow. Vice-Brown had such a case and diagnosed it as paresis, drove the poor woman into a hysterical state until the Wassermann came through. Vice-Brown is too young, and romantic. Why do I distrust romance so much ? I'm a leaden fellow.'

Adam was doing the crossword puzzle in the American newspaper.

'Here comes Elvira,' remarked Paul shortly. 'I'm glad, this sitting about makes my skin creep.'

'Don't get nervous,' advised Adam.

Elvira came up with welling eyes, sorry for herself.

'I feel sickish ; it's the heat,' said she. 'Ask for a vermouth, Paul.'

'You oughtn't to have it in your . . .' He flushed.

Adam laughed.

'What's the matter with you, Adam ? ' She called the waiter and expertly gave her order. When she had finished, 'Let's take a walk,' Paul said, 'if you feel like it, Elvira.'

'Why not ? '

They left Adam to make up to an American girl he had been eyeing for some time.

Oliver was at the Archives trying to work, puzzled, nervous, half-inclined to laugh at them all, including himself.

'With all the instruments in the orchestra, I have to pick out the triangle.'

The day passed in irresolution. Elvira spent hours with Paul reviewing the whole of their past life. She was mournful, and yet this cataloguing, adjustment of claim and blame, self-revelation, unearthing of symbols and unrecognised prophecies, the eternal game of hide-and-seek she played with all men, satisfied her ruminating mind. She remembered incidents, completely forgotten by Paul, which had occurred in their earliest married days; she resented delays, absences, forgetfulnesses which he could not even recall and certainly never intended. He said once or twice in sorry amazement :

'But, Elvira, how can you possibly remember so much against me ? How can you hoard up these things ? You know me. I never meant to wound you in my life.'

'An unconscious intention reveals itself in little things. You are not fine in the fine things of life.'

'No, I am not ; I never have been, I know it.'

When evening came, he told her that Sara had now arrived and would have dinner with them.

'How revolting !' she cried. 'Why must you make this private thing so public ? Are you so weak that you have to call in all these auxiliaries ? You're ridiculous, Paul.'

He felt ridiculous.

'Adam sent for her without my knowledge.'

'I simply don't believe it : Adam is too selfish to think of such a thing.'

'Adam loves you : he wants me to let him take you to Fontainebleau or the south for a while till you—— Elvira, have you told me everything ? You must get us all out of this frightful situation.'

She began to cry, as they sat in the garden.

'Oh, I can't stand it : you all buzz round me ! I have to decide, it is my fault, I have ruined everyone's comfort, I am the selfish one. I'm alone in the world, I have no friends. My husband blames me, my lover is suspicious of me, and unhappy. Adam is rough.

Sara, even Sara, has to come and act the big sister. I
can't stand it. Why don't you all go and leave me if
I'm such a nuisance to everyone?'

'Elvira, don't, don't. . . .'

'I can't help it.'

'I know, I know. Why don't you confide in me?'

She put her head on his shoulder.

'Paul, I've never been so miserable in all my life. I'm
going to have a baby. What shall I do? You tell me.'

They were more cheerful and arranged to have dinner
alone together. Adam could take Sara to the pictures
or show her Paris.

In the end she insisted on going home to her hotel
room with Oliver: it was only fair to talk it over with
him. She had a childish compulsion to lay her plans
and her worries at everyone's feet. He let her go
bitterly, saying: 'Elvira, you must grow up. Think
of me: I have patients waiting for me.'

'I'm a sick woman, mentally, morally and physically
sick,' she stormed. 'Call me a taxi, I'm going home.
At least Oliver doesn't tell me to bustle because his
career's waiting.'

'Good-night, Elvira.'

She slammed the taxi door.

Returning to his hotel much later, Paul went along
softly and knocked at Sara's door. She got up and
opened the door to him. She was a Yorkshire woman,
with Irish blood, tall, rosy, hazel-haired, handsome in
a yellow silk dressing-gown with a cord, strongly built,
round-bosomed, full of simple friendship and innocent
gentleness. She was a distant cousin of Paul, who had
come in to London during Elvira's absence.

'Is she with you?'

He shook his head. They were sitting on the divan
in the corner of the room.

'She went after dinner to the young fellow and I
passed the evening with friends. I will wait to-morrow
and the next day, and then I'll go back.'

She looked at him calmly, waiting for him to explain something she didn't understand.

'If I go back, Sara, do you want to go back with me? Or would you like me to leave you here a few days, to look at Paris?'

'If Elvira comes back, I will wait a few days and see how they run their lunch-rooms: if you go back by yourself, I will come with you. If you want me.'

There was a silence. Paul sighed. 'I do not think she will come back. She is pregnant. She cannot make up her mind what to do. She never can. You know her.'

'Oh, Paul: then she can't come back?'

'She is not sure she wants the baby either.'

She was timid and awkward in her virgin's inexperience. Paul explained to her all he had felt during the afternoon.

'I sat there dumbly, trying to be fair and not show the intense aversion I feel for the young fellow, his blatancy, his puppyishness, pretending to be a revolutionary: he spent a long time telling us why he was not a Leninist, or a Stalinist, or a Marxist, and not a Trotskyist either, but some shade of opinion of his own he has worked out here in between cafés and scribbling in his Archives. He was so much more serious in London.'

'He's just a boy, isn't he?'

'A brilliant boy, though, a false genius, pretty and witty. I kept saying to myself, Perhaps Elvira sees something in him I don't see, because of my prejudice.'

'That's possible.'

'We see so little in life, I don't like a sweeping opinion. We go through life erratically like a drunk motor-car turning its headlights this way and that, getting snatches of foliage. The true portrait of a person should be built up as a painter builds it, with hints from everyone, brush-strokes, thousands of little touches. I even looked at Oliver and tried to think how I would have felt if he had been my son. I should be proud of him for

being such a peacock, lovable, ingenious, mentally soft
and crooked, but so much more charming than myself.
It is only because he stole Elvira, he came between
us—that I hate him. Why do these things happen?
We could love each other so much. Even against
Elvira I feel so much resentment sometimes. And it
isn't fair : people have a right to choose their own
lives.'

He looked at her with his sad brown eyes. She said,
'Paul, Paul!' They sat half-turned towards each
other. After a silence, he went on : 'You're a very
pretty woman, Sara, and I feel such goodness in you.'

'People always say I am quite like you,' she laughed.

'Yes, you are like me.'

She had clear expressions that had never been soiled
by jealousy, hate or bitterness, the complexion of an
empty sea-pool in a sandstone rock. Some memories
flickered in her face, rippling the pool.

'Do you remember, Paul, when we first met ? When
you were at the University ? We could never look at
each other without smiling, and yet we hardly ever said
anything to each other ? '

He laughed now, laughing at her laugh.

'Yes.'

He paused over her face.

'Sara, why did you never marry ? '

Her face fell shyly.

'I don't know : I always thought I should, but no
one ever came my way. I'm too old now. There was
only Lind, and he was married.'

He said regretfully : 'A young man only cares for
a physical beauty. His pleasure drives him to marriage ;
it's not his mind or even his heart, but his——' He
stopped, looking at Sara's fearing, clouded eyes. He got
up and took a step up and down the room. 'My girl,
my girl——' He stopped abruptly and said : 'Well,
I'm dog-tired, and it'll be a couple of days before we get
out of this. Good-night, Sara, sleep well.'

She smiled. 'Good-night.'

He went out vigorously without looking back. She sat for some time, leaning forward, in her yellow dressing-gown, looking at the closed door and then letting her eyes fall to the floor. She presently got up, turned off the light, took off her gown and got into bed, moving like a sleep-walker. She sighed several times, and to shake off her sober mood began to think of the lunch-room she ran in York. Miss Sara Steele. Paul. 'If I had had any experience, I should be able to try to help you, but I am helpless,' she had said to Paul when she came to London and found him alone. 'I should try to help you, Paul; I would do anything to help you in trouble, Paul.' His hand a bunch of veins, like his old mother's. He was getting more like her as his eyes sagged and the veins came out on his temples. His face was thicker-clothed than before; white hairs were stuck in irregularly all over his head. He smiled at her with his dark ivory eyeballs, agate pupils, and the candid smile of the young University boy was still there like a fine sheen. She wanted to cry without knowing why. It was a strange and unexpected adventure that had come to her, when she took the train to London. She thought how you hesitated about making a step, for years, and how, once you took it, you found yourself being hurried on, jostled along somewhere. If one had taken that step long years ago, something beautiful might have happened. She went to sleep and had the impression all through her dreams that something marvellous had happened.

The midnight hours clanked in sordine from the belfries of the Montagne Sainte-Geneviève; the senile chimes limped out across the air with toothless infelicity and secular spleen, and yet, because of their inhuman age, passed with the austerity of a passing bell. Elvira listened to them and to Oliver's trustful breathing in the dark. When Paul had asked her if she wanted to stay with Oliver she had said yes, partly out of fright at being cast on her own resources, partly out of pique, partly out of boredom too. She awoke early to look at the fine sunlight falling through the windows and to hear the birds chattering. All her previous life in London, even the last three months here, seemed washed out in flowing water, so that gold dust remained in the pan. With a young man, she was young. She would give up the child. They would start again, children, hand in hand : they would give each other pure glances untouched by mutual blame or regret.

They got up late in the morning, and Elvira made coffee in the light-flooded kitchen which looked over the gardens of the Lycée Henri IV. The fine, large, she-eyed breeze came stirring the trees of the college, and two elder boys came leaping through the kitchen-garden and looked up at her, leaning through the barred window with a spoon in her hand : they stopped and looked at her in her Chinese robe timorously, curiously, like startled wood animals, attracted and ready to fly. Afterwards she and Oliver walked down the boulevards with linked arms. Elvira was a little depressed : she had expected a *pneumatique* from Paul. Over breakfast she said in a flat voice :

' Oliver, I must see Paul for lunch. He has his cousin Sara with him : he brought her over to look after me. He has been so kind and he is so unhappy.'

' You'll see him for supper, too, I suppose ? '

' He's still my husband, Oliver : and it may be for the last time.'

' You are right.'

' We are visiting some friends of his this afternoon for afternoon tea : naturally they do not know there is anything wrong. They think a lot of Paul : so I will go.'

' Then I will meet you at home late to-night.'

' That's it. You go to bed. Don't mind how late I get in : Paul and I must talk things over. He is perfectly fair : he wants me to choose for myself. He says if one of us is happy it is better than neither of us being

happy. Naturally we have a lot to talk over and decide.
Also, I think—that until everything is all settled we may
as well be circumspect.'

' Why not ? ' Oliver began to whistle.

' Do you mind ? '

' Aren't we going to spend the rest of our lives after
to-day together ? '

' You're so sure. You don't know the conflict in my
mind. I have to consider others besides myself. I must
see this distant cousin of his, Sara, and find out why
he brought her over : what he said to her. If you like,
though, we can meet you for the apéritif before dinner.'

' And then I go off to dinner alone ? No : I'll take
the day off and roam round, to pick up what fun I can.
Here is a taxi-rank. Where to, now ? '

She stopped on the pavement, pathetically.

' Now you are hurt. I can't leave you hurt. Oh,
what have I done ? I make no one happy.'

He took her arm and hurried her across the road to
a taxi.

' There you are, darling. Now tell me what address,
and I'll send you off. Enjoy yourself.'

He had lunch in a new café near the Luxembourg,
drank half a litre of wine and felt powerful. Plenty of
women made eyes at him. He walked along the old
streets of the Left Bank beyond the Boulevard Saint-
Germain towards the Seine. As he passed the Deux
Magots he saw Elvira, Adam, Paul and a mature young
woman sitting on the terrace. He waved gaily to them,
and going by the Abbey, soon came into the rue Jacob.
He remembered the direction of Georges Fuseaux and
wanted to see Paindebled's laces.

He saw through the window of the first floor, across
the court, a charming interior, where a diffused light
rested low on the waxed surface of an antique inlaid
chiffonier, on a copper warming-pan hung on a rich
dark tapestry paper, and on several large glazed snuff-
jars and Chinese vases, the latter being inlaid with

gold, bronze, silver, and the painted dragons and flowers in ivory, green, red and sepia enamels. Oliver stopped, pleasantly dazed, and looked in. The chamber was ceiled in wood, small beams chiselled and painted in red, blue and gold crossing at short intervals to divide the ceiling into squares. Underneath was one of those old shops selling antiquities and *objets de vertu* which are so frequent in the neighbourhood.

As Oliver stood sucking in the gloss and sparkle of the objects displayed in the living-room upstairs, a fair young woman appeared at the window between the words 'Autographs' and 'Engravings.' She placed both hands on the sill, looked up at the linen-blue sky, and down at Oliver. It was a perfectly clear day, and they could discern each other's features plainly. Oliver thought of the 'flax-haired maid.' They looked at each other boldly. Oliver's supine heart, for months in pretended chains, had risen like a lion since he had left Elvira to her finicking. He laughed to himself, rolled voluptuously on his hips. He had passed two or three remarkable-looking persons, and in the rue Jacob itself, as he lingered before a shop of illuminated MSS., a real lion had crossed him, a youth with a look of Goethe beatified, with the carriage of a toreador, with thick curled hair and eyes like amethysts, who strode past on the air, with the grand showmanship and unintentioned glory of a genius which knows its prodigies in youth. These manifestations out of the air of the divine intentions of nature towards him filled Oliver's cramped bosom, puffed away the meagre joys of the Archives and carried him lighter than Ixion into the Junoesque air.

The youthful Juno smiled at him. She put her hands together round her mouth and said, rather low :

'Hullo, young man : are you going to steal something ? '

'It's not safe to steal a masterpiece : that's the only reason I hang back.'

She laughed. 'I'm just a cartoon: but you're a charming gouache. What do you do?'

'I'm a student of history.'

'And I—a designer.'

Oliver stood there laughing, but a little awkward. The young woman said:

'What is your name?'

'Oliver.'

She lowered her voice, which was always soft but penetrating, and called:

'You could come up for just a little while if you like. For tea.'

'Thanks very much. I'd love to. Which door?'

The staircase was broad, the doors polished, with large panels. A triangular red plush seat filled the corner of each landing. No names or initials marked the dignified anonymity of these portals. The girl opened the door to him. She was young, softly nurtured, thriving. She had a pale rose flush at the moment, and a fine waxy bloom. She was singular in proportion: upon the short and elegant waist of a young girl rose a broad, arching, sculptured bosom, and, without a fault or mole, a long, full, columnar neck. She inclined towards him the whole of her bust, which was encircled, rather than dressed, in a deep net frill. On the tall stalk of her neck, her small fair head, broader at the top than at the base, with hair parted equally and ears revealed, nodded a little. Oliver instantly perceived that all her attentions, and apparently those of her parents or guardians, were devoted to her unique bosom. Her eyes rolled slowly upon Oliver. They were oval, with long dark lashes, and of a splendid transparent blue. She retired from the door and admitted him, who noted that her dress was shorter than he liked, and her feet in low-heeled shoes. There was a combination of all that he disliked with an unusual charm, of repulsive vanity with innocence and fragility. As he looked at her profile, he saw that she resembled closely a China pompadour bust, upon a small stele, and that no Dresden shepherdess ever bore a whiter, deeper, or more noble bosom, or a smaller head. When she had leaned out of the window, she had wrapped her almost naked shoulders in a dark scarf, which she had now discarded. Oliver wondered what she could be, so shameless with such dignity, so conscious without affront. She returned towards Oliver, leaning forward as ever from the waist, smiled at him hesitating at the door, and, saying 'Take care, the floor is so highly polished!' placed her finger-tips on his hand. The girl might be seventeen or twenty-two—the same disproportion existed in her bearing as in her body, a wide and perfected experience grew in a youthful mind. Oliver felt that she had not had an ordinary education, and an opposition grew in his mind between his thirsty desire to know her individuality and the fear of a strangely-endowed woman.

The large salon into which she led him looked out on the courtyard, the opposite walls and windows of which were now obscure and bluish. The room was divided by display cabinets containing MSS., engravings and varied documents. At the far end, set in white panelling, were two large frescoes in the type of Boucher. A splendid bronze-gilt candelabra, with sixty sockets bearing upright candle bulbs of small size, hung low under a painted ceiling representing a rose-covered marble balustrade looking upon a rosy-clouded blue sky in which cherubim disported themselves.

Oliver busied himself for a few minutes examining the Chinese vases, and the young woman went on to point out to him some lacquer vases, a carved pearwood reliquary on a silver and enamel stand, a white jade snuff-jar and other objects. When he glanced carelessly at the mirror in front of him, he observed at the other end of the room, the one by which he had entered, something which made him turn quickly to make sure he was not deceived. The girl smiled. On a stele stood a hamadryad, from whose small smooth waist sprang a noble bosom partially wrapped in bark. She had no arms. Upon her smooth long neck a small oval face was balanced, inclined downwards and towards the left shoulder. The eyes were incrusted in greenstone.

'That's beautiful,' cried Oliver.

The girl laughed. The laugh was surprising, clear, cold, falling from her mouth like a broken strand of glass beads on a marble table, falling and rolling on the floor.

'You are laconic: therefore you are English,' she said to Oliver, sitting on the table.

'I'm afraid to ask too much of good-fortune,' he countered. 'I hardly believe in her. I came to see her closer. I have heard of mirages. And the mysteries of Paris. You are one of her mysteries.'

She mocked. 'Not at all. Don't take it so seriously. It's just a lark on my part. I'm a designer, an artist, you know. I get stiff in the imagination, working up in the atelier all by myself. And then I sort of talk to my creations all day. I get in the habit of addressing strange creatures. Life is a wood and you are all fauns.'

'And hamadryads,' he pointed. 'It's ridiculous, of course, but it resembles you, I think.'

They sauntered about the room. He looked at her, his beautiful face and white smile close to hers.

'This is really jolly. We all feel so much more friendly than we pretend, and almost no one in the world has the courage to make a bosom friend in an instant. But I have, and you have. It's wonderful.'

At the word 'bosom' his eyes dropped and rose again above a sudden flush.

She was pleased.

'Do have an apéritif, or coffee or something. Have you had lunch?'

'I'd like a coffee: I got up early, walked a long way, had some bad *bistrot* coffee, and spent the morning eating my blood.'

She went out and shortly returned, while Oliver speculated and smiled patronisingly at himself in the glass. He was looking at the famous lace umbrella-cover when she came in. He had not noticed it before. He was not a great lover of possessions, however beautiful. She was explaining it to him, and he was explaining his interest in the lace-workers of Saint-Pierre and Calais and in the Fuseaux, when a buxom old woman in black, with a peasant cap, came in with coffee and a china service.

' Tell me frankly,' said Oliver, while drinking, ' why did you call me up ? I mean, why me, in particular ? There was a marvellous fellow, a regular Greek god, went down the street ahead of me, crossed me rather. Why not him ? It's so unconventional, anyhow, especially in a French girl. Or is all that ancient history now ? My . . . I know a French girl here whose brother runs the whole family. She has to explain all her absences, they give her a bare margin to catch the earliest train from work, and she's never out after eight. A working-class family.'

She paid no attention to this. Presently she said :

' If a strange-looking old lady comes in here, take no notice. It's my mother. She wanders a little. It's quite a history—connected with that hamadryad, by the way—I'll tell you one of these days. If she comes, you tell her that you came to see father. What is his friend's name ? Oh, Georges, Georges Fusil, no, Fuseaux ? Say Georges Fuseaux sent you. He did, didn't he ? Some other time I'll tell you the history of that hamadryad.'

They were inexplicably happy to be with each other. He said :

' I'm so glad you know we'll see each other again.'

' Why not ? '

Presently she moved to show him some of her father's peasant bonnets and fichus in lace.

She led him through a door of inlaid tulipwood into a chamber both lofty and large, in which a gallery was

divided off by a row of thin painted pillars, red and
blue with yellow and blue frets and silver notches.
Bays in this gallery, under a roof of sloping glass, contained glazed cases. In the chamber itself stood a
couch on which lay several rolls of parchment and
linen upon a Persian rug, and to one side of the
median line of the chamber stood two large antique
globes, representing the celestial and terraqueous
spheres. Round the equatorial line of each appeared
the signs of the zodiac and the rising and setting of
the sun and of the constellations. They were finely
painted and polished, and about thirty-six inches in
diameter. The globes were of the sixteenth century.
Between them a carved monolith stand supported a
compass opening in two halves, like an eggshell, the
compass within being surrounded with garnets and
topazes, the outer skin or shell being painted with the
signs of the constellations. It still pointed to the north,
and although it had been made in the early eighteenth
century, earlier copies had been found even in antiquity,
and the same appears in ancient drawings, on the forehead of Venus Anadyomene. Round the walls hung
very large maps of the world, of different countries, and
of different epochs of geographical science, the finest of
their kind and epoch. The latest ones printed in delicate
colours and minutely circumstantial ; the earlier ones
with broad names, legendary seas, imaginary lines, were
of a splendid mandarin ivory colour. The floor was of
polished wood, with a map of the Ptolemaic world
inlaid ; the ceiling was of glass, divided into squares.
The glass roof evidently served as floor to another
chamber, for a dim light penetrated the glass on all
sides, marking off in the centre the contour of a rug or
cloth lying upon it. Standard lights illumined this
chamber. At the farther end six deeply folded curtains
of plush, two emerald, two peach-coloured, two of
cloth of Chile gold, covered the wall : they were so
large that their ends were gathered up on the floor as

an imperial train is gathered, wound and splayed. Coromandel said :

'My mother's apartment is beyond there, and she has a private stairway to the library above. I will show you the library one day, when my mother is sleeping. She wakes at night and only falls asleep at four o'clock or so in the morning, awaking with nightfall.'

Coromandel seemed to have grown in beauty and dignity since they entered this chamber : her amber skin took the colour of the delicately varnished maps, her cheeks their flush, her forms were those of the legendary queens of the galaxies, her eyes the colour of the seas, her uncovered bosom displayed hemispheres comparable with the others, except that she had not had them tattooed to further the resemblance. She extinguished the standard lamps, with a sudden movement, and Oliver found himself in a strange universe of floating worlds, and ghostly countries, and islands visible in the upper air. Coromandel also seemed to have lost touch with the floor. Waves of solace and satisfaction invaded his body, and he stood half dreaming, prepared to touch any of the floating worlds if they should swim through chaos in his direction. Her pointed nails had a greenish opalescent lustre.

In the centre of the two globes, the egg of the compass floated on the dark floods softly luminous from the roof's obscure rays, and displayed more clearly a minute crystal Eros at the sign of the north, which had scarcely stood out before. Coromandel was silent. Oliver looked up and observed that the roof, being paved, as observed, with squares of glass, was also engraved with white lines in designs similar to those appearing in the first chamber, but relating to the phenomena of sunrise and sunset in the legendary personages of the ancients ; twenty-four panels surrounded the dark cloth in the centre ; the large one inset on the eastern side was engraved with the symbols of sunrise, then each of the hours was inscribed until sunset, and thereafter were the eleven dark hours. The thick translucent glass floated upon their darkness.

'I suppose there is some design in the centre of all this also,' said Oliver.

'Yes,' said the girl.

'The designs are not very clear,' said Oliver.

'They are when the sun rises,' said the girl. 'The sun falls directly on this glass roof through a skylight of clear glass.'

'It must be magnificently light here then,' said Oliver. 'It is.'

Oliver said, 'Put on the light,' and she put on the light; and Oliver, looking quickly at her, was struck again by the similarity of her skin to the yellowed tissues surrounding her. He said to her : 'You fit very well in this room, like a—topaz in a soft gold setting.'

She laughed and said : 'I have the skin of a mandarin.' She leaned her perfumed body towards Oliver, with her habit of proffering herself with each gesture. Oliver suddenly blushed, and went about the room on his toes, looking at the objects exposed and saying : 'I am amazed. I have never seen anything like this. You know the old houses of Paris are most deceptive : one would never suppose, when looking at the exterior, that these treasures were within.'

'No, no,' she assured him. 'Treasurers don't tell their tale in the market.'

After a silence, she said : 'Treasurers and women.'

A clock struck eleven in the adjoining room, slowly, as if considering between each stroke, and then making the count of the hours with weighted decision.

'But clocks do,' said Oliver. 'I suppose because, however long they count, they never have more than two dozen hours in their pocket.'

'And who wants what they've got?' sighed Coromandel sentimentally.

'Some one hour there must be that would be worth stealing,' said Oliver.

She opened her eyes wide upon Oliver, dropped the
long lashes indifferently upon her cheek, then, indolently
running one pale jade nail through the folds of the frill
of her corsage, she said : ' Perhaps you will find it at
home. That's the rule, at any rate,' with insolence.
Then, walking to the couch, she lay down there, reclin-
ing as Dresden China dolls do, with elastic grace.

Oliver said : ' You are monstrously beautiful ! '

' No doubt,' said the girl. ' My mother has disowned
me, for she says I am the daughter of a monster, that
hamadryad in the salon, to wit, but that is quite a history,
which I may tell you some day, if you should return.'

She turned off the light again, but the effulgence from
above rolled above them thicker than before, as if more
lights had been turned on. It displayed the great supple,
yellow, linen-backed map of the world which hung
above the couch. The rolls of parchment and linen
lay around Coromandel like reeds ; she did not trouble
to move them. She said to Oliver, ' Don't move them.
Why should you ? ' The girl, who was looking ab-
stractedly upwards, rolling her glassy eyeballs in the
light, suddenly reflected a brighter glow.

' Ah,' she said to Oliver, ' she's taken up the tarpaulin.'

Oliver paid no attention to what she said, but kissed
her. But observing in her eyeballs the light from the
roof above, he noticed a small shutter rolling up in each
iris and a minute black oval projecting itself over the
edge of the bright space.

' Look,' said the girl, laughing. ' My mother ! '

Oliver looked upwards with difficulty, and saw that
the centre of the glass had been uncovered, and that
through a bright square in the centre a woman with
large pale eyes and a worn face was staring at them.

At this moment Coromandel chose to recall his senses,
wandering all over the visible world, to herself, and,
foundering in a volcanic bay, he had no time to recollect
anything more than a windmill of dancing heads looking
at him from the minatory shutters of heaven. It is very

appropriate to speak at this moment of a volcanic ocean, since Coromandel had reclined among charts and soundings, and at the same moment, the large map of the world, pinned inadequately above the couch, fell down and covered them with a most unparalleled blanket; while, without, along the volcanic line from Kamchatka to New Zealand, and also on the opposite side of the Pacific, at this minute and for some quarter of an hour afterwards, slight earth tremors were recorded on the seismographs.

They talked their whole lives over. She let him out late, when the stars were shining. The rue de l'Université, lacquered, ran before him, and he ran along it waving his hat in the air. He stopped at a bar open late, and then turned homewards and took a taxi to the hotel apartment on the Montagne Sainte-Geneviève. Elvira was not yet home. It was eleven o'clock. He fell at once into dreams associated with the cherubim fed on truffles which he had seen earlier in the evening and with other inhabitants of their palpable world of painted air.

When he awoke early in the morning all his black horses had vanished. It was a strong-limbed spring morning, silver, blue-draped, soon to be hot, but the trees still not out. The old bells of the Montagne, with the sweet tintinnabulation of cowbells through trees, counted out seven o'clock to him. He turned his head. Elvira was not there. He sat up and tried to be dismayed, but he knew very well what had happened. What a woman she was! She was a monster of indecision: there was something grand and frightening about a life so involuntary. He lay back and laughed, but hot prickles of anxiety began under his skin. There was a letter under his door: he was to meet her at the Deux Magots with Paul, Adam and Sara at ten o'clock. He threw up his hands and burst out laughing. He loitered down the streets, taking a coffee at a bar, and when he got to the Deux Magots, found them all assembled:

a strain of false camaraderie united Sara and Elvira, Paul looked pasty, Adam was reading the paper. When he came to their table they all gave an imperceptible jerk and formed a band round Elvira.

Oliver said good-morning carelessly, and to Elvira, satirically, ' I hope you slept well : I positively didn't know you hadn't come home till this morning when I awoke. I got home early, went to sleep, and slept so well that—— It's such beautiful weather, isn't it ? ' he continued to Sara.

Sara, who had been looking him over incredulously, detailing him, jumped. ' Yes, it is nice,' and smiled ingenuously.

' Miss Steele, I think ? ' went on Oliver, dimpling. Sara flushed faintly and nodded. She kept her steady, clear eyes on him, and he saw a pleased surprise creep over her. They chattered on for a few minutes about the political news, and Elvira, who had been sitting there cosily but mutely, like an egg laid in a tussock, began with weary pertness :

' Why don't we talk about what we're here for ? '

Sara looked at her indignantly.

' I gather it's all decided,' said Oliver smartly.

Elvira seemed to have thought out a set speech : she began without embarrassment, naïvely :

' You see, I am fond of Paul, you can't annihilate ten years in a couple of months, and I don't want him to suffer : on the other hand, I never really made him happy ; we just lived in a sort of back garden for years, or rather, he kept on digging up the same plot of ground, and he turned me from a woman into a cabbage to orna-ment his back garden. When I was at college I got the medal in history and French, and I used to be interested in the socialist movement. At first I didn't notice what was happening to me, because I was absorbed by the physical side of marriage. I just sat there and vegetated. When Oliver came along, I noticed there was a new intellectual world I knew nothing about : I began to

feel old-fashioned. I thought to myself, Paul has made
me into a cabbage, or rather, he has given me a cabbage
shell. I am still the same person underneath as when
I was at school, but everyone else thinks I am Elvira,
the hearthside wife. I wanted to be young again. I
wanted to do something creative. Oliver kept sending me letters and asking me to be his mistress, but
I couldn't make up my mind to do anything underhand. In a way, I didn't care enough to do anything
underhand. I didn't want to decide on something and
find I had broken up all our lives. Paul and I were
living on a basis of misunderstanding : Paul was sleeping away from me, and I kept having such nightmares.
We were unhappy. I didn't want to be a cabbage-wife,
a back-yard wife. I thought, a relation like ours can't
be broken up so soon, so someone must make an experiment, and it had better be me than Paul. A man can
never remember he is making an experiment. As soon
as he loves another woman physically, he thinks he is
head over heels in love, and he will throw everything
away for her. Women have a more practical sense, a
more cynical sense of human relations. They know
nothing is worth all that bother.

' So I decided when the time came to make an experiment. I came away with Oliver. I am very fond of
him too. You can all see he has charm : no one is
asking himself or herself why I went away with him.
But it is not just charm I was looking for, it was—a
new life, a bath of the soul. I thought his charm and
love would act like cold cream, and his inexperience like
an astringent, and give me a new skin, take away my
mental wrinkles. Well, I find there is no such thing as
a spiritual renaissance, at least not for a woman. We
are too much nailed to a coffin of flesh, our souls are only
plants, they are rooted in an earth of flesh. We need
a home, security, comfort for our flesh before the mind
can grow. That is because we are the carriers of life. . . .'

Oliver listened to her simple pomp with smiling, Paul

with disillusioned, eyes. 'But in a sense, he made me creative!' She laughed. Everyone else looked askew. She went on, like a woman talking in the dark. . . . 'I have life in me now: I must think not of myself, or Paul or him, but of the future. Paul and I have a home, Oliver has no home. He wants to go somewhere out to the colonies or something of the sort and make a home. How can I, in my condition? I need peace. I have had to make too many decisions: it is not good. I should be resting. . . .'

Paul broke out impatiently: 'Elvira, what are you going to do?'

'You are not really sympathetic with my problem. It is very distasteful to have to explain oneself to people to whom explanations are a burden. You think me slow—life has frightened me. I have tried to think things out, but I need more patience than other people. I am ankylosed. You have all had your part in making me like that.'

She was ruffled: she had been avoiding the issue, complacently spreading herself out over her speech. She had two vermouths before her, and, they could see, would go on mildly eating and drinking and prolonging her navel-philosophy for a week. Sara's eyes did not recover from their startled, measuring look, but a sort of calculation had crept into them too: she looked from Paul to Elvira, stole a glance at Oliver and back to Paul. She quietly detailed all of Paul's attitudes.

At this moment Blanche d'Anizy strolled on to the terrace, and came up, impudently but gracefully intrusive.

'The whole family united! A domestic League of Nations. What are you going to do, Elvira, at last? Have you finally made up your mind? Come, I won't bother you: you have so much to talk about. *A bientôt!*'

She rejoined her men-friends in the corner, and amused, curious glances were directed at them.

' Let's get out of this,' said Adam. ' Where'll we go to lunch? Or rather, I'm going to take Sara to lunch, and you three can have lunch together.'

They paid, and the three fateful ones walked towards Montparnasse. Elvira seemed happy between her two men : she was gay with her vermouths and teased them both about their position in an outrageous manner. Both men were quiet, but Oliver fell lightly into line and began to tease her again. They went to an Italian restaurant in the rue de Montparnasse and sat at a table upstairs. The sunlight fell on the houses opposite, sparrows were building, the sun fell on the artificial roses in the vase and on the Chianti Paul had ordered. Elvira warmed up.

' It's pleasant like this : I wish we could live like this. Why can't we ? All three. If you love me, Paul, you ought to have something in common with Oliver. There must be something in common between you. Even if it's only —— ' She made an obscene remark, excited by their rivalry.

' If two children grab for one cake, they're close friends, I suppose,' commented Oliver. Paul was silent.

' They are closer friends than before,' said Elvira, ' because it never occurs to them there are other cakes in the world, it's just a passion for the one.' Her security and impudence gave her beauty a sparkle of independence. The looks of the men crossed.

' One of you has to lose me,' she answered simply : ' if you both really loved me, you'd give my plan a trial.' Her eyes, growing roots of seduction, sucked in their breaths, her prolific ego, masked in pathos, had them in its tendrils. Her eyes almost dropped a tear. ' I am all alone. How can I decide for you ? Haven't either of you any will-power ? '

' There is something in what you say,' put in Paul at last. ' But I can't do it. You must make up your mind.'

Oliver remarked :

'To me the world presents itself as a series of affirmations, my will is always decided. To you it must be odd, Elvira : you see an endless series of switches, you are a rogue-train careering over a universe of rails with no one at the signals. Now here are two signal-men : here is your chance.' He turned laughing to Paul. 'Like the old grandfather, when conscription was brought in in the last war. The mother and father came running to him : Father, what shall we do ? Bobby will perhaps be conscripted. How can we get him out of it ? The old man said, Calm, my children : it's a question of probabilities : it is all laid out before you in a comforting set of alternatives. Either Bob will be conscripted or he won't, one of the two. If he is conscripted, either he will stay here or he will go to the war, one of the two. At the war, either he will be wounded or he won't, one of the two. If he is wounded, either he will die or he won't, one of the two. If he dies, either he will go to heaven or hell, one of the two. If he goes to hell, either the devil takes graft or —but of course, the devil takes graft, like us men, and the stoniest conscription officer takes graft, so what is there to worry about ? ' He laughed. Elvira looked at him with gloomy eyes.

'And so one of you will take graft?' enquired Elvira.

'Why not : you, Elvira, will shortly pay a dividend, that is, have a child : one of us will hand in the coupon : if you choose Paul, you get back your old home, appur-tenances and income : if you choose me, I will benefit by your yearly income of £200—you can keep the wolf from the door while I pay a dividend out of books by writing another. . . .'

Paul murmured : 'You have a good business head : you ought to go into finance ! '

Oliver laughed. 'Elvira was planning the other day to get you to place me in the City. She has a head on her. Seriously, though, I should like it. What profits can books really pay? I am sick of them. I want to get my hands on sealing-wax, cabbages, coupons, bread, something solid: I'd like to go into commodity-broking. . . .'

Paul stirred himself to be polite and give the young man advice. Elvira listened intently. When the coffee came they both fell silent and looked at her. She had refused most of her lunch, suffering from indigestion. She saw them looking at her, and put her hands over her face. When she took them away, her great long-lashed eyes were full of tears.

'I am so weak,' she said. 'I love you both: I am cruel because weak. Another woman would have made up her mind long, long ago. I am heart-broken because of all the trouble I have caused you both. Forgive me when you can.'

'So, Elvira . . .'

'I am so sick,' she said. 'The child has decided: it is you, Oliver.'

Paul counted the money out of his wallet, his large hand shaking slightly.

'I'm glad it's decided,' he said. 'I'll go down town, get my business done, and we'll catch the night train via Dieppe. I'll ask Sara if she minds. I don't want to stay another night in this town.'

Elvira asked: 'Is Sara going back with you?'

'She came for me.'

Elvira shrugged her shoulders and got up lazily from the table. She pulled on her little new gloves, which Paul had bought for her that morning, smoothed them, and looking sarcastically at Paul, remarked:

'I see you will console yourself: as well I didn't choose the other way.' She laughed at Oliver. 'You call women a trade union: it's a trade union where everyone is watching for the other's job.' To Paul's pale protesting face she laughed: 'Don't make those big O-eyes, Paul: I see as far as a bat. What do you bet your " distant cousin " doesn't return home to her greasy pots and sandwich-cutting so fast ? ' She gurgled at all her jokes.

Outside Paul raised his hat, saying, ' I'll get in touch with you this afternoon,' and strode stormily down the street.

Oliver put Elvira into a taxi, laughing. ' You are a little devil ! '

' You don't half know me,' she threatened. ' I'll lead you a life.'

They went straight home. In the taxi he said : ' I believe you intended to stay with me all along.'

' I don't know : but when I saw Sara hanging round him and the understanding that existed between them, I said to myself, if he is substituting so easily, it is all over between us. Who wants to sleep at night with a corpse ? '

' Perhaps you're mistaken.'

' I'm not : he doesn't know it yet, perhaps : he's too devoted to me still, after all. But she knows it. She's a thirty-year-old virgin : they're awake to any man. And then I know what he likes, quiet, peace, a pastoral view.'

She said : ' Listen, let's go to his hotel. No, we'll drive home, and I'll send him a note. No, wait, I'll write to Mary first and tell her to pack up all my things, my linen, the summer curtains, a basket of old linen I have—I'll need it. I'll tell her to send it on.'

' Why, we'll get everything we need for our home, dear.'

' No : these are mine. Why shouldn't I have them ? They cost enough to replace, and we ought to economise if we're going to set up house. It costs enough. I know : you don't—yet. Then I'll write to Paul, asking him to send the things on. We'll put them in storage until we get a proper home. No : we'll put them in storage in London. I'll write to a friend of mine—you know, Bessie, who just got married. She can keep them for me in her cellar.'

'Why, dear, leave them in Mecklenburgh Square till we go back to London.'

'No, I want it all cleared up : nothing left behind. And there's no reason why his new consoler should be fussing round with my things.'

'You women with your darling rags.'

'Nonsense, you men don't know the value of such things : you don't need them. We need ironing-sheets, dusters, silver-cloths, old linen for wounds, old towels for cold-cream. . . .'

He stopped up his ears.

'Have them, have them all!'

They both laughed.

'Ye gods, a woman is property incarnate.'

'Oh, we are of the earth, earthy.'

He laughed at her and held both her hands. 'Earthy little hands : then I'll give you all the property you can grasp : you shall have everything you want, stuff, rags, towels, dresses, silver, rings, carpets, furniture. I'll keep on piling up property, and you can sit happily, in Nirvana, on top of everything, queen of the Great Heap. I will, I will, I promise. I'll devote my life, you ravishing mercenary, to piling up property for you. There, does that make you happy?'

'It really does,' she said. 'I love things I can touch. I am realist.'

They laughed all the way home, and she was very happy all the evening with the vast fantasia of property he spun for her amusement. She said, at the end : 'It's wonderful how you understand me : Paul never understood me. He made some mossy ideal out of me, a mossy dead woman like that statue we saw in the Beaux-Arts, a cabbage. To you, I am just a human being. I like that. There are no disappointments, just a gradual understanding. You understand women well for a young man : you must have had a lot.'

'You wouldn't be pleased if I said you were the first.'

'No. Tell me about the others.'

He teased her, telling innumerable tales of flirtations, crushes, adorations, student friendships, casual unions. She listened to him with more tenderness and respect than before.

'And is that all? You can't think of just another little one or two? It's such a few, a mere twenty or so.'

'That's all, and now fidelity, world without end, amen.'

'And you've said that before!'

'I may have said it before.'

'Well—after all—Paul kept himself pure, as he said, till he married me. Imagine it!' she said with spite. 'He promised his mother. She died when he was fourteen. That's why he's so clumsy. Imagine a sawbones' apprentice with those ideals!' She lay back across the bed, and shrieked with laughter. She got up, saying: 'Look, why should I write letters? I hate writing letters about a dead horse: I'll go to Paul's hotel now and see him and tell him to send me all those things. I'll tell Sara to see to the packing of them. She'll see that she won't walk into my slippers.' She was putting on the rouge Oliver had bought her. 'Gosh, don't I look waxy? And I feel so sick. I think I'll drop in and see Blanche on the way back. You don't mind if I'm not home to supper, do you? You have something to eat somewhere, and after meet me at home, at ten o'clock. We'll go to bed early. I'm dead tired.'

'As long as you really come home,' said Oliver with some bitterness.

'Of course I will.'

'You were with Paul last night?'

'I was. I had to make up my mind. But I did, didn't I? This is the last time. You'll do that, Oliver, for me. Now I must go and see her: I want to frighten her. I can't bear the thought of her sleeping even one night in my sheets.'

'Hold your horses,' protested Oliver. 'You're miles ahead of the procession.'

' Then if she has any delicacy, she'll lie on the floor rather than use them,' concluded Elvira. ' As for you, I have a nose, Oliver. I'm quiet, but the bystander sees most of the fun. Leave it to me. Good-bye.' She kissed him on the forehead. ' Ten o'clock at home. They're catching the night train : they'll be gone by then. Then,' she said, unconsciously repeating one of his frequent phrases, ' our life begins.'

She moved out with the dignity of her yet-distant embonpoint. He darted after her, drew her face backwards and kissed the swelling lips.

' That's right, dearest : see Blanche. I want you to be well a little while yet. Then, when we get back to England, we start everything right.' She had a ringing laugh. ' Everything seems so easy now.'

He went back to unpacking his books, and loitered over his pile of manuscripts and his manuscript book of poems—

> John Slob, Tom Nod, Bert Snub, Gabriel Grad,
> Formed in antenatal mud,
> Four fleshes, four ideas incarned,
> Flipflop, hobnob, snipsnap, gidgad.

or ' Imitation of Eliot imitating Laforgue with Morgue '—
AM I HAMLET ?

Avete una guida delle strade per Roma e suoi dintorni ?
(Italian.)

> The empty tables stood, for never guests
> Came there, except the bankrupts whom distress
> Spurr'd on. (*Pharonnida*, B. iv. c. iii. p. 53.)

> Pois, sunt turnet Baivier e Aleman
> E Peitevin e Bretun e Norman.
> Sur tuz les altres l'unt otriet li Franc
> Que Guenes moerget par verveillus ahan.
> (*Chanson de Roland*, cccxix. l. 3960.)

> O, *Todd* !   Ich kenns, das ist mein Famulus.
> (*Der Urfaust*, l. 168.)

Debitor non praesumitur donare !   (Latin.)

The poem (enfin !) :

The gelignite and marmorite, Blest office of the Hippocrene,
Invaletudinarians roll, Their double spheres across the
  green.
The hippocratic surrogate, Neat's-leather neat, and black
  cravat,
Walks from the hips, and often lifts, With simple elegance
  his hat.

Oliver could no longer contain himself, and set out
hotfoot, manuscripts and all in a roll, for Coromandel's
house. He went up to the third floor as before, and
was instantly admitted by a small good-looking maid.
When Coromandel appeared, they went straight to the
chart-room, which, it seemed agreed, was their play-
room, and seating her on the divan beside him, he began
reading the most sonorous and luscious of his poems,
occasionally putting a hand on her leg, saying : 'Now
I don't know whether you can take this. . . . Tell me
if it's too much for you :

> 'Weailala ! Weailala ! Wawa, quack, quack :
> The splashing couriers of war,
> Through thirteen bloody floods a year
> Bring fainting victory on their back : . . . '

Coromandel grinned faintly as he read on. He stopped
suddenly, panting for praise.
'What did you think of it ? Some of it was a bit
forcible, eh ? ' He swallowed her praises, sensitive to
all her qualifications. He said pettishly : 'Not one
word of it means anything to Elvira.'
'Elvira ? '
'A woman I know in England.'
'Oh ! ' She didn't believe him. It didn't matter to
either of them. 'Let's go out,' she said later. 'It's
night.'
He hesitated.
'I have to be home at ten. A chap . . .'
'All right, but somewhere over near the Halles : I

don't know that quarter : I've spent the whole time on
the Left Bank.'

Coromandel went down wearing a large hat which
obtruded her pose upon Oliver. She repelled him by
her mannerisms, dominated him by her wilfulness.

They walked towards the rue Dauphiné, reached the
banks of the river again, and so on across the river and
across the court of Notre-Dame de Paris. It was now
full night : out of one of the smoking turrets of that
hill of stones rose a white moon, baleful, full of sorcery,
turning into a fabulous ruin the columns and flying
buttresses. They passed behind this ruin, the garden of
the fountain and the débris of gargoyles : so to the Île
Saint-Louis and back by the new bridge of Sainte-
Geneviève, past the wine market to the ancient seat of
the University of Paris. Oliver drew closer irresistibly
to the rue Thouin, in which his apartment with Elvira
was. He looked up from rue Thouin and saw a light
in their apartment. At the same moment Elvira came
to the open window, and behind her Paul : they were
waiting for him. What now ? Oliver laughed low,
rebelliously, clutched Coromandel's arm. They turned
about and walked down by the École Polytechnique
to the river again. Coromandel said :

' The couples in furnished rooms on a hot night filling
an hour or two with talk till they can go to bed together—
it's romantic, isn't it ? I like these warm nights, when
all these intimacies flower along the footpaths, don't
you ? I like love, I like to see it : I feel happy every
time I see a woman embraced.'

Oliver was silent. She looked at him in surprise.

The criss-crossing bridges between the islands were
dark, silent, cool, and often traversed by soft-footed,
low-voiced lovers enlaced and stopping to kiss every
few footfalls. In a grand house at the apex of the Île
Saint-Louis, where they came once more, two negresses
from the southern states of the U.S.A., turbanned,
dressed in red and blue, sang from the window of the

servants' room. In another room, the masters picked
small bones off porcelain under candles too rare for the
old-fashioned space of the eight walls ; shadows chased
each other over the painted clouds on the ceiling. The
willows meditated over the river ; the water sounded
on the moored barges. They looked back to the lights
of central Paris and at the Louvre, a great forecastle
sliding across the lights of the Place de la Concorde.
They passed the ' street of the Woman without a Head '
(now the ' rue Le Regrattier '). Oliver's voice began
in the living dark, peopled by street lamps and high
walls as they passed palaces and hotels made foetid
by the traffic of centuries ; his voice was dry and
crackling.

' Every woman is the headless woman : we love the
Venus without an arm, the leaf-winged hamadryad,
the mermaid with only a tail, a torso without any limbs
or head, but never without breasts. We are suckling
babes, in fact : the bosom is everything. In that respect,
you are the perfection of woman.'

Coromandel drooped.

' You treasure yourself as a sculptor his model : every
muscle you have ripples towards the perfecting of your
body.'

She withdrew her hand angrily from him. ' I don't
care for my body.'

She laughed. ' You men ! We suffer universally
from an unbearable ambition. That's all. You're so
smug, smirking there,' she flung at him violently.

Oliver looked pale. ' Then why haven't they ever
done anything in the world's history ? You can't explain
that away.'

She caught hold of him. ' Oh, I could break your
arm, I could choke you. Look at the vanity ! Why
hasn't the plebs done anything in the world's history ?
Because they're weak, vain, and sensual too, I suppose.'

Oliver was silent and uneasy. Then curiosity overtook
him again. He said :

'You said you would tell me about your mother and the hamadryad and the rest.'

'My mother has lived for at least ten years in the double room behind the chart-room which overlooks the rue Cardinale. She looks all the evening out of one of the windows, gibbering to herself in a querulous way about us all, about old friends we have never known, probably about people she only dreams about. You hear all day and half the night that she is having a conversation with herself, a sibilant complaint. " She—she —she said—what does she know ?—what do they know about anything ?—what is it all about ?—he—he—he runs and acts and shows and sells and arranges—what does he know ?—what will they do next ?—when will she marry ?—she is stuck-up !—he is a fool !—I said to them, It's very nice for a daughter to visit on Sundays —a little servant, a butler with good manners—some people are rich, some poor, so the world is, no justice done : some people work, some people swindle, if I'd had sense I should have swindled too and had a country house with servants—here I sit alone and she—she and he—he . . ." So she murmurs to herself all day. There is a balcony along the street. She has been dying to have a balcony like that for years, and made the architects come once. She wants to have a window-garden and water the flowers, to be seen by the street, busy watering her flowers. Isn't it pathetic, odd ? She is always dressing her hair, getting herself up ; she's ingenious too, can produce whole historical characters out of a veil, a ribbon, an ear-ring and a swathed silk curtain. She works embroideries for herself at the open windows, all dressed up with posies in her looped hair. She often has a sort of dazed beauty of preoccupied insanity and simplicity, like a very young girl, dreaming of Mimi or Manon Lescaut. She has a little allowance of her own, and cooks her own food, convinced that we would try to poison her or palm off second-rate bits on her, mask bad food with sauces and so forth. And the old woman you saw, my nurse, has to eat with her. The only person who can put up with her rigmaroles, and who visits her, is an old oil-painter who can never finish a picture. He has been working and working ever since we've known him, but he's never sold anything but sketches that friends have stolen from him and sold for him. He cries when anything is taken from him : that if they had only left it a day more he would have put the finishing touch to it, or removed some blemish. If anyone writes to congratulate him, he recoils, in anger, thinks their compliments are taunts and that they are really gloating over the faults in the picture. A most uneasy professional conscience, a little weakness. Otherwise he is quite sane, and he is very sorry for my mother. My mother's will is in his favour ! Oh, it's very little : we wouldn't even contest it. Mother's convinced that if she had met this painter before father she would have been happy all her life. She often murmurs to herself, " If only I had met him when I was a young girl ! Oh, miserable, miserable my life has been ! I met him too late ! " She's mistaken, of course : father's always been good to her, but she doesn't recognise it.

' She says I'm not her daughter. You should see her at close quarters : she is quite like me ! During a girl-hood illness she read one of Gautier's tales, and she now pretends that father begot me with the hamadryad in the salon. It is true my father has a great love for the statue ; but it is beautiful. There's another reason too : she always wanted a daughter who would darn stockings with her, and tell her jokes and scandals and count the nine-months of all the pregnant women with her. She hates brains : she calls them " snobbery." She just looks at my father and me and mutters, " Yes, yes, I'm always wrong. I'm never right : other people are always right." When I was a little girl she used to cry, and tell father and me to go and live by ourselves : we didn't want her, she was in the way. Then she began

living apart in the same house.   But she's really a gentle,
timid woman, and the real reason is quite another one.'

The Story of the Hamadryad

'Have you seen the antiquities shop in the rue Jacob,
a little way along from the rue de Furstemberg—it
specialises in Chinese jade, ebony, lacquer, silks, ivories ?
It's kept by an old friend of father's, Madame Cecilia
Laminche. She was born in the rue de l'Esprit des Lois,
in Bordeaux, that bizarre city set down among sand-
dunes under a tomato sun, where the squat fantastic
water-line, with barges, bridges, bonds, quays and
quincuncial gardens, bears against thick neutral skies
the colours of a faded tapestry. The stinking gutters
of its aged streets, joined to the sweat of citizens and
wine-barrels, sends a vast heady incense into the nostrils
of the long-whiskered sun. The steaming town blackens
your skin and cures your heart, so that it hangs afterwards like a redolent ham in your breast, nostalgic,
penetrated with Bordeaux. Cecilia lived there, a dark
brown, stout-built, inquisitive little girl, with an inflamed
love of the theatre of life, domestic dramas, the mass,
the street, the quays, the theatre, Paris. She dreamed of
three things principally, her first communion, a lover,
her first appearance on the stage of the Bordeaux Opera
as Carmen. She was a Carmen. She looked like fifteen
at eleven, and the men ran after her. At thirteen she
kept shop and helped cook for a middle-aged widower,
a second-hand dealer. At night she went to her grandmother's home, a room in the eaves of a fourteenth-
century house. Mosquitoes went mad with their singing in the rafters. She leaned out of the unglassed
window and looked down at the whole city to the south
with her enraptured, romantic, but experienced eyes.
When her grandmother died, and she was fourteen, she
slept at her work, in a closet where rats ran amongst
packing-cases, cloths and papers. The old brocanteur

tried to make love to her, but took his defeat in good part.

In the shop was that very hamadryad you saw. Cecilia admired it wonderfully, with its green eyes, and used to press her bosom into its hard chest with passion. In her mind there was quite a long history of daily passions, intercourse and domestic discussion between her and the various beautiful objects in the shop : but for the hamadryad she had that homosexual passion, filled with pure and divine fire, that young girls often have at that age. In the evenings, between seven and eight, when the brocanteur was supping, she would often run down to a bar near at hand for a glass of coffee, a coffee cognac or a glass of white wine, which the proprietor gave her, exceptionally—a sort of investment. He hoped she would leave the second-hand dealer and come and work in his shop. There was a little dance-hall behind the shop where poor workers, sailors, petty criminals and youths looking for a pick-up danced with poor work-girls and whores for ten centimes a person, per dance. Cecilia, working there, would bring in business and keep up the tone of the place, because she was straight as well as handsome. One of the waiters in the café was a very tall, very beautiful southern brunet, who, in between his hours of service, was to be seen, smartly and flashily turned out, on the streets, watching the girls who worked for him. He was not at all lazy : he was a smart waiter, if a little too proud, and he kept four or five pretty, smart, young girls working for him on the streets. He was kind but firm with them, and never forgave lost business, stupidity or slack dressing. When they got older he turned them out. He got them customers in the café, and, it was said, had his savings in Government bonds. He hoped to marry, buy a house of rendezvous, run it up, and gradually accumulate a lot of money.

He had his eye on Cecilia, but treated her with the utmost indifference : scarcely seemed to see her. He

was very much run after by ambitious girls with " class."
He always let the girl make the first step. She used to
stand there joking every night with the boss and his
wife, with the other waiter and the customers, making
tart or sweet replies, her centipede tongue never still.
One night, after a clever retort, André turned and looked
her over particularly. She slapped his face. " I am too
fine a fish for you ! I am going to have a career—in
Paris, for example." He stared still with his dominant
stare, and then faintly shrugged one shoulder. The
next day they crossed each other, walking sprightly in
opposite directions. He was polite to her. She said,
smiling : " I like you, André : I always did. But I'm
going to make a good marriage and go on the stage :
you're no good to me."

" You'll come round to me ! "

" Never. I'm going to strike some good luck one
day."

" You're well-made and pretty : but the trees are full
of such birds. To bring a good price, they have to be
caught and put up for sale."

She read books of poetry and learned passages of
Racine by heart, and declaimed them to herself over her
work. André even courted her by hanging about the
shop with a disdainful air, and walking past her with
one or other of the prettiest of his girls. She began to
fall in love with him, and was wretched. Then he asked
her to go and live with him in the couple of rooms he
had. The next day, one of André's girls came and told
her she would throw vitriol over her if she dared to go
and live with him. Cecilia wanted a lover badly, but
she realised that she would be on a footing with these
girls and have to work for him. She found him outside
the shop when they put up the shutters at mid-day for
the usual siesta.

" Well, bring your traps over now : I'll get a boy to
help you."

He was much too grand to carry anything himself.

" Who told you I was coming ? "

André darkened and stepped up to her.

" You must come now : I'm expecting you."

" I've changed my mind. I wanted love. I won't
be your victim. You're good-looking, caressing when
you want to be, and I was weak, as girls are. I don't
mind telling you I was weak, because now I've thought
out what I must do. You are a servile soul, and I am
a free soul. I will never love a base man ; I can only
love a noble man, and when I find one I'll marry him.
I can't smirch myself with ignoble amours."

André took his hands out of his pockets.

" You've been reading some novelette. Wake up,
canary-brained woman : put yourself in my hands, little
darling, and you'll have a great future. You're an ambitious girl. There's nothing you can't do. And I know
women."

He put his hands on her shoulders and drew her to
him. Her forehead only reached the V of his waistcoat
still : he caressed her.

" There, you're going to be André's girl. I'll buy
you a pretty dress to-morrow : you won't know yourself. I'll mould you from the beginning : you come to
me fresh. That's real luck for you."

She laughed stridently as she drew away.

" You're ridiculous, André. You only know the
flimsy sort of girl. You'd better start on your way.
Mine's in the opposite direction. I'm just glad I knew
you, that's all : it's a warning. You're a signpost, tall
enough to be one. I don't want to quarrel with you,
André. In me there's something that likes you very
much : when I think of you I think of your fine skin,
your shapely naked arms full of muscles, and your
naked chest, like a bronze shield. I dreamed one night
we were kissing each other naked, leaning against a
balustrade overlooking a dark pool under an immensely
high and dark dome, in which one beam of light dropped
slow drops into the pool. I've loved you ever since.

But I know you don't ever feel as you did in my dream. So I'm going to take my time and look around until I find someone who does, even if it isn't you."

He threw away the cigarette he had started to smoke.

" I do feel like that. I'm crazy about women : I go mad nearly when I see a beautiful woman I can't get near and talk to. I dream about them, too : marvellous dreams. I only go to sleep to dream about them. But I don't dream about them in the daytime. They're not so good-looking then, and then I have my work to do. You're throwing away a good chance. You think you'll get on : but you'll stay here drudging for Turnèbe : one day he'll get you, or some other trash ; and then you're done for. You'll think of me with regret. But I don't ask girls twice. I've bothered too much about you. Your head's turned. You know my address."

He went off. The next day she was walking along the Cours de l'Intendance at lunch-time. Everything was shut, the restaurants smelt of gras-double, the streets were an oven, all was blanched. She was crying over André, when she saw walking before her a tall, bare-headed youth in a long black Spanish mantle. With him was a white-haired man, elegantly dressed, who seemed to be his companion or tutor. She thought, " A Spanish prince." She crossed the street to look at the youth, whose cloak was fastened with a jewelled buckle, and whose small, bloodless, emaciated face, with its indifferent eyes, curling lip, and faint sneer of vanity, was, as it were, buckled with a prepossessing Roman nose. The old man kept talking and using his hands with restrained, fragile gestures, and looked on the ground as he walked. The youth kept up a super-cilious inattention, and took in thousands of details of the street, sky, shops, people they passed, it seemed, with his pale eye : it looked as if he was bent on making an inventory of Bordeaux and was perfectly deaf to the older man.

Cecilia, with a splendid walk, which she had spent

years developing, her bust always carried in advance,
her eyes and nostrils throwing darts at the couple, kept
up an even pace on the opposite pavement. The youth
presently made her a sign to drop behind them, and
after a quarter of an hour gave his tutor the slip, while
he was in a *vespasienne*. He took her to a café Cecilia
had never seen, and made an appointment with her for
ten o'clock on the same evening down by the docks.
He was an expert, hurried, but more gallant than André.
In his overcoat and felt hat he looked no different from
the thin pale youths of the town ; but he had an exceed-
ingly elegant French accent, that assumed by the nobility
and extra-rich, which sounds foreign, and is intended
to make them foreigners, indeed, to the common people.
They walked a little way under the dull sky, and then
turned up towards the residential district. The youth
murmured, "I have a friend who will lend me his
apartment : there is a side-door. Let's go quickly."

Cecilia recited a line of Racine :

"Dans quel trouble, Seigneur, jetez-vous mon esprit ! "

The boy glanced at her with authority.
" You know me, then ? "
She laughed again and recited :

"Rien ne peut-il, Seigneur, changer votre entreprise ? "

"What are you talking about ? " asked the boy
haughtily. "Although a prince, I'm not rich : I have
a mean allowance. Let's drop the milord : it's bad for
pleasure, bad for friendship, bad for settling accounts.
For all you know, I'm a poor Bourse-runner spending
the evening with the first Venus of the streets. Come,
dear little chicken, give me a good time : I've had a
wretched day. My tutor talking all day, my head aching,
neuralgia everywhere, lying down all the afternoon
because my medicine upset me : it's against anaemia
and ten times too strong. I'm delicate. Come, be
kind to me. To-morrow, if I can get off, and if you

have a pretty dress, I'll take you to a charming restaurant, full of fun. You'll regret nothing."

She freed her arm and ran her fingers through the black hair that the river breeze had loosened. " I believe you're a prince incognito : you look like one. You must believe me : I look like what I am. I am a virgin, and I go to no little room. I will go to the restaurant with you to-morrow, and if you can win me you can have me. But you must really make love to me. I want it so badly, to have someone really make love to me. And I am worth it ! Look at my form ! I know Racine ! I am going to Paris. You are like André, but better than him, although not so handsome. You are rich, elegant, and you are a prince. Will you do it ? But I won't yield unless you do well : unless you have so much fire that I turn to wax."

The youth had stopped in the street, and was looking her over in confusion. He half-turned to leave her.

She began to recite again :

"Ah! Ciel! quel adieu! quel langage!
    Prince, vous vous troublez et changez de visage!"

He turned back again, with decision.

"All right : I think you're a little hothead, and I don't know that I can trust you, but if you like play-acting, we'll play-act. How many nights must I work at this ? "

" It will be as short as your compliments are long."

He took her hand and placed it over his heart, breathing unequally.

"Feel how it beats ! I can't stand much excitement. I am delicate : I am of blood too refined : be kind to me."

He escaped night after night to meet her, and, to meet her play-acting pose, was himself fantastic. One night he brought her a pair of black morocco buskins, his long cloak and a parcel of gross-false pearls, at two francs a string, the whole stock of a peddler. When

she had put them on he took a taxi and drove to the
deserted banks on the other side of the Garonne : when
the wind blew the cloak she was one of the jagged moony
clouds that thickened the whole sky that night.   They
drifted along the river-bank together, exalted with the
long whetting of their desires.   In the taxi she threw
herself round his neck in a frenzy of excitement, but
he sat upright moodily, smoothing her hair.   Then he
said :

"My tutor has wind of an affair : I have to go to
Paris to-morrow."

"Don't go : I can't bear it."

"You must come after me : I'll manage to send you
two hundred francs to-morrow and give you an address.
You must come to Paris.   You want to, anyhow."

The next day a young man entered the shop, bought
the hamadryad, paid for it, slipping the girl two hundred
francs too much, and addressed the parcel to a Paris
address, which the girl copied.

Her fleeting notions of a splendid life with a rich and
romantic lover were dissipated during her first few days
in Paris.   She walked all over the city on foot, and
found that although the youthful opulence of her
southern beauty attracted attention, she was only one
of thousands of beauties.   She went to the address
named, was not admitted, wrote a note with her address,
but in guarded terms, and the next day received the
hamadryad with the receipted bill, on the back of which
were the words "This business is concluded."   After
crying her eyes out and looking sombrely at the Seine
for a night, she took the statue to Monsieur Laminche,
who was then, as now, in the rue Jacob.   He bought
it, took her into his service, ended by marrying her.
Father saw her when she was much younger, about
fifteen years ago, and fell in love with her.   Mother
discovered the amourette through her maid, and they
had to end their friendship.   But she gave him the
hamadryad, saying that he was her only true love.

She got into touch with André again about five years ago. He appeared to be courting her for a while. The husband, old Laminche, was trying to spy on their conversation one day as they stood outside the shop discussing the arrangement of the window. He fell out of the window, broke his head and died. Since then, Madame Cecilia carries on the business most successfully herself, and as a thriving side-line has gone into the white-slave trade to Buenos Ayres with André. They are making plenty of money. She's in all that shady sort of business. The profits are big, but the hand-outs are big too. Imagine that she tried to inveigle me into joining one of her little ocean trips ! Her mind's a bit unsettled now, and she is unreasonably jealous of mother. I suppose she and father really loved each other. Mother is madly jealous of the hamadryad, and long ago took out its green eyes, which she had secreted.'

They had come back to the rue Jacob. Oliver stood looking up at the dark-shuttered shop and at the curled clouds over the eaves.

' Romance justifies us,' he said. ' Otherwise our friendship would seem lunatic.'

' Nothing is lunatic in this world : everything happens,' said Coromandel. The belfries rang out ten o'clock. As they were saying good-night, a window opened upstairs and someone called Coromandel. They looked up and saw her mother, with her hair in a two-horned coiffe, leaning out of a third-floor window.

' Coro ! Coro !' said the surcharged, slow voice. 'Bring him up : I wish to see your friend.'

' Come up,' said Coro, ' just for a minute. You have no idea how persistent she is. You don't mind ? '

When Coro opened the door the mother was already there, standing in the salon, in a blue velvet dress with a silver-tasselled girdle. She looked at Oliver, with a slow, pleased parting of the lips, and at her daughter.

' I like you, young man : you may come again. I

know character, I know character. If it had been left
to me to pick, I should never have picked the wrong
one.' She smiled with ceremonial sweetness, and put
out her blanched hand. 'Come to tea: at five—one
day. Just knock at the door and come to see me in my
apartment.' She nodded graciously to them and went
out.

'Take no notice: she will forget by to-morrow,'
said Coromandel, as she shut the door.

Oliver, fresh with his adventure, went merrily to the
Latin Quarter, his poems under his arm. If there were
any constraint he would read the blessed poems and
oust any memories of Paul. But he found Marpurgo
there, playing his game, and Paul and Adam at hand.
Elvira explained : 'They all came to take us out. Paul is
going to-morrow. They've gone to telephone Sara.'
Marpurgo chaffed Elvira.

'Still wavering, but deeper in quality, still melancholy
but with more rhythmus, still quaquaversal but swinging more and more due north, our lady Aeneas, per-
fidious but pious to herself!' He lifted his pear-shaped
hand in an unconscious gesture of worship, the worship
of such a wonderful subject for his biped analysis. 'If
you wait one more night, Oliver, the lady will be with
you.'

Oliver struck the table with medium violence.

'Another night—again!'

Her soft voice developed in the warm air.

'I'm not very well. I have to have my mind at rest.
There is so much to go over with Paul. After all, we
were married ten years ; you can't cut the tissues so
fast. You have to beware of gangrene.'

Oliver sank on to the divan, stupefied : 'Elvira, you're
not real ! Do you care so much for Paul's feelings and
not for mine ? '

'You are going to have me always,' she reproved him.
'Paul is innocent.'

Marpurgo's giggle : 'And the cousin is still there.'

She looked at him, smiling bitterly over her cigarette smoke.

'Marpurgo, you're so damned clever that someone will murder you one day.'

He whinnied, and his blue eyes opened with a flash of light: his eyes were as sapphires secreted in the crevices between dark brow and high cheekbone. He rocked to and fro slightly for a moment, as if getting up an interior incantation, and with a pointed smile, cried in his cracked voice:

'Eh! Eh! The unconscious wish. Hi! Hi! She's a jelly of sour passions: make her burn, Oliver, and she'll regenerate.' He leaned forward and said almost in a whisper: 'You know, she is wonderful, the uncanny stirring silence of the zero hour. This is a crucial night for you both.' He lifted his finger 'To-night she makes a decision, and the rest of your days follow. Be kind, Elvira: no, I must call you Melanchtha.' Elvira laughed from the depths of her flattered content. 'You see,' continued Marpurgo, 'lambent melancholy, a living body of melaphyre, that is black-curtained porphyry.' He began to sing:

> 'She is cold fire like the moon,
> In reeking spirals his wits turn:
> They will marry very soon—
> Will she smother or he burn?'

He rapped smartly on the table with his signet-ring and straightened his back, smiling at them with the first human expression of the evening. His performance was over. He finished his brandy: 'Enjoy yourselves, children.' He leaned over, smiling with bonhomie. 'Avoid Paul altogether: Paul is the rocky spit which separates the sweet confluent salt of the waves: they bite at it until they are high enough to leap over. The tide's in now, isn't it?' He nodded, nodded. 'Now, I'm leaving you. Be unkind to Paul and kind to everyone: it's the last unkind action you'll ever have to do. Now, I'm to my club: I must beat that Russian girl.'

'So that's what you've been working yourself up for?'
There was the usual disdain in Elvira's voice.

'Practising cabala at the caballine spring within.'

He raised his hat with affectation and hoppled away.
Outside he met Paul and Adam. He shook hands
warmly, and coming in close to their waistcoats, advised:

'Gunther, go yourself and snatch Brunhild from the
flames of Siegfried-adulterous.' He coughed violently
till they both looked concerned. He gasped: 'I've
been trying on Elvira that sub-innuendo which women
work themselves and understand. The little pulmonary
lesion is not second sight, but it's often the eye of
subtlety: women themselves suffer from a perpetual
little lesion in morale, essential to race-perpetuation.
I like to do my little good deed, even if it's apo-
pemptic. Take her back and save her a lot of trouble.'
He saluted them and plip-plapped off, remarking as he
passed Adam: 'Adam Cupid, I see.'

'That man's a genius,' said Paul earnestly. 'Or else
it's the fever of his complaint. I've never seen such a
subtle man. You can always tell by the eyes—that
glitter.'

'Fever, malice and play-acting; that's the long and
short of him,' was Adam's conclusion.

He turned to go into the house and found Marpurgo
back at his elbow. Marpurgo smiled brightly at him and
said, 'Do you mind, Adam? I want to say a few words
to Paul.'

'What is it?' asked Paul.

'Paul, will you walk a few steps?' He leaned in
Adam's direction. 'Just a short appoggiatura of my
own, taking its general tone from the key signature of
Handhabend: Paul will be with you anon!' He waved
his hand and entrapped Paul's arm with his arm, as he
walked him off.

'Paul, it's not my nature to interfere with other people's
misfortunes. I make it a life-principle not to give advice
to husband or wife, but I felt such a thread of kin with

you (my soul of dervish or hermit colluding with your translambent probity, the inebriety of my intelligence enjoying the fantasy of your honesty) that I mentioned your case to my old friend Antoine Fuseaux. . . .'

Paul drew away and was about to protest.

' No, Paul, make no mistake, names were not named. But I have a scheme, suggested by dear friend Antoine Fuseaux, as cunning as the seraphim, he ! He is hand-in-glove with a certain high personage at the British Embassy and he has friends at the prefecture of police. He says, If your wife can't make up her mind, you really want her back and you think it's worth while, he'll have her expelled overnight. Simple ! Doesn't she sometimes go to red meetings with our young infantile left ? '

Paul went on, walking slowly.

' It's far-fetched, but not bad. But Elvira couldn't stand the shock and the shame, especially as she is now. She would never forgive me, if she ever came to know. Her self-respect is everything to her, and she likes to be on the right side of the law and of the proprieties. You see how she calls herself Mrs. Fenton now ? '

Marpurgo thrust his face into Paul's breast ; his voice rising higher, laughing in treble.

' Then simply shanghai her, my dear fellow ! Take her for a taxi-drive, land her at the Gare du Nord, get her aboard the train and keep her there till it starts. You know what she is ! She'll accept it as fate and be glad to have the " problem " as she calls it, settled.'

Paul laughed in a troubled way.

' You're perfectly right. But perhaps she loves this— boy : and what about his child ? '

Marpurgo's cracked laugh was shocking.

' Why, Paul, when you get her home, you can influence her to do anything : get rid of it. She'll cry a bit and then she'll be glad. With aboulic impairment, and passivity of gestation, your male reiteration will blaze a trail through clogged nerves, and suggestion's impact will startle compliant impulses to desired end : the vagrant

illusion is fled, you have battled with and vanquished
the constant faun of married women's dreams, *the young
lover*, you don domestic felicity once more like a wool
chlamys.' He giggled. 'The satiric paranymph won't
even ask your thanks ; his jubilations and hallelujahs
for his old friend will even be concealed beneath habitual
sardonic mask—which you alone, friend, did not see—
you saw clear through to my real man. I'll just be glad
to see you reunited—"*blest office of the epicene,*" what ! '

'You're perfectly right about Elvira,' murmured Paul.

'Or we can get the prefecture to put Oliver out
instead.'

'I shouldn't like to do that ; Elvira's my concern,
not this student.'

'Well, think it over : I must run to my chess club.'

They had come back to the house in the rue Thouin.
Paul shook hands :

'You're really a good friend. Come and see me,
anyhow, in London.'

'I will. By the way, your cousin—what a dear girl !
So faithful ! Where is she to-night ? '

'At the hotel, I think. She wouldn't come to the
rue Thouin. She has an idea Elvira resents her being
here. Women are moody, you know. Elvira is so
sensitive, too.'

'Of course; why not ? Well, ring me to-morrow at
the Fuseaux place, if you have anything to say. You
know ! ' He nodded. Paul looked up at the lighted
windows in the house but took a turn around the Panthéon, before he could make up his mind to go up. He
finally went to a near-by café, wrote a note, and taking it
to the maid-of-all-work in the house, asked her to deliver
it upstairs. Then he walked for hours through the streets
of Paris.

Elvira opened the note and read :

DEAR ELVIRA,—I must return to London to-morrow
morning : we are catching the nine o'clock train. I don't
suppose you will be able to get up to the station. Then,

good-bye. Write to me what you want me to do and I will
make arrangements for you. I hope we will soon meet
again in pleasanter circumstances. I must regard our marriage as dead now. I do not speak of any pain I may feel
myself. I know quite well you have not been happy and
that you have had to take your courage in both hands to
do what has been done. I can only counsel one thing : if
you love this young man and intend to be his wife, do it
boldly ; don't waste any more time in hesitations. Build
up a new life, which, I hope and will always hope, will be
happy and complete.—As ever,   PAUL.

Elvira collapsed, cried and groaned, ' What have I
done to all of you ? What is such a life worth ? Let me
throw myself out of the window, and end two miserable
lives.'

Adam presently tired of comforting her and left for
home, saying, ' I will ask Paul to give me the money
to take you away for a few days, until you are rested. I
am sure your mind is not made up. How would you
like to go to Barbizon ? I've never seen it.'

He went off. Elvira was tired, went to bed, and was
soon sleeping soundly.

When Marpurgo got to his chess club he could not
find his opponent. He was fatigued, and sat at a table
over a black coffee, humming to himself for a while,
and perusing the latest copy of the *Revue Critique*, from
which he got curt, workmanlike criticisms of all the
latest in philosophy, history and letters. Presently he
stuffed it in his pocket and went off to Paul's hotel, where
he went upstairs and listened at Sara's door. He took
on a serious expression and knocked at the door with
his stick.

' Who's there ? ' said a muffled voice.

He named himself, and the door was presently opened.
Sara had been crying and had ink on her finger. Marpurgo looked round the room, nodded at Sara and shut
the door carefully.

' May I sit down ? '

Sara put the inkwell over a sheet of paper written on two sides. Marpurgo, leaning on his stick, looked at her kindly and penetratingly.

' You're unhappy, Sara.'

' Why should I be ? '

' Who knows why we should all be unhappy ? We nearly all are : happiness comes too late, or too early, or not at all.' He looked at her closely. ' Sometimes it comes, but we cannot seize it because we are too honest.'

' How can you be happy if you do harm to someone else ? '

He nodded. ' Some don't let that trouble them.'

She was silent, her face full of emotion. He said softly :

' You know, I think Elvira's behaved very badly. To-night's a fatal night. More lives than Paul's, Oliver's and hers hang in the balance.' She said nothing, looking at him with the steadiness which precedes a silent one's confession. Marpurgo laid down his stick and sighed to himself. He said gravely : ' I see things better than most people, perhaps : first, because I'm not afraid to admit any hypothesis : second, because I know many suffer who don't yammer, and I look for clues in faces, in silent, good, self-sacrificing lives.' He looked at her with admiration. ' Third, I suppose, because I'm a very sick man. . . . You were writing a letter ? ' . . . She was lumpish and he skimmed on : ' You are the woman he should have had : you would give him rest. Thou shalt give him rest who stayeth his trust in thee. He trusts you. Men are slow, blind and faithful too long to the dead—dead years, dead youth, dead emotions, dead souls, my dear ! '

Her eyes were full of tears.

' I think what you say is true, but I have no right to interfere in their lives. It is their life. He told me his first duty is to her : she is helpless, alone in the world —perhaps she needs both of us. I told him to do whatever is necessary.'

He looked around the room and saw her valise packed, the letter on the table. He pointed to it.

'Seneca says, When a woman thinks alone, she thinks evil. It's not true of you. You are going to give him up, even your friendship. Woman, woman! The son of Sirach said : There are three things in nature, the tongue, an ecclesiastic and a woman, which know no moderation in goodness or vice, and when they exceed the bound of their condition they reach the lowest depths of goodness and vice. . . .' He smiled at her. ' Do you count me your friend ? '

'Oh yes.'

'You are right. I am. Count on me. If you ever want advice or help, write to me. I am on your side.'

She looked at him curiously : she was not used to effusion. Paul, for example, was as quiet and long-suffering as herself. When he went, she looked out of the window. It was warm, and children still cried out in the streets. On a street bench a mother was knitting a yellow sweater for her baby boy. The trees were in early leaf, so that a gentle, faint colour rose through the lamp-lighted branches, like the olive fluorescence of a brunette. Sara, looking at the people standing at the bus-stop and on the boulevard seats, and at those visible through the glass screen of the café, thought she saw the scatterings of a population of Saint-Sebastians, of twisting torsos, slightly agonised, with briars twining round them. In the dark of the griping thorax, each carried a little aromatic pot of heart, from whose glossy thick leaves blood dripped. They were lonely, as she was : they were perhaps nearly all just losing their lovers, or longing for one hopelessly, alone in the world, feeling they were missing everything. How can a whole world miss everything ? She had no idea. Elvira took everything, and people said how helpless she was, how she needed help. . . .

She thought she would go down to the café herself. She was afraid to stop and listen, day or night, to the

importunate knocking in her breast. How musically
the old night waves cockled round the dyke. If the
dyke broke, there would just be an unromantic, rheumatic wading ankle-deep through mud for the rest of
her life. She did not know anyone who was sinful, had
run away and had an illicit love. When Paul returned
he would explain to her calmly what preparations he
had made. She would explain to him calmly that she
would travel back alone : he and Elvira could get off
whenever they liked to England.

When she got back to the hotel a light was burning in
Paul's room. She went to her room and lay down on
the divan, her heart beating heavily. She heard his
steps in the corridor, and his knock. She looked at him
breathless. Paul took her hand and looked at her with
a faint, resolute smile.

' I am going to divorce her and they will be married.
We go home to-morrow.'

' Oh, Paul ! '

' No, no : I am glad. And she is right. So few of
us are ever truly happy. Don't think hardly of her.'
He added : ' You have been worried about me, I know.'
She smiled. ' I want you to help me. Elvira wants you
to pack up all her things, linen, silver, music, and send
them on. She always loved her own things, she loves
property.' He laughed. ' We must put them all in,
mind you, every little rag, every doyley : she knows to
a stitch what she owns and she's quite impassioned
about it. There is not to be one single duster of hers
trailing round the house. She was much more explicit
and emotional about the teacloths than about Oliver,
upon my soul.' He slapped his powerful thigh, and
laughed as if at a kitten. ' And the minute we get home ! '
He laughed again.

Sara's voice said firmly : ' I'll do it : she needn't
worry.'

He took her hand.

' Good-night, Sara. I'm going to have a good sleep.

I need it, so do you. I told the boy to call us at seven in the morning.'

Oliver surprised himself by saying joyfully at the Archives the next day, to a student friend :

'I am going to be married ! '

'Beautiful, young, rich ? '

'Twenty thousand francs a year rente,' translated Oliver. 'Two hundred pounds a year.'

The student shrugged his shoulders. 'I will find someone who can keep me till I become professor.'

'It's better than nothing,' deprecated Oliver.

'Scarcely,' shrugged the student, whose shoes were run down and socks run up. 'It would be better to get a widow—a bigger dowry and more complaisance.'

'She is—a—widow,' faltered Oliver, in spite of himself.

The student stared at him, and one could see what he was thinking.

'A crazy foreigner—but completely crazy, oh, la-la ! ' He shrugged his shoulders, muttering : 'If I had an angel-mug like yours, I'd make my fortune, old thing.' He looked several times at Oliver, shrugging and muttering to himself.

Oliver told Elvira the story when he got home, only leaving out the 'widow.' Elvira did not laugh, but said, like an old woman, with a pinched face :

'Here all is money : even the young men sell themselves,' she quavered. 'If I'd known that art myself—but I was an idealist. I believed in ideal love, spiritual affinities. What a fool a young girl is. Now I know it's just pleasant habit, compromise, indolence, self-deception. Isn't it ? ' She tickled his temple, at his grave look. They both roared. She tried to get out of him exactly how he had described her to the Archives fossicker.

*   *   *   *   *   *

Marpurgo went to the train to see Paul, Adam and Sara off. But Adam was not going. He had persuaded

Paul to let him take Elvira to Barbizon, for the air, as soon as her little operation was over. 'She has promised faithfully to go through with it, and I'll see she does,' said Adam. At the last moment Paul said to him : 'If you're—er—in Paris, and see Elvira, would you mind dropping me a line at my address to let me know how it's going ? It's all over, you know : but she's been my wife for so long. I don't want her to be unhappy. She can always call on me.'

'And on me,' said Marpurgo. 'I'm your friend, Paul : there are sympathies and antipathies outside malevolence and benevolence.' His eye wandered to Adam. 'People hate me to whom I've done nothing but good. I've never harmed a human being, but I'm convinced that some of my friends would stick to me even if I stole their wives. Their bank-rolls—that's another question : there I answer for no man.' He stared at Adam, trying to calculate what Paul had given him for Elvira's holiday. He twinkled good-bye, and his little hunched back trundled him down the station. Paul looked affectionately at him.

'A strange fellow, lives in intimacies : admits those emotions we all feel but won't admit.'

'A soft-shell egotist,' cried Adam, helping Sara on to the train. 'Get aboard, Paul.'

Marpurgo went towards the office, self-engrossed, his lips moving. Georges called :

'I thought you were coming in early this morning.'

Marpurgo coughed and shrank together.

'I can't get up early, even in this fine spring weather. Humidity height is bad for the lesion : I was born for the nocturnes, the chiaroscuro, but a soggy lung makes indwelling constant, for relief, sustenance, it insists on the dry fresco of midday.' He sighed. Georges impatiently showed him an account.

'I say, who did you send all those telegrams to in Calais and Lyon ? Do you keep a harem or are you running a race-tout business ?'

Marpurgo waved them away.

'Have you ever heard the delightful little English word, *perquisites*? Love me, love my perquisites. What are you going to do? If you don't like it, Georgie, take it as a valedictory. I'm a man with the tastes of an anchoret Sultan, put it that I drink the Circean cup and keep my eyes clear and throat clean.'

Georges steadfastly presented the account-sheets to him.

'If you want more salary, ask Tony for it, not me: or work for commissions. That's not the way to do it.' He threw the sheets on the table and turned to some other work. Marpurgo seized the sheets, tore them, threw them on the carpet and stamped on them.

'Shadows of covetousness and jealousy poorly concealed. If Tony has any objections he can state them —not you!'

'I can get younger and cheaper men,' cried Georges in a rare fit of rage. He recalled himself, 'All right, let's talk business.'

Marpurgo was drawn with spite: 'Oh, our young friend! I thought Endymion's smile would work a *rapprochement* with Jove's assistant, whose inferiority complex festers! So Glintchick charmed Dogamanger! Once more avaricious taciturnity is mulcted by free-handed urbanity. Oh, wonderful, wonderful!'

'Let's get down to something I can understand,' said Georges. Marpurgo picked up his hat: 'I'm not well. The sepsis of hate halts phagocytosis. I must breathe: I am choking!' He rushed out. An hour later he hailed Antoine from a near-by café and drew him in for a coffee. After discussing some business matters, ridiculing Severin, telling a few anecdotes and giving important opinions on the political situation, Marpurgo said: 'Personal antipathy, detestable animal malice, which works half-unconsciously, will destroy me yet.' He coughed. Antoine said: 'Oh, you mean Georges? Oh, how many times have I to tell you he's just a grouch,

Annibale ? I never listen to a goddamn word he says. Don't worry. You're safe with us. Take the day off, Marpurgo ; you're jittery.' He laughed, sprang up and left. He came back with a frown : ' Oh, by the way, if you are feeling better this afternoon, drop in. I've got the plans from that young inventor, you know : drop in. We'll look them through. The poor sap is willing to sell them right out now, to get a couple of guilders, poor devil. You see, Marpurgo, where you'd be if you didn't have a nose for money ? This chap's got brains as good as yours and mine probably. But no knowledge of men.'

Marpurgo sneered pleasantly into his cigar-smoke behind Antoine's back. Antoine had a violent quarrel with Georges as soon as he got in, about Marpurgo's expenses. He pretended to throw the expense-sheets into the wastepaper basket. However, in the afternoon, he shut his door and went carefully through the items.

CHAPTER VI

EVERYONE was back from the Whitsun week-end. The air was full of excitement. The journalists in the cafés sat divinely alone, and scribbled and wrote, came and went, bought the newspapers and telephoned. Blanche, in the d'Harcourt, parodied, to the general applause, the Folies star Mistinguett. The old jokes circulated about her and Cécile Sorel, Marie Marquet and Joséphine Baker. Andrew Fulton had only drunk part of his first Pernod and was still querulous. He told a mean story about two frequenters of the café, music-lovers : it was a shotgun marriage, he said, and they never paid for the gramophone records they made such a display of. Septennat, Blanche's elderly but still imposing sweetheart, put in, ' What's happened to the pretty little dark woman with the broad cheekbones and hips, the runaway wife ? '

' They went away for the Whitsun week.'

' Babyface wanted to take her away from—All This.' parodied Andrew Fulton. ' We're not good enough for her. She's an innocent Englishwoman. When she comes back she's going to have—by the way, that reminds me of something. What became of the five hundred francs she deposited with you, Blanche, for the little affair ? What's your rate of interest ? Can you believe the Western woman gave Blanche five hundred francs to arrange a little business for her ? Satan finds some suckers still for idle Blanche to do.'

Blanche opened her purse and got out her powder-puff.

' I ordered this powder-puff at the Galeries Lafayette, *une vraie occase*—thirty francs. I told them to send it

the very day before, and I hadn't a sou to pay for it.
In the evening she gave me her five hundred francs. One
hundred francs was my split in any case, although she's
rather foggy, you know ; she wasn't very clear about that,
neither was the *sage-femme*. It began that way: then one
thing and another came along. I had to get a new costume
for the act Levasseur got me. (My little Blanche knows
Madame's daughter : they are taking their first communion together. It's quite a little family affair.) Did
you see me, by the way, Septennat ? What a filth thou
art, thou art as faithless as a dog. I work for my living :
it's more than this Western woman does, the dear little
thing. You sit here and ogle her, I believe.' Blanche
was never more engaging than when spilling her scurrili-
ties : her long lips and eyes curved with pixie charm
while her tongue was black and bitter. Septennat seemed
wounded ; he passed a thick silk handkerchief over his
colossal bald dome.

' My dear friend, I was there the first night : I took
you to a champagne supper after and took you home.
You bumped into the taxi door and had a bump the size
of a pigeon's egg on that lovely right temple. You were
as drunk as Queen Victoria. I'm a father to you. I really
get no thanks, but I'm not one to complain.'

' Did you like my act, my dear friend ? '

' You're a witch on the stage, Blanche.'

' But not off ? '

' Everyone knows you have already brought down my
grey hairs in sorrow—not one left ! '

' Oh, and the little flower of Étampes ? '

Septennat laughed roguishly. He had been seen
coming back from Étampes in a third-class carriage,
with a robust negroid beauty of seventeen, sulky with
surfeit.

Andrew, slightly more fuddled, said to Blanche :

' And there is that pathetic story of the young medical
student from Brittany now in Charenton on your account.'

At this reference to an unspeakably scandalous story,

they all laughed. Septennat lifted his glass to her, grandly drained it dry. Septennat alone had his brain clear. He had a satirical column to write before midnight. Blanche, drunk, cried :

'Stop looking like Henri IV, Septennat : you've worn off your pimento.'

'At least I was cradled in a shield.'

'The shield that shields nothing,' murmured Andrew, now reaching good-humour.

'A vacuum,' commented someone else.

'Never a vacuum when I'm there,' amended Septennat cheerfully.

There entered, through the open door, the tall satiric blond man with the blond satchel, Blanche's friend. He ran a news and statistics service. He had the sour insouciance of a pedigreed dyspeptic. He smiled at them all but one, a sudden, unexpectedly charming, weak smile, a confiding, timid smile with the corners turned up to ape superiority. To Septennat, his rival with Blanche, he gave a grave bow full of ironic pretensions. He was removed from Blanche by two men, and pretended to be indifferent to her. He moved forward a chair to put his satchel on, and roughly slammed it against Septennat's leg.

'Well, Herriot split the socialists at Clermont-Ferrand, and Léon Blum by a volte-face is reuniting the extreme left : Lebrun and Doumergue can congratulate themselves on their statesmanship.'

'Tournefeuille will beat volte-face,' remarked Septennat. 'Not that the two chiefs are any more than Guignol figures, but because Barthou is foreign minister, Germany is becoming presumptuous, and with a show of large-minded diplomacy in foreign affairs we can encourage a chauvin reaction.'

'I admire Tardieu,' said Blanche. 'What vigour. He is the secret power behind the ministry.'

Septennat shook his wise head that had seen many ministries and many careers.

'Like most of his profession, he overreaches himself. The Stavisky cheque will sink him.'

'It's a frame-up, a maffia,' cried Blanche, quite drunk. She went on to talk about all the *canards* she had picked up that day from friends of hers, from Lemesurier, a deputy she knew intimately ('she and Arlette, Madame Lemesurier, were intimate friends'), from her brother Fred, in the Ministère de la Guerre.

Blanche had had at various times the idea of making a career for herself and swaying ministries as the 'good friend' of a great political or industrial careerist. But her brains were superficial, her looks were going and she lived hard.

To these warm-hearted friends Oliver entered, now, alone.

'Here's the lover,' Blanche whispered.

He had a serious, tired look. He had got a little plumper and lost some of his rosy colour. He glanced round the café, saw them, and came towards them in a lack-lustre way.

'He looks as if he has been making love all the afternoon,' said Blanche's blond lover, who instinctively detested him. 'Just look at the sloppy shuffle.'

'No, I was shopping with his lady,' volunteered Blanche.

'No obstacle.' Andrew now pleasantly dripped with Pernod and moustache. He grinned at Oliver and gave him his hand: 'Hullo, pal; how are you doing?' Oliver sat down beside him, ordered a drink and credulously asked Blanche what Lemesurier thought of Léon Blum's 'common front' agitation.

Blanche spluttered, 'Léon Blum is a dirty Jew: the Government is rotten because it's full of dirty Jews and freemasons.'

'Rubbish,' said the blond satchel coldly. 'It's half full of Tartarins.'

'*Méridionaux* are not Frenchmen,' cried Blanche. 'They are loud-mouthed dirtiness from the south.'

'It has pure Normans and Bretons,' laughed blond satchel.

'Bretons are Celts and Normans are Scandinavians, they are not Frenchmen,' cried Blanche.

'And the only Frenchmen come from Château d'Anizy.' They all laughed at her.

'Ah, Oliver, thou art my only true friend,' she said good-humouredly. 'Thou comest from such a little land which yet is split into many nations. Canst thou understand a Somerset man, a Lancashire man? Thou hast told me, not at all. After all,' she told the group, 'in a monarchy individuality still exists, they do not try to boil everyone into a common equality, a vulgar republicanism.'

One by one they dropped away as seven o'clock approached. Presently, Septennat took himself off, after kissing her hand, and Maurice Blane, the blond satchel, remained with Oliver. She asked him with disdainful verve :

'And you, little one, dine with your family to-night?'

'I'm afraid so, m'dear : some friends of my dear wife Suzanne's from Prague, a honeymoon tour, I can't miss them. Suzanne's brother has turned up too. Suzanne is as suspicious as a burglar-alarm, and I believe wrote to him.'

'Then go,' said Blanche. 'I know these brothers. One knows them. The gimlet eyes of Freudian lovers.'

She had once been an intimate friend of Suzanne, too.

Maurice stalked out, from the door smiled a liverish blond smile, and waved a lank, manicured hand stained with recent ink. Blanche snickered :

'This Suzanne makes herself ridiculous with her suspicions ; and he—a mollycoddle. I have never been more than a good friend of his, out of pity. When he was down and out I fed him. Underneath he's kind and soft.'

'Ça se voit,' grinned Oliver. 'But why isn't he more explicit? I'm tired of Berl's bourgeois onions of refine-

ment. Take off layer after layer and you find the real man.
It's only eventually good for the bodysnatcher who'll
sell him to the med. school after death.'

Blanche leaned back :

'Buy me some Gaulois, Olivair. Are you dining with
this charming Elvira to-night ? '

'No.'

'I thought not; in fact, she told me so ! ' She laughed.
'Where is she ? '

'She's in bed : she said she'd been shopping all the
afternoon and felt tired. She'd ordered her dinner and
sent me out. I got your *pneu.* when I came downstairs.'

She spoke through her cigarette and the smoke.

'You don't know why ? '

'By Jove, is it—she didn't go to the *sage-femme*? I am
sorry, I didn't realise ! what a blundering thickhead I am
—I ought to go home.'

Blanche called the waiter and muttered through her
cigarette again :

'Keep calm : she's better off for the moment alone,
and I want to tell you what to do. She knows nothing
and neither do you.'

'Gee, you're the best of friends, Blanche.'

His eyes were moist with gratitude. 'She's an odd
girl : she didn't hint a word to me.'

'She only decided this afternoon. She got tired shopping; she felt sick and she suddenly said, " Oh, I can't
go through with it," so I popped her into a taxi and off
to the nurse's before she could regret. She hesitated at
least ten minutes in the street below the surgery, as it
was, until I said, " Well, here you are, you may as well
go through with it : be a sport," and she said, " What's
the odds, I'll do it." And there you are, *mon ami.* Do
I get a vote of thanks or not ? '

'It is rather a relief,' said Oliver. ' You know . . .'

'I know, I know. And now, let's celebrate ! And
will you take me to dinner as a reward ? '

'Ten dinners.'

She called the waiter : ' Another Campari for me, a Pernod for Monsieur.'

' A brandy,' corrected Oliver.

' What a vile habit ! '

Blanche explained with her nervous hands : ' You know, she is sweet, your Elvira. I should never like to see her in trouble. I love her like a sister. I love you two. And I do not want to see you make mistakes. The mistakes—I know them all. Oh, la-la ! I told her this very afternoon, Oliver is a beautiful, eligible young man, brilliant and a careerist : and yet faithful and true. He could have any woman at all, I told her, you foolish woman : realise how lucky you are. You know this little woman ! She said, " I wouldn't move hand or foot to hold any man : he'll stay with me if he loves me. I'm an idealist about love. It comes to you. You can't call it : you can't recall it." She said that. It is touching, I think. But I said to her, " Love is a tête-à-tête : a third person spoils it : a child is a third person. It is the woman's fault. She loves the child more than the father." " I should never do that," said she : " there are lover-women and mother-women—I am the first sort." We said all this in the street under the nurse's window. I do not want your lives to be spoiled.' Her fine, painted eyes misted with alcoholic sentiment.

' You're a great friend, Madame d'Anizy ! '

' No, Blanche ! Yes, I feel we will be great friends. But you must be careful of me. I have a great weakness. I spend money. I am sorry to say I spent almost all of that first five hundred francs Elvira gave me. I was in despair, they were going to throw me into the street. Then I have been owing a doctor's bill for two years. He has gone on treating me, but after all he is a poor man. He is old, seventy-two, with a darling old wife and three grown children. The usual history, all the money of the family invested in the eldest son, to make him a career. He is a doctor. There are so many, alas ! He makes what an ordinary shopkeeper would make. They could have saved the University and initial expenses. The most comic little salon you ever saw. You would worship it! For a student of periods! Sèvres china, bits of wedding silver, a souvenir pearl-handled knife, a real lace-mat, all in a cabinet, old recovered Empire chairs with dust-covers, a picture of an anatomy lesson, a picture of a butterfly-collector with his specimens, two long tapestry curtains.' Blanche was feverishly garrulous, a spindle of theatrical graces.

'Poor fellow: when he comes to see me, he takes off his two celluloid cuffs, puts them on the table, and after-wards dusts them and puts them on again. A man could not attend a woman with more delicacy and modesty. I know he has spent almost all the money he had saved establishing his son as a doctor : that son is a no-good and still lives on the old people. Then their daughter married, and they gave a small dowry—twenty thousand francs—pitiable. Since then the two old people have been living on bread and franc-a-litre wine, and he still goes running out at seventy-eight! When I first developed my cough and thought it was bronchitis I went to him. He told me to be careful. How could I be careful? My husband had just left me: I had the child! I sang until I could only sing husky and parlando : I went on the stage naked: I undressed for the men who took me home. What do you expect? To earn one's living and keep a child in Paris! And I am resolved to give my little girl a dowry: she will live bourgeois. Bourgeois! They can laugh : it is very pleasant to know you will have the same roof over your head ten years hence and will have bread and meat in the larder, wine in your cellar. I see nothing wrong with it. At any rate, *ma petite Blanche* will have it. And money to get the right sort of husband when she grows up. She will go to a convent finishing-school, too. For that, you see, I need money.'

'I thought you had a dead little boy,' said Oliver.

'No, no, that was before I married,' she hurried on. She smiled a gentle, rueful smile at him.

'I was married,' she said. 'He left me : he began by sending me a hundred francs a week, then fifty, then nothing. I could have forced him to send more, if I had had the money. Then I thought, It is my child : I will provide for her. Now I have this piece of land I am buying near Château d'Anizy. She will live there in her holidays. Hein ? I live for Blanche.'

He murmured : 'You're a brave woman.'

'I know what they all say about me : but a woman does not live an irregular life for nothing. One must know the reason, hein ? '

'You are quite right. This chattering café crowd make me tired with their scandal-mongering. You feel they know all about people but the truth.'

'I hate them,' confided Blanche. 'But I must meet people, and especially people like these who know managers and who take me to cabarets and restaurants. There I can perhaps pick up a backer or get a better job. It's business.'

'It's a tough life for you.'

'If you hadn't taken me to dinner to-night, I should simply have gone hungry,' said Blanche cheerfully. 'Oh, don't say anything, I'm used to it. I have a pretty figure that way, eh ? I haven't a sou, to tell the truth. But no matter. Perhaps to-morrow I'll find something. Elvira is very sweet. She bought me a pair of steel-grey silk stockings : otherwise I should have been up against it for to-morrow night when I dance at my new place. You must come and see me, dearie,' she said, burlesquing, affectionate, charming, suddenly changing her play. He laughed, blushing a little, flattered.

'You bet I will : you're a pretty woman, Blanche. You've got dash, verve—er, what do they call it ?—you know, éclat ! '

She smiled and half shut her long-fringed eyes :

'I am glad you think I am a pretty woman, Olivair, because I like you. You are not like English I have seen, lanky like a skeleton, with hollows in their temples and cheeks, with bad complexions, water-coloured eyes and teeth in the wind : you are quite different. I did not know there were English like you.'

' There are lots of 'em,' laughed Oliver. ' Haven't you heard the old tale about the Celtic strain underneath ? I'm it. Elvira too.'

' You are of one race with our Bretons, then ? Oh, how curious ! I had a very dear friend, a Breton : he could hardly speak French. He was an artist and I lived in his atelier two years with him and my little baby. I was never so happy before or after. His name was Hervé. Poor Hervé ! He was very strange. You know there is much insanity in the Bretons, nearly as much as in Angleterre. At last he went mad completely. Now he is in the madhouse.' She nodded. ' I loved him : I was furiously in love with him. The Celtic race has fire —and charm—and wit : and also a childlike quality which is endearing in a man.'

Oliver leaned back in his chair and detailed her charms with shining, narrowed eyes. At last, she said, taking her fur and bag abruptly :

' Olivair, *allons diner* : I am dying of hunger.'

' Where you lead, I'll follow,' answered he prosaically, tramping out behind her, his shoulders swayed back curiously, with a cocklike swagger. On the pavement he took her arm : ' I hope your Maurice doesn't shoot straight.'

In the semi-darkness all her charms came out, her tendrilly hair drawn back, her long-laid fringed eye, her pencilled brows and scarlet lips ; she murmured, pro- voking, ' Maurice doesn't shoot, he justs gets shicker : they say also that the English don't stab, they go to law : is that so ? ' The lovely face of a bird of prey glinted at him. ' But you're Celtic : unpredictable.'

He puffed his chest and laughed : ' Who knows ? I've only made one bad break in my life, and that astounded the populace.'

' You mean Elvira ? '

'Uh-huh.'

'But she's a beauty : men will do anything for beauty.'
Her stage accent appeared : 'It is a *lampe* ; you arr
moss (moths) ; you broil yourselves in ze *lampe*. It is a
poison ; you arr but ratis ; you eat ze poison.' He
looked at her in admiration, for she was reciting in a
low passionate voice a verse of Baudelaire :

> 'Je serai ton cercueil, aimable pestilence !
> Le témoin de ta force et de ta virulence,
> Cher poison, préparé par les anges ! Liqueur
> Qui me ronge. Ô la vie et la mort de mon cœur !'

She translated, 'I will be thy coffin, sweet pestilence !
The witness of thy strength and virulence, dear poison,
prepared by the angels ! Liqueur that gnaws me. O,
life and death of my heart !' The evening air was still
fresh. Oliver shivered.

'It is impressive ! The poison is passion !'

'And syphilis,' she said in a husky whisper. 'He died
of syphilis.' After a moment, she added : 'But for most
of them it is one and the same. Who can escape it ? My
husband poisoned me, Maurice has it, Andrew is falling
to pieces with it.' Oliver's arm stiffened, but he made an
effort and did not withdraw it. 'No one can escape,'
said Blanche, drunk and sibylline.

They walked through the narrow old streets round the
Marché des Quatre Vents, where the mediæval houses
belly out at the first storey, towards the giant side of
Saint-Sulpice. Oliver shook himself and laughed.

'You exaggerate.'

She said : 'My life is different from yours : who can
say I exaggerate ? I see differently. Men have killed
themselves for me. One man left his wife and children
for me. The artist, the Breton, went to the madhouse.
*Eh, après tout, pourquoi ce triste Hervé ? Ils sont tous fous à
lier.* Zey arr oll a shingle shott.'

He was silent.

She went on playing a part : 'I damn men, and I love

on-ly ze *débris, les épaves, les âmes damnées,* ze dreunken
bomss. I laike zose oo av soffer, oo av *chagrin,* I embrace
a such man wiz passion, I av secret embraces forr im.'
She laughed : ' *Parbleu !* I forgot it was you for a
moment, Oliver. I don't want to lead you astray—*Dieu
m'en garde !* I love this little Elvira.'

' We're both drunk,' giggled Oliver.

A fourteenth-century house stood out on the street.
They came round it into a corner. Oliver seized her
arm and kissed her.

' Now, enough, no more,' said she. She continued :
' My nights are full of flame, and terror : I must always
sleep with a man, any man, to know a still midnight.
A new man is better than an old friend, for his contentment and surprise is better : I know all the methods,
all the tricks, all the profane kisses and embraces. Then
he is intoxicated with me till I have shown him all :
then he tires of me. But until then, I have peace.'

Oliver laughed boyishly.

' The seven deadly sins ! When I used to go to
Sunday school, they seemed like stale dead crusts : I
thought a mean ratlike tribe of thin-blooded moral self-
polluters went in for them. I never saw them as they are
—in their majesty—whew ! ' He laughed again. ' You
Circe ! How you French women know how to talk !
There isn't a woman of my nation living who knows how
to talk like that. If they did, would it suit them ? They
haven't the *diablerie.* Whereas you, light or dark, innocent or—sinful—you all have the magic line.'

Her nostrils spread, she looked round quickly with
her kestrel-face :

' All ? Then you know some others ? '

He laughed proudly, a sort of dove's cooing in his throat.

' I know one other.'

' Ah ! Your mistress ? '

' No. Ask no questions and you'll hear no lies.'

' Ah ! The hidden fire : I knew it,' she exclaimed.
' A friend of Elvira's ? '

His gay laugh came again.

'No: aren't you a woman, though! Curiosity killed the cat. There is no other woman. I said that to make you bite.'

'I take leave to doubt it,' she said, but dropped the subject. 'Look, here is a little Corsican restaurant, not dear, where they make excellent cutlets and have good cheap red wine: I often go here. You are a student. I won't let you spend money on me.'

Through dinner he got her to recite some more Baudelaire to him; she recited when it came to the coffee:

> 'Quoique tes sourcils méchants
> Te donnent un air étrange
> Qui n'est pas celui d'un ange. . . .,

Although thy wicked brows give thee a strange air which is that of no angel, sorceress with provoking eyes, I adore thee, O my frivolous, my terrible passion! With the devotion of the priest for his idol. The desert and the forest perfume thy wild tresses, thy head has the attitudes of the enigma and the secret. Round thy flesh the perfume prowls as round a censer: thou charmest as the evening, nymph warm and tenebrous.'

She finished and laughed at him, showing her white teeth.

'Tell me, what do you think of me? Not pretty at all, eh?'

'Not pretty,' he said, rather hoarsely. 'But I can imagine that you can be maddening. You are a clever woman,' he continued as if unwillingly; 'you know how to call up a sort of cramp and rage inside a man.'

She laughed, and said with the most charming of accents: 'I will let you alone, though, for the sake of Elvira, whom I love. She is a sweet woman, Elvira, and not like me: good.'

He said umbrageously: 'Who said I wanted to be left alone?'

'I insist. You must stay in your character. If you

sank into vice, you would never get up again; it is not the breath of your nostrils. You must live and die respectable. A respectable man gone wrong is not amusing at all: you would bore me, or any other woman.'

She pulled on her fur rather coldly, and with it her airs of '*grande dame.*' She said, when she got out, 'Now you must go home and wait on Elvira: you must not keep her waiting: she is so dependent on you. Neither you nor she know anything about adventure.'

He said: 'You have a rendezvous, in other words.'

She shook his hand graciously, friendly again.

'There, let us remain comrades. It would not be safe for me to spend much time with you; I should get to like you too much. There is Elvira, and we are friends. And then, I am glad she is there. Otherwise, I should sleep with you one night or another and that would be the beginning of a passion for me and the end of our friendship. I must avoid true passions as much as possible.'

He stood still, unwilling to let go of her hand.

'Blanche, how many women like you are there in the world? I don't belong to myself any more: the ground is slipping from under my feet: are you what you seem? Or do I seem very naïve to you? I wish I had got to know women when I was a boy.'

She smiled and almost whispered: 'I wish I had been thy first: if I had known thee early, I would have been kind to thee and thou wouldst have had nothing but joy in thy youth.'

'Let us say you are the first—to-night.'

She laughed provokingly:

'No, you couldn't stand me: I am wine too strong: *je porte à la tête*; I have been the mistress of Paris' most celebrated libertines; I have been through four-day orgies and never slept, never stopped drinking, never stopped loving, and never tired.' She laughed at him: 'Will the little brazier take heat to the volcano!'

'You're teasing me, Blanche, and you know what you're doing. Don't be cruel!'

'Shh! it's for your own good. You know the Frog Princess? In the daytime, when you have seen me, I am only an ugly frog, ugh! At night you have never seen me. I know better than you that it would turn your head. Stay tranquil, go back to your gentle dream. I am a nymphomaniac. I drained Hervé to his last drop of blood: I sent him to Charenton. There! that is the truth. I tell you for your own good. Now, you can only hate me! You must never tell Elvira: she cannot conceive a woman like me: she is snow, I would not mark her with the tiniest spot.'

Oliver leaned his head on her arm for a minute.

'I must do this, my head is whirling. If you want to send me to Charenton, you are going the right way about it. Blanche, you are tormenting me: I don't believe you care twopence for Elvira. How can you, a woman like you, rich with love, passion and experience? Why, beside you she is a Sunday school miss.'

Blanche answered with guttural satisfaction:

'Nonsense, she is a good woman: she is my friend. Now go to her.'

'I can't. I must go with you, Blanche. This evening I am madly in love with you only.'

She became businesslike. 'No: what do you think of me, my God! with that poor dear at home waiting for you.'

Oliver took off his hat abruptly:

'Well, good-night; you have another rendezvous.'

She laughed: 'Good-night, *cher ami*: I have another rendezvous—but one of these nights I will be yours—yes, I think so.'

'Blanche!'

'Yes, not yet, love like wine must mature. Different vintages have different maturities. Not yet. Soon.'

He shook hands once more, and went on his way, very excited. He thought, Blanche, Coromandel, Elvira: Lord, I am like thistledown in their breaths: when one

says Come, I come, or Go, come I still.' He wondered
about her age : ' She must be thirty-one, Elvira is
twenty-eight : Coro only is my age, and less—twenty-
one.' Like a breath from a brazier, a thought burned his
cheeks and inflamed him. ' Blanche would let me be her
lover if I insisted : she would, I am sure.' He moved on
and left this thought where he found it : but in the night,
he dreamed he was straining Blanche to him in a great
and unearthly joyful passion. Elvira was cool, sorrowful.
Next morning he waited till a girl-friend came, then left.
He went to see Coromandel, took her to lunch at the
Quatrième République, where he and Elvira never went,
and spent the afternoon with her wandering along the
Seine. He told her his plans, discussed his essay, asked
her opinion about his going into business. He described
Marpurgo at length. He left Coromandel at her house,
and as they approached saw a smallish familiar figure
walking slowly up the street with its back to them.
' *Tiens*, there is Marpurgo,' cried Oliver. He thought
Coromandel started. ' Didn't you see that man who just
turned the corner ? We met him most curiously on the
way over. Here he comes back again. Funny wanderer.
He spends whole nights walking round the streets of this
quarter, I have heard. He is lonely. . . .' He turned to
look and found the door closing on Coromandel :
' Coro, heigh ! ' The door shut. He looked round and
saw Marpurgo on the other side of the street, looking at
him. Each raised his hat. He crossed over : ' Hullo :
where have you been ? Is this one of your stamping-
grounds ? '

' How is your work getting on ? ' asked Marpurgo.

' I've finished the reference work.'

' You'll be going home soon, then ? '

' I suppose so ' ; he sighed without thinking.

' It's hard to leave Paris, eh ? She has many beauties
—and furies,' said Marpurgo in a melancholy, thoughtful
way : then, ' I thought I saw you speaking to someone
in the street.'

'A young lady : a student—I met by accident on the way home,' improvised Oliver.

Marpurgo was thoughtful : Oliver grew alarmed. At last Marpurgo said :

'And how is—your lady ? '

'All right ; with friends : so I took a walk.'

'Where are you for ? '

'Nowhere.'

Marpurgo said : 'Let's go to a new district—since you're free. I am free, till evening.'

His voice was intent. Oliver thought, 'He is on his high horse : he is going to open for me his pack of secrets, the strange old peddler.' He looked sideways at Marpurgo's thin face. They walked in silence for a time. Evening thickened ; the long lights stretched across the polished macadam : the obscured Paris star-sky glimmered, the leaves blew with the noise of declining waves, the taxis passed, lurking, prowling, the long cross-streets of the Left Bank wandered away with their high pale façades and chinks of light through curtains.

Presently Oliver heard Marpurgo say philosophically, as if reasoning with himself :

'One has to be bred in the north, and dream of the lightnings of the thick low-lying sky, and the northern lights, and arise with one foot planted in the northern marshes, in a land of canals, grey rivers, soaked meadows, short summers, foggy winters, to love for ever and to death that soft, sooty, tender, distant landscape. The clear light of a rainless grey day, the terracotta furrows and raisin-brown fields, the chrome clay, iron-filled sand, the black loam and blown flats, the brick-pits filled with water, the long morasses, the floury cement cuttings and deep fields of rank grass, teach a thousand muted shades to the native eye : dun, dull, grimy-white, olive, lavender, smoke-blue, spring-yellow, burnt-sienna, horizon-blue—these are the brightest of their shades. The nights sooty, the evenings livid, the midday linen, the mornings pale ; what a land of water and mist is that. And the woman who is like that, brown like their winter woods, dusky like the four-o'clock winter twilight, melancholy, restful, dreamy-cold as their leafless woods. There are men who will ruin their lives for her, and men who, finding in her what is not in themselves, will wrestle to win her and then be disappointed.'

He was silent, then said : ' Oliver, what a profound starry night it is! It is a long time till morning, and every hour weighs heavily if you have regret on a night like this. It is a close, poisoned Paris night. There will be many this summer. France is electric.'

Oliver said, ' Do you want a bock ? Let's sit down. I'm suddenly tired : it's the air.'

' If you like.'

They sat down. ' I have been wanting to see you,' began Oliver nervously, but in a matter-of-fact tone. ' I have almost all my notes from the Archives. It is about the assemblage, the collation. I want to know whether you would treat it in a purely serial fashion, or as essays, topical, the development of the different branches of proletarian thought, and whether you would close with rectifications or strew them throughout the errors which now appear in history books. I am beginning to think that my ambition is to write a semi-honest history book and get it accepted by the schools.'

Marpurgo sipped the aerated water he had ordered.

' If you show me what you have, I can give you some idea,' he said. ' Of course, the easiest thing would be for me to write it for you. I'm a wow at that sort of thing. But if I write it for someone else, a young student, they generally don't do so well; they get the remark, " You might have read Oldtimer & Weatherall's manual with profit," or, " It is impertinent to theorise before you know the groundwork of the subject," and so forth. But then you're a M.A. already, of course. That makes a vast difference.'

Oliver looked up, amused. ' That sounds like a dirty crack.'

'It wasn't intended so. You're an academic type.
You'll get on.'

'I must. I have no fairy godmother.'

Marpurgo sneered into his aerated water : ' Paul was
a gold medallist too.' He looked at Oliver. ' If I'm not
mistaken, I saw you taking a young lady home in a very
friendly manner : a friend of Elvira's ? '

' A friend of mine : unknown to Elvira ; any harm in
that—in Paris ? '

' Coromandel Paindebled, I think ? '

' You know her ? '

' No. I know her father's shop. He has old laces ;
I am a lace-buyer. When I was there buying the other
day, she came down to call him and he told me her
name—Coromandel. Strange name. Have you known
her long ? '

' A chance acquaintance.' He grinned maliciously.
' One of those romances of your city of light and love.'
He fired. ' But, by james, it was a strange story from
beginning to end. No one would believe it.'

' She is a strange girl, it seems.'

' Unique.'

' You do well with women.'

He put on a naïve voice. ' Strange, you know : I used
to be so gauche : now, I find I have a certain something.
The French women bring it out in you. Any beautiful
woman does, but the French women especially. I almost
wish I'd been born French. Perhaps I was. There are
people born out of their country who feel like a fish out
of water all their lives.' He glinted darkly in the half-
light, inwardly pluming himself and thinking : ' With
this fellow I must be careful : he's capable of going to
Elvira and making trouble.'

' Have some more beer,' said Marpurgo.

' I can't : Elvira must be home by this. I must taxi
there : let's go there.'

' I'll share the taxi with you : then I have a rendezvous
—perhaps only with false-seeming.' His meditative pipe

kept to its old themes. 'I have an intuition—we live
in a hall of mirrors. We crook our little fingers, and
distorted wraithy gestures answer us.'

When they passed the café no one was there except
Maurice, all pale discordant shades of a hang-over, drearily
getting drunk again in a corner and studying his private
news-sheet. 'Maurice is not a man, but a reflection in
a *demie-blonde*,' said Marpurgo giggling.

'I dislike that fellow.'

'That means Blanche has gone off with Septennat or
one of her other enchanted swine.'

'The café should pay her as *allumeuse*.'

Marpurgo looked at him in the lamplight, his pale
pinched face and eyes dodging sickeningly in his infirm
malice.

'I'll let you go home to your beloved,' Marpurgo said
with false tenderness.

'Good-night, when shall I see you again ? About the
essay ? '

'I'll play chess with you here to-morrow, if you can
get away.'

'Good, cheerio.'

Marpurgo watched him walk away and then made off
rapidly across the open place and down the rue de
l'Abbaye. He never looked round. Oliver followed him.
He presently reached the Paindebleds' shop, and stood
on the opposite side of the street, looking up and down
the house. The shutters and panes were all open, but no
lights were visible. Marpurgo took a few steps up and
down in front of the house, looking at the tulip-bloom of
heaven peppered with star-dust, looking down at his
boots, well-polished, and at his long nails, always rimmed
with dirt.

'He's wormy,' whispered Oliver. 'He's just a
breeding-ground of nostalgias. Coromandel is another
one, fine lace is another.'

He went and left Marpurgo mounting guard there.

'I'm a fool,' he said to himself pleasantly. 'Coromandel's unattached, and she likes me : she'd make a good wife. Poor Elvira ! I won't read her my essay to-night, at any rate : I'll have that much self-control.'

When he got home Blanche had just put Elvira to bed. Oliver could not resist saying to Elvira :

'You are always lovelier at night than in the daytime : your great underbrush eyes—when I make money I'm going to buy coloured sheets and pillow-slips for you to lie on, black, cream, damask.'

Blanche watched them eagerly, and then left, saying : 'Now, look after her ; amuse her ! '

'Oh, I will.'

He read her the scene in the lying-in hospital in James Joyce's *Ulysses*, then some of his poems ; then he said, 'Now we're going to set up house soon. I was looking at all the prices of things to-day, since you're going to be here for a couple of weeks and I'll have to go shopping.' He turned over the paper and found the market page, began guffawing. 'Listen to this ! Are you all right ? Do you like this ? Does it amuse you ? Tell me when you're tired ! ' He read out, with the same rapid sonorous eloquence. Her eyes opened wider and wider, her face set, her nostrils moved. Presently tears rolled out of her eyes, but he took no notice, he went on reading. After a column he broke out :

'There, how's that for an evening's entertainment ? Anything else, ma'am ? anything else I can show you, ma'am ? Anything you say done free and obliging. How's that for a faithful, loving husband ? Why, by james—you're crying, Elvira ? Are you in pain ? '

'No.' She bit her lip and began to sob.

'What is it ? '

'Nothing at all.'

'There is something.'

'You get me here, you batten me down and you shout at me : you enjoy yourself. I'm in pain,' she said indignantly.

He was all gentle rebukes, explanations and apologies.

At the end she smiled and rubbed her fingers through his curls.

'I'm mean to you : you're too young. Only a solemn old fellow like Paul should have all this trouble.'

She laughed maternally at him.

'I asked Paul if, supposing I went back to him, he would get you a good job in the City. He knows all sorts of business-men who are his clients. Now, I only said " supposing." '

'How cold-blooded you are ! '

'E-eh, wait a minute ! There, now. I had a letter from him to-day : you can read it. He and Sara have packed all my things, and they are in the cellar awaiting my instructions. That sounds final, eh ? '

'I wrote to the Dean to-day telling him how much longer I expected to take, and telling him I did not want to compete for the second scholarship. I want either to be made lecturer in London or in a provincial University. So after some preliminary tacking, the good ship E. & O. will soon be scudding before a fair breeze.'

He kept her company every evening for seven days, bought her books of poems which he grandiloquently read, instructed her on market-prices, got right through his library notes, and had done a fair section of *Ulysses* when Blanche arrived and long-suffering Elvira sent him out for the evening. He had not been out for a week. He had had no idea that the world was so beautiful in the evening. He bought the papers eagerly. At Bucharest the three foreign ministers of the members of the Little Entente, Titulesco, Yevtitch and Benes, were confirming their solidarity with France and her politics. The hot summer was drawing near, and the air was humming with the usual French political swarm of conjectures. Oliver felt at home. After supper, which he took in the Corsican restaurant Blanche had introduced him to, he walked under the mallow-leaf sky. He came past the mouth of the rue des Quatre Vents. Girls kept speaking to him : the streets swarmed with them, as the air with

pollen. He passed under the lamps, and his ripe youth
shone out in the dirty vulgar street like the visit of an
angel; his well-cut clothes, fancy tie and polished shoes
were apparent too. At a doorway standing above a step,
he started back. A girl was harbouring there, silk legs
glistening under a short frock. Her thick, short, bronze
hair was brushed in curls around a beret, her milky skin
was brushed with artificial colour, the moving iris of each
eye glowed in the filtered light, her varnished feet tapped
as she hummed. He had seen that in a glance, and was
passing, when a voice came out of the doorway :

> ' Je suis belle, ô mortels ! comme un rêve de pierre,
> Et mon sein, où chacun s'est meurtri tour à tour
> Est fait pour inspirer au poête un amour——'

She stopped murmuring this chant of beauty as he
came closer.

' Have you a rendezvous with someone ? ' he questioned.

' With everyone,' she answered, looking at him with
scorn. She had green eyes. He said softly : ' I am lonely.'

' You have no lady-friends ? '

' Three. What was that you just recited ? '

She laughed, flattered.

' Did you like it ? '

' It is beautiful.'

' It is Baudelaire,' she said.

Oliver started.

' Baudelaire ! That's strange. I heard another woman
recite Baudelaire to me a week ago.'

' A woman like me, doubtless.'

He smiled. ' Do you all do it ? Is it part of the
ritual ? '

' You are a student ? Yes : I can see it.'

He was enchanted. ' But do you all learn poetry ? '

She said : ' I am hungry, my darling : buy me some
supper and I will tell you about the poetry.' They
walked to the Boulevard Saint-Michel, and on a café

terrace, where she saluted two or three other girls and spoke to the waiter affectionately by name, she told him : 'Baudelaire loved us, girls like us, and in return we sometimes learn one of his poems as a bait—a bait,' and she took a large bite of steak, 'a bait for men. And after all, he was right. Am I beautiful ? '

'Yes,' said Oliver.

'I am beautiful,' she took up, still eating. 'I am without a fault, you will see, if you are nice to me : the young girls without a spot, brought up in their schools, are beautiful often, no doubt, fed on milk and roses, but how many would be beautiful walking the streets every night, eating the filth I eat, living as I live ? How many ? Not many. It is right that poets should write for those women who shine even in the slush of the streets ! '

She finished her dinner, smiled at him, took her glass of wine and leaned back, rounding the double curve of her side and stretching her little foot in its cheap high-heeled shoe : under the long, black-pencilled eyebrows, her clear green eyes moved roving over his face, enamelled with youth, with satisfaction.

'We make a nice couple,' she said contentedly. 'When I am so young, I hate to appear on the streets with an old fellow.'

'How old are you ? '

'Sixteen.'

He smiled at her and was happier in her company than he had been with Elvira, Coromandel or Blanche. On the way home he said gallantly : ' You are more beautiful than all the honest women I have ever known.'

'And as honest as all the beautiful women you have known.'

'And as witty as any,' he said.

Her metallic, impudent, assured laugh tailed him up. 'I have much more spirit than body, but it is not so beautiful : fie, it is hideous, my spirit : I am glad you can see the body and not the spirit. I have seen horrors : my life is hideous : I will end up—can you think how ?

There is not a dog's body floating down the Seine that will end up worse than me. I will end there too.'

He asked lightly, selfishly, to stop this talk: 'I thought all you girls saved money and then retired to a little farm?'

'Not me: I live and die with my beauty. Should I give a child this body and this ugly mind I have? Should I bring a little boy or girl up on a farm in the country on milk and fresh meat and vegetables, and then, with its wicked twisted soul, drop into the mud of Paris? No, no, a thousand times no; no, no. I know it all, my friend: no. Ah!' She stamped her foot. In a minute it had passed over and she was at his side again, the graces shuttling over her members, her face, speech, and form a tissue of seduction. She said:

'Dear friend, will you stay with me all night? it is a lovely night, and we are such a nice couple.'

He grew troubled.

'I would, but I must go home: someone expects me.'

'You are not married already?'

'Yes.'

'Oh, how foolish! What, she was rich?'

'No: just pretty and kind.'

'H'm: a bourgeois woman?'

'Yes.'

'And she lets you out at night?'

'She is sick.' He explained the affair.

Happily, she took him along her accustomed beat to show him to her friends and sisters. In the dark of their way sometimes soft ironic or harsh sardonic voices called. 'Is he handsome, though?' 'You have picked up a novice?' 'A fat one!'

They reached the tiny hotel. She trotted in ahead of him with a businesslike tapping, swaying her hips: she said a word to the gentle, curly-headed proprietor reading the political news of the evening paper, and nodded to his wife, who returned her greeting pleasantly: the proprietor looked quite like Paul. The window surveying the stairs was clean and prettily hung with a lace curtain. She preceded him up the stairs. At the top of the stairs he came face to face with Adam Cinips on his way down. Neither acknowledged the other.

*　　　*　　　*　　　*　　　*　　　*

Blanche had run away early to a rendezvous, and Elvira lay expecting Oliver to return. Suddenly impatient, she got up, dressed and went out. She walked as far as the Odéon, looked at its billboards, stood in a queue to buy a ticket, and felt so weak that she walked home again. On the way she stopped at a bar for coffee. A big, drunk German artist tried to make her. She stumbled home. Oliver was not there.

Elvira lay upstairs listening to the noises of the hotel, slow to go to sleep. The young man next door brought home a woman : they kept making familiar sounds for an hour or so, then the door opened and the girl crept downstairs. An American girl, resident in the hotel for long months, brought home an American friend but could not induce him inside the door : some acoustic freak brought their words, carried on mostly in an undertone, through the opened window to Elvira's ears :

' You don't care a rap for me : I just suit your purpose.'

' That's not true ; we've always been good friends.'

' Friends ! I don't hear from you for a week, and then when you want to have a good time you come and pick me up.'

' Hush, I've got to work : I can't come every night.'

' You use me and then you won't even give me the money for my room. You know I'm broke.'

Some people coming down the street reduced the young man to a frenzy of pleading, and in a minute Elvira heard the soft sound of money changing hands. The door opened and shut, and someone came upstairs. In her fright, and helplessness, Elvira began to imagine Oliver in a brawl, gone to a communist meeting and locked up, run over, drunk and insulting the police, run off with another woman, anything. New pains, a spasm coming every ten minutes, had begun early in the evening and were now intense : the back of her head throbbed, her heart beat heavily and she was fevered. The hot-water bottle bought by Blanche (Blanche had not given her the change) was cold at her feet. The sleeping-tablet Blanche had got her had not sent her to sleep. The people who lived upstairs and always came in last in the house, now came in. She heard the loud panting of their great Dane, and in a minute the unruly thumping as it jumped about the floor. She heard them soothing it and then it gave no further sound. They must have tied it in the bathroom. They were lovers. She heard the sound of their steps, their subdued laughter.

She only was alone. She was like the American girl. She was alone and disgraced here. Suppose Oliver did not come all night ? What would they think of her downstairs ? She blushed, and cried in her fever. She could see the sullen sky with its lack-lustre powdered stars. Never had she seen so high, so ominous and still a night. Now, she felt sure, Oliver was with another woman. She turned, cried into the pillow, pressed her hand to her forehead : ran her fingers through her hair hanging in lank sweaty ringlets. Unable to bear it any more, she began to groan softly. Then the hotel, suddenly grown quiet and gone to sleep, frightened her. She got up, put on her dressing-gown, took out a French grammar-book and began to read.

' Quelques adjectifs perdent le son nasal dans la liaison. Ex. : Divi(n)-nenfant,' etc.

She looked up at the still, breeding night, the sound-less, close-wrapped night, and imagined it full of a thousand bedded loves, millions of murmurs in the dark of rooms, square miles of tumbled pillows, and some-where amongst them Oliver's seraphic white smile, which could be seen in the dark, smiling into someone else's knotted hair and little ear. Pure tears of suffering fell down her face. She got back into bed shivering some-what in her fever. When she got back to bed the torments of the bedridden and helpless returned to her. She thought, ' As soon as I can get up I return to London. I won't stay at the mercy of an irresponsible young man. Paul would never have left me in this pass.' She sobbed a long time out of pain and self-pity, and became quiet again, listening to the steps in the street. She thought: ' He has met with an accident : he will be torturing himself over me.' Her pains eased a little after a few hours, and she fell half-asleep. She did not hear him ring.

She woke to see an easily-recognised dark shape in the opening door.

' Oliver ! Oh, Oliver ! '

He held her closely without a word ; then exclaimed : ' Darling, you are burning.'

' Oh, Oliver, where have you been ? I was nearly out of my mind with fright.'

He told her a history : an accident, two taxis colliding in the Boulevard Raspail at the corner of the rue de Rennes : there had been a man seriously wounded and he had had to go to the station and give evidence : then he had thought the man dying and gone to the hospital with him. His story was convincing : he had actually seen a car graze another car at the corner of the rue de Rennes.

' I am in such pain,' she moaned. ' You were away when I was in trouble.'

He looked at her, haggard : ' How can I be such a fool— so unkind ? I ruin everything. I should have thought of you before all else.'

But he was too tired. He became fretful. ' My dear, how could I know ? You know I didn't know.'

He got into bed and they both fell thankfully asleep. Her last thought was, ' I cannot leave him even so.' She had never felt so close or dear to him.

Her escapade brought her pain, fever and impatience. She had the metritis that Blanche had warned her of. She had recovered sufficiently in a fortnight to go out for an automobile ride to the Bois de Boulogne with the contrite Oliver. Oliver was all aflame on account of the marked *rapprochement* between France and Russia at this period. He also talked continually of the Saar plebiscite, to take place in the following year, which had already begun to loom in all political columns. Elvira tried to rouse her estival mind to these problems, but as they drove through the splendours of the Bois and Oliver clamoured and rejoiced, she put out a gloved hand.

'Oliver, this is our only summer: let's forget the world and politics.'

He tried to please her. She dreamed and smiled her slow smile when the sun glinted or children played.

'I feel so young, Oliver dear. I feel like sixteen. The rich grass smell brings it all back. Oh, you're happy when you're young and know nothing.'

'You know nothing now.'

When they got home they found a telephone message from Georges Fuseaux asking them to dinner, at the Pyramides. After the usual automobile ride they ended at the Duchesse café. Georges was embarrassed by the presence of Elvira, whom he had already condemned as 'just an ordinary housewife with high-school ideas in her head,' and awkwardly offered Oliver a small position in the firm to learn the business, help with the accounts, and eventually become a junior buyer.

'Think it over, think it over,' urged Georges.

'Did Marpurgo say anything about me?' Oliver could not help asking.

'Don't talk about that spongehead,' groaned Georges. 'No, he doesn't know, and please don't mention it to him. Otherwise the proposition is off. This is my business. God, that fellow would like to think it's his. It's just to counterbalance his influence with my brother —we want some other blood in the firm. A two-man firm is no good: you need strangers, new blood. We need new blood. Now, I don't want Marpurgo to discuss this till it's all settled. Antoine does the hiring and firing, but he likes you.'

They went home jubilant. Oliver laughed.

On the doorstep, in the street, they found Adam, very dashed.

Elvira flew to kiss him. ' Adam, when did you get to Paris ? '

Adam eyed Oliver and then answered sulkily, ' I've never left Paris. I had some money saved up and I blewed it all. I'm hungry,' he added plaintively, ' and I haven't paid my hotel bill. Can you take me in ? '

Elvira was all concern and Adam was their guest for two weeks. At the end of that time, Elvira got tired of him and telegraphed Paul to send her some money, ' an advance on her quarter.' When she got it, she bought Adam's ticket and sent him home.

CHAPTER VII

MARPURGO one evening, perambulating round the rue
Jacob, thoughtful, with his hands behind his back and
his mind full of the unpleasant news he had heard of
Oliver Fenton's success with Georges Fuseaux, nearly
ran into a pretty young woman, raised his hat to apologise,
and started. It was Coromandel. She looked at him
without apology, with the insolence of the Paris woman,
saw nothing in the twilight but a stooping small man :
her right foot as it touched the pavement stamped with
impatience. He heard her accent, with its pampered ring,
lisp and clip, still on the balmy air.

' But—look where you're going, I beg you ! '

' What a racy style ! A woman of race,' he muttered.
He followed her at a distance. She certainly had not
recognised him.

' As an ardent student of character I must follow her
and discover her. If I ever wrote down my studies I
should be known as the naturalist of men—the modern
Theophrastus.'

He was more bowed and wrung his hands once, his
heart pumping, his tongue outside his teeth, like a miser
trying to make up his mind to go into an exchange office
and buy a gold coin.

' Hey ! If my wife could see me now, she'd swear she
was not surprised ! Marpurgo in a new rôle, that of
woman-chaser.' He saw his features in a shop-mirror
and composed his face. ' I look detestably senile. Is
this interest in the purely abstract parts of men and
women, their characters, their puerilities, their foibles, a
sign of old-age's malice and impotence ? ' He looked at

his smoothed-out face in the next shop-mirror : ' Non-sense, I've always been a gnomic philosopher, one of the dark beings. Paracelsus condemned me to pass easily through earth ; fire, water and air denied me.' He shuddered. ' Earthy, guardian of the barren, glittering mines, unglittering where they lie, not a good spirit of the mulch—in other words a miser. I feel cold this evening, and I'm hungry. I'll have a good meal and a liqueur. Bless the French for warming the soul of man, his stomach. There she goes. Now is she eating alone ? It's queer.'

Coromandel had entered a slightly expensive restaurant on the quay at the corner of the rue des Saints-Pères—Lafon's. He went in and sat at the next table. She glanced at him casually and did not recognise him. She had a book of Albrecht Dürer's designs and pictures, and was lightly drawing in in geometrical forms the composition of ' the Flight into Egypt.' When her hors-d'œuvres came she closed the book and ate thoughtfully, perfectly oblivious of the restaurant and its scattered clients. The owner, old Lafon, and the waiters seemed to know her well, and called her ' Mademoiselle Paindebled.'

Marpurgo ordered an apéritif before his dinner and engaged the waiter in conversation about the diplomacy of Monsieur Barthou, then in London over the proposed Eastern pact. The waiter said pessimistically : ' He is only a cat's-paw, he is making a great fuss about external politics to draw the fires from internal mix-ups. They will presently get rid of him. We will have another change, you'll see.'

Marpurgo shook his head and his eyes roved from table to table.

' No, he is your best politician, as good as Poincaré or Clemenceau.'

' He is a friend of Poincaré,' said the waiter, taking Marpurgo's glass negligently.

' But not of you, the workers,' slid in Marpurgo.

' Ah, that, that is another matter,' said the waiter. ' We

have no friends but ourselves. It is a friendship not
of philanthropy but of necessity : that lasts ! '

Marpurgo laughed appreciatively ; the waiter went
cheerfully to get his order. Marpurgo took out of his
pocket the latest publication of the *Éditions du Carrefour*.
He did not understand it well, but he was a slave of
symbols, and this was a symbol of ' culture.' Coromandel looked at him for a moment and met his glance :
he smiled. She withdrew self-communing eyes and
stared at herself in the mirror. Marpurgo unwrapped
a brown-paper roll he carried, and took out a pencil-
lithograph of a lace-making métier, not a Leavers but
another. Coromandel did not even look at his table. He
put the roll beside him and pretended to fall into a brown
study. Coromandel, who had taken a full carafe of wine,
was now faintly flushed and scribbling faces on the
back cover of the book of designs. Her black coffee
came, and she lounged against the back of the upholstered
bench as she drank it. Marpurgo, with a busy air, took a
fountain-pen and a paper out of his pocket, and began to
itemise some notes, a, b, c, d. He hummed a revolutionary tune softly as he did so. The waiter arrived
with his coffee and liqueur. He lighted a cigar. As soon
as the intoxicant loosed his tongue and changed the colour
of the air, he leaned forward to Coromandel.

' Madam ! You sit there as if invisible nightingales
sang in your ears. I am a designer myself. May I say
that you are a fine artist, better than I shall ever be ? '

She answered with scarcely a glance sideways :

' I am a little drunk, but I knew it was you singing. I
also saw the design of a lace-making métier. I am drunk
enough to believe that the invisible fauna of the sightless
waving woods, yew, sycamore and elm, follow you in
your tracks. What are you, a poet, engraver ? How do
you know I draw ? My get-up ? I know I am a little
crazy.' She called the waiter. ' Waiter, the bill, please.'

' Wait,' begged Marpurgo. ' Take another coffee,
please.'

'You're really mistaken,' answered Coromandel. 'Why should I wait for you? I don't know you. If I'm not mistaken, you trod on my toes in the street just now—aren't you the clumsy fellow?'

'You should have been a lamp to my feet: should you blame the lamp or the feet?'

She looked at him curiously; then, as she remembered her legend, with a sparkling wonder. He was in a joyful riot of mystification.

'I have thought of you as fair in a fair dress and sandalled feet, on a yellow shore, with azure eyes, in the cloudless air, gathering up a belt of sapphires by a blue sea. I thought of you, too, a virgin with a white snood of your own hair, amidst stars and jack o' lanterns, your feet treading the margin scum of a rushy lake. I dreamed I went through the rooms of a fine castle, with seven wings and seven towers, that belonged to me, the white sun lay on the naked floors, pale-flowered spikes and racemes, grasses with their silver beards blew on the lawns!'

The waiter had long ago brought the bill. Coromandel motioned him near.

'Another black coffee.'

She looked at herself in the mirror, and then, tracing on the tablecloth, said quietly:

'Are you reciting something, or did you make that up?'

'I am telling you how, as a lamp swung to and fro in a gateway, I meditated.'

She laughed and tapped with her finger-nail.

'I suppose you fly through the air with the greatest of ease, towards the fire mountain and over the seas. You know that chapter of Zarathustra? I have an illustration to it. He is like you. I had difficulty with it: an earthy man looks so ridiculous standing upright in the air. But now I have it, he should limp forward a little, with a macabre swirl of coat-tails, a cabbalistic bright tie, a soft hat. Towards the coasts of tigers, water-rats, sampans and mosquitoes.'

He laughed.

' The Coromandel coast ? '

Without more mise-en-scène he produced from his pocket-book the folded drawing of the lamp in the gateway, and flattened it on the corner of the table.

' I found it in the rue de l'Université—one evening.'

' Did I lose it ? I have so many papers in my studio. Thank you.'

' Why no, it's mine.'

' Take it, then : I've got lots of others.'

' What is purloined she gives freely; to encourage tradesmen skeely : thief's advice is, show more thrift, lest outsiders catch your drift.'

Coromandel turned to him frankly and laughed.

' Well-timed breaths, notes writ ideally, make good catches—it's a gift.'

Marpurgo edged closer and leaned towards the other table, the lucent epidermis of his face pallid with excitement and self-intoxication; he had reached the rare corybantic hour that he struggled for, his low voice was splintered by the stridor of sorcery, he trembled with the internal dithyrambs of megalomania.

' Creation is rearrangement, choice out of chaos : we who are droppings of the winds only get joy in symmetry, rhythmus, isotropes and figments of perfection. We have no god but Ieros Logos. I used to dream of writing a treatise on universal harmony, you know——

> " In harmony, in heavenly harmony,
>   This universal frame began. . . ."

now, like Nicomachus of Gerase, I would write it for a lady who is the crystalline pith of divine proportion, the egg that floated on the waters. Eros——' His voice wavered; he raised his finger. ' I started with Pythagoras. I am like, am, Luca Pacioli, the monk " drunk with beauty," friend of Leonardo, that Protean son of genius. . . .'

Coromandel murmured : ' You are the monk of

beauty and I am the canon of Polycletus—is that the idea ? '

'You are not, but are the orchestra for platonic symphonies.' He shied away from this personal line again. 'This is Greek to you and me : we are Latins, we understand, we are Goths, drunk with eurhythmus, only joyful when we find the golden section, only at peace when we know the point in the circle that in the square and triangle stands. Why have mathematics and architecture always been deposited in sworn bosoms and protected by rites and the death-danger ? Because they betray the excellence of the human body, they are founded on our microcosm : we learn first to count five on our fingers, eh ? But it would be to teach the worship of the body and physical nature to the vulgar to teach them this proportion. Therefore for the mob a vile mysticism is invented, ridiculed by men of genius, by the elect and robust. To me there is nothing beyond the physical, I distil the rarest perfumes of abstraction from the correspondences of the flesh. I followed through, for years, the forest of religions, the labyrinths of symbols, the gardens of temptations that titillate and defeat the desirous soul by rapt analogy. I coldly profited by ecstasies and calentures, fought with my superiors and inferiors, dabbled in every art, left a sickness untended, did both good and evil to see things in their true perspective, to find the point of the circle that stands in the square and triangle. Do you know it ? All is well. Is it unknown to you ? Then your fabric is only moonshine. This simple secret, jealously guarded, is the power of science ; its withholding a means of keeping down the people.

'I was born with a hump on my back, and from the first day my eyes distinguished day from night I wanted to find out the secret of oppression. You see millions toiling for three ; the Egyptian secret that enslaved Coptic millions became the secret of Chartres and Fontainebleau. The liberation of men is the death of the intellectual as such. When everyone can construct his

pantheon from the polyhedron with 72 faces which
Pacioli recommends to us (all architects, we) for har-
monic meditations, the priest, the sorcerer, the poet is
dead.   For my sake we ought to return to the barbaric
rhythms of Beowulf, the primitive improvisations of
Daniel Arnault.

'Yes, the triumph of the people is the death of the
esoteric.   What is more beautiful than the regrets in
Ecclesiasticus, the cries of Job?   The lament of the old
over the follies of the young, of the decadent over the
crudities of the newly-risen?   You and I belong to a
world that is : we are in the autumnal shades, our world
still seems populous to us, as the banks and brooks of
Vallombrosa in the fall of the year. . . .'

Coromandel, who had not followed, nor would have
been able to follow, half the learned farrago, was
enchanted by the recurrence of names and themes, the
strange commanding tone he had recited all this in.

He seized his moment: 'Let's go, shall we?   What
do you do now?   I usually play chess, but to-night—I
suppose you have enchanted nights, but for me to-night
is something that will only come once or twice in a
lifetime.   Let's walk in this old suburb you know so
well.   There's no imprudence in that.   You were born
here, doubtless.   I feel I was born here too, though
actually I saw the light many miles away—in another
Latin country—in Turin.   I became English, it should
have been French.'

'Why should a man change his nationality?   Didn't
you like being Italian?'

'Ah—my country is no longer my country : she has
wedded a tyrant.   I renounced her, like a faithless wife,
a harlot-daughter.'

'You should have fought for your country, even in
its prisons.   I should do that.'

'My country rejected me : I was proscribed.'

'A socialist?'

He smiled.

'I believe in dictatorship beyond democracy, in the revolution that springs from the loins of evolution.'

'You mean a communist? Are you? It's interesting. I know a few—my father saw the rise of the labour movement in Calais, without belonging to it—he has the weakness of thinking an artisan must remain apart, "must not be regimented," but he's an ardent radical. I'm almost persuaded by the communists, their certainty of ultimate victory, their fires and intellects. For the doctrine, I am just reading Bukharin's *Historical Materialism.*'

He archly started. 'Really? And you like it? You should read—this and this—Dr. Gradus ad Parnassum himself.' He became feline. 'You're a singular young woman, aren't you? When you get farther along, I should recommend you to start from Marx's and Engel's starting-point and study Hegel himself: you can draw your own conclusions about historical materialism from the Hegelian dialectic. . . .' He rattled on, saw that she was listening with less attention, and began to chant, suddenly :

'Wise men are of one same sort, pianaviva, pacevalee,
Philosophers all men exhort, pensafonda, penetralee,
Teachers mummer, all amort, parvalibra, pecunalee,
Judges stummer in their court, prolegmagra, premittalee,
Glappering barristers consort, paucacrimna, picayanee,
Rentiers with nose in port, privapatria, primestralee,
Officers on their nags cavort, prijovepravo, pulcheralee,
Little men speak ever short, picvapecva pukulalee.'

Each line was recited with a different pose, accent and intonation to mimic the men described. Marpurgo was an actor in a small way, a resourceful mountebank.

'You are the most original of men ! '

He didn't answer, but started like a high-bred horse which has been flicked.

'No, but one with your fantasy should read Joseph Popper—Lenin worshipped him—his stories, not his philosophy. He has a story about a boy listening to a

nightingale in the night. I know nothing that so recalls
to me my early years, the years one is in the pulsating
zentrum and dreams he is but in the penumbra, when
ciliate rainbows strew his path like rushes. . . .' He
sighed. 'Do you want to walk a little ? I'm alone, if
you can spare an hour to a lonely man : when the dry
corn meets the flame, it burns high although it perishes
that way. Or should I say, you are the embroidered
screen on whose four panels, in an abstracted moment,
man man's fate sees suddenly. A Coromandel screen.'

'Do you know who I am ? '

He spoke gently, with admiration it seemed. 'Of
course, Coromandel Paindebled; you have had my
respectful homage since the first day. I am Annibale
Marpurgo.'

'Marpurgo,' said Coro rising to her feet and looking
at him. 'I must have known : it seemed to me I knew
you. All you said was like the faint echo of a bell ! '

'You know me,' said the gentleman, flattered and
surprised.

'I should have known it was you if I had had the
brains to think of it. I love a magical coincidence, an
improbable guess falling on its feet.'

'I met you often before, too, but it wasn't you,' said
Marpurgo coyly.

'This is no real magic—you're Oliver's friend, aren't
you ? '

'Oh, Oliver Fenton, of course ! ' His sallowness and
fatigue became apparent. 'Where is he now ? '

'Out of town for a few days : he's looking up some
town records in a library in—I don't believe now he told
me where.'

'Let's forget him,' rapped out Marpurgo. Then slily,
'Or would you rather talk of him ? When he comes
back, I must see him. He's looking for a job in England,
isn't he ? I want to help him.'

Coromandel smiled. 'Why—no ! ' She covered her
mistake : 'But perhaps he is. I don't think he's serious

yet. . . . I love him, I mean lightly, you know. But I've always thought I should really love an older man.'

' Yes ? '

' Or a young man very old for his years. He is not like that.'

' You want to be the vine climbing through the hair of the oak, so that when one is green, both are green.'

' Most young men are impulsive, simple-minded, like myself : I'd like to live with someone with a cloisonné mind : a sage, a cryptic man.' She stopped. ' I told you I was crazy. Everyone says I am.'

' The zephyr is so fresh and single-minded, let's stroll,' said Marpurgo. ' If all this is true—look at the dolphin-black heavens, and the spray—it's the one night in a thousand years, for me : I'd like to stay up all night to see it through. I drank not wine and water, but Aganippe and Hippocrene to-night ; I see I am now in a world of enchanters and angelic women. I am just holding you here by the arm, do you see, so that you can't go. Oh, what shall I do when the morning breaks greyly and your night-clouded shape is not there ? I shall want to drink up every thick pond to reach the sweet slime of the one-rooted lily, I shall climb lamp-posts to sup off the blond lights, I shall be rustling in the orange-headed trees at sunset, I shall fall into the river wrestling with the long chrysoberyl rays. They will certainly take me off to Charenton this week if you don't vigil with me a little.'

' No,' she said nervously, ' don't let me go away : if the enchanter can fall in love with smoke, what about the poor female face he brought in out of the air for his minute, that looks into the brawling broth and sees its wreathed beauty and then looks and sees his startling, starting, fearful, frightened, self-indulged beauty, his cheeks that were red, all pale with reading so late at night, and his violet eyes glinting with pride, conflict, desire, diamond-sharp like a glass-cutter ? Tears—whether she loves him or not she regrets him ever after. He should not have called her up for nothing, for an hour, for his own conceit.'

' You are too observant,' said Marpurgo.

' I ought to go home : this is painful,' said Coromandel, and shivered.

' Don't go : let's stop somewhere else, and I'll sing you into a better frame of mind.'

' I'm afraid of your songs : it's like the old-fashioned X-ray bulb that comes close to your skin till you feel as if you'll burst, and begins to sing in its supernatural mauve incandescence. And while it sings it takes a ghastly picture of your skeleton.'

' I have never loved anyone. I think I—at any rate, when I think of you I think of the skeleton within. That must be the same thing. I first saw you in your father's shop, on the stairway, then at the window. To-night I followed you. All the time, when I think of you I think of that shadowy scaffolding that holds up the dissolving flesh, as a scarecrow old sun-blanched jeans.'

She laughed.

' When I was a young girl, I used to see people's brains secreting their funny thoughts and odd impulses up there in the dark of the loft.' She touched her head. ' Come to my father's shop in the rue Jacob. Look in and there you'll see my mother, the old nurse, and myself at some time of the day.'

' You want to see me by daylight.'

' Are you visible then or not ? I have seen you as I have seen you : you can never surprise me, never change. When I saw your pure, good, gentle face ——'

Marpurgo passed his hand over his face, to hide his startled eyes.

' I knew you quite well,' confessed Coromandel innocently.

' You don't know me at all : I'm not what you think. I'll take you home. I'll sing you a song translated out of the Persian. This is how I got it. A dark and handsome young man came into my office in London one day : he

said he was a dethroned Persian prince, and showed me a
manuscript book of songs and poems of his own. He
wished only to get them printed so that he could begin
a literary career and earn his bread humbly by " singing,"
he said. He looked hungry, but I did not dare offer such
an elegant, delicate and sensitive boy money. The next
day he came back and borrowed £1. I was quite confused, and yet I half expected to wake up next morning
bound and mocked, fed and clothed in the palace of
Haroun. The next day he was arrested for some pathetic
little affairs of begging. He was actually heir to a de-
thronement. I'll improvise the Music to one.

> ' The silver hind her leafy sky
> And cool cloud-showing streams
> Deserted for a field near by—
> A lettuce-patch she deems
> More succulent than forest grass :
> Now is she fenced around ;
> Deer is she still, and yet an ass
> To leave home for no ground.'

' That's poor enough, it's threadbare verse : he
beggared your Barmecide, this Persian.'
' Oh, I paid him his pound really for the following.'
sneered Marpurgo :

> ' Women are by nature light,
> So we need them in the night :
> Women are by nature sweet,
> So we take them after meat :
> Women have a mother wit,
> And we like to father it.'

Coromandel stamped impatiently, and cried :

> ' Women go by fits and starts,
> So go tailors, verses, hearts. . . .'

' I can rhyme like that all day. With me, you must
rhyme better, Marpurgo. I am a woman and lighter,
ergo, you must dazzle me. Flourish, flash in your finale,
outdo me, outshine me, Annibale ! '

His lips murmured, as if dry ; his head nodded like a sea-bud on its shrunk stalk ; he replied in the voice that had the squall of strings :

'I'm hoarse, I'm old, I'm an odd-job man. I shouldn't be bothering you. I can see you think I'm ridiculous.'

'You annoy me with that line. Let's go home. The evening's ended.'

'It's not ended for those who are going to bed to dream, for insomniacs, coughers, those who sit up bolstered by a cushion and look at the wheeling stars wondering if Andromeda or they will first touch the horizon : not for those who have bills falling due to-morrow, or need the rent, or those with a police-cordon round the house, or for mothers with babies being born, or for women to be married to-morrow, or for the old who keep a lamp on all night, fearing to trust in the eternity of stars, fearing death's black smother : not for new lovers either, or men who have just found out their lives have been wasted, or men who have just found a new cause. For almost no one the night is ended. Is it for you and me ? '

'Do you always tell the truth ? ' asked Coromandel.

'Always when it's unpleasant. I always suppress a pleasant truth. It makes people think the path of virtue is easy. On the other hand, I like to flatter, especially when there is no reason for it, or basis for the compliment. It is such a pure fantasy.'

'No wonder you did not marry,' said Coromandel. 'Women like a surer man. You're such a simple man : why do you have all this tin armour-plate of shrewdness ? You talk all the time about autumnal shades and I don't know what else. You're green still. You want to suck out the world and you're angry ; you double up your fists and want to kill everyone just because pap isn't free.'

'I'm yellow now with wishing I had married the right woman : and because you're so silken, topaz and red.'

'You aren't married ? '

'No : I have no wife.'

They walked along slowly. The black Seine, with her long lights rolling in the new breeze, said nothing. A body covered in a tarpaulin lay on the ramp waiting to be taken up by the water-police.

'A dead man,' said Coromandel.

They looked over the stone coping on to the quays : the lights were dispersed by the rustling trees. The fresh damp air blew up. Someone walked below, looking up at them with a patch-blue face.

Marpurgo put his hand on her arm to move her along.

'To-night will be short, although I am in a fever, with thinking over all that has happened to us, and making up songs to sing to you : it will be like Christmas Eve when I was a little boy, when bands were playing carols far and near all over the district. The bed rustles at the foot as your mother puts parcels in your stocking. Soon the early light will come and you can get up : all night you lie, start up, dream and wake again in the lovely joy of expectation. Early in the morning the band plays at your great gate, at the end of the drive. They made angelic music all night and in the morning you are surprised to see their ordinary faces, like the milkman and the post-man. The night has been too short for all the expectation. So much too short this night will be for me. I can see in the north star winged trees in a leafy wood, spathe-palms and the tufty coroneted cycads, flamingoes take roots, pelicans grow in strelitzias, phoenixes take root, cannons of hexagonal crystal shoot puffs of light across a smoky pavement where a peacock pecks, all in a solitary yellow hill. Across a single bridge in a folded chapel you stand looking down, obstinately frowning, remote because I dream. So I will wake all night, not to be too far away from the reality, in dream. . . .'

Coromandel said sharply : 'Doesn't Mercutio say, "I hate a dreamer, he lies so."' She pointed to the quays. 'It's a dead man : isn't it horrible? To think that you are alive there, so full of images, breeding, talking about death and decay—but there is the truth.

I must get to know more people. I believe everyone's story about themselves. And by everything, I'm swayed. When I see the melancholy creature down there, I despise us both, you know? I wish you would advise me how to study, Marpurgo. You know people's dilemmas so well.'

Marpurgo said timidly, stooping:

' You see too much in me.'

She shook her head. ' I don't think so. Some day this week, come and see my father. He likes to talk to you.'

Alone, she clasped her hands round her breast and said with joy:

' Marpurgo ! The man outdoes his description. What will Oliver say to this ? And when he hears how he spread himself for me ! Oliver—Marpurgo ? Which of them ? ' She fell asleep overcome by the excitement of the conversation. It was a hot night with a small wind. She dreamed of Marpurgo as a smoky spiral of mystic blue, neatly bowing his way out of a snuff-jar.

' Marpurgo ! ' she called. His head nodded like a sea-bud on its sea-swirled palsied stalk, his leverine eyebrows and violet eyes twinkled. He called back unintelligibly in his inhuman stridulous tone. She woke up and repeated calmly a song she had just seen written on a livid sky in blue neon lights :

> ' Landscip's murky, grisly stars,
> Lone mastaba's ululation
> And the tintinnabulation
> Of cracked bell beneath horizon
> Ringing hissing dead's orison ;
> (Pizzicato, spiritoso !
> Pluck the marrowbones and cleavers,
> Auribus arrectis ! Weavers
> Dreadful, destined, three deceivers,
> Wind, bind, snip us. Groan, oboes, so.) '

Marpurgo stood gaping in a corner of her dream, his mouth his lung's lesion, his finger was pointed at her,

he spat at her in despite, in jealousy : 'Should Zana do
what Kubla can ? '

She cast her eyes to the vitreous roof mantled by the
cloth above, and saw the blond flaunting sun fall bleached
mellow into the chamber's pearly lack-lustre obscurity.
She remembered the visions and bodily fires of her
embraces with Oliver in that room. The floating light
rose and flowed about the walls with the lactescent murex
of great magnolia flowers.

Now she was planted in a bubbly incandescent pool :
she smoked, she calcined, she sweated rivers to quench
the fires that melt rocks : she froze with such resolution
that she seemed lank as an icicle : she blushed, she became
dingy-white as death. Through Marpurgo she was in
love. On one side crouching, whispering, chanting,
dark, wicked, divine, stood Marpurgo. She began to
pity Oliver's crudeness a little and disdain it. Not that
Coro for a moment thought of poor Marpurgo as a lover,
but as the lonely sphinx may have regarded an earlier
and less successful Oedipus. She was in love. Only by
imagining hyperbolic and hyperborean scenes of licence,
folly and luxury, throngs of splendid women, sybaritic
men, courts, staircases, frescoes, tapestries, plate, porcelain, jewels, wild-hued cheeks, eyes flashing with zodiacal
light, spilled wines, lips smeared with sherbets, serpented
arms, agate-nailed hands, small snowy feet, like doves,
medusan locks, and angelican skies and the scattered
roses of blood and the ascending spirals of mystic purple,
and the wild, white-browed, dark-locked faunish youth,
and old age paunched or shrivelled with white body-hair,
lazily leering with dead-fish eyes, like almonds slit
through three green and pasty rinds, and purple mouths
ending in folds and ranges of lofty noses, whiter and
snottier than the jutting Tyrol, and love, bestial and
divine, to excess—only by these dreams could she forget
her love, fever, and the insufficiency of men.

CHAPTER VIII

MR. PAINDEBLED sat in the folds of a Persian rug at the back of the shop reading with anxious attention, in the dusk, the evening paper. There had been a special vacation vote of aerial and military credits for fortifying the eastern frontier and strengthening the air forces. His taxes had been increased that year and he had done almost no business. He wondered whether it would pay him to sell his shop and move out to Versailles in retirement. Coromandel could work even better out in that quiet town, and he would not spend the money in business taxes that could go to her dowry. The spasmodic young man courting her, the English student, did not seem eligible, even though Mr. Paindebled came from Calais, the most English of French towns. On the other hand, an Englishman did not expect a dowry. But Coromandel's son would be an Englishman, and she herself would lose her birthright. A new law had just been passed, and rigorous regulations were now in force against foreigners residing and working in France. Mr. Paindebled could not take such a son-in-law into his business unless he became French. And if he became French, he would be called up in the next war, which appeared rather close at hand, in view of the various military credits being voted. Then, it seemed, this young man imagined he was a communist. It was, naturally, a student's caprice, at the same time it might show an unruly radical kink. He was radical himself, God knew, he was the son of three revolutions, but three revolutions are enough.

Mr. Paindebled watched, through the laces, handles,

incrustations of silver jugs, piercings of marble, ivory
and jade, the evening people who went past in tatters.
The evening was grey and windy; the late-setting sun
flattened to two dimensions the roofs of the opposite
houses, and a tardy gleam lighted on the shoulder of a
Chinese jar just where it was chipped. Opposite the
antiquary, above his head, in a cupboard, were some new
fragments of Spanish lace. He wondered if his new
friend, Mr. Marpurgo, would really buy any lace for his
collection. He wondered intensely about the collection
of Mr. Marpurgo. Marpurgo was a shuttle, void of guts,
spinning out his thread endlessly. One could never
really cotton on to foreigners, even intelligent ones, and
even Latins of another breed. The Italians are always
charming, windy, fretful, untrustworthy. The Spanish
too, are untrustworthy. So are the English. And
Marpurgo was English and Italian. Coro had teased
about Annibale Marpurgo, who it appears was a friend
of this Oliver also. She rhymed

> ' L'Italien anglicé,—
> Deux fous, un satané ! '

His thoughts flew to the salon above, where the splendid
lace umbrella-cover, the stuff of dreams, hung against the
wall, facing the green-eyed hamadryad. If his taxes were
not so heavy, his life would be perfect. He now was
lucidly awaiting Marpurgo, whose stealthy complex mind
he imagined as full of anastomosing threads, a lace-mind,
one which he liked to induce to self-embroidery, seeing
the shuttles flying in the dark, hearing the click of the
battalions of threads, always advancing, watching the
Jacquard cards unfold and refold. A same design but a
long one, an old design but a stock one.

Sometimes people stopped before the window, wavering, to fill in the slow hour to dinner, or to fill a gap in
their minds—and went on. He knew how many people
to expect in a day, a week, a year. Only Marpurgo had
come in at the wrong time and unexpectedly, but Mar-

purgo was a comet. Paindebled sat there, leaning against
the tallboy, feeling through the thin skin of his finger-
tips the texture of the Persian rug. Marpurgo's slight
stoop and overcoat, which fell about him like an Arab
blanket, darkened the obscure doorway. 'Obscurum
per obscurius.'

Marpurgo looked about him, picked out Coro's father,
and with his young breaking voice that would soon
become senile, spoke.

'I have something, something which I hope you will
let me give your charming daughter, Mlle Coromandel,
a hand-painted, hand-illustrated and hand-bound book.'
He produced a folio-sized package from his coat. 'If
you will permit me ; perhaps you yourself will be so good
—no doubt she is out with her young friends.'

'She is upstairs : she will have dinner with us to-night.
You are very kind indeed. My wife is ill to-night. My
daughter must keep to the house. My wife demands her.'

'I regret very much that your wife is unwell. She
is not in bed ? '

'No. I have mounted the umbrella-piece.'

He turned on the light. 'Let me take your hat and
coat. Look at this Spanish lace : what do you think of
it ? Meantime I will put up the shutters : it is seven.'

'Marvellous, exquisite,' murmured Marpurgo. 'I was
at the auctions yesterday. Fortunate for us that everyone
is so poor, and veritable masterpieces go for very little.
Personally, also, I am against these multiplications to
infinity of the value of goods : they cannot be worth it.
Can they be worth more than he can pay who made it ?
Should they ? '

'An oyster makes a pearl ; can he pay for it ? '

'A pearl is just lumbago to an oyster.'

Paindebled closed the front door. 'Let's go upstairs
now.' He rang, and the old servant brought them port
in a blue set of Bohemian glass. They had drunk two
glasses each when the door opened behind Marpurgo's
back, and he heard Paindebled exclaim :

'Well, thou here, Amélie! Thou art better now?'

A woman stood in the doorway, a tall, strongly-built middle-aged woman, with long, silken blond hair parted and dressed in a horn on each side of a high forehead, with plump hands carrying rings, and wrists circleted with old-fashioned bracelets, and two falling cuffs of fine hand-embroidered Malines. Her hands were clasped in front of a velvet jacket while she stood calmly looking, not at her husband, but at Marpurgo. Marpurgo rose:

'Madame.'

'Monsieur Marpurgo, dear friend; my wife, Monsieur Marpurgo.'

Marpurgo raised her hand to his lips. Clusters of beautiful artificial rosebuds hung from each horn of the dressed hair, a beautiful black Spanish mantilla, in a pansy design, was folded round her shoulders. Her shoulders were exposed under the mantilla, and her velvet jacket was folded very low in front to show a bosom of mediocre grain and colour. The shoulders had a fine curve, rolling in towards the bosom, the waist was rather slender: oval eyes lay broad apart in a large oval face of peasant strain. In this eccentric lady it was easy to recognise Coromandel's mother. The husband had taken her hand and held it with a delicate firmness.

She kept looking at Marpurgo with a droop of the eyes and mouth and a faint smile, like the unconscious sick smile of a very young baby. The husband chided: 'Amélie! I am glad to see you are feeling a little better.'

The woman's unwrinkled calm face broke into a timid smile.

'I am enchanted that you visit our too-quiet home, Monsieur.'

The husband dropped her hand and tried to guide her gently to the door. She stood like a Noah's Ark dame, aspiring, one would have said, Marpurgo's atmosphere. She awoke again and said, in her flat broken voice, between two registers: 'I have been a little ill: I have been ill for years.'

The brows, edged with dark gold hair, were beautifully full, the mouth a Mona Lisa mouth, if it had not been unpleasantly compressed in the centre under a drooping nose-point. She glanced down at her shawl, smiled to herself, and looked up to see if they had noticed it.

'I shall stay,' she said to Paindebled. 'You see, I got dressed for the evening. I heard you had come,' she said to Marpurgo; 'my daughter told me your name. She heard much of you through a little friend, a young friend.'

The husband had crossed the room to ring the bell. She said in a confidential tone : 'I have not been myself for a long time. It is pleasant to see friends. I was not really ill : a sort of house-fever, a mental low-fever, as you get when you are too much in your own universe.' The golden-tinged skin was awakening, intelligence gathered over the different features in gleams, and joining, fell upon the whole mask like a light. She seemed equally to be gathering grace from her nerves, the fibres in remote points of her system, and began showering them on him with love.

'You are an expert in laces, I hear. Do you like these cuffs ?' She proffered her hand, placing it on the back of Marpurgo's hand so that he could see the lace, while with the other hand she laid it out and displayed it. Marpurgo took her hand by the tips of the fingers and gently laid it on the couch, spreading out the lace on the dark blue background of the rug. Her hands were pretty, rather plump at the base on a thick wrist, with small slender tapering fingers and a broad thumb. The line from the little finger to the wrist was the shape of an odalisque's leg from waist to little toe. One side of the face was broader than the other, and was beautiful, mild and fresh as the face of a white calf ; the other side of the face, the left side, narrower, was more shadowed, more marked by passion, and of a grave sensual seduction. The lady attracted the eye again and again for the various eccentric beauties of her face and body. Marpurgo's face

was lifted to her again and again. He withdrew his eye
to remember the symbolism of what he had just noted,
as her shoulder under the lace-shawl, her asymmetrical
face, the downward sweep of the faintly coloured mouth,
curling like a kriss, the hand, the thick silken blond
hair, the fantastic roses in it. The lady sat coolly, without
speaking, but seemed delighted with his scrutiny. The
husband, who had been speaking to a servant, came back
and said :

'Coro is waiting for you, Amélie.'

The lady rose sedately, giving Marpurgo her hand.

'Please forgive me : my daughter has something to
say to me. I will send her out to see you : she is a pretty
child : not as I am. You will see her : you must tell me
if you think she will grow to be a real beauty.'

'I will tell you,' said Marpurgo, bowing and smiling.

The lady went out with an air, much pleased with
herself and him. As she went out of the door, she half-
turned, and showed him the seductive, the left side of her
face : something in the set of the shoulders suggested
Coromandel. Marpurgo's heart went plop ! The father
took his arm and led him to the umbrella-cover, now
spread out : long tapering clusters of flowers and leaves
wheeled into the centre from the deep border, which was
a fairy surf of strings of forget-me-nots, shell-like leaves,
crescents of openwork. A ring of little birds fluttered
round the border over this surf. The tulle was machine-
made, but all the design was made by hand. Marpurgo
examined it closely, and began to praise it : keeping an
eye on it, the father discoursed rapidly and wittily on a
dozen other subjects.

Presently he asked : 'Did you notice the scarf my wife
was wearing? A hand-made mantilla : it was my
wedding-present to her. She is proud and fond of it. I
was most surprised to see her wearing it. My wife is a
little eccentric. But she was a fine lace-designer. That
was how I met her. At first she used to work with me.
Then a curious change began in her : she began to be

eaten up by ambition. She worked days and nights without a break for weeks on end, to finish a design. But she could only do uncommercial things ! She worked for a whole year once, and at the end, on my name day— my name is Jacques—she gave me a magnificent design that she had worked out ready for putting on the Jacquard machine—six scenes, the history of my life, in lace ! ' He looked at Marpurgo with a quizzical expression. ' After that she lost heart a little : Coromandel was born. She made lace herself for Coro's clothing. Then the fever got her again, but she frittered away her time, fevered and impuissant. She said she would not become a dabbler in other arts, like the bohemian sort that she hates. She gave up music, of which she is fond, and only once or twice a year tinkles on the piano : for years she has done nothing but study odd things— medicine, zoology, economics, on and off, and whenever she starts a new subject she starts a new piece of embroidery, something vast, a bedspread, a curtain ; the embroidery is to give her something to do when she tires of the book.

' It always ends, in two or three days, with her devoting herself to the embroidery entirely, and so she works at it day after day, week after week, month after month till she comes near the end, and then she falters. She sometimes lies in bed for a week and more, in a darkened room, speechless, without energy, wasted by the fever with which she has been designing, embroidering. Then she will put away that piece of work for months, and for months do nothing but sit in the garden, or if it is winter, sit in Coromandel's studio, watching her or idly playing with a pencil. At last some day, she will take up one or other of her old unfinished pieces of embroidery and finish it. And soon the terrible fever starts again.' He laughed, a bubble from the effusion of speech on his red underlip, and looked sideways down at Marpurgo. ' She was beautiful, beautiful, as a girl,' he continued, ' always with that calm, grave, and yet seductive expression. She never spoke but sensibly, she was always charitable, never gave a hard opinion without a proviso : I only feared she was a little cold. Don't you get that impression ? '

Marpurgo murmured : ' No, not exactly : your wife is a most charming lady, but . . .'

' Her parents warned me that she had a perfectly un- governable temper : they spoke of it in hair-raising terms. Yet, knowing her as I did, and seeing how mild she was, I thought they were meek people who had been scared by a couple of tantrums. Not at all : a few months after we were married, I said something to her, joking, I don't even remember now : it would have seemed nothing to anyone else. But it was true, she had an ungovernable temper. I shall never, till my dying day, forget the amazement and terror of that day : those calm, clear eyes looked at me golden with fury, insane pride, alien, animal : she did not get red but pale, alabaster-pale, and came after me quite unconsciously with the stealthy tread of a wild-cat. I was giddy four hours after, and she had violent migraine. A few months after, when I was teaching her to play chess, it occurred again. She wanted to beat me and was sure she could. She would neither eat nor drink till she had mastered several books of instructions and one by a chess champion. Then she came out one night armed for the fray ; but she had no talent for it : the theory was useless to her. She thought at first she was winning, and in the end made a series of intelligent moves (I found after they came from the end-games of the chess champion), but her memory failed her, and evidently her natural talent for it was small. I beat her. She put up the board and said nothing : but when I looked at her she was once more that poisonous pale colour. She went into the bedroom, and when I followed her she gave me that look of delirious fury. " Don't touch me, don't dare touch me." A terrible change took place and her face became the mask of a witch, evil, murderous. She went into the hall, and I heard a strange muffled bumping sound : she was beating her head against the wall. After a minute she stopped, turned round, came to me, calm again, mild, saying " I can't help it." She had the migraine again. Sometimes she is irritable, untouchable for a week : at other times nothing irritates her, and, strange to say, she is never irritated by children. She cannot stand much company, and after a little while retires to her room : the noise in the streets, the bustle of traffic also gives her bad headaches. For that reason she keeps to her room.

' I came to her one day and found her trembling and feverish : she had heard a quarrel between a young married couple who have an apartment opposite us across the courtyard. She was nervous and ready to cry all the evening. For that reason she has to stay indoors. The country does her great good : but I have my shop, we cannot live in the country, and she cannot live without me and her daughter : without us she becomes frightfully restless.' He said sadly : ' When she was a child she was much worse than she is now : I think she is improving with age.' Still talking, he unwrapped a tissue-paper and showed Marpurgo a book of Hours he had just acquired, and went on, sighing : ' When she was ten years old she held her hand in the fire till one finger was burned to the bone and the others fearfully singed and blistered, because her only brother boasted he feared pain less than she did. Then, they had to pull her hand out of the fire. It festered for months after, and did not heal for a long time, but she never murmured once in all that time. I asked her once, when she was quietly, amusedly recalling her foolhardiness, " Did it hurt you ? " " Very much," she said, " but I was obliged to do it : it was stronger than me. And every moment I burned I was more joyful, as if I pushed a knife farther into my brother." '

Marpurgo asked, rather troubled : ' Your daughter is like her mother in that ? '

The father laughed heartily. ' Oh, a little, but not in that way : Coromandel is proud, but not to the point of insanity. With Coro all that has gone into pure work-manship, and she is a first-class workman.' The father rang the bell again, and when the maid appeared, said :

'Ask Mlle Coromandel to come here if she is free now.'

Marpurgo took two or three turns up and down the room with his hands in his pockets, thoughtfully, his eyes on the floor : he feared to show the tremulousness he felt. The door opened, and Coromandel appeared, with suppressed panting, flushed.

'I just left Mamma : she is resting. She will come downstairs after dinner,' she said when she had greeted Marpurgo. She smiled at him. 'Mamma says you were charming to her : she was very happy to meet you.'

Marpurgo had never been so ill at ease. He was ashamed of himself. He flattered himself on his smooth manners. He produced his parcel as awkwardly as a boy, and said : 'Your father was kind enough to allow me to give you this book. I saw it in Blanchetière's and thought your artistic eye would be pleased with it.' She took it with excitement.

'How lovely of you ! I am so happy : I never get a present,' she said naïvely.

Marpurgo looked happy. He saw the father watching him closely and with some amusement, and he immedi-ately turned to him and began to patter learnedly about types of illustration, surrealism and so many other things that presently the father had forgotten all about that moment when they had both looked so joyful. He came back to it later on, though, and for the first time began to wonder what sort of a man Coromandel would love. 'It is not possible that Marpurgo——' he said to himself several times, stopping short each time, recrossing his legs and starting again. 'It couldn't be that Marpurgo . . . no : and yet who knows ? She's an odd girl.'

The dinner was gay, delightful : the father and daughter were a brilliant pair, full of poise : they were a perfect trio. After dinner the mother came down, in a handsome evening-gown, of silk plush encrusted on black ninon, the gown draped round the shoulders as before in an old-fashioned way : her hair was parted in the middle and dressed on the top of the head, and she wore brilliants in it now.

' You look like one of the masterpieces of Ingres,' said Marpurgo, making up now, in gallantry, for all the missteps before dinner.

The lady became radiant. Coromandel explained that her mother, in fact, admired Ingres deeply : Marpurgo then remembered that in several of his portraits of ladies, the hair was dressed in both of the ways he had seen Mme Paindebled wear. Once or twice, when Marpurgo addressed himself particularly to Coromandel, he noticed a deep shade of pain and affront cloud the mother's face, and, remembering that she rarely saw visitors, he set himself out to court her. He sang for them Arab songs and Chinese songs that he had learned in China when he had been there buying the Irish-pattern lace which is now made there. He told them stories of China—the cocoon raising, on which whole villages of hovels live, the anxieties of good and bad years, the usurers, closed mills, little girls sold for a few handfuls of rice, the floods, famine, the revolution. Coro's face was a flame of joy, wonder and enthusiasm : the mother listened with a deep expression of joy and seemed inexpressibly flattered by his attentions : the father listened with approval ; and presently they got on to politics. Then the lady's attention wandered, and presently, saying she had a headache, she excused herself, begging Marpurgo to come soon and entertain her—' they saw few friends so kind and interesting '—and asking for Coro's arm as she left the room. Marpurgo fancied she looked at Coro with a little jealousy, suspicion or pique. At any rate, Coro did not appear again until Marpurgo was about to leave, and then she excused herself, saying her mother had required her constant attention, her headache had been so bad.

The next day, at his hotel, he received a note, in large

pretentious handwriting on lavender monogrammed paper, from the mother, begging him to come to tea on the following Saturday, and to forgive the nonchalant invitation—' she was so out of the world and saw so few people.'

Marpurgo meanwhile was disturbed because it was clear that both parents thought him too old to court Coromandel, and he had as a rival Oliver's great beauty and charm. As he played his games in the various chess cafés and in the chess-club in the rue de la Sorbonne, he pondered what he had better do to ruin Oliver's chances with Coromandel. He wanted Coro to think he had a high moral character, and so he could not take all of the avenues which immediately invited him. He decided to go and see the mother on Saturday, for the sake of finding out more about the family. He also thought it likely that Coromandel would be there simply to keep her mother company. He had already perceived that the mother had developed a violent fondness for him, and he knew he would have to minuet with a delicate step to avoid engaging her too far in love or annoying and wounding her. He was glad he had heard already how passionate and unreasonable she was. Her face rose before him, larger than Coromandel's, more irregular and coarser but at times commanding : the delicate long face of the father had modified this face in Coromandel. He dreamed about the young girl, and at times it seemed impossible that she would think seriously of him : he looked ruefully in the café mirrors, as he sat there or moved in and out in his cloak. Before Saturday he bought a new hat, a black one, and pearl-grey gloves, endeavouring to look more French : he found that he looked younger. On Saturday he turned up with a nosegay for the mother, and was disappointed to be received alone by her in her own sitting-room, with her maid in attendance. Coromandel was at an art class, the mother said, and was going for supper to what is called a ' *surprise-party*,' a gathering of young things in the house of one or the other, to which everyone takes food or drink. The mother mentioned the beauty of the book Marpurgo had given Coro, watching his face surreptitiously, and then said casually that she was much sought after by young men, but they had yet to find a youth of suitable position, and that Coromandel herself was proud and difficult to please : in fact, she had several times said that she had not the slightest intention of marrying for a long time.

' I think a daughter should stay near her mother,' she remarked soulfully.

Marpurgo, with the noticeable but indescribable flickerings and movements of an animal stalking its game or being stalked, all attention and charm, succeeded in turning the conversation without allaying the mother's suspicions : presently in the charm of his conversation, she had forgotten her dawning jealousy. He found it expedient to play a dangerous game, to court her and flatter her insistently : by the end of the hour she was content and her heart at rest. She showed him her laces and designs for laces, the pretext of his visit. He left, promising to come soon to dinner. When he left he remarked to himself that the mother could be, on occasion, when the discontent and restlessness had left her face, a beautiful and striking woman. He was in a difficulty : he felt he could not see Coromandel now as he had seen her before, unknown to her parents, now that he had become their friend. He would have to take her advice and speak to her father as soon as it was possible. In his eyes she was so full of youthful charm and talent that her chances of marrying her admirers must be numerous. He wanted to impress himself upon her and not frighten her with any suggestions for the future, or proposals of a serious kind. It was a laughable thing, that although he knew her mind, and her maturity, he had always in his mind her youth, and so, it seemed, her freshness, innocence and softness.

Thinking about it now, he walked up and down until

it was near twilight, and then, in his restlessness, he went
to Oliver's hotel to see him or Elvira and hear whether
he had been out. If he found her alone, he intended to
sow seeds of doubt in Elvira's mind. Always before him
stood the triumphant youth. He began to think of his
old age and of how few warm fruitful days remained to
him. Then, with a rush he began to accuse Coromandel.
She might have waited in to see him, not left the house
bare like that with nothing but a sentimental middle-aged
woman to entertain him. And again, what did Coromandel really care for him ? He was almost her mother's
age. He was so restless that he paced up and down in
front of the door of the flat Oliver and Elvira had taken
by the month in the old house in the rue Thouin.

They were out. He went there before he went to
work the next morning.

The cleaner let him in. He called ' It's Marpurgo ! '
and Elvira's voice came from the bedroom :

' Oh, come in, Annibale ! '

She was sitting before her glass, and saw Marpurgo
standing hatless in the doorway. Her dressing-gown
was carelessly open.

' Come in, Marpurgo ; you're not intimidated by a
woman's throat, are you ? '

He sat down behind her, looking at their reflections
in the triple mirror.

' Don't move, Elvira, I like to see your image this way.'

' You're dressed to kill : who is your quarry ? '

' I'm sorry you're not out this lovely summer weather.
Are you two going to the country ? Yet you have a
lovely colour when the rest of us are as yellow as jaundice
or red as apoplexy.'

She smiled and looked at herself, speaking to him and
making slight graceful movements among her toilet
articles.

' Help yourself to an apéritif, or some brandy : there's
some in the dining-room. Jeanne will find it for you
if you can't.' She sneezed.

'A cold? Funny weather for colds now : it seems as hot as an oven, and you begin to sniffle.'

She shook her tendrilled head, damp with the heat of a bath.

'I wore my nightdress under my pillow, and that gives me a cold. Andrew Fulton's girl says she never wears a nightdress summer or winter. She seemed to think I was an old fogey.'

'Where's the man of the house ? '

'At the Archives to verify some dates. It's quite as boring to listen to Oliver's trade-unions as to Paul's cases. Why are men's jobs so boring ? I darn Oliver's socks, I darned Paul's socks. At home I studied German to please Paul, here I look up the verbs in " Salammbô " to convince Oliver I'm not lazy. Only at home I had enough linen, and here I have wine with every meal. It's odd, isn't it ! I think life is a pattern, and you have to weave the thread you're intended to.'

'And that's how you spend your days ? You spend them in reposing, in quietude, in philosophy, in stitching, reading, gilding refined gold, in waiting for your man to come back, in happy pensiveness without anticipation or remorse ? You are really a happy woman, Elvira ? '

'More or less : I suppose so. I'm not actively un-happy, at the moment. That's because I have time still. I still have time. Paul won't let me divorce yet. He says I'm a child : he will wait. If I made a false step now, it would be too late in after years to regret it. I should be too old then. He writes to me once a week.'

'If he stopped writing, would you mind ? '

'I think so.'

'If someone else darned Paul's socks, your old home was closed to you, you saw your old friends clustering round a new ménage, Paul's tenderness raining on the head of another woman, Paul's face lighting up in the evening at some other girl's smile ? You will never regret that settled life, the retirement of English life, the peace of living lawfully, the countryside in the twixt-season, the gardens, long-fingered trees, the late high spider-light of summer, the soot-faced houses and Georgian porches ? '

' In a way, I have had enough of Paris and yet I know I'll regret that too. Oliver will be going home soon. Then he says he'll look round for an apartment straight-away, in Gordon Square or some nice place. We'll send for my household things and I'll be just as happy as before.'

' Paul is very kind to you : so are they both.'

' He is very kind to me : I suppose people would say, too kind. But I don't see why not ; we have always been friends. What good does it do to take umbrage ? '

' He is too kind to you.'

Elvira withdrew chillily.

' Yes, that's what you all think. A woman has no right to freedom. She is someone's property. She has no right to tolerance. Blanche d'Anizy said months ago, A woman has to fight for everything she has, fight or scheme. That's true. I used to sneer at women with their cheap truisms. Travel and learn.'

' Oliver is such a charming fellow. I am sure you'll be happy with him in your new life in London. You have been wise. You'll be surrounded by young people. Oliver won't make as much money as Paul for some time, but he has the advantage of not loving furniture too much for its own sake. I fancy he has a little I.W.W. in him— the mobility of the hobo, you know. You should see the world with him. But then, travelling with a loving faithful husband is like having a home away from home all over the country. And you will always move in radical circles where the people are much kinder than in the conformist world of Paul. And a delightful woman, yourself, who is anxious to develop her mind and take an interest in things, will be very happy, I should think.' He leaned forward impressively : ' I rarely talk of personal physical attributes. I don't think they're important ; beauty is of the mind. Oliver is beautiful, impulsive ; he could turn any woman's head and easily fall a victim to their advances—that is one's first impression. It is illusory. One sees that though he has the charm of a Don Juan, the brilliance and headiness of Julien Sorel, he has yet the fidelity of the Chevalier des Grieux.'

Her face was serious, but she watched him carefully. He looked unspeakably crafty.

' Who was this Chevalier ? '

' Not Maurice,' he teetered, ' he's too old for you to know, you child. He was the faithful lover of Manon Lescaut.'

' Is that your impression of Oliver ? '

' Yes, some might think him an easy prey for women— his soft cheek, lustrous eye, dimpled chin, you know, the old wives' indicia !—but I think he's a splendid fellow, splendid.'

' He may be a splendid fellow and still run after women. I know that means nothing to men. They are all masonic brothers when it comes to that. But as for Oliver, he's a boy. I think I know him well enough to know if he ever trifled. He could not keep anything from me—yet.'

' After all,' said Marpurgo, laughing heartily, ' you are a woman of experience, and gifted with everything needed to make a woman delightful. I am sure you can twist us all round your little finger.'

After a moment's thought, she said, after unconsciously examining her little finger with care :

' I'm used to speaking frankly. I think nothing is gained by skirmishing. I believe you came here this afternoon to tell me something, or give me some advice. I'll ask you for it. What do you think yourself I should do ? '

' Advice is never taken, I never give it.' Marpurgo was prompt. The child's method she used, of facing him down, was easy play for him. ' No, no : you love Oliver, Oliver loves you : that's all there is for you to think about at present. Paul must plead for himself. I came to see how you both are. I am going to London on Wednesday next, and would be of service if I can do

anything for you—or Oliver, of course. I thought of
calling on Paul : he asked me to. I took to him immediately. I imagine everyone does. I'm going straight
from here to the home of a friend of mine, Monsieur
Paindebled—funny name, Paindebled, Wheatbread, isn't
it, really?—who is interested in laces. He has the
strangest possible household—most curious. A half-mad
wife, who dresses up like portraits by Ingres, a talented,
beautiful daughter who is a good designer, also slightly
touched, if I'm any judge. The father is an affinity.
Mademoiselle Coromandel, that's the daughter, is as
blonde as you are brunette, like a corn-tassel, a brilliant
intellectual girl. She speaks English very well. In fact,
she is rather interested in some English student here, I
believe, a student of economics—one of those things
everyone studies in his post-graduate pre-professor year.
I never asked his name. He works at the Archives. No
doubt Oliver knows him. There can't be too many
English students down there—even though Paris is the
dream of the English race ! '

' Oh, I hate it here,' she said passionately. ' It's no
home for us. The French have closed family circles, and
unless your situation is regular and you can come out in
the open, you sit with a lot of Anglo-Saxon loafers and
drink aperitives.'

' Well, I had better be going if Oliver is coming. I
hope you and he will soon be settled. You see too little
of each other now, don't you ? He works so hard ; and
these political discussions in cafés which keep him out
. . . a woman must hate men for their politics ! May I
come and take you both out—a little party before I leave
—on Monday ? We'll go to the Bois : just afternoon
sports-dress—everyone wears it now. We can pick Oliver
up anywhere just as he is. Ask him if there is anything I
can do for him in England. You can't just drop there out
of the blue, can you ? You have your friends to make all
over again. And you have both so much to think of and
decide upon.'

'I'll give you a letter for Paul,' said Elvira. 'Don't tell Oliver. It irritates him. Good-bye. You're not a real friend, Annibale : you're always playing some game, but I can work in with one of your moves, and so I will.'

He kissed her hand : 'I really worship you, Elvira.'

The concierge knocked at the door just after he left with a *pneumatique* from Oliver saying that he would not be in for lunch : he had gone to see Georges Fuseaux. Georges had located a new, elegant and moribund café with expensive food and bad service, and was trying to convert one or two bosom friends to it. In order to get Oliver to his café for lunch, he had promised to speak to Antoine about him as soon as Antoine had come back from his projected holiday.

'I want to get you in to learn the work : Marpurgo may decide to pension himself off. We'll give him twelve months' salary, but we don't have to see his mug round the place as well as pay him.'

'You're getting rid of Marpurgo ?'

'Oh, I suppose he can talk himself into another job. I hear he's been canvassing for one with a promoter here, I forget his name, who's trying to develop a French news-service linked up with some New York stock-pools. It isn't that he's interested in stocks, but he likes to get round and talk to people ; he likes to have two strings to his bow, and he can't bear to play a straight game with anyone.'

'You're not prejudiced against him, by any chance ?'

'I know him. Don't worry : I'm always the grouch, but I know a *duplicit* man when I see one. That goof just hates even to take his liquor straight. It's a wonder he doesn't have his hair curled.'

In the afternoon, Oliver, whose work was practically finished, and who was taking a ' holiday,' wandered over to Coromandel's studio. He cast a beggarly thought for a moment in Elvira's direction, but he thought, ' She loves tea, and no doubt Blanche will be in as usual to borrow some shoes or safety-pins or twenty francs.'

Coromandel made him sit still while she worked on a cartoon she was going to send in to *Le Canard Enchaîné*.

Oliver lay back on the couch and grinned to remember his quarrel with Elvira in the morning. She had said :

' The day's so long for me : there's nothing to do.'

' Study your French. I thought you were going to get a teacher's diploma ? '

' I'm not a schoolgirl and not a dabbler. I like to do a thing thoroughly, full-time. That course is no use. I'm just wasting time. I need an interest in life. If you have a settled life, a home, you are organised, but if you're a hobo, you need something internal to organise you.'

' I can just see our laundress across the road worrying about that.'

' Men have made me what I am. I was born into a social setting. You talk like a schoolboy, full of maxims. Get work ! That's your innuendo, isn't it ? Well, why should I ? I can live parasitically and I will. If you don't like it, you can marry a laundress.'

She had been, as always, half-mocking. He had lunged round the room : when he came near her, she pushed him impatiently. ' Oh, go and study your lesson-books. You bore me.'

When he had softly opened the front-door of the flat, after closing it loudly, and peeped in, she had been sitting dismal before her looking-glass, her soft lips shaping soundless words. He murmured, ' The darling ! '

' What did you say ? ' Coromandel looked vaguely over her shoulder and went on working.

' I said, You darling ! '

She went on drawing.

Four o'clock arrived, they went out and took a stroll. It was a moth's-wing evening with liquescent lights, a cool air blowing. Already the people who live in attics had returned and turned on their twinkling lights. Meanwhile Elvira, returned from afternoon tea, waited for her lover Oliver. From the roof-terrace she saw the great gold lunar plate rising over the Luxembourg, through the fine dust and the air thickened with the corollas and pollen of the trees at the riverside and the Lycée garden. She gave a resounding sneeze. The birds, scared, in dozens rose, made their metallic noises, wheeled, settled, only to rise once more in a knot and settle farther off, and so to rise again and cry. A bat flew back and forth in the dusk of the street; under her window two swallows swooped from their seat. The dark began to grow in the sky in sudden pulsations of deep blue, as if pumped through a vast, invisible, arterial system above, or as flocks of reindeers going to pasture at a distance over the hills. The night in the garden thickened, the birds fell asleep at last, and the traffic rolled up and down in swift, hooded binocular streams. Elvira, sitting by the open window, breathed out of the air the rarest kind of perfumes, and saw in the sky streams of small blue flowers, and clouds of honey and a perpetual dry but redolent rain of delights clustered around her and stuck to her like bees. She had the impression that the stars, so small in the unmargined sky, were reflected in her hair, which she polished nightly with a silk cloth. She had been a beauty when a girl, and now, after a happy afternoon browsing over the tea-cups with her professor of French who, she saw, had warmed to her, she felt the full intoxication of beauty sure of its empire. Poor Oliver was walking the streets, miserable because she had sent him out: he did not return, so that he need not wait in an empty house until she came back. At the same time, she might have taken him with her : she could have said he was a student at the Archives, a friend of Paul's. It was true, too. How lovely the evening ! How Oliver had worshipped her when he first was with her alone : how she ensnared him with her practised married wiles, frankness, tender brutality of speech, the little armoury of pet names and expressions she had slowly woven with Paul, the caresses, and savant libertinism. To her he was a child : he could never escape her if she wanted him. She almost fell asleep in the balmy air. She was not sure that small animals did not keep popping their wild, docile heads incorporeally out of the thick air and that white, dun or black creatures of strange heraldic forms did not walk along the air on various planes.

When he came home she was surprised to see how cool he was. He asked about the professor, and did not seem at all jealous or hurt. She asked him where he had been and got a vague answer. She pondered on that. They had dinner in a students' restaurant and then walked towards Notre-Dame. The moon was above them sucking the life out of everything, yet still bloodless like an old man: its avaricious eye watched the round-limbed river and tried to dance in its sight.

' That's lovely, isn't it ? '

' Yes, lovely.'

' Once a girl told me that love was like a night-sky, with stars. Then I did not know, but now I know she was right. She loved me, poor wench. This air is intoxicating.'

' It is spring lingering.'

' In the spring, eh ? ' He murmured, ' " In the spring a young man's fancy lightly turns to thoughts of love." I'm so happy to-night that even that sounds like poetry.'

' It's as good as any other poetry : it's true.'

' Yes, poetry is true. Gee, that's a discovery for me, Elvira. Poetry is true. To-day, walking along the quays, I found a chap with a whole stack of English books. There was Thomas Carew. I looked in and turned at once by chance to a poem which began :

> Let fools great Cupid's yoke disdain,
> Loving their own wild freedom better ;
> Whilst, proud of my triumphant chain,
> I sit and court my beauteous fetter.

I bought the book. One is always so sure one's right. When I think of the people I laughed at for their love-affairs, and realise now that I was simply on the other side of the fence, that was all ! Elvira, my dear, you are so beautiful, no wonder I went back on my whole philosophy in a single hour, when I knew you. The strange thing is that even when I first heard of you, I was moved. There is in the same book another poem with the line—that is all I remember—

Question: Whence springs love? Answer: From beauty.

Your beauty was a fact so evident that all my foolish arguments collapsed like a house of cards. Beauty spreads its atmosphere far and wide, far beyond the range of sight.' She leaned on his arm. 'But that is hard on me: I am not beautiful: I am nothing but a poor scholar.'

She answered softly: 'I like that. You are so young and honest: you question everything. You could lead me. I need someone to lead me. I am helpless by myself.'

'Darling, when you speak like that, I—I simply go wild. I never knew what it was to love a woman, a real woman. Oh, you mean everything to me. Say you love me?'

'I love you, Oliver. My life was dead before you came. I had nothing to look forward to. Now I am starting life with a young man with ambition. We will go to a new country.'

'Then you are decided? Oh, you put new life into me. I have everything to live for. I will work for you: all my life will be something to lay at your feet.'

'It won't always be like this,' said Elvira. 'We will have to go back to normal life, we'll have to get a proper apartment and settle down. Paul will have to divorce me. It won't matter; we're going so far away. Anyhow, I don't mind about that, do you? That doesn't mean anything to us?'

'No,' said Oliver heartily, thinking with dismay that if there were a scandal he could never get a position in a university, college or in extension work. The smaller the college and the university, the pettier their restrictions.

'Can you get a position easily if you're mentioned as
co-respondent?' asked Elvira.

'H'm, well, that's another question,' said Oliver,
grinning and looking into her face, which was on a level
with his. 'There's the rub. But we'll manage somehow.
If the hypocrites won't take me, or if the 'varsity kicks
me out, I'll do something else. I'll be a clerk, or I'll go
somewhere where we're not known. Don't worry.
We'd have to scrape along for a few years till I got my
footing. You wouldn't mind that, would you?'

'Oh, I'd love it: to start afresh. I don't mind working.'
Her soft-skinned face had a look of innocent enthusiasm.
He stopped on the Quai d'Anjou where they found them-
selves, and, lifting her chin, kissed her with passion.

'You don't know what you do to me, Elvira! To
think that the night I walked into your dining-room, I
walked into the arms of fate.'

'Don't we always?' she said thoughtfully.

As they walked on, he could tell that she was thinking
over the evenings in Mecklenburgh Square and wondering how the house was going now that she was away,
whether they were even now at this hour gathered round
the fire, talking, devising. They both sensed that with
her gone, they would talk about their professions,
politics, markets, the sciences, all the more to rouse
Paul from his sorrows. The picture of Paul sorrowful
appeared to them both. When they got home Oliver
noticed that Elvira looked in the letter-box. He smiled.

'Expecting a letter?'

'Oh, no, old habit!'

Before they went to bed, she said: 'I really ought to
write to Paul: after all, we are amusing ourselves and
he is worrying over there. It's only kind.'

'Yes, it's only kind.'

*   *   *   *   *   *

After several moments of darkness, during which he
was thinking, 'I suppose at some point in the road, one
would throw away a bag of gold for the sake of walking

free,' he began to chafe with a rising passion. He had practically no money left. He thought: 'By Jings, if I had a bag of gold——'

Elvira, with that telepathic appropriateness common in marriage, murmured in the dark:

'We can't go to the pictures again this week, Oliver, really. You spend so much on books and pamphlets. It goes out in five and ten-franc pieces. We don't notice it.'

Oliver bit his lip and thought of the opulence and riotous furnishings of Coromandel's studio-floor. He had said to her that afternoon:

'You wouldn't marry a skunk-cabbage like me.'

'Who knows?'

He had been surprised at how near he had come to a proposal. He thought now: 'I had better watch my step.' At one moment he wanted to throw himself into her arms and leave Elvira to pick her way home, the next he thought: 'Bind myself to this authoritative young woman—she might go crazy like her mother!' Coromandel had watched him with impatience and bitten her lip. So she, too, wanted to marry him. Surely they inoculated all girls with the idea of marriage to get them as single-minded and uniform as that? Elvira said in the dark:

'Then our washing cost thirty francs this week, and we pay four francs fifty centimes to the *femme de ménage*, that's because we're foreigners. In our own country we could live on much less.'

'Elvira, darling, don't let's talk about money now. I hate money. I want to love you. I don't want to talk about the washing. I never want to discuss money with you.'

'No, you leave all that to me, of course. I can't count on a scholarship to keep me while I write peptonised socialism.' He recognised his own phrase.

'Well, a man who emits poison-gas against himself deserves to be scorched.'

'We won't get anywhere with your wisecracks. I do wish you'd be serious. You said you'd abide by my ideas : you'd do anything to make me happy. You really haven't done a thing. You're always thinking of yourself. To you I'm just a necessity, like bread or meat.'

He was silent, and then murmured : ' Really, is it as bad as that ? '

' Oh, what a wild-goose chase ! How do I know what you do all day long ? '

He flung himself over on his side. ' Jesus ! '

She began to cry. He sulkily took no notice, till he heard harsh breathing. He turned on the light and was scared to see her stretched out as if in a fit, hands clenched, eyes rolling, lips bitten. He spent an hour in the greatest distress before she fell into a sleep, broken by shudderings. He lay back in the dark with staring eyes, a terrible fear and aimlessness in him. But presently he slept calmly.

The next day Elvira was cold to him, and yet had so surely a trace of tears that he felt half water himself. He took no notice of her, however, and left the apartment abruptly after the traditional kiss. He wanted to wound her badly, but couldn't think of an excuse. He didn't think she would go back to Paul now—everyone has some shame, he repeated—and if she does ? He set his face in a disagreeable expression. He went to the Bois de Boulogne, and walked there, looking at the shallow brooks, feeling affection for the sparrows and the varieties of fungi on the tree-trunks. He had lunch, smiled at the girls, sat on an urbane café chair planted in the midst of the forest, calculated a sparrow's life was not worth living because of the fearful way it looked round when trying to take a little sip of water from a runnel.

The sun declined, his heart began to beat, and tears to rise from his heart. He walked faster and faster through the woods, examining the opalescent skies between the leaves, leaning sentimentally over lakes and observing the foolish dignity of the swans. A male swan deployed its feathers and swam boldly about to attract the attention

of a very dirty, and quite indifferent, female on the bank.
A male pigeon, heavily banded, glossy, and apparently
the hero of the band, unsuccessfully chased a number of
females, with whom much more modest gentlemen were
later successful.   Oliver followed the repulsed hero
several rods, and threw a twig at him as he walked off.

A number of passing women reminded him of Elvira.
He thought of her, so gentle, so tender, so faithful.   He
was inexpressibly touched.   He wished she were there
so that he could press her hand, take her head on his
breast, her dark head, so shapely, so girlish.   He would
protect her from this time till their old age.   He
imagined them having children.   He desired Elvira's
presence and unimaginative propositions.   His arms
ached and his feet impetuously took every turn that the
path offered them, as if round the next corner he would
find, immaterial but complete, the object of his delusions.
With nightfall this need became so great that it shot up
within him like a beanstalk, and his spiritual powers
increased.   So profound was his passion that everything
unrelated to it seemed puny.   Coromandel he derided,
Paul he disdained, he wondered how he had ever been
able to desert the apartment with Elvira there, his jewel,
his salvation.   With impetuous speed, his hat in his hand,
he rushed along the path now thick with twilight and
with the rich amorous perfumes of the laden boughs
and with the twitterings of sparrows, until a taxi overtook him, when with breathless voice he gave the address
of the apartment in the rue Thouin and threw himself
on the cushions, his heart beating fast, his head reeling
with desire, his hands clasped, his eyes closed.   He
ascended to the apartment and clasped Elvira to him.
She had forgiven him.

' Elvira,' he said, ' I was walking in the Bois just now.
The swans' feathers are arranged in octaves, the spurting
leaves in trinities, the clouds fly through the interstices,
one, two, three, and then a flock—like sheep threading a
rank meadow ; the birds sit side by side, in twos ; there

before me the path stretches like the stem of a tree branching alternately, one, pause, two, a pause, and so forth ; and the branches beginning with one, soon wind and gyrate into their high complexity and finish at the apex, many multitudinous threads woven round one distaff, and so woven and so shuttled across the warped sky as to make a seamless damask issued from a master loom. The grass sprang in its families, the earthworms laboriously emerged with regular gyrations from their burrows, the motor cars rushed past, shells of mystery, but in reality most wearily constructed bodies whose very source of life was purchasable at the next pump station. I thought—suppose I should know your body with the same accuracy, suppose your pattern and our ecstasies were manufactured at so many thousands a day !—and I wished it were so, so that the imperfections in us would have never existed, and our joys might be perfected from the first day and increase in a mathematical proportion of wildness, velocity and climax. I loved you with arithmetic, for if the animals love by sensation, I don't see why we should not go to the heart of the matter and love mathematically. For that's how the world appears to me. You know when I clasp you to me, I think of the teeming cells of your body, of the unthreaded laby-rinths. I count your heartbeats ; all that's numerable seems to me an exquisite and exciting mystery, all that's mysterious seems to me poor and worthless. I know the slow responses of the mammary glands, the tre-mendous pulse of the matrix, the head turning from side to side, the hair falling equally on each side of the elliptical brows, the black-centred eyes rolling rhythmic-ally, the surging breathing. When I stand in the wood, so built up with complex tissues, and so enervated, so articulated with its limbs, the light pours through its bodies and through yours, showing the green and red fluids ; exquisite amphorae of musky wine.'

Elvira listened silently, and when the spring seemed to have dried up, she said tranquilly : ' Do you love me ? '

'Yes,' said Oliver, more fiercely than she had ever heard it.

'Why do you leave me so long alone? I am so lonely.'

'I know. I feel your loneliness, I suffer with you. I exult in your loneliness which makes you cling so close to me. When I am away from you, and I know you are waiting for me, I love you so ardently that I am rooted to the spot with pain, my soles burn the grass. I wish to enjoy our common loneliness for a while, so that we can be closer united.'

Elvira drew slowly away from him, and put her face in her hands.

'What is it, Elvira? Now, tell me, beloved.'

'You don't care if I am lonely as long as you can think about it and amuse yourself with my being in love with you.'

'Elvira!'

'You don't, you don't.'

He endeavoured to soothe her, but an extensive, if yet light, shadow of fear was rising over her apprehensive heart. She began to watch, calculate, divine, fear, construe, suspect. He would leave her when his spiritual ambition demanded some other object of passion, or some sacrifice, or some austerity. She couldn't keep him. For the first time in her life she knew the cruel feeling of helpless abandonment. She had no faith in his talk about mathematical love. While she turned all things into the substance of love, he turned even the strongest passion into something abstract. The same evening he looked at her with a dark liquid look, something too sentimental, and said :

'You are a strange, passionless negative, Elvira. I am a positive. Conclusion—together we make nothing.'

'Why do you say nothing? I somehow can't bear to hear you say nothing.'

'No, nothing is a beautiful idea—it avoids conflict, it avoids responsibilities, it has no past, no future; it does not struggle, or lament, it just lives in the instantaneous present and contemplates its tranquil nullity.'

' Yes, I am nothing,' said Elvira in a depressed voice. ' Who knows, who knows, what will come to us, where we will be this time next year—no, a month from now ? '

' Don't cast a spell upon us, Elvira ! '

' I'm not superstitious. You are. Men pretend to be reasonable, but they are very superstitious. Everything is an omen.'

The evening passed sadly, like many. Oliver found himself bathing in this dark air with a relish, as if he were tasting a thing he soon would be deprived of.

Elvira became more apathetic, disconsolate and pessimistic. One day she said :

' You look at all the women on the boulevard ! '

' I like them.'

' You don't look at the men.'

' The women have something the men haven't.'

' Men are always looking women over as if they were chattels.'

' These ladies don't seem to mind.'

' All men are the same,' said Elvira, petulantly. ' Even if a woman does everything for them, they look out of the corners of their eyes at every other woman.'

' Ocular infidelity no cause for divorce,' said Oliver shortly.

When he came into the room from the bathroom, she sat thoughtfully on the sea-trunk, which stood in front of the windows. Her long brows drooped to her very cheekbones and, rising like a bow over the eye, dropped to the nose where they met. He drew her up to him, kissed the centre of her low forehead, smooth and oval like a stone rubbed on the shore, looked affectionately into her eyes. He quizzed her. She shrugged her shoulders and then placed her cool moist mouth on his forehead. He closed his eyes.

' Elvira ! '

' Yes ? '

' Never leave me ! '

' Why ? '

' You are all I have in the world. I have no country, no friends, no religion, and if you fail me, no ambition.'

She said nothing. At last he heard a cool voice saying : ' You should be ambitious yourself. You should have an internal fire.'

He replied : ' I haven't. It wasn't put in me.'

' What is the matter with you ? Sometimes you have so much to say. Other times, you say you have no future. No man has a future who talks like that.'

' I need a constant. You are that. Your brows are two arrows, with them I shoot straight.'

She wrote a letter to Paul that evening :

' I miss you and our home : it is not so easy to break up a marriage, is it ? I don't know what to do. He depends so much on me, I am his whole life outside his work. It does not seem fair to him, nor to you either. You seem so far from me, but when you are near I don't feel as if anything has happened : I feel as if we are still married. I suppose we always will be in one sense. I don't suppose I will ever come as close to Oliver as I was to you. He will never understand me as well; I will never again have that feeling that we have eaten the same bread and salt. I had it with you. What have I done ? Messed up three lives ? God help me. None of us is happy. A friend will bring you a letter from me in a few days. You remember Marpurgo. Be careful what you say to him. Don't trust him too much. He is always paddling his own canoe. He hates Oliver. Male jealousy, I suppose. He pretends he is going to look for a flat for us, but we're not so settled as that.'

She wrote a note to her brother, Adam :

' Marpurgo is going to England on Wednesday next. Call in at our house and find out when he's visiting Paul. Find out what his game is. He's got something up his sleeve. Find out how Paul feels too. I am worried about him. I suppose I still love him in a way. I cannot say that I am not so happy now as I was before, only I didn't think about all these things before. Do you need any money? If—I'm not sure what our plans are—but if we get a flat in London, you could come and see us in the week-ends, couldn't you? I wouldn't want to be all alone when I first land there. I hope you are well. Does Sara look after Paul properly? I think often about him. Has she found her snack-bar yet? She's an enterprising girl. I wish I had some of that enterprise in me. I'd get on better. A girl can have men without marrying, God knows.'

She went to bed completely rested and satisfied, and the next day, Sunday, was as cheerful as a groundlark from morning to evening. They went out and walked about with hands clasped, Elvira loosing the cool pearls of contemplative wisdom she felt fertile of. She satisfied her passion a hundred times that day by small touches, accidental contacts and remarks about his person. They avoided both of their habitual cafés and walked into the thirteenth arrondissement where Oliver had some work-men friends. He liked to walk along the streets where fighting had taken place, to look up the headquarters of the International Labour Defence, the revolutionary locales of each quarter, find the co-operatives, praise the workmen and workwomen, philosophise about the French character, and say that if he had not been born an Englishman he would certainly become a naturalised Frenchman.

' You can fight for this country : it is always in danger, but always worth spilling your blood for.'

' Why France in particular, and not any native land ? ' she asked. ' You're Gaul-bitten.'

' What a lovely evening ! '

' Every evening is a lovely evening in summer.'

' How bright these new coffee-bars are ! Look at that merry Latin woman chaffing the men. Aren't they all comrades ! '

' Yes, but they're all the same, and I don't pretend to

like what's proletarian. They have a very coarse, fleshy beauty. That's typically French. They're sensualists and materialists. What do the French call a fat woman? *Une belle femme, Une riche nature.*'

' I like a fat woman myself. I suppose that's the mother-love coming out in me! Wait till you see mother!'

' Oh, I don't want to. She'll never forgive me. She'll think I'm a baby-snatcher. Mothers always think their sons are at least ten years younger than they are, anyhow. Do we have to go through this family-introduction business? Can't we just be ourselves? You say yourself the family is breaking up. Don't let's go back into the tribal game. We'll just meet once or twice and that's all. I couldn't bear a mother-in-law. Paul's mother died when he was fourteen. And mine is too busy with her other children to bother about me.'

' I never thought of all that. I'm sure you may be right. Gosh, see that boy and girl right ahead of us? They can't leave off kissing. Are they happy?'

' They can hardly wait to get home.'

' Kiss me, darling.'

' It's so horrible to kiss in public. It makes love cheap.'

' All right, oddity. Old-fashioned puzzle-head. Balmy muff. What an impulsive creature it is! Saying a word of affection to you is like dropping a match in a gas-tank.'

She was greatly flattered and soothed. When they had supper she said :

' To-morrow we have to go to dinner with that old Man of Gotham.'

' Old nuisance. Wait till he finds out that he's getting the sack. He'll put arsenic in my coffee.'

' He's too subtle for that. He'd think of something better.'

' I'm glad he's going to England. I don't like it. Georges has a grudge against him, although there's justice to his side.'

' Well, Marpurgo's got another job, hasn't he ? '

' Jobs as grand vizier to Chu Chin Chow aren't so hot ! And that's all this great financier is. Besides, great financiers are lying low at present in France. Everyone's beginning to suspect that Stavisky didn't blow up because he was the biggest fraud of the year, but because he was the smallest. He wasn't the *pape*, but a *soupape*.'

She had to go to dinner with the family of a professor who was Paul's friend. They did not know anything about Oliver and he had to spend the evening alone. He sat gloomily in the d'Harcourt irritated at the indignity. Then Blanche dropped in and picked him up and, after she had retailed all the scandal she and the boulevards could invent about the ministers, judges, juries and functionaries of the state, she took Oliver home to eat with her. There, without enchantment or poetry, they fell into each other's arms. Oliver got home at three in the morning with an aching head and told Elvira he had been drinking because she left him alone. She rather liked the idea.

CHAPTER IX

To Marpurgo, nervously and guilefully waiting for
Oliver and Elvira, Coromandel's mother in retrospect
had the aspect of a South American parrot, gawdy,
beaked, talkative, idiotically malign, peering through the
clotted leaves, and behind, an atmosphere of bloody
sun, fever heat, misanthropic snakes, and blood-diving
mosquitoes : the climate of Coromandel, in other words.
He fanned his brow with his handkerchief, called for ice.
He had dreamed about snakes the night before. He had
dreamed about a boa-constrictor last time in Calais before
he met Boutdelaize. That had put him on his guard, and
he had not been taken in by Boutdelaize. Last night,
Marpurgo dreamed he was going through a swampy
copse, and from every branch hung and swayed serpents.
He had had a most unhappy, wretched day. Antoine
Fuseaux had left for his holiday on Saturday, and Georges
had made divers unfriendly hints. Georges hates me,
whispered Marpurgo. He wished he had not been so
free with Coromandel's mother ; he saw now much
clearer than then the danger of doing so, saw the storms
that would arise when Coromandel's mother found out
that he liked the daughter.

'Is it worth it ? For a soul-friendship ? I put Clara
off till after I come back from London, but she'll be here
then, and I can't leave her alone when she's here. Is it
worth while starting anything with Coromandel ? She's
above mere dangling for marriage : she understands life
like a man. But not Clara. I've missed everything in
life.'

Oliver came into the café, quickly looking for

Marpurgo, and came gaily across the room holding out
his hand.

'How are you? Elvira says will you excuse her?
Andrew Fulton's girl is sick in bed and Elvira felt she
ought to go and see her. Fulton's girl was awfully good
to Elvira when she was in bed herself. Fulton's taking
her to supper. Will you forgive her? Shall we just take
a bite round here, or will you let me take you to the Bois?
You've been our host so often.'

'As you like. Let's stay in the city then for supper,
and go to the great boulevards after supper : men about
town, for once. What will you have? '

'Anything. A Pernod. I'm becoming hardened.'

'In all ways. The way you look at pretty girls now
makes my blood run cold.'

'Purely Platonic. Do you remember a night over a
month ago, when Paul and Adam were here and you left
me to my fate? '

'Quite well.'

'Ha, ha. I saw you run off with a young lady, you
gay Lothario. It appears you secretly go walking with
young ladies *bien élevées*, all unknown to the family, as I
suppose. You're a secret chap, aren't you? Or is it
just immaterial sentiment? "Still is the night, the street
is deserted," a Heine nostalgia? You old fraud. And
you pull a long nose at me. I'm interested because I had
a sort of *velléité* for the young lady who lives in the house
you stopped before. Those things come and go, you
know—you know, of course. She's a friend of mine and
an engaging girl—cultivates the intellect (" Don't trouble
yourself," he begged himself, " our friend here knows
very well what you are talking about "). Well, at various
times I thought I was in love with her—with both, you
know. When I saw you there I was in a state, although
I hardly think—however . . . My head was whirling, and
when I saw you paddling off up the street I could have
punched you.' He drained his Pernod. 'Then I thought,
If the lady prefers Marpurgo, it's a good hand skinned

for naught. I stayed away from her for a bit as if she
had betrayed me. Men are irrational. Elvira was somewhere : I had dinner with Blanche one night : she left me
flat. I went off in a calenture. I was just passing through
the tropic of Capricorn at the moment. I am a moody,
temperamental person. Suddenly out of a doorway, on
a quiet side-street, cooling my aches and pains like magic,
I heard a pretty murmur—some lines of Baudelaire's
being murmured in a woman's voice.' He looked at
Marpurgo with burning eyes. ' She was a beautiful
whore, take my word for it. She told me all the girls in
Paris learn bits of poetry and read the political news, to
be able to talk to men like human beings and not like
bowls of dough.'

He sighed. ' When I got home, at four in the morning,
I found that Elvira was ill in bed : she had got up
suddenly : she suddenly made up her mind, that day.
Inapposite decision ! She either makes none or the most
inexpeditious ones ! Poor Elvira. You know those
northern days in spring, a few gleams at dawn, a spot of
blue, clouds, grey, gleam, wind, a drop of rain, a moment
of fire at sunset, a grey evening, and suddenly, at midnight, a pure clear vault, with a few lovely puffs of cloud,
and timid, tremulous stars by the thousand ? Elvira !
When my fuscous cloudy beauty clears, how long and
deeply and tenderly you can look into her smoothly-
rolling but reasonless universe ! Marpurgo,' he continued, leaning forward ardently and taking Marpurgo's
hand, careless of the few curious glances directed at
them; 'don't hate me: I am young.' His voice shook
with drama and pity. 'I am brilliant but indiscreet. Give
me a chance. You see I am not thinking of letting
Elvira down.'

Marpurgo withdrew his hand pettishly.

' I know this young lady, Mlle Coromandel Paindebled : she is the daughter of a friend of mine, an
antiquary.'

' I know the old man, too. Marvellous piece of lace,

marvellous statue he has in the living-room. Queer old woman the mother, isn't she ? Oh, I often go there. I'm persona grata with everyone from the cat up. I have tea with the dear old crazy girl. She thinks I'm aspiring to Coro's hand. I'm not. Coro never thinks of such a thing. She's a jolly inspiring girl.'

' She must be a dear friend of Elvira's.'

' Oh, you nasty thing ! Well, well, Marpurgo ! I keep my girls apart. I'm a wise man. And I don't do harm to either. I'm going to England soon, too—unless a little affair turns out well here, but I don't think I'll be bothered with it.'

' A job ? '

' Oh, maybe. But what do you think of Coro, eh ? Isn't she an extraordinary woman, full of harmony, although out of drawing ? She whips me up to do something. And dear Elvira, much as I love her, and although she is my woman, Elvira has not that quality. Elvira's function is to put you to sleep. I say, I'm drunk, aren't I ? Why don't you stop me talking ? I'm talking rot, aren't I ? '

' No, you're just getting sensible. Go on.'

' I like to sleep, and that's why I like her.' He shook his plump shoulders, blew out his plump cheeks. ' An Oedipus situation. You're a Freudian, aren't you ? '

' And I am Laius, I suppose ? '

Oliver simpered, pretending to be amused, but was really confused.

' Laius was the father of Oedipus, and he slew him,' said Marpurgo cuttingly. ' But you're a scholar.'

Oliver said :

' Of course. . . .' He stared at Marpurgo and his eye brightened. ' I say, that's rather acute of you. There is something in it . . . twisted . . . but . . . Marpurgo, you know you're a damned clever man, a damned clever man. I am quite sure you've never lived up to your genius-capacity.'

Marpurgo was flattered, and allowed a wrinkle of good-humour to appear round his mouth.

Someone walked across and stood beside Oliver, saying : ' Hullo, Olivair : and where is the darling ? '

Blanche was introduced to Marpurgo, whom she was dying to know. She asked after Elvira minutely in a tone of the oldest friendship, and got the conversation on to common friendly matters and easy political comments, as if they were all at home. Oliver mentioned that Marpurgo had invited them both to the Bois, because he was leaving the city. Blanche was excited.

' Oh, did you ? Oh, that is lovely of you. Elvira would have been so happy. The Bois is exquisite on a night like this. And poor dear, she has been so sick and so lonely, but she would send Olivair to his work. She is a good wife.'

Marpurgo took them both to the Bois and promised to go the next afternoon to see Blanche's act. He would taxi her to her night-club to-night too. They came back from the Bois, dropped Oliver and went to the night-club. Marpurgo drank one glass of champagne and took Blanche to a café afterwards. She had an omelette and beer. He drank a Grand Marnier and watched her with delight.

Blanche d'Anizy began to flatter Marpurgo, and talked about some old lace that her family had kept for generations : she had it off pat, but made the mistake of talking pseudo-technicalities to a technician. Marpurgo looked at her with salty amusement, letting her run on and inducing her to drink two *fines*. He was in his element, making an easy survey of human frailty. He sent the waiter for cigars of a special kind. Blanche, feeling that her lace-talk may have been at fault, named the various personalities sitting round the café, took an interest in Italian politics, supposing Marpurgo to be an Italian, mentioned her political informant, Lemesurier. Marpurgo took a pleasure in pretending to be her meat now, talked with her in a low voice, making satirical remarks, catty innuendoes, leaving his sentences half-uttered and finishing on *mots à double entente*. Blanche

was in her element, and began to swim along with easy
strokes : she was half-drunk, too drunk at any rate to see
that Marpurgo was amusing himself. She began to tell
dirty stories. She detailed the whole story of Oliver and
Elvira, as she had seen or guessed it from the beginning,
giving it the most scabrous turn : she told him how they
all laughed at them in the café : how she kept her friends,
the ' personalities,' *au fait* with this poor little romance,
and how they had made bets about its possible termina-
tion. Marpurgo laughed wickedly to himself. She then
told Marpurgo that Oliver had syphilis and had made
love to her in a taxi last week, but she had repulsed him
with indignation, because of dear Elvira and because of
the syphilis. Marpurgo grinned more widely. Blanche,
finishing her second *fine*, ordered a beer and boasted
childishly about how she could mix her drinks. She
became melancholy then, and began to tell Marpurgo, as
to a father, the pitiful story of her life. It was not
identical with the stories told to Elvira and Oliver, but
more pathetic : she seemed to have been the baseball of
fate, everyone scoring runs and she scoring smacks.
She described all her friends with melancholy bitterness.
The more she meditated on her insecurity, the more
characterless, frail and vicious her friends seemed to her.
She leaned on her hand, her fine drunken eyes in shadow,
and foretold the short end of the affair of that ' black-eyed
flabby-dabby ' Oliver and Elvira, ' that commonplace
little housewife whose only trick is to talk slow and
childish to make them come to her.' Her life was wasted
on Lemesurier, who had deflowered her at sixteen,
promised to marry her, married instead a large *dot*, so
that in madness she had married the unfortunate Englishman. She picked up courage again, however, and began
to sparkle, laughing herself at her malignant shrewd
descriptions of her friends. At the end she was describing
her present plight with amusement : Lemesurier was
financially embarrassed at present, being an indiscreet
speculator, her other friends had left her stranded, liked her

company, but instead of the regulation cheque at Christmas, for instance, had sent her gloves and stockings. She had had to spend what she earned at the cabaret on stockings and a new dress (and she earned little, she worked there for the prestige and the hope of picking up some wealthy follower). She was flat broke. She asked Marpurgo for a loan. Marpurgo, who had been touched very frequently in life, had seen it coming, and now he smiled a curved, satiric smile, but pleasant withal.

'Madame Blanche : I am not easily touched by life-stories—especially in cafés.'

She smiled, sensing a bargain, a hardened, a gay, shameless borrower, who never had any intention of repaying, but who did not mind giving something in return, or doing some service, especially if it was a worthless or scandalous one. He smiled at her, in understanding.

'You are a woman of charm, understanding and experience, and like some other women of your sort I have met, you know what life is like : you have no illusions—I should say you have the same view of life as a business-man. I don't mind financing you—in a limited way, if you'll do something for me. I want it done discreetly. I am fond of Elvira : I came over on the train with her when she was coming to meet Oliver, and I very soon found out their secret. She seems to me a helpless creature ; she is a beauty and has charm, and she is as limp as an only child and has little confidence. She can keep Oliver, but she must not live in a fool's paradise : she must learn the sort of man he is. The sooner she goes back to London the better. Now,' he said, settling down to confidences, of which he was excessively fond, 'Oliver has been taking walks with a very handsome and talented young French girl, with a *dot* and doting parents. The father and mother are friends of mine : I met the father in the lace-business. Oliver met the girl I don't know how, by accident, because she lives in this quarter, I suppose. She does not know about Elvira, of course : she thinks he is a student studying here in bachelor quarters. I surprised them one evening coming home late as I left the house, where I had been playing chess with the father. I said nothing, naturally, to my friends, both for their sakes and hers, but I have been wondering what should be done. I now see an opportunity : I will bring the young lady to this café, my privilege and pleasure as a friend of the family— besides, she is the age my daughter would have been, if I had had one ! '—he laughed lightly, and a faint sus- picion dawned in Blanche's eyes—' introduce her to you, and you will make an appointment with her for the next day here for an apéritif. She has been a student at the Sorbonne and is perfectly free to go about by herself, although they are a good old-fashioned family : you will invite Elvira here at the same time, introduce the two, make some introductory remark such as that " Madame's husband is studying at the Archives " and so forth, and then leave them to find out the matter themselves. Thus, Elvira will be warned, and my friends will be spared any trouble.'

Blanche considered this for a while.

' Of course,' she said, ' it would not be a bad idea—in my opinion—for Oliver to marry a young girl of family, with money : he wants to be a student and he is lazy : he will need some money for the next few years. What is she like ? Pretty ? '

Marpurgo said : ' Young and very fresh-looking, with the milky charm of young girls, you know. Her mother is a strangely handsome woman, with a sort of big-boned Flanders charm, sedate : the father is handsome, mer- curial and must have been a most beautiful youth. There is a little of them both in the daughter. But she is witty, and has flashes of inspiration which would attract an intellectual strutter like Oliver,' he laughed.

Blanche's feeling that Marpurgo was interested in the daughter and her dowry, deepened, but she went gingerly, to make sure.

'If she is pretty, witty and wealthy—but poor dear
Elvira ! Of course,' she said, leaning forward confiden-
tially, 'I have always thought it a foolish escapade.
Imagine a married woman, with a husband in his position,
running away, like a schoolgirl, with a student seven
years younger than herself- -and probably she has lied
about her age : she would in those circumstances. I
think,' she said reflectively, ' the best thing would be for
you to write to the husband and tell him. Or no, that
would not do. Wait, I will think of something.'

Marpurgo smiled.

'I like my idea best : aren't you anxious to see what
will come of it when both women find out ? '

Blanche brightened. ' Yes, you are quite right : they
will both be sore as hell. What will they do? Let us do
that. After all, it amuses and it does no one any harm.
Whichever one marries him had better look out for him
—such a philanderer.' She began to giggle. Then, with
the warmest gesture of the evening, she held her slender
hand with its polished opal-tinted nails to Marpurgo.
'It's a bargain : I do not know what your object is. I
do not think it is what you told me, because you are a
clever man : but I do not care. What do I care for them ?
Both honest women, and both will think I am a louse,
nothing but a little louse, because I had hard luck and I
earn my living by men—and what do they ? Look at
that lazy, torpid Elvira ; so I do not care for them : they
can both go to hell. You are helping me out, and so I
will do what you say. Am I right ? Besides,' she
twinkled, ' we are of our sort : I know it : I spotted you
the first moment, and that is why I came across to see
Oliver this evening. Otherwise—no : he bores me : he
is a frightful bore : I don't give a damn for him. Now,
how much can you lend me ? '

'How much do you want ? '

She looked at him straight.

' At least a thousand francs for current expenses and
past bills, that is to begin with.'

He grinned.

'Hold your horses! Here are two hundred francs down.'

She laughed carelessly : ' And you expect me to help you out ? '

'What good are you doing me ? However, if the results are good, the recognition will be there.'

' Well,' she said, calmly putting away the two hundred francs and getting up, with her hand extended, ' I trust you.   I have to, and if I don't, what's the odds ?   I am two hundred francs to the good. Good-bye.' She smiled at him with all her charm.   ' When will you bring me the young lady ? '

' I can't say : I must make arrangements, consult her : she is often out of the house altogether, at classes, parties, dances : I see her very little. Perhaps to-morrow.'

She scribbled her address on her card, and left. Marpurgo said to himself : ' Now I must act quickly. It must be soon, soon : I must get rid of that painted turnip of a student with his red cheeks and black hair.'

He took Elvira out to lunch next day, and went for a long walk with her afterwards, praising her knowledge of Paris, looking in shop-windows with her : then went into a bookshop and bought her the *Mercure de France*, which flattered her.

' How is Oliver getting on ?   He must be nearly finished now ! '

' I'm tired of asking him.   He likes maundering in libraries ; but he's got to reach finality, soon.'

Marpurgo's lips curled as he heard a shadow of Oliver's pompous phraseology : but he went on the more eagerly putting words into her mouth :

' Philander philanders in mind, heart and body : he's likely to turn out a liberal-fascist of the dazzling arriviste type, unless you guide him with your commonsense and sincerity. The instinct of youth for truth led him to you, the healthy instinct of cat for catnip, cow for cowlick, crapulent for purgative moved him before he became

entirely identified with licking his own chops. You can
save him, or no one. He has a natural taste for por-
nocracies, but by accident he met an honest woman :
now you must rule. He's a purple-patch type : let his
brain-children be porphyrogenitous. . . .'

' What's that ? '

' Born to legitimate purple . . .' he carried on with a
sleeve-snicker.

Elvira laughed, and said slowly, with catches in her
voice :

' A taste for pornocracy, but by accident he met an
honest woman—dishonestly.'

' If he meets another honest woman—honestly,' continued Marpurgo brutally, ' he'll go flat out for her.
Now, I wouldn't want that to happen. I think too much
of you, I respect you too much to see that happen.'

She said coolly : ' Do you have to let that bother you ? '

' Escapades are like jags in a temperature chart : taken
together they give you the norm and you can't get along
normally without them. But a heat-wave is not a jag.'

' So you sense a heat-wave ? That's very interesting.
Who's the woman ? '

' I know nothing,' said Marpurgo smoothly. ' I just
saw him in the street walking very affectionately with a
young girl. But I think he has an affectionate way with
all women : doubtless it means nothing. No doubt he
had a kind sister and mother.'

' Thanks for the tip,' said Elvira drily. ' I'll go and
have a water-wave, and I'll see about his heat-wave.'

' Good,' said Marpurgo with his habitual air of baffled
plotter whose instruments must leave him to act, to his
regret. He called a taxi and put her into it.

' I admire you ; you're one of those feminine girls who
know that Guerlain works better than H_2SO_4.'

' What's that ? Arsenic ? '

' No—suicide ? You'd never do that ? ' he said with
conviction and surprise.

' Marpurgo, get into the taxi. I want to talk to you.

To the Café d'Harcourt! Marpurgo, now tell me why you hang round us and torment us! I want to get to the bottom of this.'

He looked at her insolently.

'I'm a virtuoso in decadence, disintegration, mental necrosis: if I sit at home, I corrode myself: I can't work in a vacuum. Out, I gather little eschatological flowers to meditate in the hectic nights of the bacillus of Koch. Each of your sorrows is for me an hour of nepenthe: in that hour I build up an endoped dome of misery and failure, doubt and dissolution, ridicule and insufficiency beyond inferno, Eblis, opium, Xanadu. . . .'

'Have you got a match, Marpurgo?'

'I don't smoke now—my lungs, you know. Wait!' He knocked on the glass and stopped the taxi, jumped out and presently came back, smiling gently, coughing, with a box of matches. 'And now, dear lady, let me leave you: you have your water-wave, scent behind your ears, eh?' he gestured.

'What's her address? I'm going there,' said Elvira.

'I don't know: I merely saw them in the street,' he replied, meaning to appear insincere.

'You're as slippery as a snake,' she said, puffing out smoke. 'I'll get the secret out of you yet. Come and see me to-morrow, Marpurgo. I'll be at home at three-thirty.'

'The ladies' hour: you should see Oliver then, not me.'

She shrugged. 'To attract Oliver is no diploma: you're different.'

'Even my enraged lymphocytes can't conquer my enraged virtue; with me it's perpetual Ramadan: strict fasting till sunset.'

She drawled insultingly: 'I wonder you never married, then.'

'Fantasy's my copulative.'

'How enervating! I think you're a fraud, Marpurgo: but I'll confess you to-morrow. You'll come, I know.'

'I'll come, and with tribute : that's your style. Men are your tributaries and you're the sea.'

'I don't want your tribute : bring yourself. I'm lonely enough : and I hate that café crowd.'

'Good : I'll come, and catch the late train. You'll have a message for me, too, for England. I wanted you to know this before I left, but only just before, so that you could make up a strong decision on the spur of the moment.'

'You're right, Marpurgo.'

He sent a *pneumatique* immediately to Blanche d'Anizy to her club, asking her to meet him at six at the Deux Magots. They would go from there to the antiquary's shop and if possible meet the young lady in question. He was sure Blanche would turn up. He returned to his office in the rue du Faubourg Montmartre cheerfully smoking his cigar. He did nothing all the afternoon but told amusing tales to the accountant and went out twice for coffee. About five, when he was preparing to leave, Georges dropped in on him.

'Hullo, Marpurgo : I hear you've got a better offer from Severin ? You've been hanging round with heavy swells in the rue de la Paix recently, they tell me. Why don't you take it ? You're too lively a personality for the lace-business. It's more your line.'

Marpurgo bit his cigar thoughtfully.

'I told your brother, privately, that I had had an offer : but it was in the course of conversation. He said to me, We need you, Marpurgo : you don't want to be mucking round with that type of cheap promoter. He suggested a rise in salary, and we agreed on the amount, but it was to be left over till his return.'

'I know all about your private conversations. You seem to think this is a vending-machine for salaries.'

Marpurgo took his cigar out of his mouth, and whipped round to Georges, like a snake.

'A man's worth his money or he isn't. If he is, the courtesy of business relations would suggest to any man of ordinary feeling that he gets it and his expenses without nagging and backbiting. You're incapable of that. You hate me. I know it. I wish you'd nurse your grudge in silence. I don't mind being hated : any man of ability gets plenty of that commodity : but I prefer the compliment to be tacit.'

Georges was unruffled. In fact, he was pink with a pleasant decision.

' Well, I can't. I'm interested in making money. I'm part of the firm, but I don't regard it as a milch-cow like you do.'

' We all know you've looked after yourself well.'

' I do my best to look after the firm well, for Antoine's sake. And if you don't like the way *I* run things you have an alternative.'

' You'd like to drive me to it. I get on well with Antoine. He's not parsimonious, no hoarding soul : his is a beautiful nature, he is generous, and he buys personality, not accountants. You don't get business through adding-machines.'

' It's my punch,' said Georges with good-humour, ' and it's below the belt. Antoine went away because he's too kind-hearted to give you your walking-ticket. He left me to do it. I'm the bounce in this firm. I'm sorry, Marpurgo, but it's so. You'll get a year's salary and everything's wiped out between us.'

' Who've you got in my place ? '

' We're getting a new man, and perhaps a sort of supercargo : we haven't enough personnel.'

' You can take two on, but I've always got to go ? Well, I know quite well from what quarter this wind blows. I deny your power to fire me. I'll stick around till Antoine comes back. Or rather, I'll go through with this trip to England—Antoine was agreed on it, we talked it over together—and I'll come back and see Antoine.'

' Do what you like. Don't forget I'm a partner. You can talk to Antoine, of course. In the meantime, you'll

get a year's salary. If you like to work during part of the
year, it's O.K. with me, just as long as you don't stick
around here and don't send in any expense sheets of
any kind.'

Marpurgo was lime-white, and faint. He sank into a
chair.

'Get me some water, Georges, please. I can't stand
enmity. Not physical enmity. Inhumanity is not in my
nature : I don't understand it in others.'

Georges moved off grudgingly and came back with a
glass of water.

'There you are. I'm sorry if it was rather a blow.
But you've seen it coming, Marpurgo. I wish it had
been while you were in England.'

'No, I prefer to take it like that, in the breast. But—
as if I could have seen it coming! Antoine and I have
had some of the friendliest, kindest and most fruitful
conversations the last few weeks. I'm sure Antoine is
incapable of conspiracy, of duplicity. It's so evident this
has been a put-up job—and by you, Georges! Your
work isn't dexterous, but it's like you. However, I can't
believe in dramatics. I'll see Antoine, and I hope he'll
convince you, Georges, that this hideous prejudice,
treachery and sapping, all based on a pure physical
antipathy, should not be allowed to ruin a good business.
I'm known as the Fuseaux man from Lyon to Saint Gall.
They're happy to see me, to hear my stories, have my
dinners : those dinners you so pettily count mean
thousands of francs of goodwill to the business. . . . If
you're getting in a supercargo, as you say, get him in :
but give him to me to train. I'm the only man who
knows your business through and through. I don't say
you can't get along without me—I haven't that popular
illusion, but I say you'll lose ground for a long time if
you fire me.' He looked up pallidly. 'And the successor?'

'You wouldn't know him.' Georges laughed rudely.

'Oliver Fenton,' Marpurgo said clearly, grasping his
stick. 'Eh?'

' I'm answering no questions.' Georges walked out.

Presently he left the office. He had his appointment with Blanche at six. Never had an appointment come so badly.

He telephoned to Coromandel, met her at the Deux Magots, introduced her to Blanche and left the two women together. He could not hear what he was saying himself or what they were saying. He had gone deaf with anxiety. He got cramps so badly that there was no question of going to England till the next day. He went to a picture-show and did not see the pictures. He coughed all night, and turned over in his head a thousand schemes and conjectures. As soon as it was light he got up and began to walk the streets. It was true that Georges had promised him a year's salary, but his expenses were enormous, his tastes very luxurious and his invalid wife was coming to town. She was nothing more than a pleasant whim when he was well off, but if he were poor and had to live with her, and she could no more go to those delightful watering-places that he had kept her in for years, life would be unbearable. He knew. His father had been a poor french-polisher, his mother sick and a hypochondriac : he and his brothers had grown up amidst squalls and filth. He fell on to a street-bench and watched a concierge putting out a garbage-tin, sluicing and sweeping. He talked to himself.

' Fate will get Georges, as it has got everyone who has ever opposed me or crossed my path with evil intention. Justice triumphs, in some strange mechanistic way. Everything is linked up in our lives. Disaster has inevitably followed in my path, hitting me, but hitting more violently, to death often, those who have hated me.'

He thought of his youth. He had never been handsome, as Oliver was : he had then been thin, active, with a white face and clear eyes with slaty lights, the face of a student and mystic. He had studied Sanskrit and thought of founding a theatrical troupe ; he had known all the

Elizabethans and had written fourteen plays, all profound, paradoxical, symbolic. His family and all his relatives had regarded him as the intellectual ugly duckling, he who had been their swan. He had begun a book of accounts at twelve. He had a page for each relative, beginning with his father and mother, and had entered on each page the insults and injuries each had done him. The page was divided in two columns : on one side were the insults and injuries ; on the other side was an 'impartial' itemisation of the traits of the individual. A police captain, a cleaner, the butcher, all sorts of people had appeared in his book of accounts. When insulted he usually kept still, thoughtful, indifferent. Afterwards he would relate the incident calmly to a friend and smile. 'I will show them.' His whole life was a thirst to show these perpetual enemies, through misunderstanding, how wrong they had been, how foolish and shallow. Those who despised him would be put to shame, those who did him wrong would be put out of the way. He had often said to people :

'The world is full of angels and devils : the angels shoot arrows for those fated to them, the devils injure those who are fated to them.'

He would laugh at this fantasy, but he firmly believed it whenever he was in misery. He thought of Coromandel. What a pity he had not met her when he was young and their ages had been nearer. He imagined her as having lovers, young, brilliant, intellectual men, in a galaxy around her floating flared skirts and her long smooth dancer's limbs. He sighed and looked round him. He had a good four miles before him to walk back to his habitual café. He went into a little chauffeurs' bar and drank some bad coffee mixed with powdered milk. It heartened him. When he thought Oliver would have gone out, at ten o'clock, he went to see Elvira. She was surprised to see him.

'Hullo, you don't work any more ?'

He twisted his face into a lamentable smile.

' Yes : and where is your lover ? '

She looked at him drily.

' What makes you such a scheming old sinner, Mar-purgo ? Oliver assured me there is no other English student in the Archives, and that the girl in the street was Blanche. We met Blanche later in the evening, and she agreed she had been walking with him, even holding his arm ; telling him how faithful he should be to me. Without any prompting. Do you like evil for its own sake ? It's really very interesting. You've picked the wrong subject in me. Or rather, I enjoy it, in a way.'

He shook his head.

' My dear, perhaps I am swayed by a certain mistrust of Oliver's talents. A young man makes the mistake of mistrusting good fellows, hearty chaps, and an old man makes the mistake of mistrusting the scholars. It's natural. You're a lovely lady. I don't want you to have any trouble, that's all. Shall we conclude a peace-treaty ? I'm miserable to-day ; I did not sleep all night. I was too fevered to go to England. I'm not too long for this little scheme of things, I'm afraid. I want to enjoy myself while I'm here. May I lunch with a pretty lady to-day ? '

' Me ? If you like. Oliver has gone to see some men in the city.'

' Get on your bonnet and shawl then, and let's walk out. The day's cooler.'

His stick tapped about the room. He sank on to the divan.

' I'm dead weary.'

She brought him some brandy.

' Oliver always has it here.   Drink some.'

He drank.

' Oliver's in business, then ? '

' Oh, I don't know ; it's problematic,' she drawled.

He took her straight to a café and telephoned Blanche. She yawned through the telephone :

' You bore me with your plots : I only got to bed at four.'

'Come and have lunch, and bring Coromandel with you. I know she's always in for lunch. Mind you, I have nothing to do with this. You walk in by accident to Lafon's. Let Coromandel suggest it. She goes there. You'll find me there with the lady.'

He came back. 'I was just telephoning my office. I'm too ill to look in this morning. They're so decent to me : they treat me like a partner more than an employé. In fact, I've never considered myself an employé.'

He was amused by the coldness of Elvira's face, thinking, 'This little lady's a cool hand : she knows Oliver is at the Fuseaux.'

He went on : 'I was telling Georges yesterday that I am going to bring my wife to Paris and settle her here, if she can stand the climate.'

'Your wife ? Is she the skeleton in your cupboard, then ? '

'She's quite plump, pretty, gracious and loving, on the contrary. But a permanent invalid. She's devoted to me.' He unfolded a paper from his pocket. 'I am glad that we shall not be separated this autumn. In the autumn you only console me :

> " *What if its leaves be falling like my own ?*
> *The murmur of thy mighty harmonies*
> *Would take from each a deep autumnal tone,*
> *Sweet though in sadness.*" '

He looked at her with an inexplicable triumph. 'That's quite a tribute. Because we have lived together very little we have for each other the love and understanding of old friends. You understand that : it is the feeling no doubt you have for Paul and Paul has for you. It is a consolation in the fall of the year.'

She took out a letter from her purse.

'Here is the letter for Paul. You didn't call yesterday. Tell him I am well and hope he is.'

'You're not sending him anything—a memento ? '

'No. Why should I ? He wouldn't understand it.'

'I see : I see.'

'No one would suspect you of being so sentimental.'

'None understands me, my dear. You all half understand—you perhaps most of all—besides my wife Clara.'

'Why have you never mentioned your wife before ? It's so queer, it seems to me.'

He delicately shifted his feet.

'Who can understand these delicacies of the soul ? I can't explain to everyone why we live apart, why she is ill, how long she is ill. I can't split into dubious banalities the exquisite strangeness of our relation. She is my good angel : I like to pretend that I am crafty and cold : she knows I am not.' He touched her gloved hand finely. 'Let us go, my dear. Do you know the little restaurant Lafon on the quays ? I think you will like it. I know the head waiter there : he will do things for me.'

CHAPTER X

AFTER the lunch, Marpurgo left, pretending he was going
to the rue du Faubourg Montmartre, and Blanche left
later after piloting the two women, who had taken a
liking to each other, to the Café de Cluny. She considered
this café strategic : it was near Elvira's home and also
Coromandel's. Elvira had *Jean Christophe* under her arm,
and the two were discussing literature when Blanche left.
Marpurgo had given her a hundred francs under the table
during lunch, but with a pained air. Coromandel was in
high spirits, piqued and intrigued by this friend of Marpurgo's of whom he had never breathed a word. Elvira
was irritated to know that Blanche was also a friend of
this Mlle Paindebled of whom Marpurgo had spoken,
but had never mentioned her.

'I do not often come to a café,' said Coromandel. 'I
am afraid to. It's too easy to become an habitué. I have
my work.'

'In Montparnasse, Matisse, Othon Friesz and—lots of
painters, go regularly to cafés. It doesn't cramp their
style, it seems,' intervened Elvira.

'I suppose one can work anywhere under any conditions. You are studying here yourself, I think, Madame ?
French, is it not ? '

' Yes, I was going to take the full course at the Alliance
Française, but it appears it is too childish for one who
knows as much as I do. I can read it so well and know
all my grammar, but I can't speak.'

' You should go to the Institut du Panthéon.'

' Unfortunately, I am thinking soon of returning to
England.'

'But if you wish to become a teacher of French . . . ?'

'My time is not my own. Like most married women,' Elvira said, with slight emphasis, 'I have to consider another.'

'Your husband is here, too?'

'Yes.'

Coromandel examined her closed expression and, after a moment, murmured:

'There is a certain charm in a café. It's a kaleido-scope: a parterre of artificial flowers uprooting them-selves in a slow ballet.'

'Yes, you see life in coloured pictures: through the apéritif glasses.'

'Crystal-gazers. They find out about the nature of truth and the primaries of life: the atom is dissolved in wine and perpetual motion invented over a draught-board.'

'My husband said the very same thing to me,' drawled Elvira. 'What is it, a quotation, what? I must scold him: I thought he made it up.'

Coromandel flushed, and looked at the small, dark, gentle-seeming woman who was changing instantly and becoming her antagonist.

'I thought I made it up. What does it matter? If mathematicians can invent problems at the same instant with continents between them, and Leverrier and Adams came to the same conclusions independently, your hus-band and I can think of this paltry joke at the same time.' She looked cheerfully at Elvira. 'It shows our minds are limited: similar streams of thought end in similar platitudes.' She bowed, imitating the prince in the *Fledermaus*. '*Je vous exprime toute ma platitude, Madame!*'

'Yes, but I don't care about perpetual motion, especi-ally the draughtboard kind. But it amuses me to sit here and read till my husband comes to collect me. I'm rather lonely here. I'm a true woman. I never discuss these things. To me it seems futile. I suppose to you I seem

futile. I have a direct mind. I can't sit and thrash out
to-day everything I came to a conclusion about yesterday.'

'What woman can? And yet I have a weakness for
it, when I'm not working.'

'Oh, you wouldn't if you were married to—if you
had a—if you married a man like my husband. I've
heard all these things over and over again for years : not
here but in my home in England.'

'But I've heard there are no cafés in England—that the
reason for its intellectual dullness is the absence of coffee-
houses—that there has not been a brilliant social age
since they died,' said Coromandel.

'Yes—my husband says that too,' confessed Elvira.
'I don't know if it's true. I suppose all people say the
same things.'

'I heard it from an Englishman,' said Coromandel.
'You are English, aren't you? I like the English very
much. I get on with them ; they are charming people,
and quite continental.'

'You think so?' said Elvira, without gratitude. She
hated to have her nationality guessed. She was swart,
and small-boned, and imagined she would be taken for a
Central European.

'I am French,' said Coro, to cover the hurt. 'I have
never travelled anywhere, but I do desire very earnestly
to do so. I am very anxious to see England.'

'It's very vulgar in many senses,' said Elvira, 'and
many foreigners don't like the approximate, dispersed
way of talking. Others find it amusing.'

'You don't like England?' said Coro curiously. 'It's
strange, I think there are many lovers of France among
the English.'

Elvira, who had been making a great effort to impress
the forward stranger, was chilled by this.

'Certainly, we all have the same verbal pattern,' she
replied. Coro smiled.

'No Englishman likes England,' Elvira cast into the
basket of scraps further.

'Not even the beggar in the Strand ? '

'You mean the "Lord of India,"' responded Elvira, curiously hoping to mystify her.

'Yes.' To relieve a slight hostility Coro noticed, she continued : 'That reminds me of an amusing story, sentimental, that I heard : A friend of a friend saw a beggar in the Strand, and being sorry for him, and a poet, composed a sonnet upon his condition, which he sent to a provincial paper. He vowed if he was paid for it, he would give half the money paid to the beggar. Alas— you guess the conclusion ? '

'Yes,' said Elvira, faintly mocking. 'Students are poor, his sentiments had no better coin. He received say thirty shillings for the sonnet, and gave the beggar—alas— none. And next day passed him with commiseration.'

'You pity everyone ? ' said Coro.

'Only myself,' said Elvira. 'I only know myself, and I cannot get outside myself. It is a sickening wrench for me to think about other people. I wasn't made that way. I cannot, for instance, bear to have people tell me their troubles.'

'Perhaps you have had many.'

'We all have problems of adjustment and self-expression.' Coro listened to her glib abstractions in surprise. 'If I had a function I could organise my life better,' continued Elvira.

'You can easily get one,' said Coro, laughing. Nothing could be quainter than Elvira talking over her idleness in the dryasdust scholastic idiom she had picked up from the men she had lived with.

'Perhaps so, but I have no energy for co-ordination. I am too oppressed, I think, by my coldness and isolation in the world ; the isolation of a person with no self-confidence. I envy those who are creative. I often wish I could create. Do you think music or literature is more satisfactory ? '

'I don't know : musicians are rare,' said Coro.

'If you have a function you avoid subjective relation-

ships,' continued Elvira dismally : ' you are not negatively suggestible to your environment.'

Coromondel laughed. Elvira took umbrage :

' I suppose I seem a defeatist to you. You have your
career. I've been over-protected—isn't that the latest
way of saying you've never had to meet the issue ? '

' I think it likely,' said Coro.

' All women are alone.'

' But you are married ? '

' Yes, but a man is—wrapped up in his own comforts ;
you have to coddle him or he runs off after the next warm
breast ; men are children. I have no children, but I
think it is as well ; I have had two husbands, and it is
lonely.'

' I am sorry,' said Coro, ' but I cannot feel lonely even
alone.'

' You cannot know till you are married. A woman
sleeps until she marries : no one can judge *a priori*.
You're not lonely till you're married. After that, if
you're alone you feel as miserable as a baby feels who is
hungry for the breast.'

Coromandel smiled at Elvira's shrinking, sombre,
nuggety little passion.

' No doubt you are right. I will find out, as you say,
Madame ! '

' You want to get married ? I thought you were too
intellectual. Do you want to give up your independence
for a man ? '

' I never thought of it that way.'

' Perhaps you will be lucky. Some are. I was always
different, a stranger in my world ; even at the age of
twelve—I was very pretty and good, but I could not
display affection to other children and teachers. I only
wanted to display good manners ; I wrote in my exercise
book to make them think me strange—" I am an anar-
chist ; in anarchism the government will be blown up."
I was kept in for that.'

Coro looked at the oval face, similar to the refined,

practical, melancholy faces of China beauties in Chinese actor-dolls.

'You had passionate instincts.'

Elvira was offended at the laugh, but she drawled on, eager to talk on that pathetic subject of her lonely heart.

'I was not passionate : I was rather negatively passionate. I immediately gave up : I am a defeatist in passionism. I never had a great passion, only an immense but quite lifeless passion for my own troubles ; melancholy I am.'

Coro said maternally : 'They should have called you something sweet and mournful, like—I don't know—Melanchtha ! I heard of someone called that somewhere. Perhaps in a book.'

'That's a strange name !'

'When I was a young girl, very young, I first fell in love with Philipp Melanchthon. But Melanchtha is beautiful —it is mellow, dark live water, it suggests the antre.'

'I think it hideous,' said Elvira briefly. 'Since you're applying it to me.'

Coro, encountering an inferior will and girlish character in a nature instinctively subtle, sombre and critical, was unruffled by differences. She pursued the conversation in curiosity. Some strange consonances, or consonant echoes, had come to her ear from that instrument. She was unaware of the reason for her interest, but she found the question guiltily seductive ; wrong to interpellate, sweet to discover.

'You need women friends perhaps ?'

'A husband saves me from the distressing necessity.'

'You don't like women,' said Coro compassionately.

'Tamed, muddled, muddy, fleshly, man-engrossed,' was the rhyme and reason of Elvira's objections. 'I suppose' (with a pleasant gleam of white teeth and her sweet smile) 'you will say what everyone does, a woman is judged by the opinion of her sisters.'

Coromandel laughed outright.

' Oh, I think you've been injured by women friends some time.'

' Only men have done me harm.'

' That surprises me, really. You are very charming.'

' Well, I should say that Mr. Marpurgo who has just left us, although grossly deceitful, is my only true man-friend.'

' And your husband, of course ! '

' One can never trust a husband : one can only manage him.'

Coro took in her suggestive, mournful, bovine, breeding look. It burdened her, seemed to creep on to her shoulders with the assumption of squaws' burdens, little household fights, venal bargaining. Coromandel rested from the conversation, which had become a passage-at-arms. Elvira noted the look and was glad to find offence in Coromandel. She sank back against the seat and tapped a cigarette.

' By the way, where did you meet Blanche d'Anizy ? I suppose you're old friends ? She dances beautifully, doesn't she ? '

' I don't know. I didn't know she was a dancer. To tell the truth I only met her yesterday, through Marpurgo.'

' I thought you were old friends.'

Coro noted the lady's great, soft, perplexed eyes, confined in the bloodless orbit of the face, ill-weighted by her smooth but irregular forehead. What mystery did she face ? Why was she forced to go on with this conversation ? She said with an effort to appear bland :

' What do you do in the afternoons ? You study ? '

' I generally wait here for my husband to come from the Archives, where he is finishing a thesis.'

Coromandel felt suddenly she worshipped this woman : she had a strange desire to cry and kiss her forehead. She felt like a chimney, some understanding of the lady was rushing through her, and yet she hardly knew what she understood. She looked on Elvira as one looks on a simple, foolish, dirty, lustful dove in a compliant green forest. Elvira rebuffed her with aversion and fatigue :

'But if you must get back to your work, don't let me detain you. I just sit here and ponder. You couldn't spend an afternoon like that, could you? I suppose work is a great consolation. I wish I had talent like you, I shouldn't be bored.'

'I have no talent, indeed.'

'Oh, yes you have. Anyone can see it, in the way you walk, the way you talk. Only people who are sure of making their way are like that. But I have no talent. I'm just empty, an earthenware bowl: you're——'

'You're a pot of basil,' said Coromandel. 'I can't bear to hear you talking like that. Why do you try to convert yourself to your own worthlessness?'

Elvira looked obstinately down.

'I don't know why I bored you with myself. I'm not worth talking about. Do you want any coffee?'

'Come home with me and have tea. I'll make it myself. I know there are some delicious cakes at home. Won't you come? I have a very pretty studio. Do you like fabrics? There is a rolling glass roof which lets in the light. Come, and I'll show you my drawings. Will you let me make a sketch of you?'

'I'm superstitious: it's unlucky,' protested Elvira. 'I've never had a photograph taken either except for passports. Thank you very much indeed, but my husband may be early from the Archives to-day because Mr. Marpurgo is leaving for England to-night. They are friends.'

'Another day, then: I'm just near here—Paindebled, the antiquary in the rue Jacob. Perhaps you know it.'

'No, we never walk in that quarter. But if we meet again, I'll be glad to accept your invitation.'

'Bring your husband too, if he is free.'

'Oh, Oliver, that's my husband, will be free all day soon. You come here sometimes, don't you? Let's put it off till we meet again. I—I think we're moving to another apartment. You don't mind, do you?'

She was worried by Coro's look of astonishment: the

French are very formal—perhaps she had been too off-hand. What did it matter? This young girl would be a bore with her drawings. They were going to England soon. She apologised :

'I am so sorry : it sounds so abrupt. But—our plans are rather formless. He's like that. So am I. I suppose that's why we get on. Oliver is a natural I.W.W., he says.'

She had regained all her self-confidence, without knowing why : perhaps because this highbrow young girl seemed to be getting ready to go. Elvira bridled with professional manners : she would go home before she met her husband. They left together. The little woman parted from Coromandel outside the café and went straight ahead, slightly bowed over her stomach, her broad hips swaying, looking neither around nor behind. Coromandel bought an evening paper at the kiosk, acting automatically and without any feeling at all. She watched Elvira's progress down the street, while thinking to herself. . . .

'But I'm mad : her name is Mrs. Western. It's simply an astounding coincidence ! All the same, I wish her husband's name had been Roland instead.'

Elvira ascended the Boulevard St. Michel. Coromandel walked slowly after her, then faster and faster, as she kept disappearing in the crowd. She turned into the rue du Panthéon. The splendidly serried façades of the old houses swept round too, like engraved battlements. Elvira turned down the rue Thouin and entered an old house there containing furnished apartments. Coromandel knew that Oliver's ' bachelor ' apartment was in the rue Thouin.

'No, this is too much : it is the same, it must be. Well, well ! Damme if he's not making a complete fool of me ! And of her. That cherub face ! I'm going to have some fun.' But she was furiously excited. When she got home she could not settle down to work at all. She polished all the copper and silver work in the place, old balm for tired hearts.

Immediately after leaving them, Marpurgo, exhausted, had sunk down on the nearest *bistrot* terrace to compose himself and think out his plans. Would he go to England to-night or not ? Would he wait and fight Oliver on his own ground ? The whole thing was ridiculous. Oliver was not a danger, but the unknown buyer that Georges had picked up. He went once more through the list of possibles. He ordered a Grand-Marnier and wrote three letters, one to Antoine Fuseaux at Vichy, one to Severin at Nancy, whither he had gone for financing, one to Paul Western, describing Oliver's double treachery, denouncing his character and picturing Elvira's tragic plight. He would be in England to-morrow, the letter said, and he would call immediately on Paul. Paul was not to act, telephone, telegraph or write to Elvira before that. He must lay all the facts before him. He, Marpurgo, was out of a job on his account ; he had an invalid wife coming to live with him in Paris : the shock of learning his financial misfortunes would affect her gravely. All Elvira needed was firm persuasion, and no brothers, cousins, friends, lovers—only her understanding husband. She herself had said only yesterday that no one would ever be as near to her as Paul. And so forth.

His decks cleared, Marpurgo finished his second cigar, and decided not to go to the Fuseaux' office but to seek out Oliver. The accustomed intoxication of the cigar carried him off cheerfully. He called for Oliver at the Archives and took him out.

' Alecto, Megaera and Tisiphone send me for you,' he lisped to Oliver, ' Orestes—or should I say, orexis ?—I left school at fourteen. I can never understand how a man of twenty-three can sit out a sunny day on his coccyx.'

Oliver, plump, ruddy, drowsy, blinked good-humouredly at him.

' Let's have a drink. I'm dry as a bone. I feel like a silverfish. Why don't you get me a position in business, Marpurgo ? '

Marpurgo's eyes narrowed.

'Why don't you get yourself one ?   Anything would be better than this . . . coprophagy.'

Oliver yawned.

'The scarab ate dung and was sacred : I belong to the sacred dung-eaters myself : the State supports me.'

'Yes, but you can't support and propitiate your three furies on your stipend, can you ? ' asked Marpurgo.

'What three furies ? ' Oliver awakened and looked curiously at his interlocutor.

'Elvira, Coromandel, the occasional whore.'

Oliver yelped cheerfully : 'You bitter old Puritan ! I believe you're in love with Elvira.'

'I despise women, all women : I never write about them, think about them, speak about them. I only court them and make tools of them.'

'You're a fearful ascetic, Marpurgo. *Ergo bibamus !* What'll you have, brandy ?   I can't drink those sweet French drinks : we drank nothing but rum, rye, gin and slivovitz at college. Garçon ! Two *fines maison* ! '

'For me, just spa-water : quart-Perrier, garçon.'

'Oui, monsieur.'

'It's marvellous to be out of doors this lovely weather. I ought to go and take Elvira out. I suppose she's at home. She's a lone girl. I don't give her enough attention.'

'She's not a girl, but a woman,' answered Marpurgo. 'You must beware of her. She's an intake girl : she'll absorb your life entirely if you're not careful. You're an easy giver : you'd give anything rather than fight about it.'

'That's true : it's funny too, because I think I'd do well in business. I've got a good business-head and I'm hard underneath.'

'Yes, but you're not an annexation-type : you'd make money for others. You're not constipated, are you ? '

Oliver laughed.

'No, and yet I'm not a spendthrift. I don't like to

think about money. I'd like to go into business just to
make money easily, you know : so as not to know where
it comes from. In scholarship, you've got to strain over
every penny so that your whole life is absorbed by money.
You can't buy a car, you can't have tailor-made clothes,
you can't have children, you can't buy the books and
pictures business-men buy, your wife's dressed like a
frump—and *you're* the aesthete ! What a contradiction !
It goes without saying business-men are more cultivated
than we are : they have the money. Now I reckon with
my background and my love of material comfort, I could
get somewhere in business. I've been thinking it out.
Then, look at Elvira : she loves goods. It's a pity we
weren't born in the merchant ages : we'd make a
wonderful couple in a cloth-house.'

Marpurgo looked suggestively at his eyes and at the
emptied brandy-glass.

' Why aren't you working to-day : are you pensioned
off now ? ' cried Oliver.

' No, I still produce sales for a living,' said Marpurgo.
' I'm not in the hocuspocus business yet, although I
could do it better than anyone. In fact, when I was
fourteen I deliberately left school because I saw I was
going to do too well at it : I knew their game. I didn't
want to be chief flamen to some paper Jove.'

' You could have done research,' said Oliver.

' If the clear call isn't there, the rest is a shadow-dance,'
said Marpurgo. ' And with me—I could have done it,
but I could never get into that state of self-intoxication
when my little ciphering seemed of world-shaking
importance.'

' I don't take it seriously like that—I'd like to do a good
job, that's all,' said Oliver seriously. ' Whatever I do,
I'll do a good job : while I'm doing it I think it's really
valuable, I can get quite earnest about it, but afterwards
I realise it's just one among many. There are lots of
jobs in life. Of course, I realise that isn't the point of
view of a fanatic, and I'd rather like to be able to be a

fanatic at times : it helps. I get rather blue at times : I
feel something of a squudge. I've a good mind to go
away down south with Elvira when I've finished this,
before I go back home, just to recreate something of the
romantic atmosphere we started out with—or rather, I
started out with. She's very happy and faithful, you
know, if you give her a direction. That's all she needs.
She needs to believe in one. Left to herself, she just
goes spinning darkly on on her own pivot. She groans
at night, asleep, and I wake her up, asking her what she
was dreaming about : she often says, " I dreamed I was
alone in a howling wilderness with no one and no lights":
or she dreams she's on the edge of a precipice, and can't
make up her mind to fall over or go away.'
  ' Naturally a man in love sees a woman different from
others, and in a sense creates her differently : we create
our mistresses.'
  ' She doesn't seem like that to you ? '
  ' I'm not interested in her : therefore I can see, without
self-reproach, that she has the single-mindedness of a
one-way street—enter without return—and the selfish
foresight of a pampered girl. But she has one weakness :
she loves her habits and she loves to create new comfortable ones. She is weaving you into her cocoon.
Don't break in on her weaving : she'll be hurt and she'll
hate you. Her strength in weaving is such that she'll
build up your life for you.'
  ' My head's bad. What are you talking about, Marpurgo ? Let's go and eat.'
  ' Delighted. But you ring your lady first, I want to
talk to you alone.'
  Over dinner Marpurgo made Oliver steadily drunk :
his backbone and skull were tingling : he sat up straight
and felt exhilarated, serious : his eyes and ears were
wide open.
  ' How the devil did I get so intimate with you, Marpurgo ? ' he asked, rollicking. ' You come in like a
demoniac old grandmother, bandying our fates, giving

advice, diabolically near the truth, pestilentially impertinent. No one has any privacy with you around. You're a vulture picking the eyes out of romance, baring a man's brains before he's dead. You're moody, cloudy, terrifying, cryptic, and full of assorted tags as a crystal-gazer.'

As they came over the sill of the restaurant, Marpurgo replied between his teeth, softly : ' Yes, but you're easy to see through, Oliver : immodestly easy.'

' You despise me ! Oh, Christ ! That's funny. I've always been the admired coxcomb. Why ? Is it because I'm dirt or you're superior to everyone in general ? '

Marpurgo's tone of hate broke in on his hilarity.

' You're an oscillating hedonist, a Cyrenaic : your haunches pull you back towards your chair and your stomach pulls you forward towards your dinner : hence you develop the requisite amount of rhythmic motion necessary for physical happiness. You're a pure physical function, docile to your moons, appetites, secretions : you think to give your brain the little bit of exercise for which it was, by Lamarckian generations, fitted. Religiously, you're a eudaemonist : in economics, a utilitarian, I'm sure : Marxism is just the newer label for a smart young man who must be up to date. You're a coward, not because you're anaemic, but because you don't want your sweet tick-tock disturbed : you're the summit of well-bred nonentity, as is a patched Great Dane. Elvira will gently but consummately henpeck you : don't worry, so will every other woman who can keep you. Coromandel would . . .'

' So you do know . . .' said Oliver.

' I know nothing : you told me the name just now.'

' I must be frightfully drunk,' murmured Oliver. ' But you're quite right : this girl is a hectoring kind : splendid but overbearing, and even Elvira, although she's timid, easily led, and hardly has an opinion of her own, she manages me : I am a softy.' He laughed. ' What difference does it make ? '

' How can you live like a slob, talk piffle, write plapper, posture, take the easy road, when you have ability ? ' nagged Marpurgo. ' You run round to workmen's meetings, so as to be in the swim : people tell you you're generous, kind, simple, and you let yourself be persuaded; but I know you for what you yourself know, when you're stocktaking—an inkpot-valiant . . .'

' Hold your horses, Marpurgo : I have some news that ought to please you. I've been offered a job in business.'

' In France ? '

' In England.'

' Take it, then.'

' Thanks ; I will.'

' And who has Georges Fuseaux picked for your new boss ? When the fungus joins hands with the kernel-worm, some interesting work is afoot. I'll be charmed to see what you two make of it.'

' Marpurgo, I had nothing to do with it.'

' Really ! I know your type, Oliver ! I know how with your half-feminine manner you get your way in scholarship as well as in life. The completely, coldly egotistic wiles of a woman. You care for no one in the world but yourself; you are wormy in head, heart and body—in soul, if there is a soul. You will regret this. No one has crossed my track but has been struck down —not by me, but by retribution. I lie with putrefaction every night : but putrefaction is my friend, and in return slowly dissolves the vertebrae of my enemies.'

Oliver grinned.

' But, I say, Marpurgo, you are coming it strong. Everyone dies without your aid, I think.'

Marpurgo wheezed with laughter.

' Oh, you've got courage, when you're drunk ! ' They had got up. Marpurgo said : ' You'll even get on for a certain time, but you can't go too far with that fake-learning of yours. The world may be full of *arrivistes* like you, but their age is past. You're somnambulists walking in a world of phantoms : you're shadows.'

Oliver laughed drunkenly.

'Marpurgo, you're the king of shadows. Why are you bothering me? I've done you no harm. I only kept it a secret so as not to annoy you. Besides, I wasn't sure.'

'That doesn't interest me: the less said about the Georges-scab the better. I'm not a specialist in skin diseases. He's an ignorant, turbid Goth, with the antipathy of the clod for anyone who can put two ideas together. I've often thought of fumigating out the place: why do you suppose I smoke these big cigars? But he doesn't interest me, that bigoted bastard. You interest me, the prairie flower of the intellect. Would you like to know how you appear to me?'

They were walking rapidly down the sordid rue du Roi de Sicile and turned into the rue de Rivoli, here known to its poor Jewish tradesmen and costers as 'Rivolagass.' It is a streaming thoroughfare. Oliver was burning to deliver himself as rapidly and rashly as he could of his new ideas. His whole life was gathered together for this great spring into a world formerly closed to him and which he perceived he must die in, or soon quit again for the calm orderly academic one which suited him best. He had to stop and breathe a little once, leaning heavily on Marpurgo's arm. His breathing could be heard, and sweat beaded his forehead. Marpurgo was solicitous, he coughed intermittently, and replied to Oliver's remarks with the quick intuition and soft flattery of a woman.

He conversed continually with Marpurgo, but his thoughts were towards the river. If he could gain the leafy quays, he felt his trouble would be calmed for a time. It was getting dark. He had migraine, and was too drunk. Other voices seemed to join in the responses of Marpurgo: his sense reeled: scenes which he had seen long ago, and strange fancies, and reminiscences of old romances floated before him through the dark, momentarily: he thought a pack of wolves ran at his side, while the largest, with white fangs and lolling

tongue and dripping mouth, ran on before him; he
thought an army rising out of the dust swarmed up a dark
hill topped with ancient white stones; he thought a
lizard as large as a crocodile lay across a dry river-bed,
and the engulfed water from the river ran back along
the ooze and the roots of the nympheas; he dreamed he
saw a pallid globe in the sky, a balloon which suddenly
expanded like a Chinese cup carved in six sections of
walnut wood, and from whose silver interior burst
brilliant fireworks; he thought he observed at one side
of the street a host of squat dark hairy creatures waddling
fast after a buxom woman with large larval eyes.

Marpurgo said to him, plucking his sleeve, 'Faster,'
and he strode on. Suddenly, with a groan, he slipped,
and a woman with a loud cry ran past him: she had
suddenly ducked up from a garbage-bin she had been
examining and had struck her elbow in his diaphragm.
Marpurgo picked him up, and when he recovered his
senses he discovered that he had reached the Pont-Neuf.
But all elation had left him: he leaned against a rail
with Marpurgo, scarcely aware of his presence, and
watched the lights rolling round him, conscious of cruel
fatigue. But he said to Marpurgo:

'I never had such a night as to-night. I am not myself.
Literally.'

'Go home now,' said Marpurgo.

'Come with me!'

'Yes, I intended to.'

Halfway up the Boulevard St. Michel, Oliver said,
'I'm faint,' and they went into La Source, a gay students'
café, full of mid- and eastern-Europeans. There was a
great clatter, so that conversation here was as private as
in a desert. Oliver sat down with Marpurgo, and
having recovered a little, said whimsically: 'Annibale,
what am I?'

Marpurgo leaned forward, on the arms of the arm-
chair, gathered into himself.

'A somnambulist; you fell off a wall. You'll pick

yourself up and go on sleep-walking. Never fear. She's
a somnambulist too. You all are. And your talk is the
talk of sleepers. One day you'll all be burned alive in
your houses. You and even I belong to the club.'

' What club is it ? '

' The Somnambulists' Club.'

' I don't quite understand ! '

Marpurgo started with the usual claptrap, but swaying,
worked himself into a paroxysm.

' Life is a dream : we are trying to wake out of it.
Science of ordinary life is lunacy to us, vice versa. Who
knows when the intellectual paroxysms and wild excess
cerebrations called philosophy, which has nothing to do
with true symbolic thought, will be turned over into the
content of some new Budget of Paradoxes ? I prefer to
be a somnambulist. I walk on the edge of precipices
safely. Awake, I tremble and run back to the skylight,
enter the little attic room, never accomplish the journey,
remain all day crouched over the books. At night one
rambles. Have you ever seen a city asleep ? If you took
off the roofs of the city, what do you think you would
see ? Logs, stones, congelations, corpses ? No, you see
fits and starts and groans and convulsions, grimaces and
clutches, twitchings and hoppings, staring eyes and
working throats, rolling eyeballs, murmuring mouths.
That is what we call sleep ! Now the somnambulists
deny this horrible sleep. We sleep in the daytime : at
night we live under the guidance of the soul, which is
always trying to break the bonds of those hag-ridden
slumberers ! With the Somnambulists you will see men
really awake—or Lunatics ! '

' I have never seen these wakers, perhaps, before,' said
Oliver calmly, but neither his drink nor the busy scene
around could prevent him from shuddering slightly.
Upon Marpurgo's face appeared the rapt, strange and
lost expression of a man communing with his own
angels. He had a large nose which seemed to point
the way for him and to be symbolic, like a great wing

of fantastic flight, or of resolution arising not from
Oliver's mind but from the Verb presiding over the
breath that first blew into his clay. How strange it is,
thought Oliver, to see an ordinary human being suddenly
transformed by the insanity which lurks in him : transformed into Disorder, apart from all restraints and con-
veniences, taking his place with Evil (that is, what is
strange, hostile, and unknown, and foreign) : to pass at
our side mute but speaking endlessly to himself in his
own symbols which have served him, unconscious as he
is of it, since his birth : how rare he seems and how awful.
Is that what I am now ? Transformed by an accident.

When Marpurgo began to speak again, it was with the
voice of internal enquiry of a person speaking to himself :
he questioned and never stopped for a reply : he submitted his own replies and elaborated, and retraced his
steps and made references to things that Oliver had
no knowledge of : he spoke of the instant flash of sanity
in the dark night of the mind, he spoke of the glistening
back of the dolphin cleaving for a moment the dark
waters of the ocean. There was a constant reference to
some white object appearing for a moment in tumult
and multitude.

Oliver felt himself getting rather drowsy. He roused
himself and broke in on Marpurgo's soliloquy.

'You know, you no longer fear a thing you understand, in the same degree ? For instance, ever since my
earliest days, I have feared a pale living corpse lying on
the floor beside me as I lay dreaming in bed, a silent
shadow-man—death or my thin soul. When I try to
recall him, all sorts of memories circulate, such as the
house where we first lived, a vacant lot beside it, my
father creeping into the room late at night, my father
tired but boringly sanguine. The Polish baker who had
ulcers, with a rag round his hair, had that face, a ghoul,
a skull. In the daytime the sight of a person with one
of these deformed faces is the one thing that puts me
into the primitive state of terror : I am sure I am going

to die. At night, it is somehow no longer so terrible.
Because in the day he is a lurking danger, at night he
promenades with the rest of the phantoms, and with
myself. Who is he ? Some poor wretch I saw long ago ?
Ever since my earliest days I have feared the deaths of
poverty, ulcerated stomachs, cancerous mouths, skinny
skulls with absent eyes, stringy veins, rasping breaths, the
horrors of old age and disease when their foul breaths
must collide with your own. I can't stand them. They
are a crowd of ghouls on my track sure to get me in the
end. I finally invented means of waking up and of
staying awake while still reposing, such as counting,
breathing deep, saying my name, and so forth. Thus I
managed to " stay awake " or preserve my sanity, while
still in the bonds of sleep. I invented the means of trying
to envisage my phantoms. At first when they escaped
me I almost screamed with terror : since, when I manage
to see them clearly, I am better off. At last I met him—
two years ago. A strange creature who hung round
coffee-dives in my old town. A deathly creature with
the " hippocratic facies," the skull face. I don't know
his real name. They used to call him " Jean-Jaurès."
The first time I met him, my heart gave a thump. Love,
real love, as I know it now, has exactly the same effect
on me. The old phantom, feared, in the flesh.'

' The Somnambulists' Club, of which you are a
member, you uneasy soul, is full of such phantoms.
You know, with your ambition, Oliver, you are only
trying to force the door of a dead-house. We are dead
but not disintegrating. We are so recently dead that
day-old memories of us walk the earth in our recent
footsteps. Our footprints are still in the dust of streets,
they have not been swept out of buildings. Our voices
are still in the air, like the voice of someone I heard
recently somewhere, I forget now, perhaps Dr. Western's.
You have heard of Munchausen's " frozen sounds." It
is like that, preserved. Living people still think we are
speaking. Our hands are still at cross-roads, pointing

one way and another. A hand has a strange effect on us, we are impelled to obey it. I always remember the hands of people as separate from their bodies : it seems such an active, useful, demonstrating and helpful member. A person with folded hands—like Elvira, Oliver—there is no help from them.'

Oliver looked puzzled, half-enticed. He said : ' Tell me about your club, that I am trying to gate-crash, it seems.'

' You are a dead soul, Oliver. You are fooling your-self with all these ideas of revolutions and these friend-ships with revolutionaries. It doesn't fool anyone but you.' His hate whistled through his teeth. ' You are corrupt like me. You can't be the workers' friend : you'd deceive them as you deceived your other friend— Dr. Western. You've got to be like me. You've got to be a mealymouth.'

' I won't,' said Oliver, leaning his heavy head on his hand.

' Look,' said Marpurgo cunningly. ' You will see a quiet dark suburban street. Your future home with the dark lady, say. A light burns in the front room of one of the semi-detached villas, or up-to-date apartments under the orthodox gable or cornice. Go in at the front door, and hang up your hat and coat. Push open the door. I am with you. We are there. There are about twenty persons we know, in ordinary dark clothes, with their hats off. Their physiognomies are various, but a Chinaman would not be able to distinguish them. Their ages vary, their colourings and status are the same. For you they are all living cancers : for me, well, my par-ticular fright.

' You have been there often, do you remember ? On the mantelpiece is a clock, with, on one side, an ikon of St. Vitus, and on the other, one of St. Columban, the one the representative, in the heavenly third estate, of dancers possessed, and the other of the weak-minded, both saints elsewhere without votaries.'

'The lamp,' said Oliver politely, 'which is in the shape of a crescent moon, undoubtedly indicates lunacy?'

'What,' said Marpurgo, 'how can you think so? Is not the moon the best regulated, the fittest and most easily observed of all heavenly bodies? Is it not itself the regulator of tides, clocks, calendars and maladies? Does it not therefore march mankind on its road better than any other dragooner in the world? No innovator, the moon: no burner of hides and addler of brains, like the sun: it takes the sun's fierce unmoderated light and strains it through its fine cool net. Is there anywhere else a finer symbol of wisdom? How calm its face: its character, modest but bright! Then its benefits—how should humanity get about at night but for the light of the moon? It is well known that the sun only shines in the day, when there is no need of light! Also, all creatures that live by the light of the moon are, as I said, figures of wisdom: the owl, the bat, and the moth, the symbol of the soul.' The loiterers in the café were looking at Marpurgo, whose voice had risen.

'Why, I humbly beg pardon of the learned assembly,' said Oliver, seeing that the members looked at him suspiciously. 'The fact is I am somewhat fatigued: walked far, had no supper! Have you a carafe of water? I am not quite myself!'

One of the members, who was small, lean, furrowed, with white hair and waiter's clothing, rose and said disagreeably: 'Have you introduced somebody who did not go to bed to-night?'

'Not at all,' said Marpurgo hastily. 'Here,' he said to Oliver, 'drink,' and he handed him a glass containing a dark liquid, purple red against the light.

'What is it?' asked Oliver, hesitating.

'You don't have to drink it,' said Marpurgo. 'You please yourself. It has this quality; if you drink of it with a person, you become confused with him, and you do not know which of you it is until the insobriety wears off. It is the devil's elixir, got out of the Pierian Spring.

Some of the members find it helps their theories, if they mix their brains with other people's for a night.'

'I shall drink—with myself,' said Oliver. 'Thus I mingle my blood with the same noble strain, like the Ptolemys.'

He drank all the wine (for such it was, a sort of heavy sweet Palestine wine, with sherbet) at a gulp. He did not notice any great change : he observed things as always with vivacity. Voices struck his tympani with such a delicate trembling that they even seemed to have a separate being, apart from throats and air : they wended their own way lightfoot over the stepping-stones through the labyrinthine canals, they laughed in his brain.

'Is our brother *in nubibus* pleasing to you now?' enquired Oliver of the ferrety gentleman.

'Yes,' said he, irritably. 'So pleasing—so charming— I fear—I fear, I don't know what, he has the charm of the veritable *effugator daemonum*.'

The company said ' Hist ! ' and drew their coat collars round their necks.

Oliver began talking to various persons, to appease the company, so he went to the irritable man who had made the remark and shook hands with him. Or so he dreamed.

A great many of the persons present seemed to be interested in heavenly bodies.

' And why not ? ' said Marpurgo. ' The heavens can be sounded with the imagination, but the earth only with infinite patience and labour.'

One man asserted that the sun was made of ice, since a piece of ice produced the same result as a burning-glass ; but beside him sat a lean, infatuated man who continually warned his hearers that he was a teacher of mathematics, better informed than his opponent, and that he had discovered that the sun was an electric space from which the planets sucked their nutriment. Another member said that comets were the spawn of volcanoes, spat out of their bellies, and that they fell back like the devils into the belly of the infernal Porteress, only to be spat out again. He had an opponent who cried out that he was a false scientist and an immoral rogue, for he (the speaker) had shown him a thousand times that comets always appeared in certain conjunctions with certain signs of the zodiac, and that their appearances marked the days of Creation (since the extent of the Days had never been told), that they would finally appear to announce the Sabbatical Jubilee : ' The ancients, who were wiser than we—for we talk of the youth of the world, but it is we who are in the young age of the world—believed that comets foretold some august event, the death of a mighty prince, the fall of a people, of a false faith.' The comets, he said, were not bodies, but were the lights flashed from a crystal mirror by the Lord, who wished to warn us : we were blind, but he was busy working out the secret semaphore. Another warned his hearers solemnly against the Scarlet Lady, the Great Incubus, Genf, and wished to debate whether this latest abomination was due to the spells and conjurations of secret warlocks and vile covens of sedition throughout this present world, or the malevolent influence of celestial bodies in unhappy conjunction, or indeed only from the wickedness of men themselves : whether Genf herself had not been conceived, in her unnatural beauty, by the coition of devils, and prinked out to seduce and entice humble men, by the artifices of such parents. He was answered that Genf was sick to death for her sins, but would be reborn again, as he knew by a secret revelation. But on all sides was strife and dissension, some people calling Blasphemy, some Shame.

' What do you think ? ' he asked Marpurgo.

' I am thinking,' said Marpurgo, ' that bees never live singly, but in swarms, and if they choose to live in a bonnet, they make honey there, no doubt.'

' Marvellous,' said the cometic prophet : ' a great mind : he talks in the symbolic language.'

' Talking of symbols,' said a sandy fellow, of about fifty, and over six feet in height, ' I am a countryman, so I look at these things with a fresh mind. It seemed to me, when I first went to college, that the philosophers just sit there spinning words . . .'

'Certainly, boundless ruffians, infinite lying black-guards . . .' said one of the fellows.

'No, no,' said the first speaker, 'they're quite innocent, they don't know it themselves : so I thought, to help everyone out, and to get down to clear thought, say, as in algebra . . .'

'Certainly, as in algebra . . .' agreed the listeners.

'One should use not words but symbols in philosophy; viz. for God a triangle, for infinity the mathematical symbol, for Man a bifurcated symbol like Λ, for the soul §, for acquisitiveness % and so forth.'

'Pah!' said one of the assembly, 'why bother about earthly philosophy when I have a direct revelation from God? I understand that language which our brother is trying to concoct from his comets. It is simply a compound of Sanskrit, Greek and Aztec with some interpolations of Yiddish, but I can't give away the secret. I have sealed it up, and if the State will not buy it from me, it will go as a legacy to my daughter. The only thing is, that to punish men for their blindness and deafness to the word of the Lord, I have arranged the language alphabetically, and each time the State refuses to pay me my price, I destroy one whole letter of the alphabet. What is left becomes therefore infinitely more precious. My daughter will have an inestimable treasure.'

'Tell us one word,' said Marpurgo.

'Timeviol,' said the man.

'Which means?'

The man leaned forward and whispered through his hands : 'The sacred word for temple! Hush!'

Marpurgo learned that one member had gone to an observatory and begged to see the Red Planet which he was sure was the Hell of the system ; he thought Jupiter one of the gates of Paradise. He believed that the new planets being discovered were not really there before, but had lately been put there by God, as he created new souls. One man affirmed that the moon was not a solid body but was the image of the earth ' refracted ' in the ether, and its face was the shadow of the Himalayas. Another said the stars were the heads of angels and the milky way the chief road to heaven. Still another asserted that the binary stars were married and produced offspring, which were the comets and falling stars : others were certain that the planets and all the heavenly bodies were inhabited in one manner or another, and offered proofs thereof. The gentleman next to Marpurgo explained ardently that atoms themselves were worlds, and had other worlds within themselves, and that each and all of these microcosms were inhabited, and that, indeed, we ourselves were but the atom of an atom in a giant molecule, that we might be disintegrated some day by a curious Titan : our only salvation lay in the companionship of like myriads. When people died, he believed that they had simply been disintegrated in some enormous chemical laboratory, and could very well be integrated again in some other part of the universe. But his neighbour, while inclining to a belief in the habitation of atoms, asserted that innumerable forms of life existed, and that no single atom was like to any other atom, nor was its (presumed) astronomy, geometry, politics or natural science anything like that of any other body in the universe. From a purely spatial standpoint, how could it be ?

' Ah, deary me,' said Marpurgo, holding his head, long ago slightly streaked by long nights of study, ' and is there so much more to be learned by the curious ? And is it all nothing after all, and likely to be put out of joint by some slight effervescence in some awful retort ? '

He looked so lugubrious that a gentleman of the cloth with snuff in his beard took him aside and promised to explain to him his infallible system for beating the wheel at Monte Carlo :

'It is true that it is weighted,' he said, 'but I have calculated the chances upon that too. Also I have very secret information about the internal structure of the Company! That is much more important, believe me! Look for the Hand of the S.J.! Yes, it belongs to the Pope, and no Protestant can win and certainly no atheist. This is quite well known at Monte Carlo, but the people go on playing. By fascination : they are there against their will : ah, ah, yes. Somebody has an anti-Christian power. Somebody is in league with his Infernal Majesty. There they sit : you can see they have a secret foreboding of their end. They fix the banker at the table with their haunted eyes, as if he were some demon ordered to fry their livers : yes, sir, and they mumble as if reciting some holy mumbo-jumbo, but a lot it helps them. They work out their little systems, graphs, tables and progressions, but *I* know the weighting of the wheel : none of them can win. Except—you know who! After all, in this age of mathematics, figures talk : this is conclusive : it is no mere chance that *non-Catholics have lost consistently over a series of years!* My own observations.'

'And Jews ?' said Marpurgo.

'Well,' said the man, 'I have reached another Machiavellian trick practised on mankind : *the Jews are themselves secret adherents of Rome!* You may look surprised, but I have found this out. I began by working on the position of the Great Pyramid.'

Marpurgo felt uncomfortable with this man, who seemed to have far less of his wits than the others, although he had noticed before that the mere thought of the Great Pyramid usually knocked a man off his base : he stood on his head to look at its base. He looked about the room : everyone seemed to direct themselves eventually at Oliver, who appeared somewhat flustered. Apart from the others sat three gentlemen of severe demeanour. Marpurgo asked who they were, and was told that they were newcomers. One founded the whole history and mystery of the world on 'internal rhythms' which included heartbeats, dances, calendars and millenniums ; another had discovered the Fourth Dimension and accused Professor Einstein of cribbing his theories, being a very embittered and cantankerous fellow, therefore, and hard to talk with ; and the third denied the existence of mind, thought that art, governments and inventions were the communications of demons through human automata, and thought he was the head demon. Everybody had a demon, but demons were rare, and sometimes one demon was given possession of several thousand or several hundred thousand bodies, which he moved like a skilful marionettist. Other demons had all they could do to work one body : Lenin and Einstein had one demon each.

Oliver moved over to Marpurgo and said : ' What, after all, is the purpose of this assembly ? Their opinions are not really remarkable. Any score of persons you pick up in the street any day have opinions and beliefs more unaccountable. There are countries where this is state policy. This is but cuckoo lore.'

' They have foisted themselves upon us, ever since we started the club : they tyrannise over us—and you haven't seen half. Hardly any of my intimates, the ones I founded the club with, are here to-night. But you must excuse me : seven o'clock approaches : I have to deliver an address and the members are in a heckling mood. I hate to speak to them on a night like this.'

Oliver found a seat. Rats ran about in the upper storey, bats squeaked in the garret, and shingle fell off the roof. Marpurgo opened a walnut concealed in his hand, wherein were his notes concealed on a chain of silk-paper. There were two carafes, one containing ego and the other nego. Marpurgo drank from one and the other indifferently to revive himself during his discourse, for he was dark, insubstantial, trembling and truculent as an affronted ghost. The carafe of wine filled again of itself. After rustling like dry leaves, they settled themselves. He spoke.

Discourse on the Immateriality of the Earth and the
Reality of the Beyond

' Pagans, heterodocts, nonjurors, calvinists, catholics, sciolists, smatterers, dabblers, obscurantists, state-co-ordinaters, you who make a domiciliary visit of hearts, beds, purses, ballotboxes, you thumb-wrenches, tax-screws, conscience-purges, spruikers, lickhaunches, parademen, truncheoners, gunmen, sabremen, tarrers, tiaras, featherers and fezes, you cowls, masks and sacred aprons, nosethumbers, treble-singers, double-facers, monomaniacs, you smutsnickerers, sluthavers, pillars of all orders, bridegrooms of paralogy, asses, racists, ignoramuses, erotics, exotics and obscure poets, flower of the fanatic world, now yours, soon lost ; I know very well that you will accept without proof my argument that the world is insubstantial and inane, a big-swollen nihility, air compressed by the devil into a borrowed and delusive form ; but there is a man here who is not quite sure of it. He comes from another land, a very coarse materialist place where they hardly believe in metaphysics at all, but where I am glad to say the astral planes are getting a good hold. Still he is consanguineous, or at least a fosterchild of our father : he came here a stultiloquent knight-errant determined to find out that the substance was a shadow, but he goes the wrong way about it. Still he is on the limen of our world. Perpend, then, and learn that with us the world is a shadow cast by the moon across the nightly road of the stars, and if you, tarnished stardust, can come easily to the knowledge, it is because your parents made you superstitious, you worship your mother, you live by taboos, your coddling Alma Mater, learned in many a cantrip and cabala, milled a he-goat into a sieve and fed you with the milk, and you are now devoured with a wonderful matriotism for capricious folly.

' Come, cheer up, you deadbones. When were ever the humanities more widely diffused ; yet was ever spell-

casting, crystal-gazing, table-rapping and evangelism
more fashionable than now ? '

(The audience cried, ' No, no : bless you, go on :
Amen. Bless you, Amen ! ')

' Amongst us, I mean, of course. The Church, which
used to be material, and have proper pursers, and
fabricate its stories out of the whole cloth, and never care
a rap, has become meticulous, fearful and scientific. Was
ever such a paradox ? The earth is overflowing with
grain, and more people are starving than ever before, the
intelligentsia are denying the intellect and crying for death
in battle, grain that was never planted makes men rich in
the fields and poor on the exchanges, schoolmasters deny
the rod, women marriage, librarians silverfish, financiers
gold. Now, if there were a world, were such things
possible ? No. Therefore, Oliver, there is no world and
we are phantoms.'

(' It is true ; how true ! Go on : Amen. Bless you,
bless you,' called the Somnambulists.)

' Yes, such a world were impossible, unless it was
watered by rivers of lightning, ruled by Prester John,
colonised by Atlantides, its roads straddled by Don
Quixote and its seas by the Flying Dutchman. Only in
those conditions could it exist, and if you contend that
it exists, it must be in those conditions.'

But the audience was displeased, murmuring : ' What,
after all, we exist ! And my great masterpiece, better
than Rubens', is it nothing ? '

' And my empire, greater than Prester John's, composed of freemen working in slave-camps, and using for
currency bellows which can be inflated and deflated at
will ? '

' What ? and my theory of astral planets ? '

' Nothing : my theory of frozen stars ? '

' Nothing : me, the Galileo of the creative erg ? '

They swayed towards Marpurgo. At the same time,
certain objects in the chamber, having become persuaded
that they were of the same creation as the philosophers,

made remarks. The clock said : ' Rhythm is the solution of the riddle of the universe : flux and reflux : there is no eternity but pedantic measured feet. By listening to the tick-tick of my pendulum you will guide your lives happily and suitably to a satisfactory stop : then the watchmaker of the world will pull you to pieces, rub you up, take out the fluff and start you off again, or put your best spring into some other clock : what of that ? Who wants to live too long counting out days and minutes, days and minutes ? And don't think,' he said severely, ' that I am a mere pendulum : I have my morality, which is strict. Keep your face bright and clear so that all men can read there your conclusions : keep your hands in clear view, and no man will fear you : go neither too fast nor too slow, and no one will overtake you, and no one will see your backparts and so ridicule you : and as for innovations—I have one based on commonsense : let all counting be done in twelves, a pox on the stupid metric system ! '

The spittoon called out lazily and satirically : ' Well, well, old pissface, if you have no posterior, you must have a queer front : I prefer not to think of such an anatomy ! Or I should say I have such notions floating round in my head as I cannot show to the present company. I am all for ejaculation, for my head swarms, yes, literally swarms with ideas, and every one of them pregnant. I understand the very guts of every man, and if I gave my advice (but why should I ? I don't care and you wouldn't heed), your apothecaries and your sawbones would go to the devil in a week, and your proctors and sublunatic doctors would get dizzy with gripes from absence of dinner—a very strange item, not included in their traumata. But a lot of greybeard loons, ineradicable poxes, insupportable windbags like you . . .'

The spittoon was suppressed, and they then heard the carpet speaking in a deep worn humble bass : ' The attention he receives has given him a swollen idea of himself, I am afraid. Spit on me instead, I have no objection : I submit to anything, I raise no questions :

I am even willing, for your convenience, to have my very beautiful false Aubusson design masked with dirt and expectorations : for, after all, in my humility I support all things, the furniture, your bodies. I stand insult from you, but I support you, it is my mission. I keep you warm : I am kind to others besides you, although you don't know it : I harbour fleas and slaters : I am much appreciated by dogs : but I say nothing, I lie here quiet and the darkness floats about me : so I sink into forgetfulness.'

A footnote in one of the books on the bookshelf began to speak in a precise, whimsical voice, with the most erudite diction : he cited thousands of authors, he told anecdotes, he went back and made corrections on himself : he spoke a very queer language for the most part, which sounded like sucking and spitting and seemed like : ' Cf. q.v. et seq. pp. etc. ib. id. e.g.' Everybody found him insupportable. The members began to call out : ' What's the matter with you ? You've disorganised the whole club : you've upset the whole system of things. Out upon you ! Order ! No order here ! We're free ! Who is it that's the Jonah ? Walpurgis : Fenton ! '

The moon-lamp swung out impertinently and touched Oliver on the nose so that he started back burnt. The audience laughed. They swayed towards Oliver, tried to prick him, pull him by the taggy ends of his clothes. Marpurgo's whinny sounded from the peaked top of a giant shadow. Oliver tried to think of Marpurgo's name, but it wouldn't come. He was afraid to fall into the gulf of that giant shadow : his stomach whirled, all whirled about him : his head danced with the waltz of giant spindles. Suddenly he found Marpurgo's name : it was MANARAGO BLUREPIN ! The dancing ceased. A cold silence fell. Oliver fell asleep in the arms of a corpse, he thought.

Elvira, who had helped Marpurgo to bring him in, put a coverlet on the floor and covered him with a

dressing-gown. Then she burst into tears, put her hands
over her face and turned her back to Marpurgo.

' What shall I do ? I had no idea he was like this. He's
just a drunk. Oh ! Marpurgo. You missed your train
through him, too.'

' Go home,' urged Marpurgo gently. ' Go home, go
back to Paul. I can't befriend you much longer. I am
a dying man : my death will be hastened by—but I can't
tell you that in this hour. I will stand by you till you
make your arrangements. I'll see you through. There,
my dear : this is enough. Go to Paul. I'll see him
to-morrow. What will I tell him ? '

' Oh, I don't know,' moaned Elvira. ' I can't make up
my mind. I must hear what Oliver has to say. You see,
he's giving up his academic career for me. I'll write to
Paul. I'm all alone. Oh, dear.'

' Christ, I've got a hang-over,' cried Oliver, awaking
the next morning.

' I think you owe me an explanation,' said Elvira
coldly, looking up from a letter she was writing and
scratching out. ' All night I stayed awake thinking about
our future. Do you get intellectual satisfaction out of a
jug ? You're a complete man : you can read and riot.
That's wonderful. You get a sexual fulfilment out of
humiliating a woman. Paul, at least, never did that.'

Oliver said, ' Give me an aspirin, will you ? '

She went on writing and consulting Paul's letter.

CHAPTER XI

THEY had breakfast in the café. Oliver felt ill, and they quarrelled. Elvira said :

' Paul hopes we are happy.'

' He's very kind, I'm sure.'

' You'd rather he wished we were unhappy ? '

' Not at all : I'm not malicious.'

Elvira held her tongue. Then she said childishly :

' You see that Lesbian over there ? She tried to make me the other day, before you came in : she's been looking at me ever since we came here. I pretended to play her game, and when you came in, I said, " So sorry, but there comes my husband ! " The girl I met yesterday is a queer sort too, ambivalent, I'd say. She gave me such looks. I suppose that after the war Frenchwomen got used to sharing a man, or to each other.'

' Frenchwomen ? Why not Englishwomen ? You've always been gallophobe.'

She looked at him idly.

' You're paying for your disgusting spree last night. Imagine poor Marpurgo having to miss his train.'

' Poor Marpurgo ! I thought woman's intuition always taught her her enemies. He hates us like poison.'

She teased him :

' It amuses me so much when I am here waiting for you sometimes, that some of the men try to catch my eye. I look like a little broody hen to them, they want to give me some fun. So kind. By my indifference I pretend to be interested.' She glanced over at the men on the opposite but distant bench—a dark, middle-aged Bulgarian who assailed his small world with ideas for

magazines, some friends of Blanche's, a sedate clean
senility with a white stock-tie who read all the newspapers of every political colour from morn till eve.

'I like a café,' she said. 'It's like a cinema, like a
ballet. Isn't it wonderful how one can pass the time?
Imagine if we had spent all the hours we have been in
this café studying something—we could have learned a
new language.'

'We could.'

'It's funny: here we are, two respectable people, but
you sit round like a wastrel, sick from a drunk, and I sit
waiting for men like a prostitute.'

'It's funny, all right.'

'After all, we're both in the same game, in the end.
You're living on what you can get by retailing a sort
of scholastic small-talk, and I'm living by yessing men.
I'm luckier than they are, that's all. That's why the
marriage system holds up under all the attacks. The
profits are better than free love. That's why the bourgeois system holds out. That's why it will hold out.'

'My, how you inspire me!'

'But I prefer one man to a lot,' concluded Elvira.
'It is safer and there is something in it, an affection
which gets wider and makes you more sensitive. I used
not to care for anything in the world before I was
married. You don't know till you're married. Now
I feel for myself and for you too. For no one else.'

'Are you sorry for Paul, perhaps?'

'No, not really: men can look after themselves.'

'You're better than you make out, Elvira. I remember many kind things you've done. Those children you
used to send shirts to, the servant to whom you gave an
extra month's pay, the sick woman in the shop.'

'Yes, well, you have to do those things for women.
But I really didn't care for their sufferings. I've been
under an anæsthetic all my life. It's easier.'

'One ought to be less attached to others and crueller
to oneself,' murmured Oliver dolefully.

'I only believe in cruelty towards others.'

'Let's go,' said Oliver. 'I must go down town. I
had a rotten time with Marpurgo last night. He found
out all about the changes. I'm going to tell Georges
Fuseaux it's all off. He made me feel such a rotter, I
want to commit suicide even now.'

'That's your hang-over.'

He walked away. Elvira went placidly shopping for
some trinkets, like a bee gathering honey. Oliver
said to himself: 'I haven't a friend in the world to
confide in.' He walked some time under the flaky sky,
his heart palpitating. 'Oh, Elvira, you sunken river,
with drowned lamps silting down, do you wish to
engulf me too?'

His work was finished: he had no heart to buckle
down and get it in order. He hated the final upgrade
pull of knocking the thing into presentable shape. He
had been sick as a dog when he got up. He wanted love,
some sort of ministration. She had left him lying on the
divan until he grew tired of the game and got up. He
had said: 'I know I'm a pig, but you ought to be
sorry for me.'

'Why should I? You made yourself sick. I've
got too much to think about. I have my own troubles.
I never imagined you would let me down like this.'

'Don't take it so seriously. You're the only girl
in the world who'd take a bend so dramatically,
gloomily.'

'It's true: I'm always melancholy.'

'Oh, don't say that again, Elvira! You've said it a
thousand times.'

'You must bear with me, I'm always melancholy.
I can't help it! If you turn against me, I have no one.
I'm all alone in the world. I had a husband, you separ-
ated me from him. I had a child—where is it?'

He had started to tell her, pretending to laugh, about
Marpurgo's attacks of the preceding night, and she had
protested:

'I don't want to hear it, really, Oliver, I have so much
to think of this morning. I know Marpurgo is what
you say : I knew before you. He would have told me
all his troubles, too, if I'd encouraged him. I stopped
that, and now he only tells me the positive side of his
life. It does look pretty dirty, what you've done down
at the Fuseaux. I know it's not your fault. I suppose
men's world is different from mine.' Then she had been
silent and morbidly satisfied. Presently she had peeped
again :

'I suppose a woman, to be completely rounded, should
taste a lot of men's individualities : in a way I believe
in free love.'

'For men too ? '

'Men have it anyhow.'

'Well, one of these days perhaps I'll present you
with a co-wife.'

'I wouldn't ever do that, if I were you,' Elvira had
said with the air of a prim, proud little girl.

'Solemn Melanchtha ! '

She had repeated *Melanchtha !* in a tone of surprise
and had fallen into reverie.

Oliver now thought he would call upon Coromandel :
she would give him a drink and she would console him.
She very nearly worshipped him, although she was so
high-spirited.

She opened the door to him with a smooth manner,
and when he attempted to kiss her, she suddenly shouted
at him ' Nonsense ! ' clapped her hands in his face, and
puffed like Boreas with fat red-and-white cheeks. 'I don't
want to see you, Mr. *Western,*' she said. 'Oliver, imagine
you deceiving me ! I ought to be cast down, and I'm not,
and yet I'm horribly cast down. Oh—" *J'ai du génie enfin
—pourquoi mourir.*" *Vingt-dieux !* Western, get out of
here ! '

Oliver said : ' I'm not Western : I'm not married to
her. Let me explain.'

The door shut and Oliver went. He was far too sick

to go and see Georges. He wrote him a note, told him
that Marpurgo had blackguarded him all the evening,
and that he thought he ought, in honour, to give up the
job. He was too sick to sit in a restaurant for lunch. He
took a taxi and went out to Blanche's flat in the Champ
de Mars. Blanche was in bed, but got up, made him
some more breakfast, and treated him for biliousness.
In his misery he told her all his troubles, about Elvira,
Coromandel, Marpurgo and Georges Fuseaux. Blanche
laughed gently.

'I knew it all, darling! All. Don't you trust that
Marpurgo. He got me to bring the two girls together
yesterday so that they would find it all out and you
would have a domestic volcano. But it seems it didn't
work. He hates you, darling. He hates everyone. He
promised to give me a thousand francs for doing it;
and he gave me three hundred. I hope he loses his
job.'

Oliver opened his weary eyes.

'Christ! It's Satan's invisible world revealed.'

'You go back to England as quickly as you can,
darling. This dirty little world, that I hate, is getting
you. You are a fine young man, you are full of promise:
you are eloquent, you love mankind, you have genius,
I know. You go back to England with that dear little
Elvira and make her happy. Unless you don't think
it works so well as it did before.'

'She's so aimless.'

'She is a dear little thing, and she loves you both:
that's what's the matter. Now, you sleep, Oliver, and I
will come back after my act and make you early supper:
then you can go home cured, and you won't feel so bad
about anything.'

Elvira received a *pneumatique* when she got back from
lunch, saying:

Dear Madam,—I have a friend working in the Archives,
Mr. Oliver Fenton. It cannot be that he is a friend of your
husband, Mr. Oliver Western?—C. Paindebled.

Elvira sat at home and ate olives and chocolates alternately. She also wound herself, slow, cold, beautifully-diamonded, as a snake, round the problem, and colder and more forbidding grew her brow. She began to smoke, and was presently smoking the chamber full of her resentment, desolation and increasing resolution.

'What a damned traitor!' she cried, beside herself with impatience. Her smoke-trails, as she paced about, were like wraiths waiting about the ceiling to topple on Oliver's much-cursed and oft-coddled black topknot. (You sinful, swart, shallow skull, you oval nut with dark shrivelled juicy sweetmeat inside, already consumed by too much passion and irregularity!)

'He's a failure,' cried Elvira aloud. 'A failure, that's all. Paul isn't really, after all. He has a position, he's respected: he doesn't chase every skirt he sees. He sees too many of them, that's a comfort. Oh, how debasing!'

She bit her fingers, and presently her mouth trembled, her chin wrinkled and she cried. When Oliver came back, rested and reassured, he said to Elvira, sitting there with her ash-trays and dish of olives, half-read book and empty box with gilt paper:

'Ellie, I'm a-weary to-night.'

Elvira lowered her lids and remained obstinately cool.

'Ellie, I feel sort of cheerless, without much faith in the future. A man has not those strong roots in life a woman has.'

This speech by fear generally roused her, but she remained unmoved.

'Ellie! My dear! You must confess me. I am afraid I am a sort of perpetual wanderer through life, no pillar of fire or even of cloud is in front of me, not even a will-o'-the-wisp, nothing but some wreathy wraith of hope that in the end I shall find something worth living for, or be worthy of the only cause worth mentioning, the people's cause.'

Elvira studied her lap through long lashes charmingly close to her soft-paste cheek.

'What's the matter?'

She looked up at him with almond eyes and an alien look. She said, dropping the words as if they were pearls from her small mouth, that was often incapable of speech :

'Then, if you lose ambition here, you'll find it with some other woman. Like all men.'

Oliver's heart went ker-flop.

'We'll go to England soon, and then you'll be happy. I've written to Fuseaux refusing the job.'

'And does the blonde young lady go too? Your mistress, I mean?'

She began to turn over a magazine, but seeing that her hand was shaking, she closed it again.

Oliver replied low : 'You met her yesterday? Why do you call her that? You are inventing a whole story.'

'Did you promise to marry her?'

'Certainly not. Did she say so?'

'Not exactly. She just sent me this.' She handed him the *pneumatique*.

'Well, you seem to know all there is to know. That is all there is to know. And she just kicked me out.'

'I wish I had her guts.'

'Yes. I wish you had, Elvira. I wish I had. I suppose I have.'

'Everyone's the same. We're all caught. Look at Marpurgo. You know he has a wife? She's an invalid, and lives at Geneva or some such place. I suppose he's got some girl on the side, he keeps it so quiet. Oh, we're all the same. I wish I could die. I'm useless to anyone, even myself. So are you.'

'I won't believe it's true. I've gone astray, but I'll come back. I'll crush back the vast sensuality and lethargy that has invaded me lately.'

'Yes, you. Only you! I know you lived with her.'

'Elvira !'

'She wrote to me—that French girl, your Coromandel. She had no fear to write me that impertinent note. That told me all.' She turned her eyes, now like rolling, dark, retributive floods, on her lover. ' You can't stay here with me to-night. You'd better go to her.'

' I love you.'

' You love me the more for deserting me and betraying me. Leave me now again. Go to her, so that you can have more pleasure out of the thought of me sitting here alone, waiting for you.'

' She will never see me again.'

' Well turned. She won't see you, otherwise . . .'

' Listen . . .'

' You bring me into shame and then disgrace me with another woman . . .'

' Into shame ! Elvira, listen . . .'

' I am listening,' said Elvira suddenly. ' What explanation have you to offer ? I should be pleased to hear it.' But she began to tremble violently again. She listened, nevertheless, with bitterness and a sudden jibing shrewish wit. She rose and began to pace the room. Oliver followed her.

' Elvira, dear, sit down.'

She refused, and her small mouth, round and purplish, sank, almost invisible in her face, as she compressed her lips.

' You're not worth her, even. I believe you told her you'd marry her.'

He looked tenderly and reproachfully out of his soft untruthful eyes.

' You took me from Paul to this poisoned atmosphere of treason, hate, insecurity. I have no home, no future, nowhere to go, no friends. Look at Blanche ! I'm everyone's footstool. I haven't even you, for who knows now when you won't go off like the miserable gipsy you are, and leave me, your old woman, and old discarded *mistress*,' she shuddered and stopped, ' your old woman, haggish, peaked, yearning, lonely, deserted, ridiculous. How do I know you won't marry Coromandel or any flimsy that flutters in your eyes some scraps of book-learning? Because you worship that, you pedant. If you had hated me you couldn't have acted otherwise. But no, you're my lover, a fine lover, a lover! Did you ever care anything for me but lust? Don't make that face. I call a spade a spade. I know you get up from our bed, almost from my arms, in the middle of the night, and run through the streets after that woman, half-dressed even, with your hair ruffled with sleep and lust, lust! the one helping out the other with a film of charm: you come home pale, wan, tired— your work was hard! You go to working-men's meetings in the evenings, the Salle Bullier, the Vel d'Hiv;—oh, how I've been fooled—and how do you return? Full of anecdotes, new arguments, stories about men, vulgar jokes, like you used to in London? No, you straggle home late, without a word, washed-out, idle, like some jellyfish waiting for the next high-tide, and then in the morning you begin to sparkle up with high-sounding new phrases, not your sort at all, poetic, snobbish. And the worst is—are they original? No, you get them from her. You imitate everything: pick up everything. You haven't a spark of originality. You're just a grubber. She is your Ligeia.' Elvira hesitated, searching Oliver's face, fearing she had used the wrong word. She took up dubiously. 'Your nymph in the grove. I've been nothing all these months but a poor wife at home, sitting silent and catching flies while you go over there, a few yards away—she was careful to put her address, wasn't she?—and listen to her bragging. That's a pretty picture. A pretty picture! You're a painter, you paint me in ridicule. Go, go! I hate you. Oh, I am so alone! You have ruined me. Go and try to ruin her. But she's too independent. That's how she got you. You're weak. You can't resist a bold woman.' She sat down on a stool in the corner, sobbing, moaning. 'I'm all alone. I have no one in the world.' Her voice rose, and she began to shriek. 'I, God, what shall I do? I'm all alone. I'll die! I'll die! Who cares for me?'

He sat there disconsolate, saying from time to time :
' Hush, Elvira, they'll hear you ! ' She only answered :
' I've ruined my life.'

He rose. ' You want me to go ? '

She said nothing. He moved towards the door,
dragging his feet. Before he laid his hand on the door-
handle, she moaned : ' Don't leave me ! How can I
stay alone and think of all this ? The people next door
must have heard us. What will they think ? Don't leave
me.'

He said wearily : ' I'll stay if you want me to ; but
Elvira, you've invented all this, every bit of it. You
women are wonderful at drama. You're all Siddonses,
all poets.' He kissed her. She pushed him away, but
with pats, petting and kisses he persuaded her into his
arms, and she soon fell asleep from exhaustion.

He sighed and, after a while, tiptoed out to get some
fresh air. The urbane old moon with bloodless, ivory
face, in tuxedo and mantlet, with a kerchief round his
head, a black eye and an opera-hat, so tall and so black
that none could see the top, went home to bed elegantly
tipsy with lights, empearled bosoms, shining coiffures
and late suppers, over the waxy pavements. Oliver trod
in his steps, scratching his brains. The moon trailed
paper garlands after him and, staggering from side to
side, cast leery shadows from cornices, filled the passages,
gratings, eaves and chimneys with warm goblin-drenched
darks, put eyes in attic windows and put to shame and
cried fie to the cozy red lamp glowing behind a hundred
shutters. He whistled a bar, and the cats shrieked and
the dreaming stallions whinnied. He flung up his claw-
hammer over his wrists and put his hands in his pockets.
He peered a moment at the clock on the Ministère de la
Guerre, he footled through the colonnades of the Hôtel
Crillon, he blew his nose vulgarly as he strode over the
Arc de Triomphe, so that silver flecks danced through
the air. He sneezed thrice. Cirrus clouds appeared over
the Bois de Boulogne. He shivered, and so did the

tramps trying to sleep in doorways and on seats. He
went home to bed beyond the Champ de Mars, and
Oliver, who had been following the moon several hours,
came home cold, drenched with moonshine, singing the
beatitudes. He also sneezed and blew his nose, and,
entering softly, found that the moon had other deeds to
his name, for Elvira lay asleep on the divan, where she
had been watching the cool, silent street, and the lingering glim lay on her peeled breasts, as if on the heavenly
twins of satiety and renewed desire. 'Gaze then, my
little one,' said the moon, over his shoulder, as he fastened
his nightcap, ' before I draw the blind and your happiness
is over.'

Oliver kissed Elvira, who started up with her hands
to her breast. She looked at him, with disordered hair,
and began panting. He saw her cheeks were pale and
her eyes very dark.

'My love !'

'Where were you ?'

'I had a headache. I took a walk.'

'I am so unhappy ; I am so unhappy here. I want to
kill myself.'

'You break my heart ! Have pity on me and tell me
what I can do : I'll do anything. I can't stand it,
Elvira.'

'You think of yourself : you should think of me.
You have a future. My life is over.'

'You must have courage.'

'Ah—I am so *mortified*—to death !'

'You regret—it all ?'

'Yes. You love her, Oliver. Tell me the truth.
Did you love her for even a moment ? Or did she just
flatter your pride ?'

'She just flattered me, my dear ; you know my
weakness.'

'Even so, I'm going to leave you, Oliver.'

He said nothing more.

In the morning there was a telegram from Paul :

'Marpurgo has told me everything: come home, or shall I come for you?'

She showed it to Oliver.

'What will I do?'

'What you must.'

He had awakened feeling tender and pitiful towards Elvira. The first hour past, however, she faced him with the cruel coldness of a desperate person unused to fighting.

'What are your own plans, Oliver?'

Oliver temporised.

She said: 'You are deceiving me again. You have some idea, no doubt, about this Coromandel. Then I am leaving you. I am going back to London to-day or to-morrow, it depends when I get the packing done. If Paul will not take me back, so much the worse. I'll go to Adam. Whatever happens, it's all my fault. Fate punishes adultery. You told me a person who remained faithful too long became a turnip—in England, that day we passed a hard field of turnips, you remember? Oh, I remember everything—well, you're a Brussels sprouts of infidelity!' She seemed quite hard. She telephoned Blanche and asked her to come and help her.

'What did Blanche say?' queried Oliver.

'She said, You are quite right, darling, if you are unhappy: you must go back to England and see Paul. At least she is a friend.'

'Well, I'll leave you to your packing.'

'Why not take a little trip over to Coromandel?' He heard her laugh as he closed the door. In fact, he would go to Coromandel; he telephoned her first from the *bistrot* and said, 'Coro, it's all a terrible mistake. It really is: this lady is going back to England this very day. A pure escapade: do see me.'

After a pause, Coro answered. 'All right, for lunch, at Lafon's.'

'Too dear for me,' said Oliver. 'Let's go to the Mabillon.'

Coro had slept all night in a ballet. First, as she lay in the dew, ghosts came tiptoeing back and forth like footless reeds round her, while down long corridors students sat and held their temples and groaned ' Ah ! ' like a musical saw ; melodies in minor keys began to weave about them, and faster and faster they rocked their shoulders and cried ' Ah ! ' The ghosts went on with their strolling : in the second ballet, an old man mourning with a shepherd's crook went leaden-heeled over the landscape, but every so long he suddenly turned himself about, lifted his skirts and did a black-faced, statuesque *pas seul*, statuesque indeed as to the upper part, abandoned and twinkling as to the lower. In the third ballet, hundreds of dancers in black and yellow with smooth black caps, like a colony of ants, did a dull measure back and forth, up and down and round about for as many hours as she seemed to have dreamed : they never varied, and their song went on for ever with the crooning train of thoughts. Sometimes, if they hesitated, a solitary singer made a musical question, or intoned a new phase ; then he had a response, and the response was taken up and ornamented and involved by all the dancers in the regiments about her. Then they fell flat, they melted into the earthskin, they vanished : once more she was left with the waste land, the long horizon, from which rainclouds now rose in puffs. It lowered, rain came, like splinters of glass ; the earth quaked, the seed, agonising to reach the air, quaked the whole earth, which boiled and bubbled about it, when it shook the dirt from its shoulders ; then it sprang up, bearing the grey seeds just fallen out of the sky upon it, not dew but seeds (whence else are they, the myriad seeds which come from a single sowing?), and in a trice Coro found herself lying, a golden maiden among golden tracts and nodding swathes and cornucopias of grain : these fell into her mouth, and with a great relish and great hunger she began to eat. As she held the ear of wheat to her mouth, she felt its texture,

and nothing had been more pleasant in life. On the
borders of the wheatfield now appeared blue clouds, blue
mountains, green meadows and untrimmed orchards of
apples, a ciderous, earthy, waxy smell passed through
the air. . . . The landscape was bathed in brilliant
light, as brilliant as the latest and most experienced
morning of the earth breaking on a cultivated landscape,
and Coro said to the wheatfield this cannibal word :

' Thou art a dish of sweet apples, the crown of the
orchard, the blood of the vat, the robe of the table, a
feast to the eye : thou art a white wheaten loaf, a silver
cloud fallen, a cloud of gold risen, like locusts in myriad
filling the bins, a white river from the dribbling maw of
Leviathan, soft as milk, white as milk, a salute to the
morn, a staff to the hungry, the yellow-curled king of
the board. Thou art a swarm of sweet odours from nut
trees, apple trees, wheatfields and paddocks, from clover
and sainfoin, wild barley and meadowsweet, from
birds, bees and beetles and tree-singing frogs, from
grasshoppers, flies, crushed beetles and cockchafers, that
fly with twined limbs through the deep glassy air, the
food of our nostrils, the pulse of our hearts, the substance of dreams.' But as she proceeded thus long-
windedly to apostrophise some creature she didn't see
nor even think of, she awakened and found the bright
morning sun streaming into her chamber. She took her
clothes from behind a long black linen curtain : she
cast her black coverlet stencilled with griffins, pelicans,
foxes, salamanders, cranes, ostriches and bandicoots over
the foot of the bed.

Oliver telephoned : ' I love you.'

Coromandel cried into the telephone : ' I just dreamed
a poem : Thou art a dish of sweet apples . . .'

' You man-eater,' commented Oliver.

At lunch Coro was gay and had lost her memory for
yesterday. He could not get a word in edgewise about
his escapades, and he did not hear a reproach. Coro
told him she was going to the country for a few days,

took her valise from under the restaurant table and went out ahead of him. She had called a taxi. She said : ' Will you hop in, and we'll talk while I go on an errand. I'm going rather a distance, to Saint-Germain-en-Laye. Can you do it ? Or are you busy this afternoon ? '

' Well, I'm not busy—I'd like to drive out there. It's so frightfully close in Paris.'

' I have a cousin out there : he can drive us back, or lend me his car. He's a car salesman.'

' That's fine, then. I'd love to go—with you ! You're the best friend I've ever met among women.'

She mentioned Marpurgo. Oliver laughed. ' Oh, I just found out something : he's a dark dog. He's got an invalid wife on Lake Como, a permanent invalid. He never mentions her.'

' He would have a sick wife : he loves transformation scenes of frailty. He's a very strange man. I'd like to know him better. He promised to take me to Calais to see through the factories. I am glad you told me about the wife. I hardly feel like doing it. '

Oliver began to relate tales of Marpurgo. They laughed over his mannerisms, his possession, his inspired manner of discourse.

' Marpurgo had a crush on you,' said Oliver, ' I know it. That's one time when he didn't worship frailty.'

She smiled rosily and slily.

' I was enchanted by him at first : he is marvellous in his way. But I've learned too much lately. I'm going to get out of all this.'

' All what ? '

' This sort of company : these gabblers, illumined failures, heroes of invalidity, these poets of detraction, these artists for art's sake. I never was in it much, and I'm on the wrong track. I'm giving it all up.'

' Me too ? '

' You too. Elvira will be happy, won't she ? ' He cleared his throat, but she said : ' Don't blame me, you are to blame : you are a gay Lothario, aren't you ? And

worse than that, you are really very severely to blame.
I will not hear a word from you on the subject.' Oliver
licked his lips. ' Am I really to believe that Elvira is
going back to her husband ? It'll be better for you if
she does ! '

' Yes ; I'm going to steer clear of women for a while.'

' Ah ! '

She changed the subject. She smiled sidelong at
Oliver, and she really looked very well that day. She
took off her hat and gave him the sensation that she was
leaning towards him, although she was not. She said it
was too sunny, and lowered the blind on her side of the
car. She said drowsily to Oliver, on whom she saw
their dinner wine sitting heavily too : ' I am so sleepy,
villain ! Why do you so misuse your Coromandel ? '
Oliver was seduced. ' The farm is yet some distance off,'
said Coro. The sun shone hot, bewildering the eyes
and arousing the same juices in human bodies as he
arouses in grapes : the sun was on fire : he should have
cooled his ardour, on him is great blame. Coro held
her watch in front of Oliver's eyes : they had been on
the road three hours. He put up the blind in a hurry
and looked out through a screen of tall trees into the
broad unfenced country : a windmill turned on the
horizon, they were passing through the outskirts of an
ancient town built on a hill ; on the hill was a Roman
tower ; round the town were notices, ' Nomads must
not camp here,' so on both sides, and in a moment they
sped through the town and out into the country.

' Where are we, in God's name ? ' said Oliver, staring
at Coromandel.

Coro spoke to the driver, speaking so fast and sibilantly in French that Oliver could not follow her.

' Wait just a moment,' said Coro.

In a few minutes they turned into a sideroad and
went along this at a very great rate : Oliver craned
his neck.

' Coro ! '

She smiled at him so tenderly and kindly that he became less alarmed.

'Have a little patience, you will be happy,' said she.

'I must get back soon, you know,' said Oliver.

'We are not very far,' said Coromandel, 'and Saugrenelle's a fine driver, you'll not be hindered getting back : and perhaps you'd better not come to the station with me. Indeed we have now turned right round ; I know the road perfectly, we shall be in in half an hour.'

They continued to run into the heart of the country.

'Coro ! '

She smiled again : 'We are in Burgundy.'

'What are you doing ? '

'Running away with you for the night,' she said roguishly. 'No harm's done, and you're leaving me anyhow, for a few weeks ; grant me this favour.'

'I must be back to-night,' said Oliver. 'Poor Elvira will worry : she worries so about me.'

'I sent her a telegram,' said Coro calmly, 'as from you, saying you had to go to Le Havre to meet some professor.'

'Coro ! '

'It is all right,' said she equably.

'All right,' said Oliver. 'To-night, then—you should have told me, though : but I must get back to-morrow.'

'Four hours from Paris,' said Coro musing.

They came to a small farm belonging to Coro's father. The house had expected them, and all was prepared. In the evening they drove to the neighbouring town and amused themselves. He chuckled to himself, had twinges of conscience about Elvira, and resolved to pay out Coro for this trick. They returned to the house. He went to his room, very large, sparely furnished, with polished floor and rich curtains. He looked out over the orchard : a peach tree loaded with fruit had split in two and lay still fresh under his window : on one side stood a row of seedling frames, and on the other a flower-bed leading to an arbour covered with ivy,

beyond which stood a small vinery. In the centre
grew peaches, nectarines, comquats, loquats, almonds,
mulberries, Japanese plums. The earth was strewn
with small plants and humble flowers, but in the
centre grew roses and dahlias. It was a very simple,
honest, countrified, sweet and nectarious orchard. The
uncoloured flowers moved scarcely in the transparent
shade, the stars like volcanic dust flew above, but Sirius
blazed. Sounds came from the night's faintly beating
heart, and if all was still, sweet crystal bells, like those of
a ghostly yucca, seemed to ring in the transparent air,
and to be one with the ghostly shades. Shortly, he perceived another star, a geaster at the end of the orchard
brighter than a cluster of glow-worms. It wandered
along the paths, carrying the upper pink mask of a man.
He spoke under his voice occasionally, walked slowly
as if to a funeral, with his head bent : once or twice he
turned and, looking into the tree-thick dark of the paths,
spoke. The light was only a candle : the man moved
like a mute, a black mantle hung from his shoulders.
He came closer, and Oliver withdrew a few paces, but
he stared : he saw the man was old, thin, bent, grey,
melancholy—and though alone, he was talking to himself. Oliver's heart beat fast. The man went past
slowly, with his head bent, murmuring, and held the
candle steady. Oliver peered behind, for he fully expected to see a coffin. None came. In two minutes
Coromandel came along the path, also with a candle
and her head bent, but Oliver saw she was searching
for something. He called her softly.

'Who is that man ? '

'Charpy, the gardener.'

'Have you lost something ? '

'My bracelet.'

'Leave it till morning ! '

'See the faint sky ? I fear rain.' She shielded the
candle with her hand and looked up at him with hospit-
able enquiries. Then she said : 'Now I look up and

you look down from on high,' in her accustomed literary phraseology.

'For the last time,' he answered without thinking.

'Why ?'

He apologised. 'I am tired, I spoke unconsciously.' He offered to hunt for the bracelet, and went down to her. In the distance Charpy still moved.

'Has he been with you long ?'

'Certainly.'

Oliver wished to see his face, but as he said the word the man moved into the garden tool-house, and when they reached it, had disappeared.

'He has gone up to the loft to bed,' said Coro. 'To-morrow you'll see him.' She yawned : they stood wearily side by side. She bade him wait for her while she put a watering-can in the tool-house, and he stood there, looking at the stars and trees, leaves and earth, whispering familiars of Coro. He looked at the house, example of all he would have desired at another time, and turned his back on it.

Love for Elvira, yearning, receptive, unassuming, compliant, strangely sensual, strangely modest, suddenly burned in his heart. At this hour Elvira was probably sobbing to herself quietly on the dusky pillow above the midnight street. Coro stood in the tool-house, built of undressed wood and smelling sweetly of bulbs, earth, seeds and raffia strands, and looked out at the stars over the barn through the farther door. Suddenly her soul burned for adventure, for traversing the Saint Bernard Pass, dipping into mountain villages, for viewing Siberia, flying with flying hair and garments through the air, for the bustle and elbowing, and manners and vanities and flatteries of thousands of people, poor and elegant. Outside stood this humble clay, this Oliver of such poor conquerable stuff, to which she was now in some sort bound. She brushed some earth from her hands. Disagreeable was bondage, and charming youth and liberty : and then, what was she, to be intriguing

for a flabby soul like this, one so ragged and in-
harmonious? Marpurgo now—Blanche's Septennat—
she imagined numbers of polished, subtle men of
genius to whom she could have given her hand and
heart. She came slowly out of the tool-house, and
said to Oliver: ' Do you think Elvira is suffering?
Would you rather return to her? If so, I beg you to
go, take the car: I feel sordid and confined here if I
think she is in pain.'

She was pained, but the idea of freedom from Oliver
and from reproach blew with a keener breath than any
other. Oliver looked surprised. She put her hand be-
seechingly on his arm: ' To-morrow morning, go to her:
it is true, she loves you, she is not so strong as I am.
Take her to England.'

Coro stood straighter and straighter, her eyes rolled
with celestial softness, like two bright continents in the
beam of everlasting mercy. Oliver took a step backwards. Then he stepped forward swiftly, kissed her
hand, and left her standing under the peach tree. Oh,
sweet peach-blossom that scattered in spring, with such
traditional sweetness and rosiness falls the rain of
generous love on my spirit and the night-airs on my
bosom! Lulled by all intimations of joy, nobility, and
the highest sensual gratification, Coromandel climbed the
stairs to her chamber and almost fell asleep by her window:
but Oliver, who went also straight to his window, saw
Charpy retrace his path with the same gait and mien. A
parchment skin was drawn tight over the skull.

' I've an evil foreboding,' said Oliver. His heart beat
hard all night and he had bad dreams. In the morning
Coromandel calmly drove him back to town. He felt
humbled, and yet more peaceful for the night in the
country. It was very early. All was grey above, the
sky the colour of a dove's breast. When they arrived
in Paris there was a crayon light, with the same flights
of doves in heaven to colour the sky faint blue. The
youthful and elegant town shook her bracelets, the

garden ruffled her loaded canopies. The Place de l'Opéra was like quicksands and undertows with regiments of all ages and kinds drifting back and forth across the roads as the circular traffic stayed and went. There stood the solid cavernous sepia Opera-house, and down the Boulevard de la Madeleine the thick old rich Chinese pavilioned and lanterned scene, with the stuff of boughs above. There was Lancel's corner-shop, with a large inverted lily in its glass bed, the first sun on the windows of the Grande Maison de Blanc. The people tapped to work. The sky was now the colour of a clear pool paved with pale smoked faience. High above the mansards were the thin filaments of night-signs—Fumez-les-Gitanes, Marivaux, Pathé-Polydor, Eversharp, Le Touquet-Paris-Plage. Oliver had been distrait. They had breakfast in the Café de la Paix, enticing with gold columns, twined red roses and painted ceilings. Some touts and conspirators were taking coffee there already.

'I'm going to leave Paris,' said Oliver quietly. 'I can't bear it. I'll mourn for Paris all my life. I'll hate to see it in the *News of the World*. Paris is the country of the heart. You are lucky to be a Frenchwoman.'

'I am,' said Coromandel : 'I should never be anything else.'

'There is much unrest here; no one is tranquil here, but I would spill my blood a thousand times to defend France.'

'So would I,' said Coromandel.

'You don't believe in glory, and yet everything you do is glorious.'

'A man should love his own country.'

'My country has no people, or so few with a birthright, that is what I mean.'

'They must get their birthright.'

'Yes. I wish we could have married, Coromandel.'
She said nothing.

'Did you love Marpurgo at all ? '

'A little. I love lots of people.'

'You're not upset to find out we've both deceived you?'

' How did you deceive me ? ' she asked with unslaked pride. ' I live and learn, that's all. I love living, I love learning : nothing will ever abate me.'

When he got home, he found the apartment empty and Elvira's trunks gone. There was no letter. He flung himself into a chair. He sat there for several hours. Then he went out and found Blanche. Blanche said :

' Chérie, you will come and stay in my apartment. Do you care ? I do not care. We will be brother and sister. Don't go back there. I'll go and get your clothes. I'll leave the address for your letters to be sent on here. Don't see that miserable café crowd, either. I love you, Oliver : I'll take care of you, till you're better.'

On Saturday she brought home some champagne, tinned food, sausages and cakes. They did not leave the house until Wednesday morning. Anyone who came to the door found it locked, and they answered no knocks. The concierge, versed in Blanche's ways, did not raise the alarm either : she just went to the door and listened from time to time. She hoped this last young gentleman of Mme Blanche was rich.

On Wednesday Oliver tried to get his papers together. He typed, nursed himself, typed, and lay on the sofa all day. Blanche did not return till one o'clock in the morning, and then she scolded him because he had not gone to the bank. He went next morning. A fortnight later he had no money left at all, and was reduced to selling his pigskin case, gift of University friends. Two days later, Blanche found him a room in a very cheap hotel, ' quite near.' It was in Grenelle. He did not hear from Blanche for three days. One evening he walked over, and when there was no response to his knock, he went round to the courtyard to look in. The lights were on inside, and Blanche was having a party with two amiable gentlemen of colour. Oliver walked up and down along the Seine. Then he went back and asked the concierge if there was any mail for him. The lights were out in Blanche's apartment. There was no mail.

CHAPTER XII

His father sent him some money to return to England.
Oliver moved to the Panthéon quarter again.   The
saucers on his table multiplied : it presently became
a necessity and not a whim for Oliver to wait for one of
his acquaintances.   The contents of the café whirled as
if in a heavy swell.   'A heavy swell,' said Oliver
meticulously, and at that identical moment one appeared
in the doorway.   Oliver hailed him.   It was Andrew
Fulton, looking extremely cocksure and somewhat
defiant.   He summed up Oliver's flushed cheeks and
moist eye before he shook hands.   Good fortune had hit
Andrew in a tender spot : his mother had died and left
him $12,000.   Andrew gossiped about wines, theatres,
vaudeville, politics, fashions and low squib-romances.
'I understood you and Mlle Blanche were . . .'
   'Oh, that's all over : she consoled me, wiped me out
and then threw me out.'
   'Do you want another pretty ? There's a charming
little Scandinavian girl I know . . .'
   'No, no more women.'
   Andrew had lost a thousand francs at Auteuil although
he had studied form for a week.   He had a millionaire
American woman 'interested' in his poetry.   He began
to laugh, and told Oliver a splendid joke.   He had just
assisted home a young English girl who had run wild.
She was dead drunk : she would never know.   Would
Oliver like to go upstairs and see her ? He had just taken
another chap.   Oliver quarrelled pettily but hotly with
Andrew, and they parted in a huff.
   Oliver found a couple of students to coach in French :

the father was willing to pay a tutor's fees to have the younger boy, aged seventeen, off his hands in Paris. The boy was stupid. At times Oliver felt like sending the young fool into a stupor that would hold him for three days, or of plastering him up with some girl, but he could not do it. He was not Andrew Fulton. He was lonely, too. He had met Blanche several times, but they were both broke and had no money for each other, and so no time. He spent the idlest and poorest life, and daily said, ' I must go back to England at once,' as if returning to England would set him on his feet. He had hoped at first to hear from Elvira, but she had sunk wordlessly into his past. The months went on, the term began, Oliver had heard nothing from his University. He was ashamed of his essay now, and began to make notes for a new one on the Uneven Development of Capitalism. He went to all the meetings he could to try to pump enthusiasm into himself. But he still hung on to his notion of a career.

It was now winter, and as his hotel was insufficiently heated, and his clothing was greatly reduced, Oliver spent most of his day on the terrace of the same café in the Boulevard St. Michel. The terrace was enclosed with glass and warmed with brasiers.

The weather was growing colder. His pupil was talking of taking a trip to Corsica to get a little warmth. Oliver half hoped to be invited, although he was tired of the miserable boy, and half feared he would be torn away from his agreeable café terrace and his morning journals. His world was as far removed from commercial and scholastic life as possible. A few of the younger persons in the café attended the Beaux-Arts. One of the older men was a journalist : many of the French habitués were indeed business men and doctors and lawyers, but Oliver did not know them. All the people in his circle were virtually fainéants : yet for the sake of being in the swim they discussed the movements of the stock exchanges and racial riots and so forth in a hole-in-the-corner way.

None of them had that grip on the hard world realised by a ten-year-old newsboy. Oliver was older in experience than most of them, and was poorer, and this mordant and snarling world which squirmed in his feeble grip took a great deal of his attention from their paradoxical discourses of nothinglets.

He moved again to poorer lodgings. Oliver had to warm his hands in the lukewarm water in his room before dressing in the morning. The landlady pitied him and gave him an old red coverlet to wrap round his feet when he read in the evenings : he never entered till late, and then he went straight to bed without washing, for he feared the cold so much. Some mornings were so cold that he did not wash till midday when he returned. He noted with shame that his personal habits grew less fastidious : he attributed it to lack of morale, thus doing the work of the furies with the pleasure of supererogation, but it was due to lack of food. His pupil left without paying him for the last month's tuition. This was to be paid upon his return. Oliver wished he could hibernate as forest animals do ; it would save in every way, and he cared for nothing but sleep. He sat for hours now, without saying a word, staring, somewhat owlishly and slightly fuddled, at the passers-by. He had no more money to buy pamphlets.

The morning of the first fall of snow, he felt giddy when he came downstairs. He frequently felt giddy in these days, but the attack that morning was serious. Incipient pains made themselves felt in different parts of his body. Christmas was approaching. One day Oliver lifted his troubled eyes and saw Marpurgo coming towards him between the tables. Oliver frowned. At the same moment, due to his excitement, he became giddy again, so that he was comforted when Marpurgo shook his hand, smiled kindly and sat down.

' Will you have a coffee ? ' Marpurgo invited.

Oliver was glad to see him.

' You should go back to work,' said Marpurgo.

'Work! That means more archives and essays. I was so happy when I got the scholarships. I saw years of freedom ahead. Now, I see no bird ever walked more cockily into a trap.'

'Every profession is a trap unless you get to the top. You sowed your wild oats.'

'Domesticated oats, but they took root in me.'

'I was there,' murmured Marpurgo. 'Paul regards me as a friend : she—as usual—is suspicious, uncertain, and lives for the moment. She had just got her linen up from the cellar and was going through it. Sara had long gone north to her sandwich-shop in York. I think there was a minor tragedy there.'

He ruminated : 'There is always someone who suffers in this kind of story. In every grouping, there is the untold tale.'

Oliver said nothing : his cheeks had lost the rose, his eyes were less glossy, his lips blacker.

'And you, Marpurgo, are you better?'

'My comrade is still the worm. My wife could not stand Paris, and I found we were better apart. She is back in Como and—dying, they tell me. I must go to see her. My finances have taken a precipitous decline. The Fuseaux brothers, of course, are desolated, but my pride prevents me from accepting their offers. They're not doing so well, of course : a firm run on those principles—better for you that Antoine didn't take to you. Antoine is a sweet fellow, he likes you or he doesn't, though. He likes me, but I can't live at a man's pleasure. Reminiscent of the harem. I don't want a tenderloin steak in the business. Eh? You, by the way, would do better that way, the way you're built. Eh? Well, my wife is dying, and I suppose I'll soon be a real, not a grass widower. Meantime, I am in touch with some friends—something rather secret for the—relations in high places : I've always been pro-British, you know, and I'd be glad to serve them. I have certain capacities. I sing my song, I dance my mental hula-hula. Some people think, An old luxurious ham-sitter—just the man to do certain things. You may also have heard of Severin. In the meantime, he helps out through a thin period. This confidential Government stuff (Foreign Office, of course, but never mentioned in the affair: non-committal nonentity, Mr. B. Jabez, private Iraqi interests, that sort of thing, you know how the British work) suits me : if I'd had money, and not been side-tracked by airy loves, arts, philosophy, I should have gone that way. There's none so crooked and clever as the English : a remarkable race. History's three enigmas—the rise of a minor Essene-heresy which became the Christian religion: the rise of science in the dirt-hovels of the Goths against the congelation of the superb Mandarin culture: the rise of a miserable, cold, infertile island in the German Ocean, half-barren hills, populated by a mixed race, often invaded, surrounded by enemies, the Scottish, the Welsh, the Irish, the French, the Dutch, to its position as balancer of Europe's powers, the first of the Empires. What a people ! What accounts for it ? I am proud to be a Briton.' His voice had risen, he looked round furtively, lowered his voice, tried to look Secret-Service.

Oliver finally said : ' Elvira—how is she ? Does she look well ? Did she ask you anything about me ? '

' No. She looks very well.'

' Funny, isn't it ? I suppose petty daily habits dominate our lives more than the great passions of fame and romance.'

Marpurgo bent on his walking-stick to hide the amusement and raillery in his eyes.

' It's written, Some women are foxes, some vixen, some birds and some field mice. St. Bernard says that their face is a burning wind and their voice the hissing of serpents.'

' Ridiculous,' said Oliver. ' He should have had a look at one once in his life. You know, I always imagined her surrounded by little animals, yet she hated animals. When she was here—you know we disagreed in a matrimonial way—we were really married, I take it. I can't

forget her. I used to lie awake in paroxysms of regret,
think of all I'd done and said. I could have managed
everything so differently. I'd throw myself on the bed
and hold the cushion, a hundred times call it Elvira. I
felt the grain of the skin or smelt the natural oils. I
walked up and down till the whole room and the house
and that dirty court of Blanche's and everything wrapped
itself round me. I yearned after dark thick sour-forests,
deep in humus, where I could hold the rough bark and
put my head in the hollows of roots, so that they could
plant their claws in me and their adventitious roots would
descend to bind me, out of the air. Even my head burst
and bounced like the rock on the side of the ravine,
sundered by a tender fossicking root, and its specks of
gold in the quartz veins are revealed. I am all naked like
the skeleton on the trees which points in the direction
of the buried treasure. In my forehead is ambergris. I
scent out the room and ascend among the tree-tops in
clouds of steam and venom; I am striated like the python,
red and yellow like the daubs of savage races; I am all
fevered as fruitful earths touched by the careless savage
male sun and becoming pregnant. I float over the forests
of the earth, and the ascending poisons and descending
rays pierce me, and rains and humours pour from the
vents of my body in my misery. Look, how I sweat!
For days I have sweated as easily! There she stands,
drooping, lurking, gentle, dark, innocent, culpable, in
the undergrowth of some thicket: she casts her eyes upon
me and thinks, What a lout! he didn't even know how
to win me. It's true; I never won her, I never won
anyone. I'm a dull, thick-headed and thick-handed
plodder.'

Marpurgo put his hand on his temple.

' You're in a fever, you'd better take care of yourself.
Have you eaten to-day?'

' No, I didn't care to. I've made such a mess of things,
I haven't any interest in eating. I wouldn't care if I
passed out right now.'

Marpurgo put his hand on his wrist.

'Well, you're going to eat now; and then home. You get your doctor's degree and you strike out afresh. You'll feel better when you leave this hotel. Flats, cities, streets are the death of man.' While Oliver was putting on his coat, Marpurgo smiled his pointed smile and intoned : '*And I have found a woman more bitter than death, who is the hunter's snare, and her heart is a net and her hands are bands. He that pleaseth God shall escape from her, but he that is a sinner shall be caught by her.*'

Oliver shrugged his shoulders.

'When he says her heart is a net, he must mean the inscrutable malice and avarice and glacial cold which reigns in her heart: it's from birth, it's unconscious. Next time (and there will be a next time, because now I want to be married, I must live with a woman) I'll choose a woman who is no woman, just an easy-going comrade, one with no wiles, who can manage me. I'm tired of struggling.'

A bead of saliva appeared between Marpurgo's lips. He put his hand to his chest as if stifling.

'Are you ill?' said Oliver.

'Naturally. I would become ill if I were not.'

'Why?'

'That's what makes me so intelligent.'

'Rubbish. You're the fox that lost his tail. An old fox! How is Elvira? Is she well?'

'Yes, but not happy. She took up her life with Paul exactly where she laid it down. She harasses him, is restless. A Dr. Penn now hangs around in a pitiable way. Apparently a suitor.'

Oliver lay back and laughed to himself.

'Alma Mater! She changes not though everything else changes: she changes everyone, but changes not. She's lovely—but she wants everything and she's never satisfied. I thought I was going to pass out one night. I saw Elvira as clear as crystal. . . . I wouldn't say the time has been wasted. I see now. Andrew Fulton tried

to get me with the old farrago the other day : now that
crowd to me is just a parade of struggling tentacular
ghosts. When I got through with Blanche I got through
with them. I should never have gone near them, anyhow,
if it hadn't been for Elvira. Impassive, she congeals ;
dependent, she dominates. If I were face to face with
her, I'd fall again, I believe, but it's the easiest thing in
the world for me to stay away from her.'

' She's just an ordinary little house-woman, with some
foolish social and personal pretensions,' sneered Marpurgo. ' Like every proud, ambitious young hot-belly,
you have to pretend there's a world of delicacy and
difference in the girl you pick out. Old women pretend
the potatoes they buy are the best in the market, the
town, the world, and are only got by superior cunning.'

He cackled.

' You old devil,' said Oliver. ' Don't you hate young
men ! '

' I did, even when I was young, because I counted the
years until I should be old and despised, and found them
few.'

Oliver dreamed. ' How was the home-coming ? I
can't very well imagine it.'

' She told me in her candid way, " I don't suppose it
meant much to Oliver when I went. Men don't die too
easily. When I came home—well, Paul was very quiet.
I felt like someone coming back from the dead. No wild
enthusiasm either on his part or Sara's, you know. I
know my life is finished. They expect me to settle back
at home, and be sorry for what I've done. Chastened.
They don't know me." She was beautiful, then, Oliver ;
all her beauty came back, more vivid than ever. She
said, " Oh, I often wish I could die in the middle of the
night. There's nothing to do. Everyone says to you,
What you want is something to do, to take a resolution,
to resolve your spiritual problems. You take a step, and
what then ? It's degrading to a spirit to find itself a
woman. You have to think what your husband is

thinking of you, what his friends think. Just because one's not socially independent. It's hateful being a bourgeois. I really went with Oliver because I didn't think he was a bourgeois. But he's just the new bourgeois, the nervous, shying one who has to talk sham-socialism." Funny little woman! But you know her, Oliver, better than I do. She was quite herself. She said, " Life is so humiliating : I can't bear the humiliations of everyday life. What did Oliver do to me? Really, he just humiliated me." Your Elvira is quite a quiddity. She said, " Oliver can rebuild his life, and of course he'll soon see me as a drab little creature." Then she laughed and made me tea. She had a young cousin there, come from some part of London.'

' You mean a young man,' said Oliver, bitterly searching out Marpurgo's face.

' Oh, of course. He was young, and fearfully attracted by her pessimism. She's strangely old in her point of view. Something like myself. Not like you, really, Oliver. We Europeans are so pessimistic : it's the old blood. Old blood that has soaked itself in and out of its native soil for centuries, thinks by itself. Knows about its million death-hours. Has to struggle up again. We were saying that. The young chap was quite fascinated, I could see. He loves Paul, too.'

Oliver's lips and eyes smiled in gentle satire.

' He must be a very young pup : poor pup.'

' And there's always the physical fact at the bottom of all these things,' philosophised Marpurgo. ' She's going to study German with him.'

' She got nothing out of it,' Oliver said with regret. ' I was just mad about her. After she left, I lived with her more intensely than at any time when she was with me. How I dreamed! ' He laughed and raised up both hands : ' Oh, lawdy! Marpurgo, I'm not the same man. There was one night during my—season, with Blanche. I fell asleep completely exhausted. She's full of poetry, that girl, too—Blanche, I mean : she had set my head

going. In a way she was fertile : she started me up again.
I thought I came to a wall of glassy rock which enclosed a
forest petrified but not carbonised. Clouds of gas passed
through the branches, and I could hear no sound but of
some underground water running down to the imperme-
able strata. The clouds curdled and straked, as dreams do
in a crystal before a medium's eyes. In the glass were
single bones, translucent, which were held in suspension
at some parts like a darning in the tissue, and the dark
passage I trod was carpeted with rustling dry fossil bones,
small as if from humming-birds. Then I felt the paths
of my brain were paved with such delicate fossil bones,
as if all delicate things had died in me, and as if my
shadowy self were articulated with such delicate broochy
bones. Through the glass I saw a Bach-blue, and over
that a light spume with hooded wanderers in the mountain
rhyming ancient runes over polar bones and behemoths
entombed. Floating far down in these subterranean
depths I saw enchanted islands covered with phosphates,
kitchen-middens, barrows, fossils; there was the stark
north and the lardy south, all floating without chain and
root, through a whalebone arch, through the whalegate
of wind-blown baleine.

' Beneath them all, flowing lucidly, was the body of a
woman, crowned with flowing dark ringlets, which entered
into the crevices like poisonous roots of trees, into the
coal-seams, the deposits of ore, and worked their way
downwards to the centre of the earth. Imprisoned by her
marauding hair she lay, and turned dark, silent eyes upon
me. Her small forehead looked large as her eyes rolled,
her hair flowing from either side encased but did not
cover her naked body. Sometimes she shivered, and blue
lights played under her flesh. I dug my nails at the glassy
wall. Her dark eyes, passive and animal, did not entreat
me, but looked at me so long that I was drawn towards
her irresistibly. She began to rise towards me in delicious
perfumes, which presently became intoxicating, and even
foul and oppressive, so that my head turned. Her pale

skin became rosy and rosy, touched with golden shadows and white reflections. Her bosom rose towards me, her belly was decked with small black lilies arising from spotted green bracts which had a rich, fleshy smell. In her hair these same flowers wreathed themselves alternately with tiger lilies, and from the lobes of her ears and round her eyelids small blue flowers sprang. I saw she lay on a bed of precious stones swarming like ants, and over these her hair flowed ceaselessly. Her hands did not move, and her mouth lay still as in death and slightly parted.

'I found myself falling towards her a long way into the bowels of the earth, till I thought, so dark and peaceful it was, so the blue flowers seemed to grow round me, I must be lying enveloped in her hair. I looked suddenly before me, and saw her awful, uncomprehending eyes below me, but large and threatening like the crab rising through the sea. Her hair writhed upon her forehead. I cast myself upon her mouth. In an instant she was cold and I was grasping a stone, no, less, it had no form, it was the glass wall, no longer transparent, but changed to rock-wall. I dreamed that. Now she lies there under all, silent, entreating, without recognition, enthralled, living, tearing at my heart day and night.

'If the miner works there long with pick and shovel, will he burst open the seam in which she is imprisoned, will he root out the matrix of that awful jewel? Or will he not rather drive his pick right through her body and so kill her and leave her to rot, rotting eternally, and spreading putrefaction through the whole earth; sprouting tendrils and spotted lilies and thick-fleshed spikes of dusky bells nodding frequently as they turn and rise to obscure the sun and blue heaven?

'You see,' he concluded, 'I am brought to a standstill and headed once more in a circle by this phantom, and this phantom which is my life, buried in the earth under me : my feet circle round and round the spot where it lies.'

Marpurgo looked at him steadily, his blue eyes and yellowed skin drawing in till he looked like a wise man from under the earth. Outside in the street workmen toiled in the drains with a clink-clonk of picks and the roar and flame of the oxy-acetylene lamp; but they only heard it through the wall. The forests of dreams were waving overhead, with long plumed cypresses, pines, poplars, and yews, among whose branches the stars twinkled, the neighing of nightmares grew louder, hippic accoutrements jingled, hounds and hunters parted the low boughs, a woman dropped tears into the well. Oliver and Marpurgo listened for a space.

Marpurgo nodded at him. 'You became quite a lover.'

Oliver smiled. 'As soon as I met Elvira I dropped all my theories, attitudes, you know, about despising women; I had to get near to her. I suddenly saw that romantic men weren't such fools as I thought. It was a game to play. Then I found I was in love!'

Marpurgo laughed. 'So you went into the business once and for all?'

Oliver said earnestly: 'Yes, like I do everything. It is an experience, too. I thought, I will try anything once. So I let myself go. . . . Last night I lay peacefully, it seemed, somewhere on the lower slopes of the Tyrol. Nothing breathes upon my bed but the breeze lifting its face from the enamelled meadows. Above are the stars, small and numerous, clustering more thickly on a distant spur. Then I see her walking a long way from me, but of heavenly stature, veiled, walking through the starry night, with bare olive feet and bare round arms braceleted, and dark young Slavic face cast down, thoughtfully but archly. The wind does not disturb her hieratic curls, her feet do not disturb the grasses, but they rebound after her; sometimes she leaves a shining track across a hillside with silver footprints like a snail, around her is a light mist, and at intervals small white waterbirds paddle delicately in the dew and, among sedgy five-fingered tufts, make a mincing step or so in a half-circle round her.

But there she goes, in some brilliant colour she surely never wore, under the sepia sky, veiled and downcast and all the night, with comets. I follow her with my eyes, recumbent, and wonder what she thinks of, and what she looks for in the flowery fields and marshy meadows. When the dawn comes she vanishes, and the restless day comes telling me I am a fool and must get up, be myself, wash my face and go to work. A workaday man, if there ever was one. She has a function: she is sucking all the dreams out of me. All, all. I am empty. I feel like a blown-out egg. I suppose it is cleansing. I am not so sure. Perhaps a jog doesn't pay in any sense.'

Oliver's voice, which had been sweet in the first part of his recital, had at the last sentence become harsh again and dejected.

Marpurgo plaited his fingers on the table. He said sibilantly:

'She was just a spell of blessed self-forgetfulness for an academic drudge. It relieves, to spin from the zentrum to the periphery. That's why men go mad, too.'

'It's true, in a way. I don't know that I love her in the ordinary way. I'm just bound to her. There she burns, the cold fire in my polar season, and the northern lights dance round her icy brow and the luminous fish in her inky currents. Sometimes she is the mother of earth, sometimes a witch-maiden, sometimes the immobile, infertile, perfect image that floats in the subterranean caverns of the hearts of men, sometimes a child, sometimes herself, a woman imperfectly-heated, imperfectly-loving, querulous, necessitous. In other words, I have been in love.'

'Do you want to see her again?'

'Never—never.'

'And now what?'

'I'd go back if I had the money. I'm ashamed to write to my father. I told him I was making notes for a book of my own, the Uneven Development of Capitalism.'

'Come and stay with me at my hotel,' urged Marpurgo.

'I couldn't do that.'

'I'll try to arrange everything for you. I'm doing some business for a brilliant financier here—he'll certainly be heard of. They'll soon get over their Stavisky scare, and the venality will start up again—it'll be our opportunity if we get in first. The judges and clerks of the court must be behind with their rent: they haven't been able to touch a thing during all this.' He looked indescribably crafty and delighted. 'At any rate, this fellow will make me an advance if I tell him what it's for. Like many scoundrels, he admires the intellect. That's been my racket, my dear Oliver: in a greater or less measure, it's yours—only you're not quite so corrupt as I am, less honest, that is, with yourself. I'm alone here. Lonely and ailing. Come and keep me company."

Oliver chuckled sardonically.

'I couldn't, unless I were what I am sure you are, and could make one in the imponderable legions that ride the shadowy air of night. Oh, you imperfect villain! All you see, do, desire, say, is discoloured by your discontent. I am hopeful. You'll only try on me another Somnambulists' Club. You walked away with that. Not now. I'm not the fat puker I was then.'

Marpurgo wrinkled up his eyes joyously.

'You love to dramatise me!'

Oliver cried with enthusiasm: 'What a sunset to-night! smoke in the heavy air, thunderous clouds pouring into the sun, like sheep into the dip, and coming out red, rays, spray, smoke, fire scattered to all parts of the sky above the Venetian blue!'

Marpurgo was heavy with his dolour.

'I wonder what it will seem to me when I turn a somersault over the sun? Oliver, I feel that I am dying, and that the time will be brief and wretched. Just now I am becalmed, but in an hour or so, as it were, the wind will catch my black sails already unfurled, and I will go scudding over the horizon into the new continent of death. Even now I seem to have that sick lucidity. It comes and goes. My hour's not yet, but soon. What a strange thing, to be alive to-day and dead to-morrow! Alive yesterday and dead to-day! How can I die? I feel as if I will be standing quietly somewhere aside, and laughing quietly in my sleeve over my rotting body. It will decay, this hand will corrupt and fall into parts —what horror, what inevitability! The bloodhounds are after me, of death, I mean—here,' he cried, throwing out his hands, ' I'll distribute the morsels myself : what, they don't fall off, they don't scatter, my juices are not leaving a trail behind me! How strange ; not to-day, but to-morrow, faster than thought they will dissolve, because I happen to fall asleep and be no longer on the watch. These ears which will hear no more scandal, reproach, nor idle beguiling words, this mouth which will drink wormwood no more nor utter bitterness, nor laugh, nor quiver, this lofty forehead behind which madness has no more home, but must now fly shamed and gibbering away, and these feet, most of all, which need not wander nor hurry at the approach of night, nor foul themselves nor be broken with fatigue . . .'

' Don't talk like that, Marpurgo! '

' You've been one of my grave-diggers : you may as well hear the plaint.'

' Marpurgo, that business with Fuseaux wasn't my fault—really. I was quite unaware of the trouble you were going to have through it. I'm fond of you, Marpurgo.'

' Yes, you love me like a grave-digger. You're a modern young mind : it's your duty and pleasure to tear down old wrecks like me, to expose shams like me. Of course you like me. I'm easy to dissect. Not so easy as you think, but you'll never know the difference. What's your address ? I'll see that you get the money to go home. I'm your phantom. You bury me and go home. I'll get you the money!'

' No, I can't let you do that! '

' I'll manage it easily : I have wide-open credit in lots

of places. I have friends. Meet me to-morrow in the Café de la Paix.'

In the morning Oliver found Marpurgo looking quite well, cheerily cracking jokes with some beetle-browed Rumanians who, he said, were plotting against the reigning king. Marpurgo was on his high-horse again, and explained to Oliver, with apt satire but hazy details, some vast scheme that Severin was mounting.

'I haven't the money here,' said Marpurgo; 'but you'll get it by to-morrow at your hotel. When you get it let me know what train you're catching.'

The following day Oliver received five hundred francs at his hotel, in an envelope with an English postmark. He did not stop to think about this, but packed everything, and telegraphed Marpurgo that he was leaving for England by the Dieppe route that evening at seven and would entertain him at dinner. They had rather a pleasant meal, with Marpurgo singing and aphoristic. He went to the train with Oliver, and as it moved out, called:

'Oh, you should know, by the way, that I telegraphed Paul about you, saying I was broke, and he telephoned me and sent you the money—five hundred francs, wasn't it? What a generous heart is buried there!'

The train slid out faster and faster, leaving Marpurgo's strange giggle and bright blue eyes behind.

With the money Oliver had bought the newest issue of *Under the Marxist Banner*, and he settled down with a pleasant sigh to read. He looked out at the frozen grey suburbs they were sliding through and his heart kicked with joy: even as he sat in the train, even as he left them, they could not escape him. They could not say to him, *We are ice-bound, diseased, verminous, rotten: we are something you can't grasp, we threaten you, we have no money to pay you, we reject you.* He read in his book and a warmth grew round his heart. The intellect was his business and reason was his tool. In the country the ponds were stiff, the kitchen doors closed: smoke froze over the chimneys, the dried beans hung under the thatch.

Oliver's eyes began to dream over the empty view. The girl opposite closed her eyes and stretched out a silken leg to touch his foot by accident. The man next to Oliver began a gurgling snore which grew louder with every breath. The girl's disgusted eyes opened. Oliver shook the man, ' Monsieur ! Monsieur ! ' He awakened, looked sheepish, and went out into the corridor. ' Thank you,' said the girl. She was a beautiful young creature, about eighteen, with a face the shape of an old-fashioned shield, and thick, uncurled, wild black hair. Deepest blue eyes flew all over Oliver's person. She leaned back impulsively and then leaned forward impulsively to ask him about himself. She was a composer, and sang him there and then some songs, written by herself in the style of Hugo Wolf, to lyrics written by men in a workers' literature class in Newcastle-on-Tyne, her home town. Oliver dropped his book and his eyes were brilliant and wet with enthusiasm.

' That's original,' cried Oliver.

' This is the most brilliant age the world has ever seen,' said the musician : ' who can help but be original?' She looked at him critically.

' There are a lot of resuscitated anachronisms about,' he laughed.

' Not you or me,' cried the girl, shaking her black hair like a filly.

' How sure you are ! Tell me your name ? '

' Rosetta ! '

' I've got some poems in my bag,' said Oliver. ' Do you think you could put one of them to music ? I'll read a couple to you. Do you want to hear ? Though I don't know whether you can stand them : they refer to experiences, many experiences which will have no meaning for you, I suppose.'

She laughed. ' I don't suppose there's anything I don't know.'

As the train rumbled along he read his poems, and she tapped the rhythms.

Presently, they turned out their bags and had the red wine, sandwiches, crescent pastries and onions which they had brought between them. At the end Oliver wiped his hands on his handkerchief, leaned back and looked at her between half-closed eyes.

'Rosetta?'

'What?'

'I simply can't resist women, thank goodness.'

She looked at him with head poised, ready to toss back her hair; then said rather shyly: 'I believe in discipline.' She tossed back her unruly hair and looked at him earnestly.

VIRAGO MODERN CLASSICS

The first Virago Modern Classic, *Frost in May* by Antonia White, was published in 1978. It launched a list dedicated to the celebration of women writers and to the rediscovery and reprinting of their works. Its aim was, and is, to demonstrate the existence of a female tradition in fiction which is both enriching and enjoyable. The Leavisite notion of the 'Great Tradition', and the narrow, academic definition of a 'classic', has meant the neglect of a large number of interesting secondary works of fiction. In calling the series 'Modern Classics' we do not necessarily mean 'great' — although this is often the case. Published with new critical and biographical introductions, books are chosen for many reasons: sometimes for their importance in literary history; sometimes because they illuminate particular aspects of womens' lives, both personal and public. They may be classics of comedy or storytelling; their interest can be historical, feminist, political or literary.

Initially the Virago Modern Classics concentrated on English novels and short stories published in the early decades of this century. As the series has grown it has broadened to include works of fiction from different centuries, different countries, cultures and literary traditions. In 1984 the Victorian Classics were launched; there are separate lists of Irish, Scottish, European, American, Australian and other English speaking countries; there are books written by Black women, by Catholic and Jewish women, and a few relevant novels by men. There is, too, a companion series of Non-Fiction Classics constituting biography, autobiography, travel, journalism, essays, poetry, letters and diaries.

By the end of 1986 over 250 titles will have been published in these two series, many of which have been suggested by our readers.